RAVES FOR T
TI
THE DEVIL

"A many-layered thriller . . . And Mr.
wraps it all up with a double-whammy ending that will take even the most wary reader by surprise."

—*The New York Times Book Review*

"When it comes to espionage, international intrigue and suspense, Frederick Forsyth is a master."

—*Washington Post*

"An enormous plot that builds unfalteringly, a staggeringly well-detailed international thriller that shows him in blazing top form."

—*Kirkus Reviews*

"Vintage Forsyth: an intricate story that works!"

—*Nashville Banner*

"More flips than a trapeze artist, including a final twist that left this unsuspecting reader cursing Forsyth's cleverness—with admiration."

—*Chicago Sun-Times*

"A by-the-lapels thriller that . . . is disturbingly current, chillingly believable . . . Forsyth places a million-ton bomb in its midst and lights a fuse that crackles and races across the globe."

—*Louisville Times*

"Brilliantly conceived, chess-game of a novel . . . You will be so spellbound that . . . you cannot quit reading."

—*Columbus Dispatch*

Corgi Books by Frederick Forsyth
Ask your bookseller for the books you have missed

THE DAY OF THE JACKAL
THE DEVIL'S ALTERNATIVE
THE DOGS OF WAR
THE FOURTH PROTOCOL
NO COMEBACKS
THE ODESSA FILE
THE SHEPHERD

The Devil's Alternative

Frederick Forsyth

This low-priced Bantam Book has been completely reset in a type face designed for easy reading, and was printed from new plates. It contains the complete text of the original hard-cover edition.
NOT ONE WORD HAS BEEN OMITTED.

THE DEVIL'S ALTERNATIVE

A Bantam Book / published by arrangement with The Viking Press

PRINTING HISTORY

Viking Press edition published December 1979
2nd printing . . . January 1980
5 printings through April 1980

Literary Guild edition March 1980

Serialized in PENTHOUSE; *condensed by Reader's Digest Condensed Books*

Bantam edition / July 1980
10 printings through October 1984

Corgi Canada edition / September 1985

For information address: The Viking Press, Div. of Viking Penguin Inc., 40 West 23rd Street, New York, N.Y. 10010.

ISBN 0-552-11500-2

Published simultaneously in the United States and Canada

Bantam Books are published by Bantam Books, Inc. Its trademark, consisting of the words "Bantam Books" and the portrayal of a rooster, is Registered in U.S. Patent and Trademark Office and in other countries. Marca Registrada. Bantam Books, Inc., 666 Fifth Avenue, New York, New York 10103.

PRINTED IN THE UNITED STATES OF AMERICA

H 0 9 8 7 6 5 4 3 2 1

FOR FREDERICK STUART,
WHO DOES NOT KNOW YET

The Devil's Alternative

PROLOGUE

THE CASTAWAY would have been dead before sundown but for the sharp eyes of an Italian seaman called Mario. By the time he was spotted he had lapsed into unconsciousness, the exposed parts of his near-naked body grilled to second-degree burns by the relentless sun, and those parts submerged in seawater soft and white between the salt sores like the limbs of a rotting goose.

Mario Curcio was the cook-steward on the *Garibaldi*, an amiable old rust bucket out of Brindisi, thumping her way eastward toward Cape Ince and on to Trabzon in the far eastern corner of the north shore of Turkey. She was on her way to pick up a cargo of almonds from Anatolia.

Just why Mario decided that morning in the last ten days of April 1982 to empty his bucket of potato peelings over the lee rail instead of through the garbage chute at the poop, he could never explain, nor was he ever asked to. But perhaps to take a breath of fresh Black Sea air and break the monotony of the steam heat in the cramped galley, he stepped out on deck, strolled to the starboard rail, and hurled his garbage to an indifferent but patient sea. He turned away and started to lumber back to his duties. After two steps he stopped, frowned, turned, and walked back to the rail, puzzled and uncertain.

The ship was heading east-northeast to clear Cape Ince, so that as he shielded his eyes and gazed abaft the beam, the noon sun was almost straight in his face. But he was sure he had seen something out there on the blue-green rolling swell between the ship and the coast of Turkey, twenty miles to the south. Unable to see it again, he trotted up the afterdeck, mounted the outside ladders to the wing of the bridge, and peered again. Then he saw it, quite clearly, for half a second between the softly moving hills of water. He turned to the open door behind him, leading into the wheelhouse, and shouted *"Capitano!"*

Captain Vittorio Ingrao took some persuading, for Mario was a simple lad, but he was enough of a sailor to know that if a man might be out there on the water, he was duty-bound to turn his ship around and have a closer look, and his radar had indeed revealed an echo. It took the captain half an hour to bring the *Garibaldi* around and back to the spot Mario had pointed at, and then he, too, saw it.

The skiff was barely twelve feet long, and not very wide. A light craft, of the type that could have been a ship's jolly boat. Forward of midships there was a single thwart across the boat, with a hole in it for the stepping of a mast. But either there had never been a mast or it had been ill-secured and had gone overboard. With the *Garibaldi* stopped and wallowing in the swell, Captain Ingrao leaned on the bridge-wing rail and watched Mario and the bosun, Paolo Longhi, set off in the motor lifeboat to bring the skiff alongside. From his elevation he could look down into the skiff as it was towed closer.

The man in it was lying on his back in several inches of seawater. He was gaunt and emaciated, bearded and unconscious, his head to one side, breathing in short gasps. He moaned a few times as he was lifted aboard and the sailors' hands touched his flayed shoulders and chest.

There was one permanently spare cabin on the *Garibaldi*, kept free as a sort of sick bay, and the castaway was taken to it. Mario, at his own request, was given time off to tend the man, whom he soon came to regard as his personal property, as a boy will take special care of a puppy he has personally rescued from death. Longhi, the bosun, gave the man a shot of morphine from the first-aid chest to spare him the pain, and the pair of them set to work on the sunburn.

Being Calabrians they knew a bit about sunburn and prepared the best sunburn salve in the world. Mario brought from his galley a fifty-fifty mixture of fresh lemon juice and wine vinegar in a basin, a light cotton cloth torn from his pillowcase, and a bowl of ice cubes. Soaking the cloth in the mixture and wrapping it around a dozen ice cubes, he gently pressed the pad to the worst areas, where the ultraviolet rays had bitten through almost to the bone. Plumes of steam rose from the unconscious man as the freezing astringent drew the heat out of the scorched flesh. The man shuddered.

"Better a fever than death by burn shock," Mario told him in Italian. The man could not hear, and if he had, he could not have understood.

Longhi joined his skipper on the afterdeck, where the skiff had been hauled.

"Anything?" he asked.

Captain Ingrao shook his head.

"Nothing on the man, either. No watch, no name tag. A pair of cheap underpants with no label. And his beard looks about ten days old."

"There's nothing here, either," said Ingrao. "No mast, no sail, no oars. No food and no water container. No name on the boat, even. But it could have peeled off."

"A tourist from a beach resort, blown out to sea?" asked Longhi.

Ingrao shrugged. "Or a survivor from a small freighter," he said. "We'll be at Trabzonin two days. The Turkish authorities can solve that one when he wakes up and talks. Meanwhile, let's get under way. Oh, and we must cable our agent there and tell him what's happened. We'll need an ambulance on the quay when we dock."

Two days later the castaway, still barely conscious and unable to speak, was tucked up between white sheets in a sick ward in the small municipal hospital of Trabzon.

Mario the sailor had accompanied his castaway in the ambulance from the quay to the hospital, along with the ship's agent and the port's medical officer, who had insisted on checking the delirious man for communicable diseases. After waiting an hour by the bedside, he had bade his unconscious friend farewell and returned to the *Garibaldi* to prepare the crew's lunch. That had been the previous day, and the old Italian tramp steamer had sailed during the evening.

Now another man stood by the bedside, accompanied by a police officer and the white-coated doctor. All three were Turkish, but the short, broad man in the civilian suit spoke passable English.

"He'll pull through," said the doctor, "but he's very sick for the moment. Heatstroke, second-degree sunburn, exposure generally, and by the look of it, he hasn't eaten for days. Generally weak."

"What are these?" asked the civilian, gesturing at the intravenous tubes that entered both the man's arms.

"Saline drip and concentrated glucose drip for nourishment and to offset shock," said the doctor. "The sailors probably saved his life by taking the heat out of the burns, but we've bathed him in calamine to help the healing process. Now it's between him and Allah."

Umit Erdal, partner in the shipping and trading company of Erdal and Sermit, was the Lloyd's subagent for the port of Trabzon, and the *Garibaldi*'s agent had thankfully passed the matter of the castaway over to him. The sick man's eyelids fluttered in the nut-brown, bearded face. Erdal cleared his throat, bent over the figure, and spoke in his best English.

"What . . . is . . . you . . . name?" he asked slowly and clearly.

The man groaned and moved his head from side to side several times. The Lloyd's man bent his head closer to listen. "*Zradzhenyi,*" the sick man murmured, "*zradzhenyi.*"

Erdal straightened up. "He's not Turkish," he said with finality, "but he seems to be called Zradzhenyi. It's probably a Ukrainian name."

Both his companions shrugged.

"I'll inform Lloyd's in London," said Erdal. "Maybe they'll have news of a missing vessel somewhere in the Black Sea."

The daily bible of the world's merchant marine fraternity is *Lloyd's List*, which is published Monday to Saturday and contains editorials, features, and news on one topic only—shipping. Its partner in harness, *Lloyd's Shipping Index*, gives the movements of the world's thirty thousand active merchant vessels: name of ship, owner, flag of registry, year of construction, tonnage, where last reported coming from, and where bound.

Both organs are published out of a building complex at Sheepen Place, Colchester, in the English county of Essex. It was to this building that Umit Erdal telexed the shipping movements into and out of the port of Trabzon, and added a small extra for the attention of the Lloyd's Shipping Intelligence Unit in the same building.

The SI unit checked their maritime casualty records to confirm that there were no recent reports of missing, sunk, or simply overdue vessels in the Black Sea, and passed the paragraph over to the editorial desk of the *List*. Here a subeditor gave it a mention as a news brief on the front page, including the name the castaway had given as his own. It appeared the following morning.

Most of those who read *Lloyd's List* that day in late April flipped past the paragraph about the unidentified man in Trabzon.

But the piece caught and held the sharp eyes and the attention of a man in his early thirties who worked as senior clerk and trusted employee in a firm of chartered shipbrokers situated in a small street called Crutched Friars in the center of the City of London, financial and commercial square mile of the British capital. His colleagues in the firm knew him as Andrew Drake.

Having absorbed the content of the paragraph, Drake left his desk and went to the company boardroom, where he consulted a framed chart of the world that showed prevailing wind and ocean-current circulation. The winds in the Black Sea during spring and summer are predominantly from the north, and the currents screw counterclockwise around this small ocean from the southern coast of the Ukraine in the far northwest of the sea, down past the coasts of Rumania and Bulgaria, then swing eastward again into the shipping lanes between Istanbul and Cape Ince.

Drake did some calculations on a scratch pad. A small skiff, setting off from the marshes of the delta of the Dniester River just south of Odessa could make four to five knots with a following wind and favorable current, southward past Rumania and Bulgaria toward Turkey. But after three days it would tend to be carried eastward, away from the Bosporus toward the eastern end of the Black Sea.

The Weather and Navigation section of *Lloyd's List* confirmed there had been bad weather nine days earlier in that area. The sort, Drake mused, that could cause a skiff in the hands of an unskilled seaman to capsize, lose its mast and all its contents, and leave its occupant, even if he could climb back into it again, at the mercy of the sun and the wind.

Two hours later Andrew Drake asked for a week of his owed holidays, and it was agreed that he could take it, but only starting the following Monday, May 3.

He was mildly excited as he waited out the week and bought himself from a nearby agency a round-trip ticket from London to Istanbul. He decided to buy the connecting ticket from Istanbul to Trabzon with cash in Istanbul. He also checked to confirm that a British passport holder needs no visa for Turkey, but after work he secured for himself the needed smallpox vaccination certificate at the British Airways medical center at Victoria.

He was excited because he thought there just might be a chance that, after years of waiting, he had found the man he was looking for. Unlike the three men by the castaway's bedside two days earlier, he knew what country the word *zradzhenyi* came from. He also knew it was not the man's name. The man in the bed had been muttering the word *betrayed* in his native tongue, and that language was Ukrainian. Which could mean that the man was a refugee Ukrainian partisan.

Andrew Drake, despite his Anglicized name, was also a Ukrainian, and a fanatic.

Drake's first call after arriving in Trabzon was at the office of Umit Erdal, whose name he had obtained from a friend at Lloyd's on the grounds that he was taking a holiday on the Turkish coast and, speaking not a word of Turkish, might need some assistance. Erdal, seeing the letter of introduction that Drake was able to produce, was happily unquestioning as to why his visitor should want to see the castaway in the local hospital. He wrote a personal letter of introduction to the hospital administrator, and, shortly after lunch, Drake was shown into the small, one-bed ward where the man lay.

The local Lloyd's agent had already told him that the man, while conscious again, spent much of the time sleeping, and during his periods of wakefulness had so far said absolutely nothing. When Drake entered the room, the invalid was lying on his back, eyes closed. Drake drew up a chair and sat by the bedside. For a time he stared at the man's haggard face. After several minutes the man's eyelids flickered, half-opened, and closed again. Whether he had seen the visitor staring at him intently, Drake did not know. But he knew the man was on the fringe of wakefulness. Slowly he leaned forward and said clearly in the sick man's ear:

"Shche ne vmerla Ukraina."

The words mean, literally, "The Ukraine is not dead," but in a looser translation would mean "The Ukraine lives on." They are the first words of the Ukrainian national anthem, banned by the Russian masters, and would be instantly recognizable to a nationally conscious Ukrainian.

The sick man's eyes flicked open, and he regarded Drake intently. After several seconds he asked in Ukrainian, "Who are you?"

"A Ukrainian, like yourself," said Drake.

The other man's eyes clouded with suspicion.

"Quisling," he said.

Drake shook his head. "No," he said calmly. "I am British by nationality, born and bred there, son of a Ukrainian father and an English mother. But in my heart I'm as Ukrainian as you are."

The man in the bed stared stubbornly at the ceiling.

"I could show you my passport, issued in London, but that would prove nothing. A Chekisti could produce one if he wanted to try to trick you." Drake had used the slang term for a Soviet secret policeman and KGB member.

"But you are not in the Ukraine anymore and there are no Chekisti here," Drake went on. "You were not washed up on the shores of the Crimea, nor of south Russia or Georgia. You did not land in Rumania or Bulgaria, either. You were picked up by an Italian ship and landed here at Trabzon. You are in Turkey. You are in the West. You made it."

The man's eyes were on his face now, alert, lucid, wanting to believe.

"Can you move?" asked Drake.

"I don't know," said the man.

Drake nodded across the small room to the window, beyond which the sounds of traffic could be heard.

"The KGB can dress up hospital staff to look like Turks," he said, "but they cannot change a whole city for one man whom they could torture for a confession if they wanted. Can you make the window?"

Helped by Drake, the castaway hobbled painfully to the window and looked out at the street scene.

"The cars are Austins and Morrises, imported from England," said Drake. "Peugeots from France and Volkswagens from West Germany. The words on the billboards are in Turkish. That advertisement over there is for Coca-Cola."

The man put the back of one hand against his mouth and chewed at the knuckles. He blinked rapidly several times.

"I made it," he said.

"Yes," said Drake, "by a miracle you made it."

"My name," said the castaway when he was back in bed, "is Miroslav Kaminsky. I come from Ternopol. I was the leader of a group of seven Ukrainian partisans."

Over the next hour the story came out. Kaminsky and six others like him, all from the Ternopol area, once a hotbed of Ukrainian nationalism, and a region where some of the embers still glowed, had decided to strike back against the program of ruthless russification of their land that had intensified in the sixties and become a "final solution" in the seventies and early eighties for the whole area of Ukrainian art, poetry, literature, language, and national consciousness. In six months of operations they had ambushed and killed two low-level Party secretaries—Russians imposed by Moscow on Ternopol—and a plainclothes KGB agent. Then had come the betrayal.

Whoever had talked, he, too, had died in the hail of fire as the green insignia of the KGB special troops had closed in on the country cottage where the group was meeting to plan its next operation. Only Kaminsky had escaped, running like an animal through the undergrowth, hiding by day in barns and woodland, moving by night, heading southeast toward the coast with a vague idea of jumping a Western ship.

It had been impossible to get near the docks of Odessa. Living off potatoes and swedes from the fields, he had sought refuge in the swampy country of the Dniester estuary southwest of Odessa, toward the Rumanian border. Finally, coming by night on a small fishing hamlet on a creek, he had stolen a skiff with a stepped mast and a small sail. He had never been in a sailing boat before and knew nothing of the sea. Trying to manage the sail and the rudder, just holding on and praying, he had let the skiff run before the wind, southward by the stars and the sun.

By pure luck he had avoided the patrol boats that cruise the offshore waters of the Soviet Union, and the fishing fleets. The tiny sliver of wood that contained him had slipped past the coastal radar sweeps until he was out of range. Then he was lost, somewhere between Rumania and the Crimea, heading south, but far from the nearest shipping lanes—if he did but know where they were, anyway. The storm caught him unawares. Not knowing how to shorten sail in time, he had capsized, spending the night using his last reserves of strength clinging to the upturned hull. By morning he had righted the skiff and crawled inside. His clothes, which he had taken off to let the night wind cool his skin, were gone. So also were his few raw potatoes, the open lemonade bottle of fresh water, the sail, and the rudder. The pain came shortly after sunrise as the heat of the day increased. Oblivion came on the third day after the storm. When he regained consciousness he was in a bed, taking the pain of the burns in silence, listening to the voices he thought were Bulgarian. For six days he had kept his eyes closed and his mouth shut.

Andrew Drake heard him out with a song in his heart. He had found the man he had waited years for.

"I'll go and see the Swiss consul in Istanbul and try to obtain temporary travel documents for you from the Red Cross," he said when Kaminsky showed signs of tiring. "If I do, I can probably get you to England, at least on a temporary visa. Then we can try for asylum. I'll return in a few days."

By the door, he paused.

"You can't go back, you know," he told Kaminsky. "But with your help, I can. It's what I want. It's what I've always wanted."

Andrew Drake took longer than he had thought in Istanbul, and it was not until May 16 that he was able to fly back to Trabzon with travel papers for Kaminsky. He had extended his leave after a long telephone call to London and a row with the broking firm's junior partner, but it was worth it. For through Kaminsky he was certain he could fulfill the single burning ambition of his life.

The Union of Soviet Socialist Republics (and the Tsarist Empire before it), despite its monolithic appearance from outside, has two Achilles heels. One is the problem of feeding its 250 million people. The other is euphemistically called "the nationalities question." In the fifteen constituent republics ruled from Moscow, capital of the USSR and of the Russian Soviet Federated Socialist Republic (RSFSR), are several score identifiable non-Russian peoples, the most numerous and perhaps the most nationally conscious of whom are the Ukrainians. By 1982 the population of the RSFSR numbered only 120 million out of the 250. Second in economic importance and population, with 70 million inhabitants, was the Ukrainian SSR, which was one reason why under tsars and Politburo the Ukraine had always been singled out for special attention and particularly ruthless russification. The second reason lay in its history.

The Ukraine is divided by the Dnieper River into two parts. West (right-bank) Ukraine stretches from Kiev westward to the Polish border. East (left-bank) Ukraine is more russified, having dwelt under the tsars for centuries; during those centuries West Ukraine formed a part, successively, of Poland, Austria, and the Austro-Hungarian Empire. Its spiritual and cultural orientation was and remains more Western than the rest of the region, except possibly for the three Baltic States of Latvia, Lithuania, and Estonia. Ukrainians read and write with Roman letters, not Cyrillic script; they are overwhelmingly Uniate Catholics, not Russian Orthodox Christians. Their language, poetry, literature, arts, and traditions predate the rise of the Rus conquerors who swept down from the north.

In 1918, with the breakup of Austria-Hungary, West Ukrainians tried desperately for a separate republic out of the empire's ruins; unlike the Czechs, Slovaks, and Magyars, they failed and were annexed in 1919 by Poland as the province of East Galicia. When Hitler swept into western Poland in 1939, Stalin came in from the east with the Red Army and took Galicia. In 1941, the Germans took it. What followed was a violent and vicious confusion of hopes, fears, and loyalties. Some hoped for concessions from Moscow if they fought the Germans. Others mistakenly thought a free Ukraine would come through the defeat of Moscow by Berlin, and joined the Ukrainian Division, which fought in German uniform against the red Army. Others, like Kaminsky's father, took to the Carpathian Mountains as guerrillas and fought first one invader, then the next, then the first again. They all lost. Stalin won, and pushed his empire westward to the Bug River, the new border for Poland. West Ukraine came under the new tsars, the Politburo, but the old dreams lived on. Apart from one glimmer in the last days of Khrushchev, the program to crush them once and for all had steadily intensified.

Stepan Drach, a student from Rovno, joined up with the Ukrainian Division. He was one of the lucky ones; he survived the war and was captured by the British in Austria in 1945. Sent to work as a farm laborer in Norfolk, he would certainly have been returned to the USSR for execution by the NKVD in 1946 as the British Foreign Office and American State Department quietly conspired to return the two million "victims of Yalta" to the mercies of Stalin. But he was lucky again. Behind a Norfolk haystack he tumbled a Land Army girl, and she became pregnant. Marriage was the answer, and six months later, on compassionate grounds, he was excused repatriation and allowed to stay in England. Freed from farm labor, he used the knowledge he had gained as a radio operator to set up a small repair shop in Bradford, a center for Britain's thirty thousand Ukrainians. The first baby died in infancy; a second son, christened Andriy, was born in 1950.

Andriy learned Ukrainian at his father's knee, and that was not all. He learned, too, of his father's land, of the great, sweeping vistas of the Carpathians and Ruthenia. He imbibed his father's loathing of Russians. But the father died in an automobile crash when the boy was twelve; his mother, tired of her husband's endless evenings with fellow exiles around the sitting-room fire, talking of the past in a language she could never understand, Anglicized both their names to Drake, and Andriy's given name to Andrew. It was as Andrew Drake that the boy went to grammar school and the university; as Andrew Drake that he received his first passport.

The rebirth came in his late teens at the university. There were other Ukrainians there, and he became fluent again in his father's language. These were the late sixties, and the brief renaissance of Ukrainian literature and poetry back in the Ukraine had come and gone, its leading lights mostly by then doing slave labor in the camps of Gulag. So he absorbed these events with hindsight and knowledge of what had befallen the writers. He read everything he could get his hands on as the first years of the seventh decade dawned: the classics of Taras Shevchenko and those who wrote in the brief flowering under Lenin, suppressed and liquidated under Stalin. But most of all he read the works of those called "the Sixtiers" because they flourished for a brief few years until Brezhnev struck yet again to stamp out the national pride they called for. He read and grieved for Osdachy, Chornovil, and Dzyuba; and when he read the poems and secret diary of Pavel Symonenko, the young firebrand dead of cancer at twenty-eight, the cult figure of the Ukrainian students inside the USSR, his heart broke for a land he had never even seen.

With his love for this land of his dead father came a matching loathing of those he saw as its persecutors. Avidly he devoured the underground pamphlets that came out, smuggled from the resistance movement inside; he read the *Ukrainian Herald,* with its accounts of what befell the hundreds of unknowns, the miserable, forgotten ones who did not receive the publicity accorded to the great Moscow trials of Daniel, Sinyavsky, Orlov, Shcharansky. With each detail, his hatred grew until for Andrew Drake, once Andriy Drach, the personification of all evil in the world was called simply the KGB.

He had enough sense of reality to eschew the crude, raw

nationalism of the older exiles, and their divisions between West and East Ukrainians. He rejected, too, their implanted anti-Semitism, preferring to accept the works of Gluzman, both a Zionist and a Ukrainian nationalist, as the words of a fellow Ukrainian. He analyzed the exile community in Britain and Europe and perceived there were four levels: the language nationalists, for whom simply speaking and writing in the tongue of their fathers was enough; the debating nationalists, who would talk forever and a day but do nothing; the slogan daubers, who irritated their adoptive countrymen but left the Soviet Behemoth untouched; and the activists, who demonstrated before visiting Moscow dignitaries, were carefully photographed and filed by the Special Branch, and achieved a passing publicity.

Drake rejected them all. He remained quiet, well-behaved, and aloof. He came south to London and took a clerking job. There are many in such work who have one secret passion, unknown to all their colleagues, that absorbs all their savings, their spare time, and their annual holidays. Drake was such a man. He quietly put together a small group of men who felt just as he did; traced them, met them, befriended them, swore a common oath with them, and bade them be patient. For Andriy Drach had a secret dream, and, as T. E. Lawrence said, he was dangerous because "he dreamed with his eyes open." His dream was that one day he would strike one single gigantic blow against the men of Moscow that would shake them as they had never been shaken before. He would penetrate the walls of their power and hurt them right inside the fortress.

His dream was alive and one step nearer fulfillment for the finding of Kaminsky, and he was a determined and excited man as his plane slipped once more out of a warm blue sky toward Trabzon.

Miroslav Kaminsky looked across at Drake with indecision on his face.

"I don't know, Andriy," he said. "I just don't know. Despite everything you have done, I just don't know if I can trust you that much. I'm sorry, it's the way I've had to live all my life."

"Miroslav, you could know me for the next twenty years and not know more about me than you do already. Everything I've told you about me is the truth. If you cannot go back, then let me go in your place. But I must have contacts there. If you know of anybody, anybody at all . . ."

Kaminsky finally agreed.

"There are two men," he said at last. "They were not blown when my group was destroyed, and no one knew of them. I had met them only a few months earlier."

"But they are Ukrainians, and partisans?" asked Drake eagerly.

"Yes, they are Ukrainians. But that is not their primary motivation. Their people, too, have suffered. Their fathers, like mine, have been for ten years in the labor camps, but for a different reason. They are Jews."

"But do they hate Moscow?" asked Drake. "Do they, too, want to strike against the Kremlin?"

"Yes, they hate Moscow," replied Kaminsky. "As much as you or I. Their inspiration seems to be a thing called the Jewish Defense League. They heard about it on the radio. It seems their philosophy, like ours, is to begin to strike back, not to take any more persecution lying down."

"Then let me make contact with them," urged Drake.

The following morning, Drake flew back to London with the names and addresses in Lvov of the two young Jewish partisans. Within two weeks he had subscribed to a package tour run by Intourist for early July, visiting Kiev, Ternopol, and Lvov. He also quit his job and withdrew his life savings in cash.

Unnoticed by anyone, Andrew Drake, born Andriy Drach, was going to his private war—against the Kremlin.

CHAPTER ONE

A GENTLY WARMING SUN shone down on Washington that middle of May, bringing the first shirt sleeves to the streets and the first rich red roses to the garden outside the French windows of the Oval Office in the White House. But though the windows were open and the fresh smells of grass and flowers wafted into the private sanctum of the most powerful official in the world, the attention of the four men present was focused upon other plants in a far and foreign country.

President William Matthews sat where American presidents have always sat—his back to the south wall of the room, facing northward across a wide antique desk toward the classical marble fireplace that dominates the north wall. His chair, unlike that of most of his predecessors, who had favored personalized, made-to-measure seating, was a factory-made, high-backed swivel chair of the kind any senior corporate executive might have. For "Bill" Matthews, as he insisted his publicity posters call him, had always through his successive and successful election campaigns stressed his ordinary, down-home personal tastes in clothing, food, and creature comforts. The chair, therefore, which could be seen by the scores of delegates he liked to welcome personally into the Oval Office, was not luxurious. The fine antique desk, he was at pains to point out, he had inherited, and it had become part of the precious tradition of the White House. That went down well.

But there Bill Matthews drew the line. When he was in conclave with his senior advisers, the "Bill" that his humblest constituent could call him to his face became the formal "Mr. President." He also dropped the nice-guy tone of voice and the rumpled bird-dog grin that had originally gulled the voters into putting the boy-next-door into the White House. He was not the boy-next-door, and his advisers knew it; he was the man at the top.

Seated in upright armchairs across the desk from the President were the three men who had asked to see him alone that morning. Closest to him in personal terms was his Assistant for National Security Affairs. Variously referred to in the environs of the West Wing and the Executive Office Building as "the Doctor" or "that damned Polack," the sharp-faced Stanislaw Poklewski was sometimes disliked but never underestimated.

They made a strange pair, to be so close: the blond white Anglo-Saxon Protestant from the Midwest, and the dark, taciturn, devout Roman Catholic who had come over from Krakow as a small boy. But what Bill Matthews lacked in understanding of the tortuous psychologies of Europeans in general and Slavs in particular could be made up by the Jesuit-educated calculating machine who always had his ear. There were two other reasons why Poklewski appealed to him: he was ferociously loyal, and he had no political ambitions outside the shadow of Bill Matthews. But there was one reservation: Matthews always had to balance the Doctor's suspicious dislike of the men of Moscow with the more urbane assessments of his Boston-born Secretary of State.

The Secretary was not present that morning at the meeting asked for personally by Poklewski. The other two men on the chairs in front of the desk were Robert Benson, Director of the Central Intelligence Agency, and Carl Taylor.

It has frequently been written that America's National Security Agency is the body responsible for all electronic espionage. It is a popular idea but not true. The NSA is responsible for that portion of electronic surveillance and espionage conducted outside the United States on her behalf that has to do with listening: wiretapping, radio monitoring, and, above all, the plucking out of the ether of literally billions of words a day in hundreds of dialects and languages for recording, decoding, translating, and analyzing. But not spy satellites. The *visual* surveillance of the globe by cameras mounted in airplanes and, more important, in space satellites has always been the preserve of the National Reconnaissance Office, a joint U.S. Air Force–CIA operation. Carl Taylor was its Director, and he was a two-star general in Air Force Intelligence.

The President shuffled together the pile of high-definition photographs on his desk and handed them back to Taylor, who rose to accept them and placed them back in his briefcase.

"All right, gentlemen," Matthews said slowly, "so you have shown me that the wheat crop in a small portion of the Soviet Union, maybe even only in the few acres shown in these pictures, is coming up defective. What does it prove?"

Poklewski glanced across at Taylor and nodded. Taylor cleared his throat.

"Mr. President, I've taken the liberty of setting up a screening of what is coming in right now from one of our Condor satellites. Would you care to see it?"

Matthews nodded and watched Taylor cross to the bank of television sets placed in the curving west wall below the bookcases, which had been specially remodeled to accept the console of TV sets. When non-security-cleared deputations were in the room, the new row of TV screens was covered by sliding teak doors. Taylor turned on the extreme left-hand set and returned to the President's desk. He detached one of the six telephones from its cradle, dialed a number, and said simply, "Screen it."

President Matthews knew about the Condor satellites. Flying higher than anything before, using cameras of a sophistication that could show a close-up of a human fingernail from two hundred miles up, through fog, rain, hail, snow, cloud, and night, the Condors were the latest and the best.

Back in the seventies, photographic surveillance, though good, had been slow, mainly because each cartridge of exposed film had to be ejected from the satellite at specific positions, free-fall to earth in protective coverings, be retrieved with the aid of bleepers and tracing devices, be air-freighted to the NRO's central laboratories, be developed and screened. Only when the satellite was within that arc of flight which permitted a direct line between it and the United States or one of the American-controlled tracking stations could simultaneous TV transmissions take place. But when the satellite passed close over the Soviet Union, the curve of the earth's surface baffled direct reception, so the watchers had to wait until it came around again.

Then, in the summer of 1978, the scientists cracked the problem with the Parabola Game. Their computers devised a cat's cradle of infinite complexity for the flight tracks of half a dozen space cameras around the globe's surface, to this end: whichever spy-in-the-sky the White House wanted to tap into could be ordered by signal to begin transmitting what it was seeing, and throw the images in a low-parabola arc to another satellite that was not out of vision. The second bird would throw the image on again, to a third satellite, and so on, like basketball players tossing the ball from fingertip to fingertip while they run. When the needed images were caught by a satellite over the United States, they could be beamed back down to NRO headquarters, and from there be patched through to the Oval Office.

The satellites were traveling at over forty thousand miles per hour; the globe was spinning with the hours, tilting with the seasons. The number of computations and permutations was astronomical, but the computers solved them. By 1980, at the touch of a button, the President had twenty-four-hour access by simultaneous transmission to every square inch of the world's surface. Sometimes it bothered him. It never bothered Poklewski; he had been brought up on the idea of the exposition of all private thoughts and actions in the confessional. The Condors were like confessionals, with himself as the priest he had once nearly become.

As the screen flickered into life, General Taylor spread a map of the Soviet Union on the President's desk and pointed with a forefinger.

"What you are seeing, Mr. President, is coming to you from Condor Five, tracking here, northeastward, between Saratov and Perm, across the black-earth country."

Matthews raised his gaze to the screen. Great tracts of land were unrolling slowly down the screen from top to bottom, a swath about twenty miles broad. The land looked bare, as in autumn after the harvest. Taylor muttered a few instructions into the telephone. Seconds later, the view concentrated, closing to a band barely five miles wide. A small group of peasant shacks—wooden-plank isbas, no doubt—lost in the infinity of the steppe, drifted past on the left of the screen. The line of a road entered the picture, stayed center for a few uncertain moments, then drifted offscreen. Taylor muttered again; the picture closed to a track a hundred yards wide. Definition was better. A man leading a horse across the vast expanse of steppe came and went.

"Slow it down," instructed Taylor into the telephone. The ground beneath the cameras passed less quickly. High in space, the Condor satellite was still on track at the same height and speed; inside the NRO's laboratories the images were being narrowed and slowed. The picture came closer, slower. Against the bole of a lone tree, a Russian peasant slowly unbuttoned his fly. President Matthews was not a scientist and never ceased to be amazed at the possibilities of advanced technology. He was, he reminded himself, sitting in a warm office on a late spring morning in Washington, watching a man urinate somewhere in the shadow of the Ural mountain range. The peasant passed slowly out of vision toward the bottom of the screen. The image coming up was of a wheat field, many hundreds of acres abroad.

"And freeze," instructed Taylor into the telephone. The picture slowly stopped moving and held.

"Close up," said Taylor.

The picture came closer and closer until the entire yard-square screen was filled with twenty separate stalks of young wheat. Each looked frail, listless, bedraggled. Matthews had seen them like this in the dust bowls of the Midwest he had known in his boyhood, fifty years before.

"Stan," said the President.

Poklewski, who had asked for the meeting and the screening, chose his words carefully.

"Mr. President, the Soviet Union has a total grain target this year or two hundred forty million metric tons. Now, this breaks down into goal targets of one hundred twenty million tons of wheat, sixty million of barley, fourteen million of oats, fourteen million of corn, twelve million of rye, and the remaining twenty million of a mixture of rice, millet, buckwheat, and leguminous grains. The giants of the crop are wheat and barley."

He rose and came around the desk to where the map of the Soviet Union was still spread. Taylor flicked off the television and resumed his seat.

"About forty percent of the annual Soviet grain crop, or approximately one hundred million tons, comes from here, in the Ukraine and the Kuban area of the southern RSFSR," Poklewski continued, indicating the areas on the map. "And it is all winter wheat. That is, it's planted in September and October. It has reached the stage of young shoots by November, when the first snows come. The snows cover the shoots and protect them from the bitter frosts of December and January."

Poklewski turned and paced away from the desk to the curved ceiling-to-floor windows behind the presidential chair. He had this habit of pacing when he talked.

The Pennsylvania Avenue observer cannot actually see the Oval Office, tucked away at the back of the tiny West Wing building, but because the tops of these south-facing tall windows to the office can just be observed from the Washington

Monument, a thousand yards away, they have long been fitted with six-inch-thick, green-tinted bulletproof glass just in case a sniper near the monument might care to try a long shot. As Poklewski reached the windows, the aquamarine-tinted light coming through them cast a deeper pallor across his already pale face.

He turned and walked back, just as Matthews was preparing to swing his chair around to keep him in vision.

"Last December, the whole of the Ukraine and the Kuban Steppe were subjected to a freak thaw during the early days of the month. They've had them before, but never as warm. A great wave of warm southern air swept in off the Black Sea and the Bosporus and rolled northeastward over the Ukraine and the Kuban region. It lasted a week and melted the first coverings of snow, about six inches deep, to water. The young wheat and barley stems were exposed. Ten days later, as if to compensate, the same freak weather patterns hammered the whole area with frosts going fifteen, even twenty degrees, below zero."

"Which did the wheat no good at all," suggested the President.

"Mr. President," interjected Robert Benson of the CIA, "our best agricultural experts have estimated the Soviets will be lucky if they salvage fifty percent of that Ukrainian and Kuban crop. The damage was massive and irreparable."

"So that is what you have been showing me?" asked Matthews.

"No, sir," said Poklewski. "That is the point of this meeting. The other sixty percent of the Soviet crop, nigh on one hundred forty million tons, comes from the great tracts of the Virgin Lands in Kazakhstan, first put under the plow by Khrushchev in the middle fifties, and the black-earth country, butting up against the Urals. A small portion comes from across the mountains in Siberia. That is what we have been showing you."

"What is happening there?" asked Matthews.

"Something odd, sir. Something strange is happening to the Soviet grain crop. All this remaining sixty percent is spring wheat, put down as seed in March and April after the thaw. It should be coming up sweet and green by now. It's coming up stunted, sparse, sporadic, as if it had been hit by some kind of blight."

"Weather again?" asked Matthews.

"No. They had a damp winter and spring over this area,

but nothing serious. Now that the sun has come out, the weather is perfect—warm and dry."

"How widespread is this . . . blight?"

Benson came in again. "We don't know, Mr. President. We have maybe fifty samples of film of this particular problem. We tend to focus on military concentrations, of course—troop movements, new rocket bases, arms factories. But what we have indicates it must be pretty widespread."

"So what are you after?"

"What we'd like," resumed Poklewski, "is your go-ahead to spend a lot more time on this problem, find out just how big it is for the Soviets. It will mean trying to send in delegations, businessmen. Diverting a lot of space surveillance from non-priority tasks. We believe it is in America's vital interest to find out just exactly what it is that Moscow is going to have to handle here."

Matthews considered and glanced at his watch. He had a troop of ecologists due to greet him and present him with yet another plaque in ten minutes. Then there was the Attorney General before lunch about the new labor legislation. He rose.

"Very well, gentlemen, you have it. By my authority. This is one I think we need to know. But I want an answer within thirty days."

General Carl Taylor sat in the seventh-floor office of Robert Benson, the Director of Central Intelligence, or DCI, ten days later and gazed down at his own report, clipped to a large sheaf of photo stills, that lay on the low coffee table in front of him.

"It's a funny one, Bob. I can't figure it out," he said.

Benson turned away from the great, sweeping picture windows that form one entire wall of the DCI's office at Langley, Virginia, and face out north by northwest across vistas of trees toward the invisible Potomac River. Like his predecessors, he loved that view, particularly in late spring and early summer, when the woodlands are a wash of tender green. He took his seat on the low settee across the coffee table from Taylor.

"Neither can my grain experts, Carl. And I don't want to go to the Department of Agriculture. Whatever is going on over there in Russia, publicity is the last thing we need, and if I bring in outsiders, it'll be in the papers within a week. So what have you got?"

"Well, the photos show the blight, or whatever it is, is not pandemic," said Taylor. "It's not even regional. That's the twister. If the cause were climatic, there'd be weather phenomena to explain it. There aren't any. If it were a straight disease of the crop, it would be at least regional. If it were parasite-caused, the same would apply. But it's haphazard. There are stands of strong, healthy, growing wheat right alongside the affected acreage. The Condor reconnaissance shows no logical pattern at all. How about you?"

Benson nodded in agreement.

"It's illogical, all right. I've put a couple of assets in on the ground, but they haven't reported back yet. The Soviet press has said nothing. My own agronomy boys have been over your photos backwards and forwards. All they can come up with is some blight of the seed or in the earth. But they can't figure the haphazard nature of it all, either. It fits no known pattern. But the important thing is I have to produce some kind of estimate for the President for the total probable Soviet grain harvest next September and October. And I have to produce it soon."

"There's no way I can photograph every damn stand of wheat and barley in the Soviet Union, even with Condor," said Taylor. "It would take months. Can you give me that?"

"Not a chance," said Benson. "I need information about the troop movements along the China border, the buildup opposite Turkey and Iran. I need a constant watch on the Red Army deployments in East Germany and the locations of the new SS-twenties behind the Urals."

"Then I can only come up with a percentage figure based on what we have photographed to date, and extrapolate for a Soviet-wide figure," said Taylor.

"It's got to be accurate," said Benson. "I don't want a repeat of 1977."

Taylor winced at the memory, even though he had not been Director of the NRO in that year. In 1977 the American intelligence machine had been fooled by a gigantic Soviet confidence trick. Throughout the summer, all the experts of the CIA and the Department of Agriculture had been telling the President the Soviet grain crop would reach around 215 million metric tons. Agriculture delegates visiting Russia had been shown fields of fine, healthy wheat; in fact, these had been the exceptions. Photoreconnaissance analysis had been faulty. In the autumn the then Soviet President, Leonid Brezhnev, had calmly announced the Soviet crop would be only 194 million tons.

As a result, the price of the U.S. wheat surplus over domestic requirements had shot up, in the certainty the Russians would after all have to buy close on 20 million tons. Too late. Through the summer, acting through French-based front companies, Moscow had already bought up futures for enough wheat to cover the deficit—and at the old, low price. They had even chartered dry-cargo shipping space through front men, then redirected the ships, which were en route to Western Europe, into Soviet ports. The affair was known in Langley as "the Sting."

Carl Taylor rose. "Okay, Bob, I'll go on taking happy snapshots."

"Carl." The DCI's voice stopped him in the doorway. "Nice pictures are not enough. By July first I want the Condors back on military deployment. Give me the best grain-figure estimates you have by the end of the month. Err, if you must, on the side of caution. And if there's *anything* your boys spot that could explain the phenomenon, go back and reshoot it. Somehow we have to find out what the hell is happening to the Soviet wheat."

President Matthews's Condor satellites could see most things in the Soviet Union, but they could not observe Harold Lessing, one of the three first secretaries in the Commercial Section of the British Embassy in Moscow at his desk the following morning. It was probably just as well, for he would have been the first to agree he was not an edifying sight. He was pale as a sheet and feeling extremely sick.

The main embassy building of the British mission in the Soviet capital is a fine old pre-Revolution mansion facing north on Maurice Thorez Embankment, staring straight across the Moscow River at the south facade of the Kremlin wall. It once belonged to a millionaire sugar merchant in tsarist days, and was snapped up by the British soon after the Revolution. The Soviet government has been trying to get the British out of there ever since. Stalin hated the place; every morning as he rose he had to see, across the river from his private apartments, the Union Jack fluttering in the morning breeze, and it angered him greatly.

But the Commercial Section does not have the fortune to

dwell in this elegant cream-and-gold mansion. It functions in a drab complex of postwar jerry-built office blocks two miles away on Kutuzovsky Prospekt, almost opposite the wedding-cake-style Ukraina Hotel. The same compound, guarded at its single gate by several watchful militiamen, contains several drab apartment buildings set aside for the flats of diplomatic personnel from a score or more of foreign embassies, and is called collectively the "Korpus Diplomatik," or Diplomats' Compound.

Harold Lessing's office was on the top floor of the commercial office block. When he finally fainted at ten-thirty that bright May morning, it was the sound of the telephone he brought crashing to the carpet with him that alerted his secretary in the neighboring office. Quietly and efficiently, she summoned the commercial counselor, who had two young attachés assist Lessing, by this time groggily conscious again, out of the building, across the parking lot, and up to his own sixth-floor apartment in Korpus 6, a hundred yards away.

Simultaneously, the commercial counselor telephoned the main embassy on Maurice Thorez Embankment, informed the head of Chancery, and asked for the embassy doctor to be sent over. By noon, having examined Lessing in his own bed in his own flat, the doctor was conferring with the commercial counselor. To his surprise, the senior man cut him short and suggested they drive over to the main embassy to consult jointly with the head of Chancery. Only later did the doctor, an ordinary British general practitioner doing a three-year stint on attachment to the embassy with the rank of First Secretary, realize why the move was necessary. The head of Chancery took them all to a special room in the embassy building that was secure from wiretapping—something the Commercial Section was definitely not.

"It's a bleeding ulcer," the medico told the two diplomats. "He seemingly has been suffering from what he thought was an excess of acid indigestion for some weeks, even months. Put it down to strain of work and bunged down loads of antacid tablets. Foolish, really; he should have come to me."

"Will it require hospitalization?" asked the head of Chancery, gazing at the ceiling.

"Oh yes, indeed," said the doctor. "I think I can get him admitted here within a few hours. The local Soviet medical men are quite up to that sort of treatment."

There was a brief silence as the two diplomats exchanged glances. The commercial counselor shook his head. Both men had the same thought; because of their need-to-know, both of them were aware of Lessing's real function in the embassy. The doctor was not. The counselor deferred to Chancery.

"That will not be possible," said Chancery smoothly. "Not in Lessing's case. He'll have to be flown to Helsinki on the afternoon shuttle. Will you ensure that he can make it?"

"But surely . . ." began the doctor. Then he stopped. He realized why they had had to drive two miles to have this conversation. Lessing must be the head of the Secret Intelligence Service operation in Moscow. "Ah, yes. Well, now. He's shocked and has lost probably a pint of blood. I've given him a hundred milligrams of pethidine as a tranquilizer. I could give him another shot at three this afternoon. If he's chauffeur-driven to the airport and escorted all the way, yes, he can make Helsinki. But he'll need immediate entry into hospital when he gets there. I'd prefer to go with him myself, just to be sure. I could be back tomorrow."

The head of Chancery rose. "Splendid," he pronounced. "Give yourself two days. And my wife has a list of little items she's run short of, if you'd be so kind. Yes? Thank you so much. I'll make all the arrangements from here."

For years it has been customary in newspapers, magazines, and books to refer to the headquarters of Britain's Secret Intelligence Service, or SIS, or MI6, as being at a certain office block in the borough of Lambeth in London. It is a custom that causes quiet amusement to the staff members of "the Firm," as it is more colloquially known in the community of such organizations, for the Lambeth address is a sedulously maintained front.

In much the same way, a front is maintained at Leconfield House on Curzon Street, still supposed to be the home of the counterintelligence arm, MI5, to decoy the unneeded inquirer. In reality, those indefatigable spy-catchers have not dwelt near the Playboy Club for years.

The real home of the world's most secret Secret Intelligence Service is a modern-design steel-and-concrete block, allocated by the Department of the Environment, a stone's throw from one of the capital's principal Southern Regional railway stations, and it was taken over in the early seventies.

It was in his top-floor suite with its tinted windows looking out toward the spire of Big Ben and the Houses of Parliament across the river that, just after lunch, the Director General of the SIS received the news of Lessing's illness. The call came on one of the internal lines from the head of Personnel, who had received the message from the basement cipher room. He listened carefully.

"How long will he be off?" he asked at length.

"Several months, at least," said Personnel. "There'll be a couple of weeks in hospital in Helsinki, then home for a bit more. Probably several more weeks' convalescence."

"Pity," mused the Director General. "We shall have to replace him rather fast." His capacious memory recalled to him that Lessing had been running two Russian agents, low-level staffers in the Red Army and the Soviet Foreign Ministry, respectively—not world-beating, but useful. Finally he said, "Let me know when Lessing is safely tucked up in Helsinki. And get me a short list of possibles for his replacement. By close of play tonight, please."

Sir Nigel Irvine was the third successive professional intelligence man to rise to the post of Director General of the SIS. The vastly bigger American CIA, which had been brought to the peak of its powers by its first Director, Allen Dulles, had, as a result of abusing its strength with go-it-alone antics, in the early seventies finally been brought under the control of an outsider, Admiral Stansfield Turner. It was ironic that at exactly the same period a British government had finally done the opposite, breaking the tradition of putting the Firm under a senior diplomat from the Foreign Office and letting a professional take over.

The risk had worked well. The Firm had paid a long penance for the Burgess, MacLean, and Philby affairs, and Sir Nigel Irvine was determined that the tradition of a professional at the head of the Firm would continue after him. That was why he intended to be as strict as any of his immediate predecessors in preventing the emergence of any "Lone Rangers."

"This is a service, not a trapeze act," he used to tell the novices at Beaconsfield. "We're not here for the applause."

It was already dark by the time the three files arrived on Sir Nigel Irvine's desk, but he wanted to get the selection finished and was prepared to stay on. He spent an hour poring over the files, but the selection seemed fairly obvious. Finally he used the telephone to ask the head of Personnel, who was still in the building, to step by. His secretary showed the staffer in, two minutes later.

Sir Nigel hospitably poured the man a whiskey and soda to match his own. He saw no reason not to permit himself a few of the gracious things of life, and he had arranged a well-appointed office, perhaps to compensate for the stink of combat in 1944 and 1945, and the dingy hotels of Vienna in the late forties when he was a junior agent in the Firm, suborning Soviet personnel in the Russian-occupied areas of Austria. Two of his recruits of that period, sleepers for years, were still being run, he was able to congratulate himself.

Although the building housing the SIS was of modern steel, concrete, and chrome, the top-floor office of its Director General was decorated with an older and more elegant motif. The wallpaper was a restful café au lait; the wall-to-wall carpet, burnt orange. The desk, the high chair behind it, the two uprights in front of it, and the button-back leather Chesterfield were all genuine antiques.

From the Department of the Environment store of pictures, to which the mandarins of Britain's Civil Service have access for the decoration of their office walls, Sir Nigel had collared a Dufy, a Vlaminck, and a slightly suspect Breughel. He had had his eye on a small but exquisite Fragonard, but a shifty grandee in Treasury had got there first.

Unlike the Foreign and Commonwealth Office, whose walls were hung with oils of past foreign ministers like Canning and Grey, the Firm had always eschewed ancestral portraits. In any case, whoever heard of such self-effacing men as Britain's successive spymasters enjoying having their likeness put on record in the first place? Nor were portraits of the Queen in full regalia much in favor, though the White House and Langley were plastered with signed photos of the latest President.

"One's commitment to service of Queen and country in this building needs no further advertisement," a dumbfounded visitor from the CIA at Langley had once been told. "If it did, one wouldn't be working here, anyway."

Sir Nigel turned from the window and his study of the lights of the West End across the water.

"It looks like Munro, wouldn't you say?" he asked.

"I would have thought so," answered Personnel.

"What's he like? I've read the file; I know him slightly. Give me the personal touch."

"Secretive."

"Good."
"A bit of a loner."
"Blast."
"It's a question of his Russian," said Personnel. "The other two have good, working Russian. Munro can pass for one. He doesn't normally. Speaks to them in strongly accented, moderate Russian. When he drops that, he can blend right in. It's just that, well, to run Mallard and Merganser at such short notice, brilliant Russian would be an asset."
"Mallard" and "Merganser" were the code names for the two low-level agents recruited and run by Lessing. Russians being run inside the Soviet Union by the Firm tended to have bird names, in alphabetical order according to the date of recruitment. The two *M*s were recent acquisitions. Sir Nigel grunted.
"Very well. Munro it is. Where is he now?"
"On training. At Beaconsfield. Tradecraft."
"Have him here tomorrow afternoon. Since he's not married, he can probably leave quite quickly. No need to hang about. I'll have the Foreign Office agree to the appointment in the morning as Lessing's replacement in the Commercial Section."

Beaconsfield, being in the Home County of Buckinghamshire—which is to say, within easy reach of central London—was years ago a favored area for the elegant country homes of those who enjoyed high and wealthy status in the capital. By the early seventies, most of the buildings played host to seminars, retreats, executive courses in management and marketing, or even religious observation. One of them housed the Joint Services School of Russian and was quite open about it; another, smaller house, contained the training school of the SIS and was not open about it at all.
Adam Munro's course in tradecraft was popular, not the least because it broke the wearisome routine of enciphering and deciphering. He had his class's attention, and he knew it.
"Right," said Munro that morning in the last week of the month. "Now for some snags and how to get out of them."
The class was still with expectancy. Routine procedures were one thing; a sniff of some real Opposition was more interesting.
"You have to pick up a package from a contact," said Munro. "But you are being tailed by the local fuzz. You have

diplomatic cover in case of arrest, but your contact does not. He's right out in the cold, a local man. He's coming to a meet, and you can't stop him. He knows that if he hangs about too long, he could attract attention, so he'll wait ten minutes. What do you do?"

"Shake the tail," suggested someone.

Munro shook his head.

"For one thing, you're supposed to be an innocent diplomat, not a Houdini. Lose the tail and you give yourself away as a trained agent. Secondly, you might not succeed. If it's the KGB and they're using the first team, you won't do it, short of dodging back into the embassy. Try again."

"Abort," said another trainee. "Don't show. The safety of the unprotected contributor is paramount."

"Right," said Munro. "But that leaves your man with a package he can't hold onto forever, and no procedure for an alternative meet." He paused for several seconds. "Or does he . . . ?"

"There's a second procedure established in the event of an abort," suggested a third student.

"Good," said Munro. "When you had him alone in the good old days before the routine surveillance was switched to yourself, you briefed him on a whole range of alternative meets in the event of an abort. So he waits ten minutes; you don't show up; he goes off nice and innocently to the second meeting point. What is this procedure called?"

"Fallback," ventured the bright spark who wanted to shake off the tail.

"First fallback," corrected Munro. "We'll be doing all this on the streets of London in a couple of months, so get it right." They scribbled hard. "Okay. You have a second location in the city, but you're still tailed. You haven't got anywhere. What happens at the first-fallback location?"

There was a general silence. Munro gave them thirty seconds.

"You don't meet at this location," he instructed. "Under the procedures you have taught your contact, the second location is always a place where he can observe you but you can stay well away from him. When you know he is watching you, from a terrace perhaps, from a café, but always well away from you, you give him a signal. Can be anything: scratch an ear, blow your nose, drop a newspaper and pick it up again. What does that mean to the contact?"

"That you're setting up the third meet, according to your prearranged procedures," said Bright Spark.

"Precisely. But you're *still* being tailed. Where does the third meet happen? What kind of place?"

This time there were no takers.

"It's a building—a bar, club, restaurant, or what you like—that has a closed front, so that once the door is closed, no one can see through any plate-glass windows from the street into the ground floor. Now, why is that the place for the exchange?"

There was a brief knock, and the head of Student Program poked his face through the doorway. He beckoned to Munro, who left his desk and went across to the door. His superior officer drew him outside into the corridor.

"You've been summoned," he said quietly. "The Master wants to see you. In his office at three. Leave here at the lunch break. Bailey will take over afternoon classes."

Munro returned to his desk, somewhat puzzled. "The Master" was the half-affectionate and half-respectful nickname for any holder of the post of Director General of the Firm.

One of the class had a suggestion to make. "So that you can walk to the contact's table and pick up the package unobserved."

Munro shook his head. "Not quite. When you leave the place, the tailing Opposition might leave one man behind to question the waiters. If you approached your man directly, the face of a contact could be observed and the contributor identified, even by description. Anyone else?"

"Use a drop inside the restaurant," proposed Bright Spark. Another shake from Munro.

"You won't have time," he advised. "The tails will be tumbling into the place a few seconds after you. Maybe the contact, who by arrangement was there before you, will not have found the right toilet cubicle free. Or the right table unoccupied. It's too hit-or-miss. No, this time we'll use the brush-pass. Note it; it goes like this.

"When your contact received your signal at the first-fallback location that you were under surveillance, he moved into the agreed procedure. He synchronized his watch to the nearest second with a reliable public clock or, preferably, with the telephone time service. In another place, you did exactly the same.

"At an agreed hour, he is already sitting in the agreed bar, or whatever. Outside the door, you are approaching at exactly the same time, to the nearest second. If you're ahead of time, delay a bit by adjusting your shoelace, pausing at a shopwindow. Do not consult your watch in an obvious manner.

"To the second, you enter the bar and the door closes behind you. At the same second, the contact is on his feet, bill paid, moving toward the door. At a minimum, five seconds will elapse before the door opens again and the fuzz come in. You brush past your contact a couple of feet inside the door, making sure it is closed to block off vision. As you brush past, you pass the package or collect it. Part company and proceed to a vacant table or barstool. The Opposition will come in seconds later. As they move past him, the contact steps out and vanishes. Later the bar staff will confirm you spoke to nobody, contacted nobody. You paused at nobody's table, nor anyone at yours. You have the package in an inside pocket, and you finish your drink and go back to the embassy. The Opposition will, hopefully, report that you contacted nobody throughout the entire stroll.

"That is the brush-pass . . . and *that* is the lunch bell. All right, we'll scrub it for now."

By midafternoon, Adam Munro was closeted in the secure library beneath the Firm's headquarters, beginning to bore through a pile of buff folders. He had just five days to master and commit to memory enough background material to enable him to take over from Harold Lessing at the Firm's "legal resident" in Moscow.

On May 31 he flew from London to Moscow to take up his new appointment.

Munro spent the first week settling in. To all the embassy staff but an informed few he was just a professional diplomat and the hurried replacement for Harold Lessing. The Ambassador, head of Chancery, chief cipher clerk, and commercial counselor knew what his real job was. The fact of his relatively advanced age at forty-six years to be only a First Secretary in the Commercial Section was explained by his late entrance into the diplomatic corps.

The commercial counselor ensured that the commercial files placed before him were as unburdensome as possible. He had a brief and formal reception by the Ambassador in the latter's private office, and a more informal drink with the head of Chancery. He met most of the staff and was taken to a round of diplomatic parties to meet many of the other diplomats from Western embassies. He also had a face-to-face and more businesslike conference with his opposite number at the American Embassy. "Business," as the CIA man confirmed to him, was quiet.

Though it would have made any staffer at the British Embassy in Moscow stand out like a sore thumb to speak no Russian, Munro kept his use of the language to a formal and accented version both in front of his colleagues and when talking to official Russians during the introduction process. At one party, two Soviet Foreign Ministry personnel had had a brief exchange in rapid, colloquial Russian a few feet away. He had understood it completely, and as it was mildly interesting, he had filed it to London.

On his tenth day, he sat alone on a park bench in the sprawling Soviet Exhibition of Economic Achievements, in the extreme northern outskirts of the Russian capital. He was waiting to make first contact with the agent from the Red Army whom he had taken over from Lessing.

Munro had been born in 1936, the son of an Edinburgh doctor, and his boyhood through the war years had been conventional, middle-class, untroubled, and happy. He had attended a local school up to the age of thirteen years and then spent five at Fettes College, one of Scotland's best schools. It was during his period here that his senior languages master had detected in the lad an unusually acute ear for foreign languages.

In 1954, with National Service then obligatory, he had gone into the Army and after basic training secured a posting to his father's old regiment, the First Gordon Highlanders. Transferred to Cyprus, he had been on operations against EOKA partisans in the Troodos Mountains that late summer.

Sitting in a park in Moscow, he could see the farmhouse still, in his mind's eye. They had spent half the night crawling through the heather to surround the place, following a tip-off from an informant. When dawn came, Munro was posted alone at the bottom of a steep escarpment behind the hilltop house. The main body of his platoon stormed the front of the farm just as dawn broke, coming up the shallower slope with the sun behind them.

From above him, on the other side of the hill, he could hear the chattering of the Stens in the quiet dawn. By the first rays of the sun he could see the two figures that came tumbling out of the rear windows, in shadow until their headlong flight down the escarpment took them clear of the lee of the house. They came straight at him, as he crouched behind a fallen olive tree in the shadow of the grove, their legs flying as they sought to keep their balance on the shale. They came nearer, and one of them had what looked like a short black stick in his right hand. Even if he had shouted, he told himself later, they could not have stopped their momentum. But he did not say that to himself at the time. Training took over; he just stood up as they reached a point fifty feet from him, and loosed off two short, lethal bursts.

The force of the bullets lifted them both, one after the other, stopped their momentum, and slammed them onto the shale at the foot of the slope. As a blue plume of cordite smoke drifted away from the muzzle of his Sten, he moved forward to look down at them. He thought he might feel sick or faint. There was nothing; just a dead curiosity. He looked at the faces. They were boys, younger than himself, and he was eighteen.

His sergeant came crashing through the olive grove.

"Well done, laddie!" he shouted. "You got 'em."

Munro looked down at the bodies of the boys who would never marry or have children, never dance to a bouzouki or feel the warmth of sun and wine again. One of them was still clutching the black stick; it was a sausage. A piece of it hung out of the body's mouth. He had been having breakfast. Munro turned on the sergeant.

"You don't own me!" he shouted. "You don't bloody own me! Nobody owns me but me!"

The sergeant put the outburst down to first-kill nerves and failed to report it. Perhaps that was a mistake. For authority failed to notice that Adam Munro was not completely, not one hundred percent, obedient. Not ever again.

Six months later he was urged to consider himself as potential officer material and extend his time in the Army to three years so as to qualify for a short-service commission. Tired of Cyprus, he did so and was posted back to England, to the Officer Cadet Training Unit at Eaton Hall. Three months later he got his "pip" as a second lieutenant.

While form-filling at Eaton Hall, he had mentioned that he was fluent in French and German. One day he was casually tested in both languages, and his claim proved to be correct. Just after his commissioning, it was suggested he might like to apply for the Joint Services Russian language course, which in those days was situated at a camp called Little Russia at Bodmin in Cornwall. The alternative was regimental duties at the barracks in Scotland, so he agreed. Within six months he emerged not merely fluent in Russian but vitually able to pass for a Russian.

In 1957, despite considerable pressure from the regiment to stay on, he left the Army, for he had decided he wanted to be a foreign correspondent. He had seen a few of them in Cyprus and thought he would prefer the job to office work. At the age of twenty-one he joined *The Scotsman* in his native Edinburgh as a cub reporter, and two years later moved to London, where he was taken on by Reuters, the international news agency with its headquarters at 85 Fleet Street.

In the summer of 1960 his languages again came to his rescue; he was twenty-four, and he was posted to the Reuters office in West Berlin as second man to the then bureau chief, Alfred Kluehs. That was the summer before the Wall went up, and within three months he had met Valentina, the woman he now realized to have been the only one he had ever really loved in his life. . . .

A man sat down beside him and coughed. Munro jerked himself out of his reverie. Teaching tradecraft to sprogs one week, he told himself, and forgetting the basic rules a fortnight later. Never slacken attention before a meet.

The Russian looked at him uncomprehendingly, but Munro wore the necessary polka-dot tie. Slowly the Russian put a cigarette in his mouth, eyes on Munro. Corny, but it still worked. Munro took out his lighter and held the flame to the cigarette tip.

"Ronald collapsed at his desk two weeks ago," he said softly and calmly. "Ulcers, I'm afraid. I am Michael. I've been asked to take over from him. Oh, and perhaps you can help me. Is it true that the Ostankino TV tower is the highest structure in Moscow?"

The Russian officer in plainclothes exhaled smoke and relaxed. The words were exactly the ones established by Lessing, whom he had known only as Ronald.

"Yes," he replied. "It is five hundred forty meters high."

He had a folded newspaper in his hand, which he laid on the seat between them. Munro's folded raincoat slipped off his knees to the ground. He retrieved it, refolded it, and placed it on top of the newspaper. The two men ignored each other for ten minutes, while the Russian smoked. Finally he rose and stubbed the butt into the ground, bending as he did so.

"A fortnight's time," muttered Munro. "The men's toilet under G Block at the New State Circus. During the clown Popov's act. The show starts at seven-thirty."

The Russian moved away and continued strolling. Munro surveyed the scene calmly for ten minutes. No one showed interest. He scooped up the mackintosh, newspaper, and buff envelope inside it and returned by Metro to Kutuzovsky Prospekt. The envelope contained an up-to-date list of Red Army officer postings.

CHAPTER TWO

WHILE ADAM MUNRO was changing trains at Revolution Square shortly before eleven A.M. that morning of June 10, a convoy of a dozen sleek black Zil limousines was sweeping through the Borovitsky Gate in the Kremlin wall a hundred feet above his head and thirteen hundred feet southwest of him. The Soviet Politburo was about to begin a meeting that would change history.

The Kremlin is a triangular compound, with its apex, dominated by the Sobakin Tower, pointing due north. On all sides it is protected by a fifty-foot wall studded by eighteen towers and penetrated by four gates.

The southern two thirds of this triangle is the tourist area, where docile parties troop along to admire the cathedrals, halls, and palaces of the long-dead tsars. At the midsection is a cleared swath of tarmacadam, patrolled by guards, an invisible dividing line across which tourists may not step. But the cavalcade of custom-built limousines that morning purred across this open space toward the three buildings in the northern part of the Kremlin.

The smallest of these is the Kremlin Theater to the east. Half exposed and half hidden behind the theater stands the building of the Council of Ministers, seemingly the home of the government, inasmuch as the ministers meet here. But the real government of the USSR lies not in the Council of Ministers but in the Politburo, the tiny, exclusive group who constitute the pinnacle of the Central Committee of the Communist Party of the Soviet Union, or CPSU.

The third building is the biggest. It lies up along the western facade, just behind the wall's crenelations, overlooking the Alexandrovsky Gardens down below. In shape it is a long, slim rectangle running north. The southern end is the old Arsenal, a museum for antique weaponry. But just behind the Arsenal the interior walls are blocked off. To reach the upper section, one must arrive from outside and penetrate a high, wrought-iron barrier that spans the gap between the Ministers Building and the Arsenal. The limousines that morning swept through the wrought-iron gates and came to rest beside the upper entrance to the secret building.

In shape, the upper Arsenal is a hollow rectangle; inside is a narrow courtyard running north and south, and dividing the complex into two even narrower blocks of apartments and offices. There are four stories, including the attics. Halfway up the inner, eastern office block, on the third floor, overlooking the courtyard only and screened from prying eyes, is the room where the Politburo meets every Thursday morning to hold sway over 250 million Soviet citizens and scores of millions more who like to think they dwell outside the boundaries of the Russian empire.

For an empire it is. Although in theory the Russian Soviet Federated Socialist Republic is one of fifteen republics that make up the Soviet Union, in effect the Russia of the tsars, ancient or modern, rules the other fourteen non-Russian republics with a rod of iron. The three arms Russia uses and needs to implement this rule are the Red Army, including as it always does the Navy and Air Force; the Committee of State Security, or KGB, with its 100,000 staffers, 300,000 armed troops, and 600,000 informers; and the Party Organizations Section of the General Secretariat of the Central Committee, controlling the Party cadres in every place of work, thought, abode, study, and leisure from the Arctic to the hills of Persia, from the fringes of Brunswick to the shores of the Sea of Japan. And that is just inside the empire.

The room in which the Politburo meets in the Arsenal Building of the Kremlin is about fifty feet long and twenty-five wide, not enormous for the power enclosed in it. It is decorated in the heavy, marbled decor favored by the Party bosses, but dominated by a long table topped with green baize. The table is T-shaped.

That morning, June 10, 1982, was unusual, for they had

received no agenda, just a summons. And the men who grouped at the table to take their places sensed, with the perceptive collective nose for danger that had brought them all to this pinnacle, that something of importance was afoot.

Seated at the center point of the head of the T in his usual chair was the chief of them all, Maxim Rudin. Ostensibly his superiority lay in his title of President of the USSR. But nothing except the weather is ever quite what it appears in Russia. His real power came to him through his title of General Secretary of the Communist Party of the USSR. As such, he was also Chairman of the Central Committee, and Chairman of the Politburo.

At the age of seventy-one he was craggy, brooding, and immensely cunning; had he not been the latter, he would never have occupied the chair that had once supported Stalin (who rarely ever called Politburo meetings), Malenkov, Khrushchev, and Brezhnev. To his left and right he was flanked by four secretaries from his own personal secretariat, men loyal to him personally above all else. Behind him, at each corner of the north wall of the chamber, was a small table. At one sat two stenographers, a man and a woman, taking down every word in shorthand. At the other, as a countercheck, two men hunched over the slowly turning spools of a tape recorder. There was a spare recorder to take over during spool changes.

The Politburo had thirteen members, and the other twelve ranged themselves, six a side, down the stem of the T-shaped table, facing jotting pads, carafes of water, ashtrays. At the far end of this arm of the table was one single chair. The Politburo men checked numbers to make sure no one was missing. For the empty seat was the Penal Chair, sat in only by a man on his last appearance in that room, a man forced to listen to his own denunciation by his former colleagues, a man facing disgrace, ruin, and once, not long ago, death at the Black Wall of the Lubyanka. The custom has always been to delay the condemned man until, on entering, he finds all seats taken and only the Penal Chair free. Then he knows. But this morning it was empty. And all were present.

Rudin leaned back and surveyed the twelve through half-closed eyes, the smoke from his inevitable cigarette drifting past his face. He still favored the old-style Russian *papyrossy*, half tobacco and half thin cardboard tube, the tube nipped twice between finger and thumb to filter the smoke. His aides had been taught to pass them to him one after the other, and his doctors to shut up.

To his left on the stem of the table was Vassili Petrov, age forty-nine, his own protégé and young for the job he held, head of the Party Organizations Section of the General Secretariat of the Central Committee. Rudin could count on him in the trouble that lay ahead. Beside Petrov was the veteran Foreign Minister, Dmitri Rykov, who would side with Rudin because he had nowhere else to go. Beyond him was Yuri Ivanenko, slim and ruthless at fifty-three, standing out like a sore thumb in his elegant London-tailored suit, as if flaunting his sophistication to a group of men who hated all forms of Westernness. Picked personally by Rudin to be chairman of the KGB, Ivanenko would side with him simply because the opposition would come from quarters who hated Ivanenko and wanted him destroyed.

On the other side of the table sat Yefrem Vishnayev, also young for the job, like half the post-Brezhnev Politburo. At fifty-five he was the Party theoretician, spare, ascetic, disapproving, the scourge of dissidents and deviationists, guardian of Marxist purity, and consumed by a pathological loathing of the capitalist West. The opposition would come here, Rudin knew. By his side was Marshal Nikolai Kerensky, age sixty-three, Defense Minister and chief of the Red Army. He would go where the interests of the Red Army led him.

That left seven, including Vladimir Komarov, responsible for Agriculture and sitting white-faced because he, like Rudin and Ivanenko alone, knew roughly what was to come. The KGB chief betrayed no emotion; the rest did not know.

"It" came when Rudin gestured to one of the Kremlin praetorian guards at the door at the far end of the room to admit the person waiting in fear and trembling outside.

"Let me present Professor Ivan Ivanovich Yakovlev, Comrades," Rudin growled as the man advanced timorously to the end of the table and stood waiting, his sweat-damp report in his hands. "The professor is our senior agronomist and grain specialist from the Ministry of Agriculture, and a member of the Academy of Sciences. He has a report for our attention. Proceed, Professor."

Rudin, who had read the report several days earlier in the privacy of his study, leaned back and gazed above the man's head at the far ceiling. Ivanenko carefully lit a Western king-size filtered cigarette. Komarov wiped his brow and studied his hands. The professor cleared his throat.

"Comrades," he began hesistantly. No one disagreed that they were comrades. With a deep breath the scientist stared down at his papers and plunged straight into his report.

"Last December and January our long-range weather forecast satellites predicted an unusually damp winter and early spring. As a result and in accordance with habitual scientific practice, it was decided at the Ministry of Agriculture that our seed grain for the spring planting should be treated with a prophylactic dressing to inhibit fungoid infections that would probably be prevalent as a result of the dampness. This has been done many times before.

"The treatment selected was a dual-purpose seed dressing: an organomercurial compound to inhibit fungoid attack on the germinating grain, and a pesticide and bird repellant called lindane. It was agreed in scientific committee that because the USSR, following the unfortunate damage through frost to the winter wheat crop, would need at least one hundred forty million tons of crop from the spring wheat plantings, it would be necessary to sow six and a quarter million tons of seed grain."

All eyes were on him now, the fidgeting stilled. The Politburo members could smell danger a mile off. Only Komarov, the one responsible for Agriculture, stared at the table in misery. Several eyes swiveled to him, sensing blood. The professor swallowed hard and went on.

"At the rate of two ounces of organomercurial seed dressing per ton of grain, the requirement was for three hundred fifty tons of dressing. There were only seventy tons in stock. An immediate order was sent to the manufacturing plant for this dressing at Kuibyshev to go into immediate production to make up the required two hundred eighty tons."

"Is there only one such factory?" asked Petrov.

"Yes, Comrade. The tonnages required do not justify more factories. The Kuibyshev factory is a major chemical plant, making many insecticides, weed killers, fertilizers, and so forth. The production of the two hundred eighty tons of this chemical would take less than forty hours."

"Continue," ordered Rudin.

"Due to a confusion in communication, the factory was undergoing annual maintenance, and time was running short if the dressing was to be distributed to the one hundred twenty-seven dressing stations for seed grain scattered across the Soviet Union, the grain treated, and then taken back to the thousands of state and collective farms in time for planting. So an energetic young official and Party cadre was sent from Moscow to hurry things along. It appears he ordered the workmen to terminate what they were doing, restore the plant to operating order, and start it functioning again."

"He failed to do it in time?" rasped Marshal Kerensky.

"No, Comrade Marshal, the factory started work again, although the maintenance engineers had not quite finished. But something malfunctioned. A hopper valve. Lindane is a very powerful chemical, and the dosage of the lindane to the remainder of the organomercurial compound has to be strictly regulated.

"The valve on the lindane hopper, although registering one-third open on the control panel, was in fact stuck at full open. The whole two hundred eighty tons of dressing were affected."

"What about quality control?" asked one of the members, who had been born on a farm. The professor swallowed again and wished he could quietly go into exile in Siberia without any more of this torture.

"There was a conjunction of coincidence and error," he confessed. "The chief analytical and quality-control chemist was away on holiday at Sochi during the plant closedown. He was summoned back by cable. But because of fog in the Kuibyshev area, his plane was diverted and he had to continue his journey by train. When he arrived, production was complete."

"The dressing was not tested?" asked Petrov incredulously. The professor looked more sick than ever.

"The chemist insisted on making quality-control tests. The young functionary from Moscow wanted the entire production shipped at once. An argument ensued. In the event, a compromise was reached. The chemist wanted to test every tenth bag of dressing, twenty-eight in all. The functionary insisted he could have only one. That was when the third error occurred.

"The new bags had been stacked along with the reserve of seventy tons left over from last year. In the warehouse, one of the loaders, receiving a report to send one single bag to the laboratory for testing, selected one of the old bags. Tests proved it was perfectly in order, and the entire consignment was shipped."

He ended his report. There was nothing more to say. He could have tried to explain that a conjunction of three mistakes—a mechanical malfunction, an error of judgment by two men under pressure, and a piece of carelessness by a warehouseman—had combined to produce the catastrophe. But that was not his job, and he did not intend to make lame excuses for other men. The silence in the room was murderous.

Vishnayev came in with icy clarity.

"What exactly is the effect of an excessive component of lindane in this organomercurial compound?" he asked.

"Comrade, it causes a toxic effect on the germinating seed in the ground, rather than a protective effect. The seedlings come up—if at all—stunted, sparse, and mottled brown. There is virtually no grain yield from such affected stems."

"And how much of the spring planting has been affected?" asked Vishnayev coldly.

"Just about four fifths, Comrade. The seventy tons of reserve compound was perfectly all right. The two hundred eighty tons of new compound were all affected by the jamming hopper valve."

"And the toxic dressing was all mixed in with seed grain and planted?"

"Yes, Comrade."

Two minutes later the professor was dismissed, to his privacy and his oblivion.

Vishnayev turned to Komarov.

"Forgive my ignorance, Comrade, but it would appear you had some foreknowledge of this affair. What has happened to the functionary who produced this . . . cockup?" (He used a crude Russian expression that refers to a pile of dog mess on the pavement.)

Ivanenko cut in.

"He is in our hands," he said, "along with the analytical chemist who deserted his function, the warehouseman, who is simply of exceptionally low intelligence, and the maintenance team of engineers, who claim they demanded and received written instructions to wind up their work before they had finished."

"This functionary, has he talked?" asked Vishnayev.

Ivanenko considered a mental image of the broken man in the cellars beneath the Lubyanka.

"Extensively," he said.

"Is he a saboteur, a fascist agent?"

"No," said Ivanenko with a sigh. "Just an idiot; an ambitious apparatchik trying to overfulfill his orders. You can believe me on that one. We do know by now the inside of that man's skull."

"Then one last question, just so that we can all be sure of the dimensions of this affair." Vishnayev swung back to the unhappy Komarov. "We already know we will save only fifty million tons of the expected hundred million from the winter wheat. How much will we now get from the spring wheat this coming October?"

Komarov glanced at Rudin, who nodded imperceptibly.

"Out of the hundred-forty-million-ton target for the spring-sown wheat and other grains, we cannot reasonably expect more than fifty million tons," he said quietly.

The meeting sat in stunned horror.

"That means a total yield over both crops of one hundred million tons," breathed Petrov. "A national shortfall of one hundred forty million tons. We could have taken a shortfall of fifty, even seventy million tons. We've done it before, endured the shortages, and bought what we could from elsewhere. But this . . ."

Rudin closed the meeting.

"We have as big a problem here as we have ever confronted, Chinese and American imperialism included. I propose we adjourn and separately seek some suggestions. It goes without saying that this news does not pass outside those present in this room. Our next meeting will be a week from today."

As the thirteen men and the four aides at the top table came to their feet, Petrov turned to the impassive Ivanenko.

"This doesn't mean shortages," he muttered, "this means famine."

The Soviet Politburo descended to their chauffeur-driven Zil limousines, still absorbing the knowledge that a weedy professor of agronomy had just placed a time bomb under one of the world's two superpowers.

Adam Munro's thoughts a week later as he sat in the circle at the Bolshoi Theater on Karl Marx Prospekt were not on war but on love—and not for the excited embassy secretary beside him who had prevailed on him to take her to the ballet.

He was not a great fan of ballet, though he conceded he liked some of the music. But the grace of the entrechats and fouettés—or as he called it, the jumping about—left him cold. By the second act of *Giselle,* the evening's offering, his thoughts were straying back again to Berlin.

It had been a beautiful affair, a once-in-a-lifetime love. He was twenty-four, turning twenty-five, and she nineteen, dark and lovely. Because of her job they had had to conduct their affair in secret, furtively meeting in darkened streets so that he could pick her up in his car and take her back to his small flat at the western end of Charlottenburg without anyone's seeing. They had loved and talked, she had made him suppers, and they had loved again.

At first, the clandestine nature of their affair, like married people slipping away from the world and each other's partners, had added spice, piquancy to the loving. But by the summer of 1961, when the forests of Berlin were ablaze with leaves and flowers, when there was boating on the lakes and swimming from the shores, it had become cramped, frustrating. That was when he had asked her to marry him, and she had almost agreed. She might still have agreed, but then came the Wall. It was completed on August 13, 1961, but it was obvious for a week that it was going up.

That was when she made her decision, and they loved for the last time. She could not, she told him, abandon her parents to what would happen to them: to the disgrace, to the loss of her father's trusted job, her mother's beloved apartment, for which she had waited so many years through the dark times. She could not destroy her young brother's chances of a good education and prospects. And finally, she could not bear to know that she would never see her beloved homeland again.

So she left, and he watched from the shadows as she slipped back into the East through the last uncompleted section in the Wall, sad and lonely and heartbroken—and very, very beautiful.

He had never seen her again, and he had never mentioned her to anyone, guarding her memory with his quiet Scottish secretiveness. He had never let on that he had loved and still loved a Russian girl called Valentina who had been a secretary-stenographer with the Soviet delegation to the Four Power Conference in Berlin. And that, as he well knew, was far out against the rules.

After Valentina, Berlin had palled. A year later he was transferred by Reuters to Paris, and it was two years after that, when he was back in London again, kicking his heels in the head office on Fleet Street, that a civilian he had known in Berlin, a man who had worked at the British headquarters there, Hitler's old Olympic stadium, had made a point of looking him up and renewing their acquaintance. There had been a dinner, and another man had joined them. The acquaintance from the stadium had excused himself and left during coffee. The newcomer had been friendly and noncommittal. But by the second brandy he had made his point.

"Some of my associates in the Firm," he had said with disarming diffidence, "were wondering if you could do us a little favor."

That was the first time Munro had heard the term "the Firm." Later he would learn the terminology. To those in the Anglo-American alliance of intelligence services, a strange and guarded but ultimately vital alliance, the SIS was always called "the Firm." To its employees, those in the counterintelligence arm, or M15, were "the Colleagues." The CIA at Langley, Virginia, was "the Company," and its staff "the Cousins." On the opposite side worked "the Opposition," whose headquarters in Moscow were at No. 2 Dzerzhinsky Square, named after Feliks Dzerzhinsky, Lenin's secret-police boss and the founder of the old Cheka. This building would always be known as "the Center," and the territory east of the Iron Curtain as "the Bloc."

The meeting in the London restaurant was in December 1964, and the proposal, confirmed later in a small flat in Chelsea, was for a "little run into the Bloc." He made it in the spring of 1965 while ostensibly covering the Leipzig Fair in East Germany. It was a pig of a run.

He left Leipzig at the right time and drove to the meet in Dresden, close by the Albertinium Museum. The package in his inner pocket felt like five Bibles, and everyone seemed to be looking at him. The East German Army officer who knew where the Russians were locating their tactical rockets in the Saxon hillsides showed up half an hour late, by which time two officers of the People's Police undoubtedly *were* watching him. The swap of packages went off all right, somewhere in the bushes of the nearby park. Then he returned to his car and set off southwest for the Gera Crossroads and the Bavarian border checkpoint. On the outskirts of Dresden a local driver rammed him from the front offside, although Munro had the right-of-way. He had not even had time to transfer the package to the hiding place between the trunk and the back seat; it was still in the breast pocket of his blazer.

There were two gut-wrenching hours in a local police station, every moment dreading the command "Turn out your pockets, please, *mein Herr*." There was enough up against his breastbone to collect him twenty-five years in Potma labor camp. Eventually he was allowed to go. Then the battery went flat and four policemen had to push-start him.

The front offside wheel was screaming from a fractured roller bearing inside the hub, and it was suggested he might like to stay overnight and get it mended. He pleaded that his visa time expired at midnight—which it did—and set off again. He made the checkpoint on the Saale River between Plauen in East Germany and Hof in the West at ten minutes before midnight, having driven at twenty miles per hour all the way, rending the night air with the screaming of the front wheel. When he chugged past the Bavarian guards on the other side, he was wet with sweat.

A year later he left Reuters and accepted a suggestion to sit for the Civil Service Entrance examinations as a late entrant. He was twenty-nine.

The CSE examinations are unavoidable for anyone trying to join the Civil Service. Based on the results, the Treasury has first choice of the cream, which enables that department to foul up the British economy with impeccable academic references. The Foreign and Commonwealth Office get next choice, and as Munro had a First he had no trouble entering the foreign service, usually the cover for staffers of the Firm.

In sixteen years he had specialized in economic intelligence matters and the Soviet Union, though he had never been there before. He had had foreign postings in Turkey, Austria, and Mexico. In 1967, just turned thirty-one, he had married. But after the honeymoon it had been an increasingly loveless union, a mistake, and it was quietly ended six years later. Since then there had been affairs, of course, and they were all known to the Firm, but he had stayed single.

There was one affair he had never mentioned to the Firm, and had the fact of it, and his covering up of it, leaked out, he would have been fired on the spot.

On joining the service, like everyone else, he had to write a complete life story of himself, followed by a viva voce examination by a senior officer. (This procedure is repeated every five years of service. Among the matters of interest are inevitably any emotional or social involvement with personnel from behind the Iron Curtain—or anywhere else, for that matter.)

The first time he was asked, something inside him rebelled,

as it had in the olive grove on Cyprus. He knew he was loyal, that he would never be suborned over the matter of Valentina, even if the Opposition knew about it, which he was certain they did not. If an attempt were ever made to blackmail him over it, he would admit it and resign, but never accede. He just did not want the fingers of other men, not to mention filing clerks, rummaging through a part of the most private inside of him. *Nobody owns me but me!* So he said "No" to the question, and broke the rules. Once trapped by the lie, he had to stick with it. He repeated it three times in sixteen years. Nothing had ever happened because of it, and nothing ever would happen. He was certain of it. The affair was a secret, dead and buried. It would always be so.

Had he been less deep in his reverie, he might have noticed something. From a private box high in the left-hand wall of the theater, he was being observed. Before the lights went up for the entr'acte, the watcher had vanished.

The thirteen men who grouped around the Politburo table in the Kremlin the following day were subdued and watchful, sensing that the report of the professor of agronomy could trigger a faction fight such as there had not been since Khrushchev fell.

Rudin as usual surveyed them all through his drifting spire of cigarette smoke. Petrov of Party Organizations was in his usual seat to his left, with Ivanenko of the KGB beyond him. Rykov of Foreign Affairs shuffled his papers; Vishnayev the Party theoretician and Kerensky of the Red Army sat in stony silence. Rudin surveyed the other seven, calculating which way they would jump if it came to a fight.

There were the three non-Russians: Vitautas the Balt, from Vilnius, Lithuania; Chavadze the Georgian, from Tbilisi; and Mukhamed the Tajik, an Oriental and born a Muslim. The presence of each was a sop to the minorities, but in fact each had paid the price to be there. Each, Rudin knew, was completely russified; the price had been high, higher than a Great Russian would have had to pay. Each had been First Party Secretary for his republic, and two still were. Each had supervised programs of vigorous repression against their fellow nationals, crushing dissidents, nationalists, poets, writers, artists, intelligentsia, and workers who had even hinted at a less than one hundred percent acceptance of the rule of Great Russia over them. None could go back without the protection of

Moscow, and each would side, if it came to it, with the faction that would ensure his survival—that is, the winning one. Rudin did not relish the prospect of a faction fight, but he had held it in mind since he had first read Professor Yakovlev's report in the privacy of his study.

That left four more, all Russians. There were Komarov of the Agriculture Ministry, still extremely ill at ease; Stepanov, head of the trade unions; Shushkin, responsible for liaison with foreign Communist parties worldwide; and Petryanov, with special responsibilities for economics and industrial planning.

"Comrades," began Rudin slowly, "you have all studied the Yakovlev report at your leisure. You have all observed Comrade Komarov's separate report to the effect that next September and October our aggregate grain yield will fall short of target by close to one hundred forty million tons. Let us consider first questions first. Can the Soviet Union survive for one year on no more than one hundred million tons of grain?"

The discussion lasted an hour. It was bitter, acrimonious, but virtually unanimous. Such a shortage of grain would lead to privations that had not been seen since the Second World War. If the state bought even an irreducible minimum to make bread for the cities, the countryside would be left with almost nothing. The slaughter of livestock, as the winter snows covered the grazing lands and the beasts were left without forage or feed grains, would strip the Soviet Union of every four-footed animal. It would take a generation to recover the livestock herds. To leave even the minimum of grain on the land would starve the cities.

At last Rudin cut them short.

"Very well. If we insist on accepting the famine, both in grains and, as a consequence, in meat several months later, what will be the outcome in terms of national discipline?"

Petrov broke the ensuing silence. He admitted that there already existed a groundswell of restiveness among the broad masses of the people, evidenced by a recent rash of small outbreaks of disorder and resignations from the Party, all reported back to him in the Central Committee through the million tendrils of the Party machine. In the face of a true famine, many Party cadres could side with the proletariat.

The non-Russians nodded in agreement. In their republics Moscow's grip was always likely to be less total then inside the RSFSR itself.

"We could strip the six East European satellites," suggested Petryanov, not even bothering to refer to the East Europeans as "fraternal comrades."

"Poland and Rumania would burst into flame for a start," countered Shushkin, the liaison man with Eastern Europe. "Probably Hungary to follow suit."

"The Red Army could deal with them," snarled Marshal Kerensky.

"Not three at a time. Not nowadays," said Rudin.

"We are still talking only of a total acquisition of ten million tons," said Komarov. "It's not enough."

"Comrade Stepanov?" asked Rudin.

The head of the state-controlled trade unions chose his words carefully.

"In the event of genuine famine this winter and next spring through summer," he said, studying his pencil, "it would not be possible to guarantee the absence of the outbreak of acts of disorder, perhaps on a wide scale."

Ivanenko, sitting quietly, gazing at the Western king-size filter between his right forefinger and thumb, smelled more than smoke in his nostrils. He had scented fear many times: in the arrest procedures, in the interrogation rooms, in the corridors of his craft. He smelled it now. He and the men around him were powerful, privileged, protected. But he knew them all well; he had the files. And he, who knew no fear for himself, as the soul-dead know no fear, knew also that they all feared one thing more than war itself. If the Soviet proletariat, long-suffering, patient, oxlike in the face of deprivation, ever went berserk . . .

All eyes were on him. Public "acts of disorder," and the repression of them, were his territory.

"I could," he said evenly, "cope with one Novocherkassk." There was a hiss of indrawn breath down the table. "I could cope with ten, or even twenty. But the combined resources of the KGB could not cope with fifty."

The mention of Novocherkassk brought the specter right out of the wallpaper, as he knew it would. On June 2, 1962, almost exactly twenty years earlier, the great industrial city of Novocherkassk had erupted in worker riots. But twenty years had not dimmed the memory.

It had started when by a stupid coincidence one ministry raised the price of meat and butter while another cut wages at the giant NEVZ locomotive works by thirty percent. In the resulting riots the shouting workers took over the city for three days, an unheard-of phenomenon in the Soviet Union. Equally unheard of, they booed the local Party leaders into trembling self-imprisonment in their own headquarters, shouted down a full general, charged ranks of armed soldiers, and pelted advancing tanks with mud until the vision slits clogged up and the tanks ground to a halt.

The response of Moscow was massive. Every single line, every road, every telephone, every track in and out of Novocherkassk was sealed so the news could not leak out. Two divisions of KGB special troops had to be drafted to finish off the affair and mop up the rioters. There were eighty-six civilians shot down in the streets, over three hundred wounded. None ever returned home; none was buried locally. Not only the wounded but every single member of every family of a dead or wounded man, woman, or child was deported to the camps of Gulag lest they persist in asking after their relatives and thus keep memory of the affair alive. Every trace was wiped out, but two decades later it was still well remembered inside the Kremlin.

When Ivanenko dropped his bombshell, there was silence again around the table. Rudin broke it.

"Very well, then. The conclusion seems inescapable. We will have to buy from abroad as never before. Comrade Komarov, what is the minimum we would need to buy abroad to avoid disaster?"

"Comrade Secretary-General, if we leave the irreducible minimum in the countryside and use every scrap of our thirty million tons of national reserve, we will need fifty-five million tons of grain from outside. That would mean the entire surplus, in a year of bumper crops, from both the United States and Canada," Komarov answered.

"They'll never sell it to us!" shouted Kerensky.

"They are not fools, Comrade Marshal," Ivanenko cut in quietly. "Their Condor satellites must have warned them already that something is wrong with our spring wheat. But they cannot know what or how much. Not yet. But by the autumn they will have a pretty fair idea. And they are greedy, endlessly greedy for more money. I can raise the production levels in the gold mines of Siberia and Kolyma, ship more labor there from the camps of Mordovia. The money for such a purchase we can raise."

"I agree with you on one point," said Rudin, "but not on the other, Comrade Ivanenko. They may have the wheat, we may have the gold, but there is a chance, just a chance, that this time they will require concessions."

At the word *concessions*, everyone stiffened.

"What kinds of concessions?" asked Marshal Kerensky suspiciously.

"One never knows until one negotiates," said Rudin, "but it's a possibility we have to face. They might require concessions in military areas. . . ."

"Never!" shouted Kerensky, on his feet and red-faced.

"Our options are somewhat closed," countered Rudin. "We appear to have agreed that a severe and nationwide famine is not tolerable. It would set back the progress of the Soviet Union and thence the global rule of Marxism-Leninism by a decade, maybe more. We need the grain; there are no more options. If the imperialists exact concessions in the military field, we may have to accept a drawback lasting two or three years, but only in order all the better to advance after the recovery."

There was a general murmur of assent. Rudin was on the threshold of carrying his meeting. Then Vishnayev struck. He rose slowly as the buzz subsided.

"The issues before us, Comrades," he began with silky reasonableness, "are massive, with incalculable consequences. I propose that this is too early to reach any binding conclusion. I propose an adjournment until two weeks from today, while we all think over what has been said and suggested."

His ploy worked. He had bought his time, as Rudin had privately feared he would. The meeting agreed, ten against three, to adjourn without a resolution.

Yuri Ivanenko had reached the ground floor and was about to step into his waiting limousine when he felt a touch at his elbow. Standing beside him was a tall, beautifully tailored major of the Kremlin guard.

"The Comrade Secretary-General would like a word with you in his private suite, Comrade Chairman," he said quietly. Without another word he turned and headed down a corridor leading along the building away from the main doorway. Ivanenko followed. As he tailed the major's perfectly fitting barathea jacket, fawn whipcord trousers, and gleaming boots, it occurred to him that if any one of the men of the Politburo came to sit one day in the Penal Chair, the subsequent arrest would be carried out by his own KGB special troops, called Border Guards, with their bright green cap bands and shoulder boards, the sword-and-shield insignia of the KGB above the peaks of their caps.

But if he, Ivanenko alone, were to be arrested, the KGB would not be given the job, as they had not been trusted almost thirty years earlier to arrest Lavrenti Beria. It would be these elegant, disdainful Kremlin elite guards, the praetorians at the seat of ultimate power, who would do the job. Perhaps the self-assured major walking before him; he would have no qualms at all.

They reached a private elevator, ascended to the third floor again, and Ivanenko was shown into the private apartments of Maxim Rudin.

Stalin had lived in seclusion right in the heart of the Kremlin, but Malenkov and Khrushchev had ended the practice, preferring to establish themselves and most of their cronies in luxury apartments in a nondescript (from the outside) complex of apartment blocks at the far end of Kutuzovsky Prospekt. But when Rudin's wife had died two years earlier, he had moved back to the Kremlin.

It was a comparatively modest apartment for this most powerful of men: six rooms, including a well-equipped kitchen, marble bathroom, private study, sitting room, dining room, and bedroom. Rudin lived alone, ate sparingly, dispensed with most luxuries, and was cared for by an elderly cleaning woman and the ever-present Misha, a hulking but silent-moving ex-soldier who never spoke but was never far away. When Ivanenko entered the study at Misha's silent gesture, he found Maxim Rudin and Vassili Petrov already there. Rudin waved him to a vacant chair, and began without preamble.

"I've asked you both here because there is trouble brewing and we all know it," he rumbled. "I'm old and I smoke too much. Two weeks ago I went out to see the quacks at Kuntsevo. They took some tests. Now they want me back again."

Petrov shot Ivanenko a sharp look. The KGB chief was still impassive. He knew about the visit to the super-exclusive clinic in the woods southwest of Moscow; one of the doctors there reported back to him.

"The question of the succession hangs in the air, and we all know it," Rudin continued. "We all also know, or should, that Vishnayev wants it."

Rudin turned to Ivanenko.

"If he gets it, Yuri Aleksandrovich, and he's young enough, that will be the end of you. He never approved of a professional taking over the KGB. He'll put his own man, Krivoi, in your place."

Ivanenko steepled his hands and gazed back at Rudin. Three years earlier Rudin had broken a long tradition in Soviet Russia of imposing a political Party luminary as chairman and chief of the KGB. Shelepin, Semichastny, Andropov—they had all been Party men placed over the KGB from outside the service. Only the professional Ivan Serov had nearly made it to the top through a tide of blood. Then Rudin had plucked Ivanenko from among the senior deputies to Andropov and favored him as the new chief.

That was not the only break with tradition. Ivanenko was young for the job of the world's most powerful policeman and spymaster. Then again, he had served as an agent in Washington twenty years earlier, always a basis for suspicion among the xenophobes of the Politburo. He had a taste for Western elegance in his private life. And he was reputed, though none dared mention it, to have certain private reservations about dogma. That, for Vishnayev at least, was absolutely unforgivable.

"If he takes over, now or ever, that will also mark your cards, Vassili Alekseevich," Rudin told Petrov. In private he was prepared to address both his protégés familiarly by using their patronymics, but never in public session.

Petrov nodded that he understood. He and Anatoly Krivoi had worked together in the Party Organizations Section of the General Secretariat of the Central Committee. Krivoi had been older and senior. He had expected the top job, but when it fell vacant, Rudin had preferred Petrov for the post that sooner or later carried the ultimate accolade, a seat on the all-powerful Politburo. Krivoi, embittered, had accepted the courtship of Vishnayev and had taken a post as the Party theoretician's chief of staff and right-hand man. But Krivoi still wanted Petrov's job.

Neither Ivanenko nor Petrov had forgotten that it was Vishnayev's predecessor as Party theoretician, Mikhail Suslov, who had put together the majority that had toppled Khrushchev in 1964. Rudin let his words sink in.

"Yuri, you know my successor cannot be you, not with your background." Ivanenko inclined his head; he had no illusions on that score. "But," Rudin resumed, "you and Vassili together can keep this country on a steady course if you stick together and behind me. Next year I'm going, one way or the other. And when I go, I want you, Vassili, in this chair."

The silence between the two younger men was electric. Neither could recall any predecessor of Rudin's ever having been so forthcoming. Stalin had suffered a cerebral hemorrhage and had probably been finished off by his own Politburo as he prepared to liquidate them all; Beria had tried for power and been arrested and shot by his fearful colleagues; Malenkov had fallen in disgrace, as had Khrushchev; Brezhnev had kept them all guessing until the last minute.

Rudin stood up to signal the reception was at an end.

"One last thing," he said. "Vishnayev is up to something. He's going to try to do a Suslov on me over this wheat foul-up. If he succeeds, we're all finished—perhaps Russia, too—because he's an extremist. He's impeccable on theory but impossible on practicalities. Now I have to know what he's doing, what he's going to spring, whom he's trying to enlist. Find out for me. Find out in fourteen days."

The headquarters of the KGB, the Center, is a huge stone complex of office blocks taking up the whole northeastern facade of Dzerzhinsky Square at the top end of Karl Marx Prospekt. The complex is actually a hollow square, the front and both wings being devoted to the KGB, the rear block being Lubyanka interrogation center and prison. The proximity of the one to the other, with only the inner courtyard separating them, enables the interrogators to stay well on top of their work.

The chairman's office is on the third floor, left of the main doorway. But he always comes by limousine with chauffeur and bodyguard through the side gateway. The office is a big, ornate room with mahogany-paneled walls and luxurious Oriental carpets. One wall carries the required portrait of Lenin, another a picture of Feliks Dzerzhinsky himself. Through the four tall, draped, bulletproof windows overlooking the square, the observer must look at yet another representation of the Cheka's founder, standing twenty feet tall in bronze in the center of the square, sightless eye staring down Karl Marx Prospekt to Revolution Square.

Ivanenko disliked the heavy, fustian, overstuffed, and brocaded decor of Soviet officialdom, but there was little he could do about the office. The desk alone, of the furniture inherited from his predecessor, Andropov, he appreciated. It was immense and adorned with seven telephones. The most important was the Kremlevka, linking him directly with the

Kremlin and Rudin. Next was the Vertushka, in KGB green, which connected him with other Politburo members and the Central Committee. Others joined him through high-frequency circuits to the principal KGB representatives throughout the Soviet Union and the East European satellites. Still others went directly to the Ministry of Defense and its intelligence arm, the GRU. All through separate exchanges. It was on this last one that he took the call he had been waiting ten days for, that afternoon three days before the end of June.

It was a brief one, from a man who called himself Arkady. Ivanenko had instructed the exchange to put Arkady straight through. The conversation was short.

"Better face-to-face," said Ivanenko shortly. "Not now, not here. At my house, this evening." He put the phone down.

Most senior Soviet leaders never take their work home with them. In fact, almost all Russians have two distinct personae; they have their official life and their private life, and never, if possible, shall the twain meet. The higher one gets, the greater the divide. As with the Mafia dons, whom the Politburo chiefs remarkably resemble, wives and families are simply not to be involved, even by listening to business talk, in the usually less-than-noble affairs that make up official life.

Ivanenko was different, the main reason he was distrusted by the risen apparatchiks of the Politburo. For the oldest reason in the world, he had no wife and family. Nor did he choose to live near the others, most of them content to dwell cheek by jowl with each other in the apartments on the western end of Kutuzovsky Prospekt during the week, and in neighboring villas grouped around Zhukovka and Usovo on weekends. Members of the Soviet elite never like to be too far from each other.

Soon after taking over the KGB, Yuri Ivanenko had found a handsome old house in the Arbat, the once fine residential quarter of central Moscow, favored before the Revolution by merchants. Within six months, teams of KGB builders, painters, and decorators had restored it—an impossible feat in Soviet Russia save for a Politburo member.

Having restored the building to its former elegance, albeit with the most modern security and alarm devices, Ivanenko had no trouble, either, in furnishing it with the ultimate in Soviet status—Western furniture. The kitchen was the last cry in California-convenient, the entire room flown to Moscow from Los Angeles in packing creates. The living room and bedroom were paneled in Swedish pine via Finland, and the bathroom was sleek in marble and tile. Ivanenko himself occupied only the upper floor, which was a self-contained suite of rooms and also included his study–music room with its wall-to-wall stereo deck by Phillips and a library of foreign and forbidden books in English, French, and German, all of which he spoke. There was a dining room off the living room, and a sauna off the bedroom to complete the floor area of the upper story.

The staff of chauffeur, bodyguard, and personal valet, all KGB men, lived on the ground floor, which also housed the garage. Such was the house to which he returned after work and awaited his caller.

Arkady, when he came, was a thickset, ruddy-faced man in civilian clothes, though he would have felt more at home in his usual uniform of brigadier general on the Red Army General Staff. He was one of Ivanenko's agents inside the Army. He hunched forward on his chair in Ivanenko's sitting room, perched on the edge as he talked. The spare KGB chief leaned back at ease, asking a few questions, making the occasional note on a jotting pad. When the brigadier had finished, he thanked him and rose to press a wall button. In seconds, the door opened as Ivanenko's valet, a young blond guard of startling good looks, arrived to show the visitor out by the door in the side wall.

Ivanenko considered the news for a long time, feeling increasingly tired and dispirited. So that was what Vishnayev was up to. He would tell Maxim Rudin in the morning.

He had a lengthy bath, redolent of an expensive London bath oil, wrapped himself in a silk robe, and sipped an old French brandy. Finally he returned to the bedroom, turned out the lights, barring only a small lantern in the corner, and stretched himself on the wide coverlet. Picking up the telephone by the bedside, he pressed one of the call buttons. It was answered instantly.

"Valodya," he said quietly, using the affectionate diminutive of Vladimir, "come up here, will you, please?"

CHAPTER THREE

THE POLISH AIRLINES twin-jet dipped a wing over the wide sweep of the Dnieper River and settled into its final approach to Borispil Airport outside Kiev, capital of the Ukraine. From his window seat, Andrew Drake looked down eagerly at the sprawling city beneath him. He was tense with excitement.

Along with the other hundred-plus package tourists from London who had staged through Warsaw earlier in the day, he queued nearly an hour for passport control and customs. At the immigration control he slipped his passport under the plate-glass window and waited. The man in the booth was in uniform, Border Guard uniform, with the green band around his cap and the sword-and-shield emblem of the KGB above its peak. He looked at the photo in the passport, then stared hard at Drake.

"An . . . drev . . . Drak?" he asked.

Drake smiled and bobbed his head.

"Andrew Drake," he corrected gently. The immigration man glowered back. He examined the visa, issued in London, tore off the incoming half, and clipped the exit visa to the passport. Then he handed it back. Drake was in.

On the Intourist motor coach from the airport to the seventeen-story Lybid Hotel, he took stock again of his fellow passengers. About half were of Ukrainian extraction, excited and innocent, visiting the land of their fathers. The other half were of British stock, just curious tourists. All seemed to have British passports. Drake, with his English name, was part of the second group. He had given no indication he spoke fluent Ukrainian and passable Russian.

During the ride they met Ludmilla, their Intourist guide for the tour. She was a Russian, and spoke Russian to the driver, who, though a Ukrainian, replied in the same language. As the motor coach left the airport she smiled brightly and in reasonable English began to describe the tour ahead of them.

Drake glanced at his itinerary: two days in Kiev, trotting around the eleventh-century Cathedral of St. Sophia ("A wonderful example of Kievan-Rus architecture, where Prince Yaroslav the Wise is buried," warbled Ludmilla from up front) and Golden Gate, not to mention Vladimir Hill, the State University, the Academy of Sciences, and the Botanical Gardens. No doubt, thought Drake bitterly, no mention would be made of the 1964 fire at the Academy Library, in which priceless manuscripts, books, and archives devoted to Ukrainian national literature, poetry, and culture had been destroyed; no mention that the fire brigade failed to arrive for three hours; no mention that the fire was set by the KGB itself as their answer to the nationalistic writings of "the Sixtiers."

After Kiev, there would be a day trip by hydrofoil to Kanev, then a day in Ternopol, where a man called Miroslav Kaminsky would certainly not be a subject for discussion, and finally the tour would go on to Lvov.

As he had expected, he heard only Russian on the streets of the intensively russified capital city of Kiev. It was not until Kanev and Ternopol that he heard Ukrainian spoken extensively. His heart sang to hear it spoken so widely by so many people, and his only regret was that he had to keep saying "I'm sorry, do you speak English?" But he would wait until he could visit the two addresses that he had memorized so well he could say them backward.

Five thousand miles away, the President of the United States was in conclave with his security adviser, Poklewski, Robert Benson of the CIA, and a third man, Myron Fletcher, chief analyst of Soviet grain affairs in the Department of Agriculture.

"Bob, are you sure beyond any reasonable doubt that General Taylor's Condor reconnaissance and your ground reports point to these figures?" Matthews asked, his eye running once again down the columns of numbers in front of him.

The report that his intelligence chief had presented to him via Stanislaw Poklewski five days earlier consisted of a breakdown of the entire Soviet Union into one hundred grain-producing zones. From each zone a sample square, ten miles by ten, had been seen in close-up and its grain problems analyzed. From the hundred portraits, his experts had drawn up the nationwide grain forecast.

"Mr. President, if we err, it is on the side of caution, of giving the Soviets a better grain crop than they have any right to expect," replied Benson.

The President looked across at the man from the Department of Agriculture.

"Dr. Fletcher, how does this break down in layman's terms?"

"Well, sir, Mr. President, for a start, one has to deduct, at the very minimum, ten percent of the gross harvest to produce a figure of usable grain. Some would say we should deduct twenty percent. This modest ten-percent figure is to account for moisture content, foreign matter like stones and grit, dust and earth, losses in transportation, and wastage through inadequate storage facilities, which we know they suffer from badly.

"Starting from there, one then has to deduct the tonnages the Soviets have to keep on the land itself, right in the countryside, before any state procurements can be made to feed the industrial masses. You will find my table for this on the second page of my separate report."

President Matthews flicked over the sheets before him and examined the table. It read:

1.	*Seed Grain.* The tonnage the Soviets must put by for replanting next year, both for winter wheat and spring-sown wheat . .	10 million tons
2.	*Human Consumption.* The tonnage that must be set aside to feed the masses who inhabit the rural areas, the state and collective farms, and all suburban units—from hamlets, through villages, up to towns of less than 5,000 population . .	28 million tons
3.	*Animal Feed.* The tonnage that must be set aside for the feeding of the livestock through the winter months until the spring thaw	52 million tons
4.	*Irreducible Total*	90 million tons
5.	Representing a gross total, prior to a 10 percent unavoidable wastage deduction, of	100 million tons

"I would point out, Mr. President," went on Fletcher, "that these are not generous figures. They are the absolute minima required before they start feeding the cities. If they cut down on the human rations, the peasants will simply consume the livestock, with or without permission. If they cut back on animal feed, the livestock slaughter will be wholesale; they'll have a meat glut in the winter, then a meat famine for three to four years."

"Okay, Dr. Fletcher, I'll buy that. Now what about their reserves?"

"We estimate they have a national reserve of thirty million tons. It is unheard of to use up the whole of it, but if they did, that would give them an extra thirty million tons. And they *should* have twenty million tons left over from this year's crop available for the cities—a grand total for their cities of fifty million."

The President swung back to Benson.

"Bob, what do they have to have by way of state procurements to feed the urban millions?"

"Mr. President, 1977 was their worst year for a long time, the year they perpetrated 'the Sting' on us. They had a total crop of one hundred ninety-four million tons. They bought sixty-eight million tons from their own farms. They *still* needed to buy twenty million from us by subterfuge. Even in 1975, their worst year for a decade and a half, they needed seventy million tons for the cities. And that led to savage shortages. With a greater population now than then, the state must buy no less than eighty-five million tons."

"Then," concluded the President, "by your figures, even if they use the total of their national reserve, they are going to need thirty to thirty-five million tons of foreign grain?"

"Right, Mr. President," cut in Poklewski. "Maybe even more. And we and the Canadians are the only people who are going to have it. Dr. Fletcher?"

The man from the Department of Agriculture nodded. "It appears North America is going to have a bumper crop this year. Maybe fifty million tons over domestic requirements for both us and Canada considered together."

Minutes later, Dr. Fletcher was escorted out. The debate resumed. Poklewski pressed his point.

"Mr. President, this time we have to act. We have to require a quid pro quo from them this time around."

"Linkage?" asked the President suspiciously. "I know your thoughts on that, Stan. Last time it didn't work; it made things worse. I will not have another repeat of the Jackson Amendment."

All three men recalled the fate of that piece of legislation with little joy. At the end of 1974 Congress had passed a compromise trade-reform bill; its passage had been delayed by a controversial section that specified in effect that unless the Soviets went easier on the question of Russian-Jewish emigration to Israel, there would be no U.S. trade credits for the purchase of technology and industrial goods. The Politburo under Brezhnev had contemptuously rejected the pressure, launched a series of predominantly anti-Jewish show trials, and bought their requirements, with trade credits, from Britain, Germany, and Japan.

"The point about a nice little spot of blackmail," Sir Nigel Irvine, who was in Washington in 1975, had remarked to Bob Benson, "is that you must be sure the victim simply cannot do without something that you have, and cannot acquire it anywhere else."

Poklewski had learned of this remark from Benson and repeated it to President Matthews, avoiding the word *blackmail.*

"Mr. President, this time around they cannot get their wheat elsewhere. Our wheat surplus is no longer a trading matter. It is a strategic weapon. It is worth ten squadrons of nuclear bombers. There is no way we would sell nuclear technology to Moscow for money. I urge you to invoke the Shannon Act."

In the wake of the Sting of 1977, Congress had, finally and belatedly, in 1980 passed the Shannon Act. This said simply that, in any year, the federal government had the right to exercise an option to buy the entire U.S. grain surplus at the going rate per ton at the time of the announcement that it wished to do so.

The grain speculators had hated it, but the farmers had gone along. The act smoothed out some of the wilder fluctuations in world grain prices. In years of glut, the farmers got prices for their grain that were too low; in years of shortage, the prices were exceptionally high. The Shannon Act ensured that if the government exercised its option the farmers would get a fair price but the speculators would be out of business. The act also gave the administration a gigantic new weapon in dealing with customer countries: the aggressive as well as the humble and poor.

"Very well," said President Matthews, "I will invoke the Shannon Act. I will authorize the use of federal funds to buy the futures for the expected surplus of fifty million tons of grain."

Poklewski was jubilant.

"You won't regret it, Mr. President. This time, the Soviets will have to deal directly with your administration, not with middlemen. We have them over a barrel. There is nothing else they can do."

Yefrem Vishnayev had a different opinion. At the outset of the Politburo meeting, he asked for the floor and got it.

"No one here, Comrades, denies that the famine that faces us is not acceptable. No one denies that the surplus foods lie in the decadent capitalist West. It has been suggested that the only thing we can do is to humble ourselves, possibly grant concessions that will reduce our military might and thereby delay the onward march of Marxism-Leninism in order to buy these surpluses to tide us over.

"Comrades, I disagree, and I ask you to join me in rejection of the course of yielding to blackmail and betraying our great inspirator, Lenin. There is one other way—one other way in which we can obtain acceptance by the entire Soviet people of rigid rationing at the minimum-subsistence level, promote a nationwide upsurge of patriotism and self-sacrifice, and secure an imposition of that discipline without which we cannot get through the hunger that has to come.

"There is a way in which we can use what little harvest grain we shall cull this autumn, spin out the national reserve until the spring next year, use the meat from our herds and flocks in place of grain, and then, when all is used, turn to Western Europe, where the milk lakes are, where the beef-and-butter mountains are, where the national reserves of ten wealthy nations are."

"And buy them?" asked Foreign Minister Rykov ironically.

"No, Comrade," replied Vishnayev softly. "Take them. I yield the floor to Comrade Marshal Kerensky. He has a file he would wish each of us to examine."

Twelve thick files were passed around. Kerensky kept his own and began reading aloud from it. Rudin left his unopened in front of him and smoked steadily. Ivanenko also left his on the table and contemplated Kerensky. He and Rudin had known for four days what the file would contain. In collaboration with Vishnayev, Kerensky had brought out of the General Staff's safe the file for Plan Aleksandr, named after Field Marshal Aleksandr Suvorov, the great and never defeated Russian commander. Now the plan had been brought right up to date.

And it was impressive, as Kerensky spent the next two hours reading it. During the following May the usual massive spring maneuvers of the Red Army in East Germany would be bigger than ever, but with a difference. These would be no maneuvers, but the real thing. On command, all thirty thousand tanks and armored personnel carriers, mobile guns and amphibious craft would swing westward, hammer across the Elbe, and plow into West Germany, heading for France and the Channel ports.

Ahead of them, fifty thousand paratroops would drop over fifty locations to take out the principal tactical nuclear airfields of the French inside France and the Americans and British on German soil. Another hundred thousand would drop on the four countries of Scandinavia to control the capital cities and main transportation arteries, with massive naval backup from offshore.

The military thrust would avoid the Italian and Iberian peninsulas, whose governments, all partners with the Euro-Communists in office, would be ordered by the Soviet Ambassador to stay out of the fight or perish by joining in. Within half a decade later, they would fall like ripe plums, anyway. Likewise Greece, Turkey, and Yugoslavia. Switzerland would be avoided, Austria used only as a through-route. Both would later be islands in a Soviet sea, and would not last long.

The primary zone of attack and occupation would be the three Benelux countries, France, and West Germany. Britain, as a prelude, would be crippled by strikes and confused by the extreme Left, which on instructions would mount an immediate clamor for nonintervention. London would be informed that if the nuclear Strike Command were used east of the Elbe, Britain would be wiped off the face of the map.

Throughout the entire operation the Soviet Union would be stridently demanding an immediate cease-fire in every capital in the world and in the United Nations, claiming the hostilities were local to West Germany, temporary, and caused entirely by a West German preemptive strike toward Berlin, a claim that most of the non-German European Left would believe and support.

"And the United States, all this time?" Petrov interrupted. Kerensky looked irritated at being stopped in full flow after ninety minutes.

"The use of tactical nuclear weapons right across the face

of Germany cannot be excluded," pursued Kerensky, "but the overwhelming majority of them will destroy West Germany, East Germany, and Poland—no loss, of course, for the Soviet Union. Thanks to the weakness of Washington, there is no deployment of either Cruise missiles or neutron bombs. Soviet military casualties are estimated at between one hundred thousand and two hundred thousand at the maximum. But as two million men in all three services will be involved, such percentages will be acceptable."

"Duration?" asked Ivanenko.

"The point units of the forward mechanized armies will enter the French Channel ports one hundred hours after crossing the Elbe. At that point, of course, the cease-fire may be allowed to operate. The mopping up can take place under the cease-fire."

"Is that time scale feasible?" asked Petryanov.

This time, Rudin cut in.

"Oh yes, it's feasible," he said mildly. Vishnayev shot him a suspicious look.

"I still have not had an answer to my question," Petrov pointed out. "What about the United States? What about their nuclear strike forces? Not tactical missiles. Strategic missiles. The hydrogen-bomb warheads in their ICBMs, their bombers, and their submarines."

The eyes around the table riveted on Vishnayev. He rose again.

"The American President must, at the outset, be given three solemn assurances in absolutely credible form," he said. "One: that for her part the USSR will never be the first to use thermonuclear weapons. Two: that if the three hundred thousand American troops in Western Europe are committed to the fight, they must take their chances in conventional or tactical nuclear warfare with ours. Three: that in the event the United States resorts to ballistic missiles aimed at the Soviet Union, the top hundred cities of the United States will cease to exist.

"President Matthews, Comrades, will not trade New York for the decadence of Paris, nor Los Angeles for Frankfurt. There will be *no* American thermonuclear riposte."

The silence was heavy as the perspectives sank in. The vast storehouse of food, including grain, of consumer goods and technology that was contained in Western Europe. The fall like ripe plums of Italy, Spain, Portugal, Austria, Greece, and Yugoslavia within a few years. The treasure trove of gold beneath the streets of Switzerland. The utter isolation of Britain and Ireland off the new Soviet coast. The domination without a shot fired of the entire Arab bloc and Third World. It was a heady mixture.

"It's a fine scenario," said Rudin at last. "But it all seems to be based on one assumption: that the United States will not rain her nuclear warheads on the Soviet Union if we promise not to let ours loose on her. I would be grateful to hear if Comrade Vishnayev has any corroboration for that confident declaration. In short, is it a proved fact or a fond hope?"

"More than a hope," snapped Vishnayev. "A realistic calculation. As capitalists and bourgeois nationalists, the Americans will always think of themselves first. They are paper tigers, weak and indecisive. Above all, when the prospect of losing their own lives faces them, they are cowards."

"Are they indeed?" mused Rudin. "Well now, Comrades, let me attempt to sum up. Comrade Vishnayev's scenario is realistic in every sense, but it all hangs on his hope—I beg his pardon, on his calculation—that the Americans will not respond with their heavy thermonuclear weapons. Had we ever believed this before, we would surely already have completed the process of liberating the captive masses of Western Europe from fascism-capitalism to Marxism-Leninism. Personally, I perceive no new element to justify the calculation of Comrade Vishnayev.

"However, neither he nor the Comrade Marshal has ever had any dealings with the Americans, or ever been in the West. Personally, I have, and I disagree. Let us hear from Comrade Rykov."

The elderly and veteran Foreign Minister was white-faced.

"All this smacks of Khrushchevism, as in the case of Cuba. I have spent thirty years in foreign affairs. Ambassadors around the world report to me, not to Comrade Vishnayev. None of them, not one—not one single analyst in my department has a single doubt that the American President would use the thermonuclear response on the Soviet Union. Nor do I. It is not a question of exchanging cities. He, too, can see that the outcome of such a war would be domination by the Soviet Union of almost the whole world. It would be the end of America as a superpower, as a power, as anything other than a nonentity. They would devastate the Soviet Union before they yielded Western Europe and thence the world."

"I would point out that if they did," said Rudin, "we could

not stop them. Our high-energy-particle laser beams from space satellites are not fully functional yet. One day we will no doubt be able to vaporize incoming rockets in inner space before they can reach us. But not yet. The latest assessments of our experts—our experts, Comrade Vishnayev, not our optimists—suggest a full-blown Anglo-American thermonuclear strike would take out one hundred million of our citizens—mostly Great Russians—and devastate sixty percent of the Soviet Union from Poland to the Urals. But to continue. Comrade Ivanenko, you have experience of the West. What do you say?"

"Unlike Comrades Vishnayev and Kerensky," observed Ivanenko, "I control hundreds of agents throughout the capitalist West. Their reports are constant. I, too, have no doubt at all that the Americans would respond."

"Then let me put it in a nutshell," said Rudin brusquely. The time for sparring was over. "If we negotiate with the Americans for wheat, we may have to accede to demands that could set us back by five years. If we tolerate the famine, we will probably be set back by ten years. If we launch a European war, we could be wiped out, certainly set back by twenty to forty years.

"I am not the theoretician that Comrade Vishnayev undoubtedly is. But I seem to recall the teachings of Marx and Lenin are very firm on one point: that while the pursuit of the world rule of Marxism-Leninism must be pursued at every stage by every means, its progress should not be endangered by the incurring of foolish risks. I estimate this plan as being based on a foolish risk. Therefore I propose that we—"

"I propose a vote," said Vishnayev softly.

So that was it. Not a vote of no confidence in him, thought Rudin. That would come later if he lost this round. The faction fight was out in the open now. He had not had the feeling so clearly in years that he was fighting for his life. If he lost, there would be no graceful retirement, no retaining the villas and the privileges as Mikoyan had done. It would be ruin, exile, perhaps the bullet in the nape of the neck. But he kept his composure. He put his own motion first. One by one, the hands went up.

Rykov, Ivanenko, Petrov—all voted for him and the negotiation policy. There was hesitancy down the table. Who had Vishnayev got to? What had he promised them?

Stepanov and Shushkin raised their hands. Last, slowly, came Chavadze the Georgian. Rudin put the countermotion, for war in the spring. Vishnayev and Kerensky, of course, were for it. Komarov of Agriculture joined them. Bastard, thought Rudin, it was your bloody ministry that got us into this mess. Vishnayev must have persuaded the man that Rudin was going to ruin him in any case, so he thought he had nothing to lose. You're wrong, my friend, thought Rudin, face impassive, I'm going to have your entrails for this. Petryanov raised his hand. He's been promised the prime ministership, thought Rudin. Vitautas the Balt and Mukhamed the Tajik also went with Vishnayev for war. The Tajik would know that if nuclear war came, the Orientals would rule over the ruins. The Lithuanian had been bought.

"Six for each proposal," he said quietly. "And my own vote for the negotiations."

Too close, he thought. Much too close.

It was sundown when the meeting dissolved. But the faction fight, all knew, would now go on until it was resolved; no one could back away now, no one could stay neutral anymore.

It was not until the fifth day of the tour that the party arrived in Lvov and stayed at the Intourist Hotel. Up to this point, Drake had gone with all the guided tours on the itinerary, but this time he made an excuse that he had a headache and wished to stay in his room. As soon as the party left by motor coach for St. Nicholas Church, he changed into more casual clothes and slipped out of the hotel.

Kaminsky had told him the sort of clothes that would pass without attracting attention: socks with sandals over them, light trousers, not too smart, and an open-necked shirt of the cheaper variety. With a street map he set off on foot for the seedy, poor, working-class suburb of Levandivka. He had not the slightest doubt that the two men he sought would treat him with the profoundest suspicion, once he found them. And this was hardly surprising when one considered the family backgrounds and circumstances that had forged them. He recalled what Miroslav Kaminsky, lying in his Turkish hospital bed, had told him.

On September 29, 1966, near Kiev, at the gorge of Babi Yar, where over fifty thousand Jews had been slaughtered by the SS in Nazi-occupied Ukraine in 1941–42, the Ukraine's foremost contemporary poet, Ivan Dzyuba, gave an address that was remarkable inasmuch as a Ukrainian Catholic was speaking out powerfully against anti-Semitism.

Anti-Semitism has always flourished in the Ukraine, and successive rulers—tsars, Stalinists, Nazis, Stalinists again, and their successors—have vigorously encouraged it to flourish.

Dzyuba's long speech began as a seeming plea for remembrance of the slaughtered Jews of Babi Yar, a straight condemnation of Nazism and facism. But as it developed, his theme began to encompass all those despotisms which, despite their technological triumphs, brutalize the human spirit and seek to persuade even the brutalized that this is normal.

"We should therefore judge each society," he said, "not by its external technical achievements but by the position and meaning it gives to man, by the value it puts on human dignity and human conscience."

By the time he reached this point, the Chekisti who had infiltrated the silent crowd had realized the poet was not talking about Hitler's Germany at all; he was talking about the Politburo's Soviet Union. Shortly after the speech, he was arrested.

In the cellars of the local KGB barracks, the chief interrogator, the man who had at his beck and call the two hulks in the corners of the room, the ones gripping the heavy, three-foot-long rubber hoses, was a fast-rising young colonel of the Second Chief Directorate, sent in from Moscow. His name was Yuri Ivanenko.

But at the address at Babi Yar there had been, in the front row, standing next to their fathers, two small boys, age ten. They did not know each other then, and would meet and become firm friends only six years later on a building site. One was Lev Mishkin; the other was David Lazareff.

The presence of both the fathers of Mishkin and Lazareff at the meeting had also been noted, and when, years later, they applied for permission to emigrate to Israel, both were accused of anti-Soviet activities and drew long sentences in labor camps.

Their families lost their apartments, the sons any hope of attending a university. Though highly intelligent, they were destined for pick-and-shovel work. Now both twenty-six, these were the young men Drake sought among the hot and dusty byways of Levandivka.

It was at the second address that he found David Lazareff, who, after Drake had introduced himself, treated him with extreme suspicion. But he agreed to bring his friend Lev

Mishkin to a rendezvous since Drake knew both their names, anyway.

That evening Drake met Mishkin, and the pair regarded him with something close to hostility. He told them the whole story of the escape and rescue of Miroslav Kaminsky, and his own background. The only proof he could produce was the photograph of himself and Kaminsky together, taken in the hospital room at Trabzon with a Polaroid camera by a nursing orderly. Held up in front of them was that day's edition of the local Turkish newspaper. Drake had brought the same newspaper as suitcase lining and showed it to them as proof of his story.

"Look," he said finally, "if Miroslav had been washed up in Soviet territory and been taken by the KGB, if he had talked and revealed your names, and if I were from the KGB, I'd hardly be asking for your help."

The two Jewish workers agreed to consider his request overnight. Unknown to Drake, both Mishkin and Lazareff had long shared an ideal close to his own—that of striking one single, powerful blow of revenge against the Kremlin hierarchy in their midst. But they were near to giving up, weighed down by the hopelessness of trying to do anything without outside help.

Impelled by their desire for an ally beyond the borders of the USSR, the two shook hands in the small hours of the morning and agreed to take the Anglo-Ukrainian into their confidence. The second meeting was that afternoon, Drake having skipped another guided tour. For safety they strolled through wide, unpaved lanes near the outskirts of the city, talking quietly in Ukrainian. They told Drake of their desire also to strike at Moscow in a single, deadly act.

"The question is—what?" said Drake. Lazareff, who was the more silent and more dominant of the pair, spoke.

"Ivanenko," he said. "The most hated man in the Ukraine."

"What about him?" asked Drake.

"Kill him."

Drake stopped in his tracks and stared at the dark-haired, intense young man.

"You'd never get near him," he said finally.

"Last year," said Lazareff, "I was working on a job here in Lvov. I'm a house painter, right? We were redecorating the apartment of a Party bigwig. There was a little old woman staying with them. From Kiev. After she'd gone, the Party man's wife mentioned who she was. Later I saw a letter postmarked Kiev in the letter box. I took it, and it was from the old woman. It had her address on it."

"So who was she?" asked Drake.

"His mother."

Drake considered the information. "You wouldn't think people like that had mothers," he said. "But you'd have to watch her flat for a long time before he might come to visit her."

Lazareff shook his head. "She's the bait," he said, and outlined his idea. Drake considered the magnitude of it.

Before coming to the Ukraine, he had envisaged the great single blow he had dreamed of delivering against the might of the Kremlin in many terms, but never this. To assassinate the head of the KGB would be to strike into the very center of the Politburo, to send hairline cracks running through every corner of the power structure.

"It might work," he conceded.

If it did, he thought, it would be hushed up at once. But if the news ever got out, the effect on popular opinion, especially in the Ukraine, would be traumatic.

"It could trigger the biggest uprising there has ever been here," he said.

Lazareff nodded. Alone with his partner Mishkin, far away from outside help, he had evidently given the project a lot of thought.

"True," he said.

"What equipment would you need?" asked Drake.

Lazareff told him. Drake nodded.

"It can all be acquired in the West," he said. "But how to get it in?"

"Odessa," cut in Mishkin. "I worked on the docks there for a while. The place is completely corrupt. The black market is thriving. Every Western ship brings seamen who do a vigorous illegal trade in Turkish leather jackets, suede coats, and denim jeans. We would meet you there. It is inside the Ukraine; we would not need internal passports."

Before they parted, they agreed to the plan. Drake would acquire the equipment and bring it to Odessa by sea. He would alert Mishkin and Lazareff by a letter, posted inside the Soviet Union, well in advance of his own arrival. The wording would be innocent. The rendezvous in Odessa was to be a café that Mishkin knew from his days as a teenage laborer there.

"Two more things," said Drake. "When it is over, the publicity for it, the worldwide announcement that it has been done, is vital—almost as important as the act itself. And that means that you personally must tell the world. Only you will have the details to convince the world of the truth. But that means you must escape from here to the West."

"It goes without saying," murmured Lazareff. "We are both Refuseniks. Like our fathers before us, we have tried to emigrate to Israel and have been refused. This time we will go, with or without permission. When this is over, we have to get to Israel. It is the only place we will ever be safe, ever again. Once there, we will tell the world what we have done and leave those bastards in the Kremlin and the KGB discredited in the eyes of their own people."

"The other point follows from the first," said Drake. "When it is done, you must let me know by coded letter or postcard. In case anything goes wrong with the escape. So that I can try to help get the news to the world."

They agreed that an innocently worded postcard would be sent from Lvov to a poste restante address in London. With the last details memorized, they parted, and Drake rejoined his tour group.

Two days later Drake was back in London. The first thing he did was buy the world's most comprehensive book on small arms. The second was to send a telegram to a friend in Canada, one of the best of that elite private list he had built up over the years of émigrés who thought as he did of carrying their hatred to the enemy. The third was to begin preparations for a long-dormant plan to raise the needed funds by robbing a bank.

At the far end of Kutuzovsky Prospekt on the southeastern outskirts of Moscow, a driver pulling to the right off the main boulevard onto the Rublevo Road will come twenty kilometers later to the little village of Uspenskoye, in the heart of the weekend-villa country. In the great pine and birch forests around Uspenskoye lie such hamlets as Usovo and Zhukovka, where stand the country mansions of the Soviet elite. Just beyond Uspenskoye Bridge over the Moscow River is a beach where in summer the lesser-privileged but nevertheless very well off (they have their own cars) come from Moscow to bathe from the sandy beach.

The Western diplomats come here, too, and it is one of the

rare places where a Westerner can be cheek by jowl with ordinary Muscovite families. Even the routine KGB tailing of Western diplomats seems to let up on Sunday afternoons in high summer.

Adam Munro came here with a party of British Embassy staffers that Sunday afternoon, July 11, 1982. Some of them were married couples, some single and younger than he. Shortly before three, the whole party of them left their towels and picnic baskets among the trees, ran down the low bluff toward the sandy beach, and swam. When he came back, Munro picked up his rolled towel and began to dry himself. Something fell out of it.

He stooped to pick it up. It was a small pasteboard card, half the size of a postcard, white on both sides. On one side was typed, in Russian, the words: "Three kilometers north of here is an abandoned chapel in the woods. Meet me there in thirty minutes. Please. It is urgent."

He maintained his smile as one of the embassy secretaries came over, laughing, to ask for a cigarette. While he lit it for her, his mind was working out all the angles he could think of. A dissident wanting to pass over the underground literature? A load of trouble, that. A religious group wanting asylum in the embassy? The Americans had had that in 1978, and it had caused untold problems. A trap set by the KGB to identify the SIS man inside the embassy? Always possible. No ordinary commercial secretary would accept such an invitation, slipped into a rolled towel by someone who had evidently tailed him and watched from the surrounding woods. And yet it was too crude for the KGB. They would have set up a pretended defector in central Moscow with information to pass, arranged for secret photographs at the handover point. So who was the secret writer?

He dressed quickly, still undecided.

Finally he pulled on his shoes and made up his mind. If it was a trap, then he had received no message and was simply walking in the forest. To the disappointment of his hopeful secretary he set off alone. After a hundred yards he paused, took out his lighter and burned the card, grinding the ash into the carpet of pine needles.

The sun and his watch gave him due north, away from the riverbank, which faced south. After ten minutes he emerged on the side of a slope and saw the onion-shaped dome of a chapel two kilometers farther on across the valley. Seconds later he was back in the trees.

The forests around Moscow have dozens of such small chapels, once the worshiping places of the villagers, now mainly derelict, boarded up, deserted. The one he was approaching stood in its own clearing among the trees, beside a derelict cemetery. At the edge of the clearing he stopped and surveyed the tiny church. He could see no one. Carefully he advanced into the open. He was a few yards from the sealed front door when he saw the figure standing in deep shadow under an archway. He stopped, and for minutes on end the two stared at each other.

There was really nothing to say, so he just said her name. "Valentina."

She moved out of the shadow and replied, "Adam."

Twenty-one years, he thought in wonderment. She must be turned forty. She looked like thirty, still raven-haired, beautiful, and ineffably sad.

They sat on one of the tombstones and talked quietly of the old times. She told him she had returned from Berlin to Moscow a few months after their parting, and had continued to be a stenographer for the Party machine. At twenty-three she had married a young Army officer with good prospects. After seven years there had been a baby, and they had been happy, all three of them. Her husband's career had flourished, for he had an uncle high in the Red Army, and patronage is no different in the Soviet Union from anywhere else. The boy was now ten.

Five years before, her husband, having reached the rank of colonel at a young age, had been killed in a helicopter crash while surveying Red Chinese troop deployments along the Ussuri River in the Far East. To kill the grief she had gone back to work. Her husband's uncle had used his influence to secure her good, highly placed work, bringing with it privileges in the form of special food shops, special restaurants, a better apartment, a private car—all the things that go with high rank in the Party machine.

Finally, two years before, after special clearance, she had been offered a post in the tiny, closed group of stenographers and typists, a subsection of the General Secretariat of the Central Committee, that is called the Politburo Secretariat.

Munro breathed deeply. That was high, very high, and very trusted.

"Who," he asked, "is the uncle of your late husband?"

"Kerensky," she murmured.

"Marshal Kerensky?" he asked. She nodded. Munro exhaled slowly. Kerensky, the ultrahawk. When he looked again at her face, the eyes were wet. She was blinking rapidly, on the verge of tears. On an impulse he put his arm around her shoulders, and she leaned against him. He smelled her hair, the same sweet odor that had made him feel both tender and excited two decades ago, in his youth.

"What's the matter?" he asked gently.

"Oh, Adam, I'm so unhappy."

"In God's name, why? In your society you have everything."

She shook her head slowly, then pulled away from him. She avoided his eye, gazing across the clearing into the woods.

"Adam, all my life, since I was a small girl, I believed. I truly believed. Even when we loved, I believed in the goodness, the rightness, of socialism. Even in the hard times, the times of deprivation in my country, when the West had all the consumer riches and we had none, I believed in the justice of the Communist ideal that we in Russia would one day bring to the world. It was an ideal that would give us all a world without fascism, without money-lust, without exploitation, without war.

"I was taught it, and I really believed it. It was more important than you, than our love, than my husband and child. It meant as much to me as this country, Russia, which is part of my soul."

Munro knew about the patriotism of the Russians toward their country, a fierce flame that would make them endure any suffering, any privation, any sacrifice, and which, when manipulated, would make them obey their Kremlin overlords without demur.

"What happened?" he asked quietly.

"They have betrayed it. Are betraying it. My ideal, my people, and my country."

"They?" he asked.

She was twisting her fingers until they looked as if they would come off.

"The Party chiefs," she said bitterly. She spat out the Russian slang word meaning "fat cats": "The *nachalstvo*."

Munro had twice witnessed a recantation. When a true believer loses the faith, the reversed fanaticism goes to strange extremes.

"I worshiped them, Adam. I respected them. I revered them. Now, for years, I have lived close to them all. I have lived in their shadow, taken their gifts, been showered with their privileges. I have seen them close up, in private; heard them talk about the people, whom they despise. They are rotten, Adam, corrupt and cruel. Everything they touch they turn to ashes."

Munro swung one leg across the tombstone so he could face her, and took her in his arms. She was crying softly.

"I can't go on, Adam, I can't go on," she murmured into his shoulder.

"All right, my darling, do you want me to try to get you out?"

He knew it would cost him his career, but this time he was not going to let her go. It would be worth it; everything would be worth it.

She pulled away, her face tear-streaked.

"I cannot. I cannot leave. I have Sasha to think about."

He held her quietly for a while longer. His mind was racing.

"How did you know I was in Moscow?" he asked carefully.

She gave no hint of surprise at the question. It was in any case natural enough for him to ask it.

"Last month," she said between sniffs, "I was taken to the ballet by a colleague from the office. We were in a box. When the lights were low, I thought I must be mistaken. But when they went up at intermission, I knew it was really you. I could not stay after that. I pleaded a headache and left quickly."

She dabbed her eyes, the crying spell over.

"Adam," she asked eventually, "did you marry?"

"Yes," he said. "Long after Berlin. It didn't work. We were divorced years ago."

She managed a little smile. "I'm glad," she said. "I'm glad there is no one else. That is not very logical, is it?"

He grinned back at her.

"No," he said. "It is not. But it is nice to hear. Can we see each other? In the future?"

Her smile faded; there was a hunted look in her eyes. She shook her dark head.

"No, not very often, Adam," she said. "I am trusted, privileged, but if a foreigner came to my apartment, it would soon be noticed and reported on. The same applies to your apartment. Diplomats are watched—you know that. Hotels are watched also; no apartments are for rent here without impossible formalities. It will be difficult, Adam, very difficult."

"Valentina, you arranged this meeting. You took the initiative. Was it just for old times' sake? If you do not like your life here, if you do not like the men you work for . . . But if you cannot leave because of Sasha, then what is it you want?"

She composed herself and thought for a while. When she spoke, it was quite calmly.

"Adam, I want to try to stop them. I want to try to stop what they are doing. I suppose I have for several years now, but since I saw you at the Bolshoi, and remembered all the freedom we had in Berlin, I began thinking about it more and more. Now I am certain. Tell me if you can—is there an intelligence officer in your embassy?"

Munro was shaken. He had handled two defectors-in-place, one from the Soviet Embassy in Mexico City, the other in Vienna. One had been motivated by a conversion from respect to hatred for his own regime, like Valentina; the other by bitterness at lack of promotion. The former had been the trickier to handle.

"I suppose so," he said slowly. "I suppose there must be."

Valentina rummaged in the shoulder bag on the pine needles by her feet. Having made up her mind, she was apparently determined to go through with her betrayal. She withdrew a thick, padded envelope.

"I want you to give this to him, Adam. Promise me you will never tell him who it came from. Please, Adam. I am frightened by what I am doing. I cannot trust anyone but you."

"I promise," he said. "But I have to see you again. I can't just see you walk away through the gap in the wall as I did last time."

"No, I cannot do that again, either. But do not try to contact me at my apartment. It is in a walled compound for senior functionaries, with a single gate in the wall and a policeman at it. Do not try to telephone me. The calls are monitored. And I will never meet anyone else from your embassy, not even the intelligence chief."

"I agree," said Munro. "But when can we meet again?"

She considered for a moment. "It is not always easy for me to get away. Sasha takes up most of my spare time. But I have my own car and I am not followed. Tomorrow I must go away for two weeks, but we can meet here, four Sundays from today." She looked at her watch. "I must go, Adam. I am one of a house party at a dacha a few miles from here."

He kissed her on the lips, the way it used to be. And it was as sweet as it had ever been. She rose and walked away across the clearing. When she reached the fringe of the trees, he called after her.

"Valentina, what is in this?" He held up the package.

She paused and turned.

"My job," she said, "is to prepare the verbatim transcripts of the Politburo meetings, one for each member. And the digests for the candidate members. From the tape recordings. That is a copy of the recording of the meeting of June tenth."

Then she was gone into the trees. Munro sat on the tombstone and looked down at the package.

"Bloody hell," he said.

CHAPTER FOUR

ADAM MUNRO sat in a locked room in the main building of the British Embassy on Maurice Thorez Embankment and listened to the last sentences of the tape recording on the machine in front of him. The room was safe from any chance of electronic surveillance by the Russians, which was why he had borrowed it for a few hours from the head of Chancery.

". . . goes without saying that this news does not pass outside those present in this room. Our next meeting will be a week from today."

The voice of Maxim Rudin died away, and the tape hissed on the machine, then stopped. Munro switched it off. He leaned back and let out a long, low whistle.

If it was true, it was bigger than anything Oleg Penkovsky had brought over, twenty years before. The story of Penkovsky was folklore in the SIS, the CIA, and, most of all, in the bitterest memories of the KGB. He was a brigadier general in the GRU, with access to the highest information, who, disenchanted with the Kremlin hierarchy, had approached first the Americans and then the British with an offer to provide information.

The Americans had turned him down, suspecting a trap. The British had accepted him, and for two and a half years "run" him until he was trapped by the KGB, exposed, tried, and shot. In his time he had brought over a golden harvest of secret information, but most of all at the time of the October 1962 Cuban missile crisis. In that month the world had applauded the exceptionally skillful handling by President John F. Kennedy of the eyeball-to-eyeball confrontation with Nikita Khrushchev over the matter of the planting of Soviet missiles in Cuba. What the world had not known was that the exact strengths and weaknesses of the Russian leader were already in the Americans' hands, thanks to Penkovsky.

When it was finally over, the Soviet missiles were out of Cuba, Khrushchev was humbled, Kennedy was a hero, and Penkovsky was under suspicion. He was arrested in November. Within a year, after a show trial, he was dead. That same winter of 1963 Kennedy, too, died, just thirteen months after his triumph. And within two years Khrushchev had fallen, toppled by his own colleagues, ostensibly because of his failure in the grain policy, in fact because his adventurism had scared the daylights out of them. The democrat, the despot, and the spy had all left the stage. But even Penkovsky had never got right inside the Politburo.

Munro took the spool off the machine and carefully rewrapped it. The voice of Professor Yakovlev was, of course, unknown to him, and most of the tape was of him reading his report. But in the discussion following the professor, there were ten voices, and three at least were identifiable. The low growl of Rudin was well enough known; the high tones of Vishnayev, Munro had heard before, watching televised speeches by the man to Party congresses; and the bark of Marshal Kerensky he had heard at May Day celebrations, as well as on film and tape.

His problem, when he took the tape back to London for voiceprint analysis, as he knew he must, was how to cover his source. He knew if he admitted to the secret rendezvous in the forest, following the typed note in the bathing towel, the question would be asked: "Why you, Munro? How did she know you?" It would be impossible to avoid that question, and equally impossible to answer it. The only solution was to devise an alternative source, credible and uncheckable.

He had been in Moscow only six weeks, but his unsuspected mastery of even slang Russian had paid a couple of dividends. At a diplomatic reception in the Czech Embassy two weeks earlier, he had been in conversation with an Indian attaché when he had heard two Russians in muttered conversation behind him. One of them had said, "He's a bitter bastard. Thinks he should have had the top slot."

He had followed the gaze of the two who had spoken, and noted they were observing and presumably talking about a Russian across the room. The guest list later confirmed the man was Anatoly Krivoi, personal aide and right-hand man to the Party theoretician, Vishnayev. So what had he got to be bitter about? Munro checked his files and came up with Krivoi's history. He had worked in the Party Organizations Section of the Central Committee; shortly after the nomination of Petrov to the top job, Krivoi had appeared on Vishnayev's staff. Quit in disgust? Personality conflict with Petrov? Bitter at being passed over? They were all possible, and all interesting to an intelligence chief in a foreign capital.

Krivoi, he mused. Maybe. Just maybe. He, too, would have access, at least to Vishnayev's copy of the transcript, maybe even to the tape. And he was probably in Moscow; certainly his boss was. Vishnayev had been present when the East German Premier had arrived a week before.

"Sorry, Anatoly, you've just changed sides," he said as he slipped the fat envelope into an inside pocket and took the stairs to see the head of Chancery.

"I'm afraid I have to go back to London with the Wednesday bag," he told the diplomat. "It's unavoidable, and it can't wait."

Chancery asked no questions. He knew Munro's job and promised to arrange it. The diplomatic bag, which actually *is* a bag, or at least a series of canvas sacks, goes from Moscow to London every Wednesday and always on the British Airways flight, never Aeroflot. A Queen's Messenger, one of that team of men who constantly fly around the world from London picking up embassy bags and who are protected by the insignia of the crown and greyhound, comes out from London for it. The very secret material is carried in a hard-frame dispatch box chained to the man's left wrist; the more routine stuff in the canvas sacks, the Messenger personally checks into the aircraft's hold. Once there, it is on British territory. But in the case of Moscow, the Messenger is accompanied by an embassy staffer.

The escort job is sought after, since it permits a quick trip home to London, a bit of shopping, and a chance of a good night out. The Second Secretary who lost his place in the rota that week was annoyed but asked no questions.

The following Wednesday, British Airways Airbus-300B lifted out of the new, post–1980 Olympics terminal at Sheremetyevo Airport and turned its nose toward London. By Munro's side the Messenger, a short, dapper, ex-Army major, withdrew straight into his hobby, composing crossword puzzles for a major newspaper.

"You have to do something to while away these endless airplane flights," he told Munro. "We all have our in-flight hobbies."

Munro grunted and looked back over the wing tip at the receding city of Moscow. Somewhere down there in the sun-drenched streets, the woman he loved was working and moving among people she had betrayed. She was on her own right out in the cold.

The country of Norway, seen in isolation from its eastern neighbor, Sweden, looks like a great prehistoric fossilized human hand stretching down from the Arctic toward Denmark and Britain. It is a right hand, palm downward to the ocean, a stubby thumb toward the east clenched into the forefinger. Up the crack between thumb and forefinger lies Oslo, its capital.

To the north the fractured forearm bones stretch up to Tromsø and Hammerfest, deep in the Arctic, so narrow that in places there are only forty miles from the sea to the Swedish border. On a relief map, the hand looks as if it has been smashed by some gigantic hammer of the gods, splintering bones and knuckles into thousands of particles. Nowhere is this breakage more marked than along the west coast, where the chopping edge of the hand would be.

Here the land is shattered into a thousand fragments, and between the shards the sea has flowed in to form a million creeks, gullies, bays, and gorges—winding, narrow defiles where the mountains fall sheer to glittering water. These are the fjords, and it was from the headwaters of these that a race of men came out a thousand years ago who were the best sailors ever to set keel to the water or sail to the wind. Before their age was over, they had sailed to Greenland and Iceland, conquered Ireland, settled Britain and Normandy, navigated as far as North America. They were the Vikings, and their descendants still live and fish along the fjords of Norway.

Such a man was Thor Larsen, sea captain and ship's master, who strode that mid-July afternoon past the royal palace in the Swedish capital of Stockholm from his company's head office back to his hotel. People tended to step aside for him; he was six feet three inches tall, broad as the pavements of the old quarter of the city, blue-eyed, and bearded. Being ashore, he was in civilian clothes, but he was happy, because he had reason to think, after visiting the head office of the Nordia Line, which now lay behind him along the Ship Quay, that he might soon have a new command.

After six months attending a course at the company's expense in the intricacies of radar, computer navigation, and supertanker technology, he was dying to get back to sea again. The summons to the head office had been to receive from the hands of the personal secretary to the proprietor, chairman, and managing director of the Nordia Line his invitation to dinner that evening. The invitation also included Larsen's wife, who had been informed by telephone and was flying in from Norway on a company ticket. The Old Man was splashing out a bit, thought Larsen. There must be something in the wind.

He took his rented car from the hotel parking lot across the bridge on Nybroviken and drove the thirty-seven kilometers to the airport. When Lisa Larsen arrived in the concourse with her overnight bag, he greeted her with the delicacy of an excited St. Bernard, swinging her off her feet like a girl. She was small and petite, with dark, bright eyes, soft chestnut curls, and a trim figure that belied her thirty-eight years. And he adored her. Twenty years earlier, when he had been a gangling second mate of twenty-seven, he had met her one freezing winter day in Oslo. She had slipped on the ice; he had picked her up like a doll and set her back on her feet.

She had been wearing a fur-trimmed hood that almost hid her tiny, red-nosed face, and when she thanked him, he could see only her eyes, looking out of the mass of snow and fur like the bright eyes of a snow mouse in the forests of winter. Ever since, through their courtship and marriage and the years that had followed, he had called her his "little snow mouse."

He drove her back into central Stockholm, asking all the

way about their home in Ålesund, far away on Norway's western coast, and of the progress of their two teenage children. To the south a British Airways Airbus passed by on its great-circle route from Moscow to London. Thor Larsen neither knew nor cared.

The dinner that evening was to be in the famous Aurora Cellar, built below ground in the cellar-storerooms of an old palace in the city's medieval quarter. When Thor and Lisa Larsen arrived and were shown down the narrow steps to the cellar, the proprietor, Leonard, was waiting for them at the bottom.

"Mr. Wennerstrom is already here," he said, and showed them into one of the private rooms, a small, intimate cavern, arched in five-hundred-year-old brick, spanned by a thick table of glittering, ancient timber, and lit by candles in cast-iron holders. As they entered, Larsen's employer, Harald Wennerstrom, lumbered to his feet, embraced Lisa, and shook hands with her husband.

Harald ("Harry") Wennerstrom was something of a legend in his own lifetime among the seafaring people of Scandinavia. He was now seventy-five, grizzled and craggy, with bristling eyebrows. Just after the Second World War, when he returned to his native Stockholm, he had inherited from his father half a dozen small cargo ships. In thirty-five years he had built up the biggest independently owned fleet of tankers outside the hands of the Greeks and the Hong Kong Chinese. The Nordia Line was his creation, diversifying from dry-cargo ships to tankers in the mid-fifties, laying out the money, building the ships for the oil needs of the sixties, backing his own judgment, often going against the grain.

They sat and ate, and Wennerstrom talked only of small things, asking after the family. His own forty-year marriage had ended with the death of his wife four years earlier; they had had no children. But if he had had a son, he would have liked him to be like the big Norwegian across the table from him, a sailor's sailor; and he was particularly fond of Lisa.

The salmon, cured in brine and dill in the Scandinavian way, was delicious, the tender duck from the Stockholm salt marshes excellent. It was only when they sat finishing their wine—Wennerstrom unhappily sipping at his balloon glass of water ("All the bloody doctors will allow me nowadays")—that he came to business.

"Three years ago, Thor, back in 1979, I made three forecasts to myself. One was that by the end of 1982 the solidarity of the Organization of Petroleum Exporting Countries, OPEC, would have broken down. The second was that the American President's policy of curbing the United States consumption of oil energy and by-products would have failed. The third was that the Soviet Union would have changed from a net oil exporter to a net oil importer. I was told I was crazy, but I was right."

Thor Larsen nodded. The formation of OPEC and its quadrupling of oil prices in the winter of 1973 had produced a world slump that had nearly broken the economies of the West. It had also, paradoxically, sent the oil-tanker business into a seven-year decline, with millions of tons of tanker space partially built, laid up, useless, uneconomic, loss-making. It was a bold spirit who could have seen three years earlier the events between 1979 and 1982: the breakup of OPEC as the Arab world split into feuding factions; the revolutionary takeover in Iran; the disintegration of Nigeria; the rush by the radical oil-producing nations to sell oil at any price to finance arms-buying sprees; the spiraling increase in U.S. oil consumption based on the ordinary American's conviction of his God-given right to rape the globe's resources for his own comforts; and the Soviet native oil industry peaking at such a low production figure through poor technology and forcing Russia to become once again an oil importer. The three factors had produced the tanker boom into which they were now, in the summer of 1982, beginning to move.

"As you know," Wennerstrom resumed, "last September I signed a contract with the Japanese for a new supertanker. Down in the marketplace they all said I was mad; half my fleet laid up in Strömstad Sound, and I order a new one. But I'm not mad. You know the story of the East Shore Oil Company?"

Larsen nodded again. A small Louisiana-based oil company in America ten years before, it had passed into the hands of the dynamic Clint Blake. In ten years it had grown and expanded until it was on the verge of joining the Seven Sisters, the mastodons of the world oil cartels.

"Well, in the summer of next year, 1983, Clint Blake is invading Europe. It's a tough, crowded market, but he thinks he can crack it. He's putting several thousand service stations across the motorways of Europe, marketing his own brand of gasoline and oil. And for that he'll need tanker tonnage. And I've got it. A seven-year contract to bring crude from the Middle East to Western Europe. He's already building his own refinery at Rotterdam, alongside Esso, Mobil, and Chevron. That is what the new tanker is for. She's big and she's ultramodern and she's expensive, but she'll pay. She'll make five or six runs a year from the Persian Gulf to Rotterdam, and in five years she'll amortize the investment. But that's not the reason I'm building her. She's going to be the biggest and the best; my flagship, my memorial. And you're going to be her skipper."

Thor Larsen sat in silence. Lisa's hand stole across the table and laid itself on top of his, squeezing gently. Two years before, Larsen knew, he could never have skippered a Swedish-flag vessel, being himself a Norwegian. But since the Göteborg Agreement of the previous year, which Wennerstrom had helped to push through, a Swedish shipowner could apply for honorary Swedish citizenship for exceptional Scandinavian but non-Swedish officers in his employ, so that they could be offered captaincies. He had applied successfully on behalf of Larsen.

The coffee came, and they sipped it appreciatively.

"I'm having her built at the Ishikawajima-Harima yard in Japan," said Wennerstrom. "It's the only yard in the world that can take her. They have the dry dock."

Both men knew the days of ships being built on slipways and then being allowed to slide into the water were long past. The size and weight factors were too great. The giants were now built in enormous dry docks, so that when they were ready for launching, the sea was let in through dock sluices and the ships simply floated off their blocks and rode water inside the dock.

"Work began on her last November fourth," Wennerstrom told them. "The keel was laid on January thirtieth. She's taking shape now. She'll float next November first, and after three months at the fitting-out berth and sea trials, she'll sail on February second. And you'll be on her bridge, Thor."

"Thank you," said Larsen. "What are you calling her?"

"Ah, yes. I've thought of that. Do you remember the sagas? Well, we'll name her to please Niorn, the god of the sea." He was gripping his glass of water, staring at the flame of the candle in its cast-iron holder before him. "For Niorn controls the fire and the water, the twin enemies of a tanker captain, the explosion and the sea herself."

The water in his glass and the flame of the candle reflected in the old man's eyes, as once fire and water had reflected in his eyes as he sat helpless in a lifeboat in the mid-Atlantic in

1942, four cables from his blazing tanker, his first command, watching his crew fry in the sea around him.

Thor Larsen stared at his patron, doubting that the old man could really believe this mythology; Lisa, being a woman, knew he meant every word of it. At last Wennerstrom sat back, pushed the glass aside with an impatient gesture, and filled his spare glass with red wine.

"So we will call her after the daughter of Niorn—Freya, the most beautiful of all the goddesses. We will call her *Freya*." He raised his glass. "To the *Freya*."

They all drank.

"When she sails," said Wennerstrom, "the world will never have seen the like of her. And when she is past sailing, the world will never see the like of her again."

Larsen was aware that the two biggest tankers in the world were the French Shell tankers *Bellamya* and *Batillus*, both with a capacity of just over half a million tons.

"What will be the *Freya's* deadweight?" asked Larsen. "How much crude will she carry?"

"Ah, yes, I forgot to mention that," said the old shipowner mischievously. "She'll be carrying one million tons of crude oil."

Thor Larsen heard a hiss of indrawn breath from his wife beside him.

"That's big," he said at last. "That's very big."

"The biggest the world has ever seen," said Wennerstrom.

Two days later a jumbo jet arrived at London Heathrow from Toronto. Among its passengers it carried one Azamat Krim, Canadian-born son of an émigré, who, like Andrew Drake, had Anglicized his name—to Arthur Crimmins. He was one of those whom Drake had noted years before as a man who shared his beliefs completely.

Drake was waiting to meet him as he came out of the customs area, and together they drove to Drake's flat, off the Bayswater Road.

Azamat Krim was a Crimean Tatar by heritage, short, dark, and wiry. His father, unlike Drake's, had fought in the Second World War *with* the Red Army rather than against it, and had been captured in combat by the Germans. His personal loyalty to Russia and that of others like him had availed them nothing. Stalin had accused the entire Tatar nation of collaboration with the Germans, a patently unfounded charge but one that the Soviet leader employed as an excuse to deport the Tatar people to the east. Tens of thousands had died in the unheated cattle trucks, thousands more in the arid wastes of Kazakhstan and Uzbekistan.

In a German forced-labor camp, Chingris Krim had heard of the death of his entire family. Liberated by the Canadians in 1945, he had been lucky not to be sent back to Stalin's Russia for execution or the slave camps. He had been befriended by a Canadian officer, a former rodeo rider from Calgary, who one day on an Austrian horse farm had admired the Tatar soldier's mastery of horses and brilliant riding. The Canadian had secured Krim's authorized emigration to Canada, where he had married and fathered a son. Azamat was the boy, now aged thirty and, like Drake, bitter against the Kremlin for the sufferings of his father's people.

In a small flat in Bayswater, Andrew Drake explained his plan, and the Tatar agreed to join him in it. Together they put the final touches to securing the needed funds by taking out a bank in northern England.

The man Adam Munro reported to at the head office was his controller, Barry Ferndale, the head of the Soviet Section. Years before, Ferndale had done his time in the field, and had assisted in the exhaustive debriefings of Oleg Penkovsky when the Russian defector visited Britain while accompanying Soviet trade delegations.

He was short and rotund, pink-cheeked and jolly. He hid his keen brain and a profound knowledge of Soviet affairs behind mannerisms of great cheerfulness and seeming naiveté.

In his office on the fourth floor of the Firm's headquarters, he listened to the tape from Moscow from end to end. When it was over he began furiously polishing his glasses, hopping with excitement.

"Good gracious me, my dear fellow. My dear Adam. What an extraordinary affair. This really is quite priceless."

"If it's true," said Munro carefully. Ferndale started, as if the thought had not occurred to him.

"Ah, yes, of course. If it's true. Now, you simply must tell me how you got hold of it."

Munro told his story carefully. It was true in every detail save that he claimed the source of the tape had been Anatoly Krivoi.

"Krivoi, yes, yes, know of him of course," said Ferndale.

"Well now, I shall have to get this translated into English and show it to the Master. This could be very big indeed. You won't be able to return to Moscow tomorrow, you know. Do you have a place to stay? Your club? Excellent. First class. Well now, you pop along and have a decent dinner and stay at the club for a couple of days."

Ferndale called his wife to tell her he would not be home to their modest house at Pinner that evening, but he would be spending the night in town. She knew his job and was accustomed to such absences.

Then he spent the night working on the translation of the tape, alone in his office. He was fluent in Russian, without the ultrakeen ear for tone and pitch that Munro had, which denotes the truly bilingual speaker. But it was good enough. He missed nothing of the Yakovlev report, nor of the brief but stunned reaction that had followed it among the Politburo members.

At ten o'clock the following morning, sleepless but shaved and breakfasted, looking as pink and fresh as he always did, Ferndale called Sir Nigel Irvine's secretary on the private line and asked to see him. He was with the Director General in ten minutes.

Sir Nigel Irvine read the transcript in silence, put it down, and regarded the tape lying on the desk before him.

"Is this genuine?" he asked.

Barry Ferndale had dropped his bonhomie. He had known Nigel Irvine for years as a colleague, and the elevation of his friend to the supreme post and a knighthood had changed nothing between them.

"Don't know," he said thoughtfully. "It's going to take a lot of checking out. It's possible. Adam told me he met this Krivoi briefly at a reception at the Czech Embassy just over two weeks ago. If Krivoi was thinking of coming over, that would have been his chance. Penkovsky did exactly the same; met a diplomat on neutral ground and established a secret meeting later. Of course he was regarded with intense suspicion until his information checked out. That's what I want to do here."

"Spell it out," said Sir Nigel.

Ferndale began polishing his glasses again. The speed of his circular movements with handkerchief on the lenses, so went the folklore, was in direct proportion to the pace of his thinking, and now he polished furiously.

"Firstly, Munro," he said. "Just in case it is a trap and the second meeting is to spring the trap, I would like him to take furlough here until we have finished with the tape. The Opposition might, just might, be trying to create an incident between governments."

"Is he owed leave?" asked Sir Nigel.

"Yes, he is, actually. He was shifted to Moscow so fast at the end of May, he is owed a fortnight's summer holiday."

"Then let him take it now. But he should keep in touch. And inside Britain, Barry. No wandering abroad until this is sorted out."

"Then there's the tape itself," said Ferndale. "It breaks down into two parts: the Yakovlev report and the voices of the Politburo. So far as I know, we have never heard Yakovlev speak. So no voiceprint tests will be possible with him. But what he says is highly specific. I'd like to check that out with some experts in chemical seed-dressing techniques. There's an excellent section in the Ministry of Agriculture who deal with that sort of thing. No need for anyone to know why we want to know, but I'll have to be convinced this accident with the lindane hopper valve is feasible."

"You recall that file the Cousins lent us a month ago?" asked Sir Nigel. "The photos taken by the Condor satellites?"

"Of course."

"Check the symptoms against the apparent explanation. What else?"

"The second section comes down to voiceprint analysis," said Ferndale. "I'd like to chop that section up into bits, so no one need know what is being talked about. The language laboratory at Beaconsfield could check out phraseology, syntax, vernacular expressions, regional dialects, and so forth. But the clincher will be the comparison of voiceprints."

Sir Nigel nodded. Both men knew that human voices, reduced to a series of electronically registered blips and pulses, are as individual as fingerprints. No two are ever quite alike.

"Very well," he said, "but Barry, I insist on two things. For the moment, no one knows about this outside of you, me, and Munro. If it's a phony, we don't want to raise false hopes; if it's not, it's high explosive. None of the technical side must know the whole. Secondly, I don't want to hear the name of Anatoly Krivoi again. Devise a cover name for this asset and use it in future."

Two hours later Barry Ferndale called Munro after lunch at his club. The telephone line being open, they used the commercial parlance that was habitual.

"The managing director's terribly happy with the sales report," Ferndale told Munro. "He's very keen that you take a fortnight's leave to enable us to break it right down and see where we go from here. Have you any ideas for a spot of leave?"

Munro hadn't, but he made up his mind. This was not a request; it was an order.

"I'd like to go back to Scotland for a while," he said. "I've always wanted to walk during the summer from Lochaber up the coast to Sutherland."

Ferndale was ecstatic. "The Highlands, the glens of Bonnie Scotland. So pretty at this time of year. Never could stand physical exercise myself, but I'm sure you'll enjoy it. Stay in touch with me—say, every second day. You have my home number, don't you?"

A week later, Miroslav Kaminsky arrived in England on his Red Cross travel papers. He had come across Europe by train, the ticket paid for by Drake, who was nearing the end of his financial resources.

Kaminsky and Krim were introduced, and Kaminsky given his orders.

"You learn English," Drake told him. "Morning, noon, and night. Books and gramophone records, faster than you've ever learned anything before. Meanwhile, I'm going to get you some decent papers. You can't travel on Red Cross documents forever. Until I do, and until you can make yourself understood in English, don't leave the flat."

Adam Munro had walked for ten days through the Highlands of Inverness, Ross, and Cromarty and finally into Sutherland County. He had arrived at the small town of Lochinver, where the waters of the North Minch stretch away westward to the Isle of Lewis, when he made his sixth call to Barry Ferndale's home on the outskirts of London.

"Glad you called," said Ferndale down the line. "Could

you come back to the office? The managing director would like a word."

Munro promised to leave within the hour and make his way as fast as possible to Inverness. There he could pick up a flight for London.

At his home on the outskirts of Sheffield, the great steel town of Yorkshire, Norman Pickering kissed his wife and daughter farewell that brilliant late-July morning and drove off to the bank of which he was manager.

Twenty minutes later a small van bearing the name of an electrical appliance company drove up to the house and disgorged two men in white coats. One carried a large cardboard carton up to the front door, preceded by his companion bearing a clipboard. Mrs. Pickering answered the door, and the two men went inside. None of the neighbors took any notice.

Ten minutes later the man with the clipboard came out and drove away. His companion had apparently stayed to fix and test the appliance they had delivered.

Thirty minutes after that, the van was parked about two corners from the bank, and the driver, without his white coat and wearing a charcoal-gray business suit, carrying not a clipboard but a large attaché case, entered the bank. He proffered an envelope to one of the women clerks, who looked at it, saw that it was addressed personally to Mr. Pickering, and took it in to him. The businessman waited patiently.

Two minutes later the manager opened his office door and looked out. His eye caught the waiting businessman.

"Mr. Partington?" he asked. "Do come in."

Andrew Drake did not speak until the door had closed behind him. When he did, his voice had no trace of his native Yorkshire, but a guttural edge as if it came from Europe. His hair was carrot-red, and heavy-rimmed, tinted glasses masked his eyes to some extent.

"I wish to open an account," he said, "and to make a withdrawal in cash."

Pickering was perplexed; his chief clerk could have handled this transaction.

"A large account, and a large transaction," said Drake. He slid a check across the desk. It was a bank check, the sort that can be obtained across the counter. It was issued by the

Holborn, London, branch of Pickering's own bank, and was drawn to thirty thousand pounds.

"I see," said Pickering. That kind of money was definitely the manager's business. "And the withdrawal?"

"Twenty thousand pounds in cash."

"Twenty thousand pounds in cash?" asked Pickering. He reached for the phone. "Well, of course I shall have to call the Holborn branch and—"

"I don't think that will be necessary," said Drake, and pushed a copy of that morning's London *Times* over the desk. Pickering stared at it. What Drake handed him next caused him to stare even more. It was a photograph, taken with a Polaroid camera. He recognized his wife, whom he had left ninety minutes earlier, sitting round-eyed with fear in his own fireside chair. He could make out a portion of his own sitting room. His wife held their child close to her with one arm. Across her knees was the same issue of the London *Times*.

"Taken sixty minutes ago," said Drake.

Pickering's stomach tightened. The photo would win no prizes for photographic quality, but the shape of the man's shoulder in the foreground and the sawed-off shotgun pointing at his family was quite clear enough.

"If you raise the alarm," said Drake quietly, "the police will come here, not to your home. Before they break in, you will be dead. In exactly sixty minutes, unless I make a phone call to say I am safely away with the money, that man is going to pull that trigger. Please don't think we are joking; we are quite prepared to die if we have to. We are the Red Army Faction."

Pickering swallowed hard. Under his desk, a foot from his knee, was a button linked to a silent alarm. He looked at the photograph again and moved his knee away.

"Call your chief clerk," said Drake, "and instruct him to open the account, credit the check to it, and provide the check for the twenty-thousand-pound withdrawal. Tell him you have telephoned London and all is in order. If he expresses surprise, tell him the sum is for a very big commercial promotion campaign in which prize money will be given away in cash. Pull yourself together and make it good."

The chief clerk *was* surprised, but his manager seemed calm enough; a little subdued, perhaps, but otherwise normal. And the dark-suited man before him looked relaxed and friendly. There was even a glass of the manager's sherry before each of them, though the businessman had kept his light gloves on—odd for such warm weather. Thirty minutes later the chief clerk brought the money from the vault, deposited it on the manager's desk, and left.

Drake packed it calmly into the attaché case.

"There are thirty minutes left," he told Pickering. "In twenty-five I shall make my phone call. My colleague will leave your wife and child perfectly unharmed. If you raise the alarm before that, he will shoot first and take his chances with the police later."

When he had gone, Pickering sat frozen for half an hour. In fact, Drake phoned the house five minutes later from a call box. Krim took the call, smiled briefly at the woman on the floor with her hands and ankles bound with adhesive tape, and left. Neither used the van, which had been stolen the previous day. Krim used a motorcycle parked in readiness farther down the road. Drake took a motorcycle helmet from the van to cover his flaming red hair, and used a second motorcycle parked near the van. Both were out of Sheffield within thirty minutes. They abandoned the vehicles north of London and met again in Drake's flat, where he washed the red dye out of his hair and crushed the eyeglasses to fragments.

Munro caught the following morning's breakfast flight south from Inverness. When the plastic trays were cleared away, the hostess offered the passengers newspapers fresh up from London. Being at the back of the aircraft, Munro missed the *Times* and the *Telegraph*, but secured a copy of the *Daily Express*. The headline story concerned two unidentified men, believed to be Germans from the Red Army Faction, who had robbed a Sheffield bank of twenty thousand pounds.

"Bloody bastards," said the English oilman from the North Sea rigs who was in the seat next to Munro. He tapped the *Express* headline. "Bloody Commies. I'd string them all up."

Munro conceded that upstringing would definitely have to be considered in future.

At Heathrow he took a taxi almost to the office and was shown straight into Barry Ferndale's room.

"Adam, my dear chap, you're looking a new man."

He sat Munro down and proffered coffee.

"Well now, the tape. You must be dying to know. Fact is, m'dear chap, it's genuine. No doubt about it. Everything checks. There's been a fearful blowup in the Soviet Agriculture Ministry. Six or seven senior functionaries ousted, including one we think must be that unfortunate fellow in the Lubyanka.

"That helps corroborate it. But the voices are genuine. No doubt, according to the lab boys. Now for the big one. One of our assets working out of Leningrad managed to take a drive out of town. There's not much wheat grown up there in the north, but there is a little. He stopped his car for a pee and swiped a stalk of the afflicted wheat. It came home in the bag three days ago. I got the report from the lab last night. They confirm there is an excess of this lindane stuff present in the root of the seedling.

"So, there we are. You've hit what our American cousins so charmingly call pay dirt. In fact, twenty-four-carat gold. By the way, the Master wants to see you. You're going back to Moscow tonight."

Munro's meeting with Sir Nigel Irvine was friendly but brief.

"Well done," said the Master. "Now, I understand your next meeting will be in a fortnight."

Munro nodded.

"This might be a long-term operation," Sir Nigel resumed, "which makes it a good thing you are new to Moscow. There will be no raised eyebrows if you stay on for a couple of years. But just in case this fellow changes his mind, I want you to press for more—everything we can squeeze out. Do you want any help, any backup?"

"No, thank you," said Munro. "Now that he's taken the plunge, the asset has insisted he'll talk only to me. I don't think I want to scare him off at this stage by bringing others in. Nor do I think he can travel, as Penkovsky could. Vishnayev never travels, so there's no cause for Krivoi to, either. I'll have to handle it alone."

Sir Nigel nodded. "Very well, you've got it."

When Munro had gone, Sir Nigel Irvine turned over the file on his desk, which was Munro's personal record. He had his misgivings. The man was a loner, ill at ease working in a team. A man who walked alone in the mountains of Scotland for relaxation.

There was an adage in the Firm: there are old agents and there are bold agents, but there are no old, bold agents. Sir Nigel was an old agent, and he appreciated caution. This opportunity had come swinging in from the outfield, unexpected, unprepared for. And it was moving fast. But then, the tape was genuine, no doubt of it. So was the summons on his desk to see the Prime Minister that evening at Downing Street. He had of course informed the Foreign Secretary when the tape had passed muster, and this was the outcome.

The black door of No. 10 Downing Street, residence of the British Prime Minister, is perhaps one of the best-known doors in the world. It stands on the right, two-thirds down a small cul-de-sac off Whitehall, an alley almost, sandwiched between the imposing piles of the Cabinet Office and the Foreign Office.

In front of this door, with its simple white figure 10 and brass knocker, attended by a single, unarmed police constable, the tourists gather to take each other's photograph and watch the comings and goings of the messengers and the well-known.

In fact, it is the men of words who go in through the front door; the men of influence tend to use the side. The house called No. 10 stands at ninety degrees to the Cabinet Office block, and the rear corners almost touch each other, enclosing a small lawn behind black railings. Where the corners almost meet, the gap is covered by a passageway leading to a small side door, and it was through this that the Director General of the SIS, accompanied by Sir Julian Flannery, the Cabinet Secretary, passed that last evening of July. The pair were shown straight to the second floor, past the Cabinet Room, to the Prime Minister's private study.

The Prime Minister had read the transcript of the Politburo tape, passed to her by the Foreign Secretary.

"Have you informed the Americans of this matter?" she asked directly.

"Not yet, ma'am," Sir Nigel answered. "Our final confirmation of its authenticity is only three days old."

"I would like you to do it personally," said the Prime Minister. Sir Nigel inclined his head. "The political perspectives of this pending wheat famine in the Soviet Union are immeasurable, of course, and as the world's biggest surplus wheat producer, the United States should be involved from the outset."

"I would not wish the Cousins to move in on this agent of ours," said Sir Nigel. "The running of this asset may be extremely delicate. I think we should handle it ourselves, alone."

"Will they try to move in?" asked the Prime Minister.

"They may, ma'am. They may. We ran Penkovsky jointly, even though it was we who recruited him. But there were reasons why. This time, I think we should go it alone."

The Prime Minister was not slow to see the value in political terms of controlling such an agent as one who had access to the Politburo transcripts.

"If pressure is brought," she said, "refer back to me, and I will speak to President Matthews personally about it. In the meantime, I would like you to fly to Washington tomorrow and present them the tape, or at least a verbatim copy of it. I intend to speak to President Matthews tonight in any case."

Sir Nigel and Sir Julian rose to leave.

"One last thing," said the Prime Minister. "I fully understand that I am not allowed to know the identity of this agent. Will you be telling Robert Benson who it is?"

"Certainly not, ma'am." Not only would the Director General of the SIS refuse point-blank to inform his own Prime Minister or the Foreign Secretary of the identity of the Russian, but he would not tell them even of Munro, who was running that agent. The Americans would know who Munro was, but never whom he was running. Nor would there be any tailing of Munro by the Cousins in Moscow; he would see to that as well.

"Then presumably this Russian defector has a code name. May I know it?" asked the Prime Minister.

"Certainly, ma'am. The defector is now known in every file simply as the Nightingale."

It just happened that Nightingale was the first songbird in the *N* section of the list of birds after which all Soviet agents were code-named, but the Prime Minister did not know this. She smiled for the first time.

"How very appropriate."

CHAPTER FIVE

JUST AFTER TEN in the morning of a wet and rainy August 1, an aging but comfortable four-jet VC-10 of the Royal Air Force Strike Command lifted out of Lyneham base in Wiltshire and headed west for Ireland and the Atlantic. It carried a small enough passenger complement: one air chief marshal who had been informed the night before that this of all days was the best for him to visit the Pentagon in Washington to discuss the forthcoming USAF–RAF tactical bomber exercises, and a civilian in a shabby mackintosh.

The air chief marshal had introduced himself to the unexpected civilian, and learned in reply that his companion was a Mr. Barrett of the Foreign Office who had business with the British Embassy on Massachusetts Avenue and had been instructed to take advantage of the VC-10 flight to save the taxpayer the cost of a two-way air ticket. The Air Force officer never learned that the purpose of the RAF plane's flight was in fact the other way around.

On another track south of the VC-10, a Boeing jumbo jet of British Airways left Heathrow, bound for New York. Among its three hundred–plus passengers it bore Azamat Krim, alias Arthur Crimmins, Canadian citizen, heading west on a buying mission, with a back pocket full of money.

Eight hours later, the VC-10 landed perfectly at Andrews Air Force Base in Maryland, ten miles southeast of Washington. As it closed down its engines on the apron, a Pentagon staff car swept up to the foot of the steps and disgorged a two-star general of the USAF. Two Air Force Security Police snapped to attention as the air chief marshal came down the steps to his welcoming committee. Within five minutes the ceremonies were all over; the Pentagon limousine drove away to Washington, the police "snowdrops" marched off, and the idle and curious of the air base went back to their duties.

No one noticed the modest sedan with nonofficial plates that drove to the parked VC-10 ten minutes later—no one, that is, with enough sophistication to note the odd-shaped aerial on the roof that betrayed a CIA car. No one bothered with the rumpled civilian who trotted down the steps and straight into the car moments later, and no one saw the car leave the air base.

The Company man in the U.S. Embassy on Grosvenor Square, London, had been alerted the night before, and his coded signal to Langley had caused the car to appear. The driver was in civilian clothes, a low-level staffer, but the man in the back who welcomed the guest from London was the chief of the Western European Division, one of the regional subordinates of the Deputy Director for Operations. He had been chosen to meet the Englishman because, having once headed the CIA operation in London, he knew him well. No one likes substitutions.

"Nigel, good to see you again," he said after confirming to himself that the arrival was indeed the man they expected.

"How good of you to come to meet me, Lance," responded Sir Nigel Irvine, well aware there was nothing good about it; it was a duty. The talk in the car was of London, family, the weather. No question of "What are you doing here?" The car swept along the Capital Beltway to the Woodrow Wilson Memorial Bridge over the Potomac and headed west into Virginia.

On the outskirts of Alexandria the driver pulled right into the George Washington Memorial Parkway, which fringes the whole western bank of the river. As they cruised past the National Airport and Arlington Cemetery, Sir Nigel Irvine glanced out to his right at the skyline of Washington, where years before he had been the SIS liaison man with the CIA, based in the British Embassy. Those had been tough days, in the wake of the Philby affair, when even the state of the weather was classified information so far as the English were concerned. He thought of what he carried in his briefcase and permitted himself a small smile.

After thirty minutes' cruising they pulled off the main highway, swung over it again, and headed into the forest. He remembered the small notice saying simply BPR–CIA and wondered again why they had to signpost the place. You either knew where it was or you didn't, and if you didn't, you weren't invited, anyway.

At the security gate in the great seven-foot-high chain-link fence that surrounds Langley, they halted while Lance showed his pass, then drove on and turned left past the awful conference center known as "the Igloo" because that is just what it resembles.

The Company's headquarters consists of five blocks, one in the center and one at each corner of the center block, like a rough St. Andrews cross. The Igloo is stuck onto the corner block nearest the main gate. Passing the recessed center block, Sir Nigel noticed the imposing main doorway and the great seal of the United States paved in terrazzo into the ground in front of it. But he knew this front entrance was for congressmen, senators, and other undesirables. The car swept on, past the complex, then pulled to the right and drove around to the back.

Here there is a short ramp, protected by a steel portcullis, running down one floor to the first basement level. At the bottom is a select garage for no more than ten cars. The black sedan came to a halt, and the man called Lance handed Sir Nigel over to his superior, Charles ("Chip") Allen, the Deputy Director for Operations. They, too, knew each other well.

Set in the back wall of the garage is a small elevator, guarded by steel doors and two armed men. Chip Allen identified his guest, signed for him, and used a plastic card to open the elevator doors. The elevator hummed its way quietly seven floors up to the Director's suite. Another magnetized plastic card got them both out of the elevator, into a lobby faced by three doors. Chip Allen knocked on the center one, and it was Bob Benson himself who, alerted from below, welcomed the British visitor into his suite.

Benson led him past the big desk to the lounge area in front of the beige marble fireplace. In winter Benson liked a crackling log fire to burn here, but Washington in August is no place for fires and the air conditioning was working overtime. Benson pulled the rice-paper screen across the room to separate the lounge from the office and sat back opposite his guest. Coffee was ordered, and when they were alone, Benson finally asked, "What brings you to Langley, Nigel?"

Sir Nigel sipped and sat back.

"We have," he said undramatically, "obtained the services of a new asset."

He spoke for almost ten minutes before the Director of Central Intelligence interrupted him.

"Inside the Politburo?" he queried. "You mean, right inside?"

"Let us just say, with access to Politburo meeting transcripts," said Sir Nigel.

"Would you mind if I called Chip Allen and Ben Kahn in on this?"

"Not at all, Bob. They'll have to know within an hour or so, anyway. Prevents repetition."

Bob Benson rose, crossed to a telephone on a coffee table, and made a call to his private secretary. When he had finished he stared out of the picture window at the great green forest. "Jesus H. Christ," he breathed.

Sir Nigel Irvine was not displeased that his two old contacts in the CIA should be in on the ground floor of his briefing. All pure intelligence agencies—as opposed to intelligence–secret police forces like the KGB—have two main arms. One is Operations, covering the business of actually obtaining information; the other is Intelligence, covering the business of collating, cross-referencing, interpreting, and analyzing the great mass of raw, unprocessed information that is gathered in.

Both have to be good. If the information is faulty, the best analysis in the world will only come up with nonsense; if the analysis is inept, all the efforts of the information gatherers are wasted. Statesmen need to know what other nations, friends or potential foes, are doing and, if possible, what they intend to do. What they are doing is nowadays often observable; what they intend to do is not. Which is why all the space cameras in the world will never supplant a brilliant analyst working with material from inside another's secret councils.

In the CIA the two men who hold sway under the Director of Central Intelligence, who may be a political appointee, are the Deputy Director (Operations), or DDO, and the Deputy Director (Intelligence), or DDI. It is Operations that inspires the thriller writers; Intelligence is back-room work, tedious, slow, methodical, and, paradoxically, often most valuable when most boring.

Like Tweedledum and Tweedledee, the DDO and the DDI have to work hand in hand and they have to trust each other. Benson, as a political appointee, was lucky. His DDO was Chip Allen, WASP and former football player; his DDI was Ben Kahn, Jewish chess master; they fitted together like a pair of gloves. In five minutes both were sitting with Benson and Irvine in the lounge area. Coffee was forgotten.

The British spymaster talked for almost an hour. He was

uninterrupted. Then the three Americans read the Nightingale transcript and watched the tape recording in its polyethylene bag with something like hunger. When Irvine had finished, there was a short silence. Chip Allen broke it.

"Roll over, Penkovsky," he said.

"You'll want to check it all," said Sir Nigel evenly. No one dissented. Friends are friends, but . . . "It took us ten days, but we can't fault it. The voiceprints check out, every one. We've already exchanged cables about the bustup in the Soviet Agriculture Ministry. And of course you have your Condor photographs. Oh, one last thing . . ."

From his bag he produced a small polyethylene sack with a sprig of young wheat inside it.

"One of our chaps swiped this from a field outside Leningrad."

"I'll have our Agriculture Department check it out as well," said Benson. "Anything else, Nigel?"

"Oh, not really," said Sir Nigel. "Well, perhaps a couple of small points . . ."

"Spit it out."

Sir Nigel drew a breath.

"The Russian buildup in Afghanistan. We think they may be mounting a move toward Pakistan and India through the passes. That we regard as our patch. Now, if you could ask Condor to have a look . . ."

"You've got it," said Benson without hesitation.

"And then," resumed Sir Nigel, "that Soviet defector you brought out of Geneva two weeks ago. He seems to know quite a bit about Soviet assets in our trade-union movement."

"We sent you transcripts of that," said Allen hastily.

"We'd like direct access," said Sir Nigel.

Allen looked at Kahn. Kahn shrugged.

"Okay," said Benson. "Can we have access to the Nightingale?"

"Sorry, no," said Sir Nigel. "That's different. The Nightingale's too damn delicate, right out in the cold. I don't want to disturb the fish just yet in case of a change of heart. You'll get everything we get, as soon as we get it. But no moving in. I'm trying to speed up the delivery and volume, but it's going to take time and a lot of care."

"When's your next delivery slated for?" asked Allen.

"A week from today. At least, that's the meet. I hope there'll be a handover."

Sir Nigel Irvine spent the night at a CIA safe house in the

Virginia countryside, and the next day "Mr. Barrett" flew back to London with the air chief marshal.

It was three days later that Azamat Krim sailed from Pier 49 in New York harbor aboard the elderly *Queen Elizabeth 2* for Southampton. He had decided to sail rather than fly because he felt there was a better chance his main luggage would escape X-ray examination if he went by sea.

His purchases were complete. One of his pieces of luggage was a standard aluminum shoulder case such as professional photographers use to protect their cameras and lenses. As such, it could not be X-rayed but would have to be hand-examined. The molded plastic sponge inside that held the cameras and lenses from banging against each other was glued to the bottom of the case, but ended two inches short of the real bottom. In the cavity were two handguns with ammunition clips.

Another piece of luggage, deep in the heart of a small cabin trunk full of clothes, was an aluminum tube with a screw top, containing what looked like a long, cylindrical camera lens, some four inches in diameter. He calculated that if it were examined, it would pass in the eyes of all but the most suspicious of customs officers as the sort of lens that camera freaks use for very long range photography, and a collection of books of bird photographs and wildlife pictures lying next to the lens inside the trunk was designed to corroborate the explanation.

In fact, the lens was an image intensifier, also called a night-sight, of the kind that may be commercially bought without a permit in the United States but not in Britain.

It was boiling hot that Sunday, August 8, in Moscow, and those who could not get to the beaches crowded instead to the numerous swimming pools of the city, especially the new complex built for the 1980 Olympics. But the British Embassy staff, along with those of a dozen other legations, were at the beach on the Moscow River upstream from Uspenskoye Bridge. Adam Munro was among them.

He tried to appear as carefree as the others, but it was hard. He checked his watch too many times, and finally got dressed.

"Oh, Adam, you're not going back already? There's ages of daylight left," one of the secretaries called to him.

He forced a rueful grin.

"Duty calls, or rather the plans for the Manchester Chamber of Commerce visit call," he shouted back to her.

He walked through the woods to his car, dropped his bathing things, had a covert look to see if anyone was interested, and locked the car. There were too many men in sandals, slacks, and open shirts for one extra to be of notice, and he thanked his stars the KGB never seemed to take their jackets off. There was no one looking remotely like the Opposition within sight of him. He set off through the trees to the north.

Valentina was waiting for him, standing back in the shade of the trees. His stomach was tight, knotted, for all that he was pleased to see her. She was no expert at spotting a tail and might have been followed. If she had, his diplomatic cover would save him from worse than expulsion, but the repercussions would be enormous. Even that was not his worry; it was what they would do to her if she were ever caught. Whatever the motives, the term for what she was doing was high treason.

He took her in his arms and kissed her. She kissed him back and trembled in his arms.

"Are you frightened?" he asked her.

"A bit." She nodded. "You listened to the tape recording?"

"Yes, I did. Before I handed it over. I suppose I should not have done, but I did."

"Then you know about the famine that faces us. Adam, when I was a girl I saw the famine in this country just after the war. It was bad, but it was caused by the war, by Germans. We could take it. Our leaders were on our side, they would make things get better."

"Perhaps they can sort things out this time," said Munro lamely.

Valentina shook her head angrily.

"They're not even trying," she burst out. "I sit there listening to their voices, typing the transcripts. They are just bickering, trying to save their own skins."

"And your uncle, Marshal Kerensky?" he asked gently.

"He's as bad as the rest. When I married my husband, Uncle Nikolai was at the wedding. I thought he was so jolly, so kindly. Of course, that was his private life. Now I listen to him in his public life; he's like all of them, ruthless and cynical. They just jockey for advantage over each other, for power, and to hell with the people. I suppose I should be one of them, but I can't be. Not now, not anymore."

Munro looked across the clearing at the pines but saw olive trees and heard a boy in uniform shouting. "You don't own me!" Strange, he mused, how establishments with all their power sometimes went too far and lost control of their own servants through sheer excess. Not always, not often, but sometimes.

"I could get you out of here, Valentina," he said. "It would mean my leaving the diplomatic corps, but it's been done before. Sasha is young enough to grow up somewhere else."

"No, Adam, no, it's tempting but I can't. Whatever the outcome, I am part of Russia, I have to stay. Perhaps, one day . . . I don't know."

They sat in silence for a while, holding hands. She broke the quiet at last.

"Did your . . . intelligence people pass the tape recording on to London?"

"I think so. I handed it to the man I believe represents the Secret Service in the embassy. He asked me if there would be another one."

She nodded at her shoulder bag.

"It's just the transcript. I can't get the tape recordings anymore. They're kept in a safe after the transcriptions, and I don't have the key. The papers in there are of the following Politburo meeting."

"How do you get them out, Valentina?" he asked.

"After the meetings," she told him, "the tapes and the stenographic notes are brought under guard to the Central Committee building. There is a locked department there where we work, five other women and I. With one man in charge. When the transcripts are finished, the tapes are locked away."

"Then how did you get the first one?"

She shrugged.

"The man in charge is new, since last month. The other one, before him, was more lax. There is a tape studio next door where the tapes are copied once before being locked in the safe. I was alone in there last month, long enough to steal the second tape and substitute a dummy."

"A dummy?" exclaimed Munro. "They'll spot the substitution if ever they play them back."

"It's unlikely," she said. "The transcripts form the archives once they have been checked against the tapes for accuracy. I was lucky with that tape; I brought it out in a shopping bag under the groceries I had bought in the Central Committee commissary."

"Aren't you searched?"

"Hardly ever. We are trusted, Adam, the elite of the New Russia. The papers are easier. At work I wear an old-fashioned girdle. I copied the last meeting of June on the machine, but ran off one extra copy, then switched the number control back by one figure. The extra copy I stuck inside my girdle. It made no noticeable bulge."

Munro's stomach turned at the risk she was taking.

"What do they talk about in this meeting?" he asked, gesturing toward the shoulder bag.

"The consequences," she said. "What will happen when the famine breaks. What the people of Russia will do to them. But Adam . . . there's been one since. Early in July. I couldn't copy it; I was on leave. I couldn't refuse my leave; it would have been too obvious. But when I got back, I met one of the girls who had transcribed it. She was white-faced and wouldn't describe it."

"Can you get it?" asked Munro.

"I can try. I'll have to wait until the office is empty and use the copying machine. I can reset it afterward so it will not show it has been used. But not until early next month; I shall not be on the late shift when I can work alone until then."

"We shouldn't meet here again," Munro told her. "Patterns are dangerous."

He spent another hour describing the sort of tradecraft she would need to know if they were to go on meeting. Finally he gave her a pad of closely typed sheets he had tucked in his waistband under his loose shirt.

"It's all in there, my darling. Memorize it and burn it. Flush the ashes down the can."

Five minutes later she gave him a wad of flimsy paper sheets covered with neat, typed Cyrillic script from her bag and slipped away through the forest to her car on a sandy track half a mile away.

Munro retreated into the darkness of the main arch above the church's recessed side door. He produced a roll of tape from his pocket, slipped his pants to his knees, and taped the batch of sheets to his thigh. With the trousers back up again and belted, he could feel the paper snug against his thigh as he walked, but under the baggy, Russian-made trousers, they did not show.

By midnight, in the silence of his flat, he had read them all a dozen times. The next Wednesday, they went in the Messenger's wrist-chained briefcase to London, wax-sealed in a stout envelope and coded for the SIS liaison man at the Foreign Office only.

The glass doors leading to the Rose Garden were tightly shut, and only the whir of the air conditioner broke the silence in the Oval Office of the White House. The balmy days of June were long gone, and the steamy heat of a Washington August forbade open doors and windows.

Around the building on the Pennsylvania Avenue side, the tourists, damp and hot, admired the familiar aspect of the White House front entrance, with its pillars, flag, and curved driveway, or queued for the guided tour of this most holy of American holies. None of them would penetrate to the tiny West Wing building where President Matthews sat in conclave with his advisers.

In front of his desk were Stanislaw Poklewski and Robert Benson. They had been joined by the Secretary of State, David Lawrence, a Boston lawyer and pillar of the East Coast establishment.

President Matthews flicked the file in front of him closed. He had long since devoured the first Politburo transcript, translated into English; what he had just finished reading was his experts' evaluation of it.

"Bob, you were remarkably close with your estimate of a shortfall of thirty million tons," he said. "Now it appears they are going to be fifty to fifty-five million tons short this fall. And you have no doubt this transcript comes right from inside the Politburo?"

"Mr. President, we've checked it out every way. The voices are real; the traces of excessive lindane in the root of the wheat plant are real; the hatchet job inside the Soviet Agriculture Ministry is real. We don't believe there is room for any substantive doubt that tape recording was of the Politburo in session."

"We have to handle this right," mused the President. "There must be no way we make a miscalculation on this one. There has never been an opportunity like it."

"Mr. President," said Poklewski, "this means the Soviets are not facing severe shortages, as we supposed when you invoked the Shannon Act last month. They are facing a famine."

Unknowingly he was echoing the words of Petrov in the Kremlin two months earlier in his aside to Ivanenko, which had not been on the tape. President Matthews nodded slowly.

"We can't disagree with that, Stan. The question is, what do we do about it?"

"Let them have their famine," said Poklewski. "This is the biggest mistake they have made since Stalin refused to believe Western warnings about the Nazi buildup on his frontier in the spring of 1941. This time, the enemy is within. So let them work it out in their own way."

"David?" asked the President of his Secretary of State.

Lawrence shook his head. The differences of opinion between the arch-hawk Poklewski and the cautious Bostonian were legendary.

"I disagree, Mr. President," he said at length. "Firstly, I don't think we have examined deeply enough the possible permutations of what might happen if the Soviet Union were plunged into chaos next spring. As I see it, it is more than simply a question of letting the Soviets stew in their own juice. There are massive implications on a worldwide basis consequent on such a phenomenon."

"Bob?" asked President Matthews. His Director of Central Intelligence was lost in thought.

"We have the time, Mr. President," he said. "They know you invoked the Shannon Act last month. They know that if they want the grain, they have to come to you. As David says, we really should examine the perspectives consequent upon a famine across the Soviet Union. We can do that as of now. Sooner or later, the Kremlin has to make a play. When they do, we have all the cards. We know how bad their predicament is; they don't know we know. We have the wheat, we have the Condors, we have the Nightingale, and we have the time. We hold all the aces this time. No need to decide yet which way to play them."

Lawrence nodded and regarded Benson with new respect. Poklewski shrugged.

President Matthews made up his mind.

"Stan, as of now I want you to put together an ad hoc group within the National Security Council. I want it small, and absolutely secret. You, Bob, and David here. The Chairman of the Joint Chiefs of Staff, the secretaries of Defense, the Treasury, and Agriculture. I want to know what will happen, worldwide, if the Soviet Union starves. I need to know, and soon."

One of the telephones on his desk rang. It was the direct line to the State Department. President Matthews looked inquiringly at David Lawrence.

"Are you calling me, David?" he asked with a smile.

The Secretary of State rose and took the machine off its hook. He listened for several minutes, then replaced the receiver.

"Mr. President, the pace is speeding up. Two hours ago in Moscow, Foreign Minister Rykov summoned Ambassador Donaldson to the Foreign Ministry. On behalf of the Soviet government he has proposed the sale by the United States to the Soviet Union by next spring of fifty-five million tons of mixed cereal grains."

For several moments only the ormolu carriage clock above the marble fireplace could be heard in the Oval Office.

"What did Ambassador Donaldson reply?" asked the President.

"Of course, that the request would be passed on to Washington for consideration," said Lawrence, "and that no doubt your answer would be forthcoming in due course."

"Gentlemen," said the President, "I need those answers, and I need them fast. I can hold my answer for four weeks at the outside, but by September fifteenth at the latest I shall have to reply. When I do, I shall want to know what we are handling here. Every possibility."

"Mr. President, within a few days we may be receiving a second package of information from the Nightingale. That could give an indication of the way the Kremlin sees the same problem."

President Matthews nodded. "Bob, if and when it comes, I would like it decoded and on my desk immediately."

As the presidential meeting broke up in the dusk of Washington, it was already long after dark in Britain. Police records later showed that scores of burglaries and break-ins had taken place during the night of August 11, but down in Somerset the one that most disturbed the police was the theft from a sporting-gun shop in the pleasant country town of Taunton.

The thieves had evidently visited the shop in the daylight hours during the previous day or so, for the alarm had been neatly cut by someone who had spotted where the cable ran.

With the alarm system out of commission, the thieves had used powerful bolt cutters on the window grille in the back alley that ran behind the shop.

The place had not been ransacked, and the usual haul, shotguns for the holding up of banks, had not been taken. What was missing, the proprietor confirmed, was a single hunting rifle, one of his finest, a Finnish-made Sako Hornet .22, a highly accurate precision piece. Also gone were two boxes of shells for the rifle, soft-nosed 45-grain hollow-point Remingtons, capable of high velocity, great penetration, and considerable distortion on impact.

In his flat in Bayswater, Andrew Drake sat with Miroslav Kaminsky and Azamat Krim and gazed at their haul laid out on the sitting-room table; it consisted of two handguns, each with two magazines fully loaded, the rifle with two boxes of shells, and the image intensifier.

There are two basic types of night-sight, the infrared scope and the intensifier. Men who shoot by night tend to prefer the latter, and Krim, with his Western Canadian hunting background and three years with the Canadian paratroopers, had chosen well.

The infrared sight is based on the principle of sending a beam of infrared light down the line of fire to illuminate the target, which appears in the sight as a greenish outline. But because it emits light, even a light invisible to the naked eye, the infrared sight requires a power source. The image intensifier works on the principle of gathering all those tiny elements of light that are present in a "dark" environment, and concentrating them, as the gigantic retina of a barn owl's eye can concentrate what little light there is and see a moving mouse where a human eye would detect nothing. It needs no power source.

Originally developed for military purposes, the small, hand-held image intensifiers had by the late seventies come to interest the vast American security industry and were of use to factory guards and others. Soon they were sold commercially. By the early eighties the larger versions, capable of being mounted atop a rifle barrel, were also purchasable in America for cash across the counter. It was one of these that Azamat Krim had bought.

The rifle already had grooves along the upper side of its barrel to take a telescopic sight for target practice. Working with a file and a vise screwed to the edge of the kitchen table,

Krim began to convert the clips of the image intensifier to fit into these grooves.

While Krim was working, Barry Ferndale paid a visit to the United States Embassy, a mile away in Grosvenor Square. By prearrangement he was visiting the head of the CIA operation in London, who was ostensibly a diplomat attached to his country's embassy staff.

The meeting was brief and cordial. Ferndale removed from his briefcase a wad of papers and handed them over.

"Fresh from the presses, my dear fellow," he told the American. "Rather a lot, I'm afraid. These Russians do tend to talk, don't they? Anyway, best of luck."

The papers were the Nightingale's second delivery, and already in translation into English. The American knew he would have to encode them himself, and send them himself. No one else would see them. He thanked Ferndale and settled down to a long night of hard work.

He was not the only man who slept little that night. Far away in the city of Ternopol in the Ukraine, a plainclothes agent of the KGB left the noncommissioned officers club and commissary beside the KGB barracks and began to walk home. He was not of the rank to rate a staff car, and his own private vehicle was parked near his house. He did not mind; it was a warm and pleasant night, and he had had a convivial evening with his colleagues in the club.

Which was probably why he failed to notice the two figures in the doorway across the street who seemed to be watching the club entrance and who nodded to each other.

It was after midnight, and Ternopol, even in a warm August, has no nightlife to speak of. The secret policeman's path took him away from the main streets and into the sprawl of Shevchenko Park, where the trees in full leaf almost covered the narrow pathways. It was the longest shortcut he ever took. Halfway across the park there was a scuttling of feet behind him; he half turned, took the blow from the blackjack that had been aimed at the back of his head on the temple, and went down in a heap.

It was nearly dawn before he recovered. He had been dragged into a tangle of bushes and robbed of his wallet, money, keys, ration card, and I.D. card. Police and KGB inquiries continued for several weeks into this most unaccustomed mugging, but no culprits were discovered. In fact, both assailants had been on the first dawn train out of Ternopol and were back in their homes in Lvov.

President Matthews chaired the meeting of the ad hoc committee that considered the Nightingale's second package, and it was a subdued meeting.

"My analysts have already come up with some possibilities consequent upon a famine in the Soviet Union next winter and spring," Benson told the seven men in the Oval Office, "but I don't think any one of them would have dared go as far as the Politburo themselves have done in predicting a pandemic breakdown of law and order. It's unheard of in the Soviet Union."

"That's true of my people, too," agreed David Lawrence of the State Department. "They're talking here about the KGB's not being able to hold the line. I don't think we could have gone that far in our prognosis."

"So what answer do I give Maxim Rudin to his request to purchase fifty-five million tons of grain?" asked the President.

"Mr. President, tell him 'No,'" urged Poklewski. "We have here an opportunity that has never occurred before and may never occur again. You have Maxim Rudin and the whole Politburo in the palm of your hand. For two decades successive administrations have bailed the Soviets out every time they have gotten into problems with their economy. Every time, they have come back more aggressive than ever. Every time they have responded by pushing further with their involvement in Africa, Asia, Latin America. Every time, the Third World has been encouraged to believe the Soviets have recovered from their setbacks through their own efforts, that the Marxist economic system works. This time, the world can be shown beyond a doubt that the Marxist economic system does not work and never will. This time, I urge you to screw the lid down tight, real tight. You can demand a concession for every ton of wheat. You can require them to get out of Asia, Africa, and the Americas. And if Rudin won't, you can bring him down."

"Would this"—President Matthews tapped the Nightingale report in front of him—"bring Rudin down?"

David Lawrence answered, and no one disagreed with him. "If what is described in here by the members of the Politburo themselves actually happened inside the Soviet Union, yes, Rudin would fall in disgrace, as Khrushchev fell," he said.

"Then use the power," urged Poklewski. "Use it. Rudin has run out of options. He has no alternative but to agree to your terms. If he won't, topple him."

"And the successor—" began the President.

"Will have seen what happened to Rudin, and will learn his lesson from that. Any successor will have to agree to the terms we lay down."

President Matthews sought the views of the rest of the meeting. All but Lawrence and Benson agreed with Poklewski. President Matthews made his decision; the hawks had won.

The Soviet Foreign Ministry is one of seven near-identical buildings of the wedding-cake architectural style that Stalin favored: neo-Gothic as put together by a mad *pâtissier* in brown sandstone, and standing on Smolensky Boulevard, on the corner of Arbat.

On the penultimate day of the month, the Fleetwood Brougham Cadillac of the American Ambassador to Moscow hissed into the parking bay before the main doors, and Myron Donaldson was escorted to the plush fourth-floor office of Dmitri Rykov, the Soviet Foreign Minister. They knew each other well; before coming to Moscow, Ambassador Donaldson had done a spell at the United Nations, where Dmitri Rykov was a well-known figure. Frequently they had drunk friendly toasts there together, and here in Moscow also. But today's meeting was formal. Donaldson was attended by his deputy chief of mission, and Rykov by five senior officials.

Donaldson read his message carefully, word for word, in its original English. Rykov understood and spoke English well, but an aide did a rapid running translation into his right ear.

President Matthew's message made no reference to his knowledge of the disaster that had struck the Soviet wheat crop, and it expressed no surprise at the Soviet request of earlier in the month for the staggering purchase of fifty-five million tons of grain. In measured terms it expressed regret that the United States of America would not be in a position to make a sale to the Union of Soviet Socialist Republics of the requested tonnage of wheat.

With hardly a pause, Ambassador Donaldson read on, into the second part of the message. This, seemingly unconnected with the first, though following without a break, regretted the lack of success of the Strategic Arms Limitation Talks known as SALT III, concluded in the winter of 1980, in lessening world tension, and expressed the hope that SALT IV, scheduled for preliminary discussion that coming autumn and winter, would achieve more, and enable the world to make genuine steps along the road to a just and lasting peace. That was all.

Ambassador Donaldson laid the full text of the message on Rykov's desk, received the formal, straight-faced thanks of the gray-haired, gray-visaged Soviet Foreign Minister, and left.

Andrew Drake spent most of that day poring over books. Azamat Krim, he knew, was somewhere in the hills of Wales fire-testing the hunting rifle with its new sight mounted above the barrel. Miroslav Kaminsky was still working at his steadily improving English. For Drake, the problems centered on the south Ukrainian port of Odessa.

His first work of reference was the red-covered *Lloyd's Loading List*, a weekly guide to ships loading in European ports for destinations all over the world. From this he learned that there was no regular service from Northern Europe to Odessa, but there was a small, independent, inter-Mediterranean service that also called at several Black Sea ports. It was named the Salonika Line, and listed two vessels.

From there he went to the blue-covered *Lloyd's Shipping Index* and scoured the columns until he came to the vessels in question. He smiled. The supposed owners of each vessel trading in the Salonika Line were one-ship companies registered in Panama, which meant beyond much of a doubt that the owning "company" in each case was a single brass plate attached to the wall of a lawyer's office in Panama City, and no more.

From his third work of reference, a book called the *Greek Shipping Directory*, he ascertained that the managing agents were listed as a Greek firm and that their offices were in Piraeus, the port of Athens. He knew what that meant. In ninety-nine cases out of a hundred, when one talks to the managing agents of a Panama-flag ship and they are Greek, one is in effect talking to the ship's owners. They masquerade as "agents only" in order to take advantage of the fact that agents cannot be held legally responsible for the peccadilloes of their principals. Some of these peccadilloes include inferior rates of pay and conditions for the crew, unseaworthy vessels and ill-defined safety standards but well-defined valuations for "total-loss" insurance, and occasionally some very careless habits with crude-oil spillages.

For all that, Drake began to like the Salonika Line for one reason: a Greek-registered vessel would inevitably be allowed to employ only Greek senior officers, but could employ a cosmopolitan crew with or without official seaman's books; passports alone would be sufficient. And her ships visited Odessa regularly.

Maxim Rudin leaned forward, lay the Russian translation of President Matthews's negative message as delivered by Ambassador Donaldson on his coffee table, and surveyed his three guests. It was dark outside, and he liked to keep the lights low in his private study at the north end of the Arsenal Building in the Kremlin.

"Blackmail," said Petrov angrily.

"Of course," said Rudin. "What were you expecting? Sympathy?"

"That damned Poklewski is behind this," said Rykov. "But this cannot be Matthews's final answer. Their own Condors and our offer to buy fifty-five million tons of grain must have told them what position we are in."

"Will they talk eventually? Will they negotiate after all?" asked Ivanenko.

"Oh, yes, they'll talk eventually," said Rykov. "But they'll delay as long as they can, spin things out, wait until the famine begins to bite, then trade the grain against humiliating concessions."

"Not too humiliating, I hope," murmured Ivanenko. "We have only a seven-to-six majority in the Politburo, and I for one would like to hold onto it."

"That is precisely my problem," growled Rudin. "Sooner or later I have to send Dmitri Rykov into the negotiating chamber to fight for us, and I don't have a single damned weapon to give him."

On the last day of the month, Andrew Drake flew from London to Athens to begin his search for a ship heading toward Odessa.

The same day, a small van, converted into a two-bunk mobile home such as students like to use for a roving Continental holiday, left London for Dover on the Channel coast, and thence to France and Athens by road. Concealed beneath the floor were the guns, ammunition, and image intensifier. Fortunately, most drug consignments head the other way, from the Balkans toward France and Britain. Customs checks were perfunctory at Dover and Calais.

At the wheel was Azamat Krim with his Canadian passport and international driving license. Beside him, with new, albeit not quite regular, British papers, was Miroslav Kaminsky.

CHAPTER SIX

CLOSE BY THE BRIDGE across the Moscow River at Uspenskoye is a restaurant called the Russian Isba. It is built in the style of the timber cottages in which Russian peasants dwell, and which are called isbas. Both interior and exterior are of split pine tree trunks, nailed to timber uprights. The gap between its traditionally filled with river clay, in a fashion not unlike the manner in which North American log cabins are insulated.

These isbas may look primitive, and from the point of view of sanitation often are, but they are much warmer than brick or concrete structures through the freezing Russian winters. The Isba restaurant is snug and warm inside, divided into a dozen small private dining rooms, many of which will seat only one dinner party. Unlike the restaurants of central Moscow, it is permitted a profit incentive linked to staff pay, and as a result, and in even more stark contrast to the usual run of Russian eateries, it has tasty food and fast and willing service.

It was here that Adam Munro had set up his next meeting with Valentina, scheduled for Saturday, September 4. She had secured a dinner date with a male friend and had persuaded him to take her to this particular restaurant. Munro had invited one of the embassy secretaries to dinner, and had booked the table in her name, not in his own. The written reservations record would not, therefore, show that either Munro or Valentina had been present that evening.

They dined in separate rooms, and on the dot of nine o'clock each made the excuse of going to the toilet and left the table. They met in the parking lot, and Munro, whose own car would have been too noticeable with its embassy plates, followed Valentina to her own private Zhiguli sedan. She was subdued and puffed nervously at a cigarette.

Munro had handled two Russian defectors-in-place and knew the incessant strain that begins to wear at the nerves after a few weeks of subterfuge and secrecy.

"I got my chance," she said at length. "Three days ago. The meeting of early July. I was nearly caught."

Munro was tense. Whatever she might think about her being trusted within the Party machine, no one, no one at all, is ever really trusted in Moscow politics. She was walking a high wire; they both were. The difference was, he had a net: his diplomatic status.

"What happened?" he asked.

"Someone came in. A guard. I had just switched off the copying machine and was back at my typewriter. He was perfectly friendly. But he leaned against the machine. It was still warm. I don't think he noticed anything. But it frightened me. That's not all that frightened me. I couldn't read the transcript until I got home. I was too busy feeding it into the copier. Adam, it's awful."

She took her car keys, unlocked the glove compartment, and extracted a fat envelope, which she handed to Munro. The moment of handover is usually the moment when the watchers pounce, if they are there; the moment when the feet pound on the gravel, the doors are torn open, the occupants dragged out. Nothing happened.

Munro glanced at his watch. Nearly ten minutes. Too long. He put the envelope in his inside breast pocket.

"I'm going to try for permission to bring you out," he said. "You can't go on like this forever, even for much longer. Nor can you simply settle back to the old life, not now. Not knowing what you know. Nor can I carry on, knowing you are out in the city, knowing that we love each other. I have a leave break next month. I'm going to ask them in London then."

This time she made no demur, a sign that her nerve was showing the first signs of breaking.

"All right," she said. Seconds later, she was gone into the

darkness of the parking lot. He watched her enter the pool of light by the open restaurant door and disappear inside. He gave her two minutes, then returned to his own impatient companion.

It was three in the morning before Munro had finished reading Plan Aleksandr, Marshal Nikolai Kerensky's scenario for the conquest of Western Europe. He poured himself a double brandy and sat staring at the papers on his sitting-room table. Valentina's jolly, kindly Uncle Nikolai, he mused, had certainly laid it on the line. He spent two hours staring at a map of Europe, and by sunrise was as certain as Kerensky himself that in terms of conventional warfare the plan would work. Secondly, he was sure that Rykov, too, was right: thermonuclear war would ensue. And thirdly, he was convinced there was no way of convincing the dissident members of the Politburo of this, short of the holocaust's actually happening.

He rose and went to the window. Daylight was breaking in the east, out over the Kremlin spires; an ordinary Sunday was beginning for the citizens of Moscow, as it would in two hours for the Londoners and five hours later for the New Yorkers.

All his adult life the guarantee that summer Sundays would remain just plain ordinary had been dependent on a fine balance—a balance of belief in the might and willpower of the opponent superpower, a balance of credibility, a balance of fear, but a balance for all that. He shivered, partly from the chill of morning, more from the realization that the papers behind him proved that at last the old nightmare was coming out of the shadows; the balance was breaking down.

The Sunday sunrise found Andrew Drake in far better humor, for his Saturday night had brought information of a different kind.

Every area of human knowledge, however small, however arcane, has its experts and its devotees. And every group of these appear to have one place where they congregate to talk, discuss, exchange their information, and impart the newest gossip.

Shipping movements in the eastern Mediterranean hardly form a subject on which doctorates are earned, but they do form a subject of great interest to out-of-work seamen in that area, such as Andrew Drake was pretending to be. The information center about such movements is a small hotel called the Cavo d'Oro, standing above a yacht basin in the port of Piraeus.

Drake had already observed the offices of the agents, and probable owners, of the Salonika Line, but he knew the last thing he should do was to visit them.

Instead, he checked into the Cavo d'Oro Hotel and spent his time at the bar, where captains, mates, bosuns, agents, dockland gossips, and job seekers sat over drinks to exchange what tidbits of information they had. On Saturday night Drake found his man, a bosun who had once worked for the Salonika Line. It took half a bottle of retsina to extract the information.

"The one that visits Odessa most frequently is the M/V *Sanadria*," he was told. "She is an old tub. Captain is Nikos Thanos. I think she's in harbor now."

She *was* in harbor, and Drake found her by midmorning. She was a five-thousand-ton-deadweight, tween-deck Mediterranean trader, rusty and none too clean, but if she was heading into the Black Sea and up to Odessa on her next voyage, Drake would not have minded if she had been full of holes.

By sundown he had found her captain, having learned that Thanos and all his officers were from the Greek island of Chios. Most of these Greek-run traders are almost family affairs, the master and his senior officers usually being from the same island, and often interrelated. Drake spoke no Greek, but fortunately English was the lingua franca of the international maritime community, even in Piraeus, and just before sundown he found Captain Thanos.

Northern Europeans, when they finish work, head for home, wife, and family. Eastern Mediterraneans head for the coffeehouse, friends, and gossip. The mecca of the coffeehouse community in Piraeus is a street alongside the waterfront called Akti Miaouli; its vicinity contains little else but shipping offices and coffeehouses.

Each frequenter has his favorite, and they are always crammed. Captain Thanos hung out when he was ashore at an open-fronted affair called Miki's, and there Drake found him, sitting over the inevitable thick black coffee, tumbler of cold water, and shot glass of ouzo. He was short, broad, and nut-brown, with black curly hair and several days of stubble.

"Captain Thanos?" asked Drake. The man looked up in suspicion at the Englishman and nodded.

"Nikos Thanos, of the *Sanadria?*" The seaman nodded again. His three companions had fallen silent, watching. Drake smiled.

"My name is Andrew Drake. Can I offer you a drink?"

Captain Thanos used one forefinger to indicate his own glass and those of his companions. Drake, still standing, summoned a waiter and ordered five of everything. Thanos nodded to a vacant chair, the invitation to join them. Drake knew it would be slow, and might take days. But he was not going to hurry. He had found his ship.

The meeting in the Oval Office five days later was far less relaxed. All eight members of the ad hoc committee of the National Security Council were present, with President Matthews in the chair. All had spent half the night reading the transcript of the Politburo meeting in which Marshal Kerensky had laid out his plan for war and Vishnayev had made his bid for power. All eight men were shaken. The focus was on the Chairman of the Joint Chiefs of Staff, General Martin Craig.

"The question is, General," President Matthews asked, "is it feasible?"

"In terms of a conventional war across the face of Western Europe from the Iron Curtain to the Channel ports, even involving the use of tactical nuclear shells and rockets, yes, Mr. President, it's feasible."

"Could the West, before next spring, increase her defenses to the point of making it completely unworkable?"

"That's a harder one, Mr. President. Certainly we in the United States could ship more men, more hardware, over to Europe. That would give the Soviets ample excuse to beef up their own levels, if they ever needed such an excuse. But as to our European allies, they don't have the reserves we have; for over a decade they have run down their manpower levels, arms levels, and preparation levels to a point where the imbalance in conventional manpower and hardware between the NATO forces and the Warsaw Pact forces is at a stage that cannot be recouped in a mere nine months. The training that the personnel would need, even if recruited now, the production of new weapons of the necessary sophistication—these cannot be achieved in nine months."

"So they're back to 1939 again," said the Secretary of the Treasury gloomily.

"What about the nuclear option?" asked Bill Matthews quietly. General Craig shrugged.

"If the Soviets attack in full force, it's inescapable. Forewarned may be forearmed, but nowadays armament programs and training programs take too long. Forewarned as we are, we could slow up a Soviet advance westward, spoil Kerensky's time scale of a hundred hours. But whether we could stop him dead—the whole damn Soviet Army, Navy, and Air Force—that's another matter. By the time we knew the answer, it would probably be too late, anyway. Which makes our use of the nuclear option inescapable. Unless, of course, sir, we abandon Europe and our three hundred thousand men there."

"David?" asked the President.

Secretary of State David Lawrence tapped the file in front of him.

"For about the first time in my life, I agree with Dmitri Rykov. It's not just a question of Western Europe. If Europe goes, the Balkans, the eastern Mediterranean, Turkey, Iran, and the Arabian states cannot hold. Ten years ago, five percent of our oil was imported; five years ago, the total had risen to fifty percent. Now it's running at sixty-two percent, and rising. Even the whole of the Western Hemisphere cannot fulfill more than fifty-five percent of our needs at maximum production. We need the Arabian oil. Without it we are as finished as Europe, without a shot fired."

"Suggestions, gentlemen?" asked the President.

"The Nightingale is valuable, but not indispensable, not now," said Stanislaw Poklewski. "Why not meet with Rudin and lay it on the table? We now know about Plan Aleksandr; we know the intent. And we will take steps to head off that intent, to make it unworkable. When he informs his Politburo of that, they'll realize the element of surprise is lost, that the war option won't work anymore. It'll be the end of the Nightingale, but it will also be the end of Plan Aleksandr."

Bob Benson of the CIA shook his head vigorously.

"I don't think it's that simple, Mr. President. As I read it, it's not a question of convincing Rudin or Rykov. There's a vicious faction fight now going on inside the Politburo, as we know. At stake is the succession to Rudin. And the famine is hanging over them.

"Vishnayev and Kerensky have proposed a limited war as a means both of obtaining the food surpluses of Western Europe and of imposing war discipline on the Soviet peoples. Revealing what we know to Rudin would change nothing. It might even cause him to fall. Vishnayev and his group would take over; they are completely ignorant of the West and the way we Americans react to being attacked. Even with the element of surprise gone, with the grain famine pending they could still try the war option."

"I agree with Bob," said David Lawrence. "There is a parallel here with the Japanese position forty years ago. The oil embargo caused the fall of the moderate Konoye faction. Instead, we got General Tojo, and that led to Pearl Harbor. If Maxim Rudin is toppled now, we could get Yefrem Vishnayev in his place. And on the basis of these papers, that could lead to war."

"Then Maxim Rudin must not fall," said President Matthews.

"Mr. President, I protest," said Poklewski heatedly. "Am I to understand that the efforts of the United States are now to be bent toward saving the skin of Maxim Rudin? Have any of us forgotten what he did, the people liquidated under his regime, for him to get to the pinnacle of power in Soviet Russia?"

"Stan, I'm sorry," said President Matthews with finality. "Last month I authorized a refusal by the United States to supply the Soviet Union with the grain it needs to head off a famine. At least until I knew what the perspectives of that famine would be. I can no longer pursue that policy of rejection, because I think we now know what those perspectives entail.

"Gentlemen, I am going this night to draft a personal letter to President Rudin, proposing that David Lawrence and Dmitri Rykov meet on neutral territory to confer together. And that they confer on the subject of the new SALT Four arms-limitation treaty and *any other matters of interest.*"

When Andrew Drake returned to the Cavo d'Oro after his second meeting with Captain Thanos, there was a message waiting for him. It was from Azamat Krim, to say he and Kaminsky had just checked into their agreed hotel.

An hour later Drake was with them. The van had come through unscathed. During the night, Drake had the guns and ammunition transferred piece by piece to his own room at the Cavo d'Oro in separate visits from Kaminsky and Krim. When all was safely locked away, he took them both out to dinner. The following morning, Krim flew back to London, to live in Drake's apartment and await his phone call. Kaminsky stayed on in a small pension in the back streets of Piraeus. It was not comfortable, but it was anonymous.

While they were dining, the U.S. Secretary of State was locked in private conference with the Irish Ambassador to Washington.

"If my meeting with Foreign Minister Rykov is to succeed," said David Lawrence, "we must have privacy. The discretion must be absolute. Reykjavík in Iceland is too obvious; our base at Keflavík there is like U.S. territory. The meeting has to be on neutral territory. Geneva is full of watching eyes; ditto Stockholm and Vienna. Helsinki, like Iceland, would be too obvious. Ireland is halfway between Moscow and Washington, and you still foster the cult of privacy there."

That night, coded messages passed between Washington and Dublin. Within twenty-four hours, the government in Dublin had agreed to host the meeting and proposed flight plans for both parties. Within hours, President Matthews's personal and private letter to President Maxim Rudin was on its way to Ambassador Donaldson in Moscow.

Andrew Drake at his third attempt secured a person-to-person conversation with Captain Nikos Thanos. There was by then little doubt in the old Greek's mind that the young Englishman wanted something from him, but he gave no hint of curiosity. As usual, Drake bought the coffee and ouzo.

"Captain," said Drake, "I have a problem, and I think you may be able to help me."

Thanos raised an eyebrow but studied his coffee.

"Sometime near the end of the month the *Sanadria* will sail from Piraeus for Istanbul and the Black Sea. I believe you will be calling at Odessa."

Thanos nodded. "We are due to sail on the thirtieth," he said, "and yes, we will be discharging cargo at Odessa."

"I want to go to Odessa," said Drake. "I must reach Odessa."

"You are an Englishman," said Thanos. "There are package tours of Odessa. You could fly there. There are cruises by Soviet liners out of Odessa. You could join one."

Drake shook his head.

"It's not as easy as that," he said. "Captain Thanos, I would not receive a visa for Odessa. My application would be dealt with in Moscow, and I would not be allowed in."

"And why do you want to go?" asked Thanos with suspicion.

"I have a girl in Odessa," said Drake. "My fiancée. I want to get her out."

Captain Thanos shook his head with finality. He and his ancestors from Chios had been smuggling in the eastern Mediterranean since Homer was learning to talk, and he knew that a brisk contraband trade went into and out of Odessa, and that his own crew made a tidy living on the side from bringing such luxury items as nylons, perfume, and leather coats to the black market of the Ukrainian port. But smuggling people was quite different, and he had no intention of getting involved in that.

"I don't think you understand," said Drake. "There's no question of bringing her out on the *Sanadria*. Let me explain."

He produced a photograph of himself and a remarkably pretty girl sitting on the balustrade of the Potemkin Stairway, which links the city with the port. Thanos's interest revived at once, for the girl was definitely worth looking at.

"I am a graduate in Russian studies of the University of Bradford," said Drake. "Last year I was an exchange student for six months, and spent those six months at Odessa University. That was where I met Larissa. We fell in love. We wanted to get married."

Like most Greeks, Nikos Thanos prided himself on his romantic nature. Drake was talking his language.

"Why didn't you?" he asked.

"The Soviet authorities would not let us," said Drake. "Of course, I wanted to bring Larissa back to England and marry her and settle down. She applied for permission to leave and was turned down. I kept reapplying on her behalf from the London end. No luck. Then, last July, I did as you just suggested; I went on a package tour to the Ukraine, through Kiev, Ternopol, and Lvov."

He flicked open his passport and showed Thanos the date stamps at the Kiev airport.

"She came up to Kiev to see me. We made love. Now she has written to me to say she is having our baby. So now I have to marry her more than ever."

Captain Thanos also knew the rules. They had applied to his society since time began. He looked again at the photograph. He was not to know that the girl was a London lady who had posed in a studio not far from King's Cross station, nor that the background of the Potemkin Stairway was an enlarged detail from a tourist poster obtained at the London office of Intourist.

"So how are you going to get her out?" he asked.

"Next month," said Drake, "there is a Soviet liner, the *Litva*, leaving Odessa with a large party from the Soviet youth movement, the Komsomol, for an off-season educational tour of the Mediterranean."

Thanos nodded; he knew the *Litva* well.

"Because I made too many scenes over the matter of Larissa, the authorities will not let me back in. Larissa would not normally be allowed to go on this tour. But there is an official in the local branch of the Interior Ministry who likes to live well above his income. He will get her onto that cruise with all her papers in order, and when the ship docks at Venice, I will be waiting for her. But the official wants ten thousand American dollars. I have them, but I have to get the package to her."

It made perfect sense to Captain Thanos. He knew the level of bureaucratic corruption that was endemic to the southern shore of the Ukraine, Crimea, and Georgia—Communism or no Communism. That an official should "arrange" a few documents for enough Western currency to improve his life-style substantially was quite normal.

An hour later the deal was concluded. For a further five thousand dollars Thanos would take Drake on as a temporary deckhand for the duration of the voyage.

"We sail on the thirtieth," he said, "and we should be in Odessa on the tenth or eleventh. Be at the quay where the *Sanadria* is berthed by six P.M. on the thirtieth. Wait until the agent's water clerk has left, then come aboard just before the immigration people."

Four hours later in Drake's flat in London, Azamat Krim took Drake's call from Piraeus giving him the date that Mishkin and Lazareff needed to know.

It was on the twentieth that President Matthews received Maxim Rudin's reply. It was a personal letter, as his had been to the Soviet leader. In it Rudin agreed to the secret meeting between David Lawrence and Dmitri Rykov in Ireland, scheduled for the twenty-fourth.

President Matthews pushed the letter across his desk to Lawrence.

"He's not wasting time," he remarked.

"He has no time to waste," returned the Secretary of State. "Everything is being prepared. I have two men in Dublin now, checking out the arrangements. Our Ambassador to Dublin will be meeting the Soviet Ambassador tomorrow, as a result of this letter, to finalize details."

"Well, David, you know what to do," said the President.

Azamat Krim's problem was to be able to post a letter or card to Mishkin from inside the Soviet Union, complete with Russian stamps and written in Russian, without going through the necessary delay in waiting for a visa to be granted to him by the Soviet Consulate in London, which could take up to four weeks. With the help of Drake, he had solved it relatively simply.

Prior to 1980, the main airport of Moscow, Sheremetyevo, had been a small, drab, and shabby affair. But for the Olympics the Soviet government had commissioned a grand new airport terminal there, and Drake had done some research on it.

The facilities in the new terminal, which handled all long-distance flights out of Moscow, were excellent. There were numerous plaques praising the achievements of Soviet technology all over the airport; conspicuous by its absence was any mention that Moscow had had to commission a West German firm to build the place because no Soviet construction company could have achieved the standard or the completion date. The West Germans had been handsomely paid in hard currency, but their contract had had rigorous penalty clauses in the case of noncompletion by the start of the 1980 Olympics. For this reason, the Germans had used only two local Russian ingredients—sand and water. Everything else had been trucked in from West Germany in order to be certain of delivery on time.

In the great transit lounge and departure lounges, they had built letter boxes to handle the mail of anyone forgetting to post his last picture postcards from inside Moscow before leaving. The KGB monitors every single letter, postcard, cable, or phone call coming into or leaving the Soviet Union.

Massive though the task may be, it gets done. But the new departure lounges at Sheremetyevo were used both for international flights and for long-distance internal Soviet Union flights.

Krim's postcard, therefore, had been acquired at the Aeroflot offices in London. Modern Soviet stamps sufficient for a postcard at the internal rate had been openly bought from the London stamp emporium Stanley Gibbons. On the card, which showed a picture of the Tupolev-144 supersonic passenger jet, was written in Russian the message: "Just leaving with our factory's Party group for the expedition to Khabarovsk. Great excitement. Almost forgot to write you. Many happy returns for your birthday on the eleventh. Your cousin, Ivan."

Khabarovsk being in the extreme southeast of Siberia, close to the Sea of Japan, a group leaving by Aeroflot for that city would leave from the same terminal building as a flight leaving for Japan. The card was addressed to David Mishkin at his address in Lvov.

Azamat Krim took the Aeroflot flight from London to Moscow and changed planes there for the Aeroflot flight from Moscow to Narita Airport, Tokyo. He had an open-dated return. He also had a two-hour wait in the transit lounge in Moscow. Here he dropped the card in the letter box and went on to Tokyo. Once there, he changed to Japan Air Lines and flew back to London.

The card was examined by the KGB postal detail at Moscow's airport, assumed to be from a Russian to a Ukrainian cousin, both living and working inside the USSR, and sent on. It arrived in Lvov three days later.

While the tired and very jet-lagged Crimean Tatar was flying back from Japan, a small jet of the Norwegian internal airline Braethens-Safe banked high over the fishing town of Alesund and began to let down to the municipal airport on the flat island across the bay. From one of its passenger windows Thor Larsen looked down with the thrill of excitement that he felt whenever he returned to the small community that had raised him and that would always be home.

He had arrived in the world in 1935, in a fisherman's cottage in the old Buholmen quarter, long since demolished to make way for the new highway. Buholmen before the war had been the fishing quarter, a maze of wooden cottages in gray, blue, and ocher. From his father's cottage a yard had run down, like all the others along the row, from the back stoop to the sound. Here were the rickety wooden jetties where the independent fishermen like his father had tied their small vessels when they came home from the sea; here the smells of his childhood had been of pitch, resin, paint, salt, and fish.

As a child he had sat on his father's jetty, watching the big ships moving slowly up to berth at the Storneskaia, and he had dreamed of the places they must visit, far away across the western ocean. By the age of seven he could manage his own small skiff several hundred yards off the Buholmen shore to where old Sula Mountain cast her shadow from across the fjord on the shining water.

"He'll be a seaman," said his father, watching with satisfaction from his jetty. "Not a fisherman, staying close to these waters, but a seaman."

He was five when the Germans came to Ålesund, big, gray-coated men who tramped around in heavy boots. It was not until he was seven that he saw the war. It was summer, and his father had let him come fishing during the holidays from Norvoy School. With the rest of the Ålesund fishing fleet, his father's boat was far out at sea under the guard of a German E-boat. During the night he awoke because men were moving about. Away to the west were twinkling lights, the mastheads of the Orkneys fleet.

There was a small rowboat bobbing beside his father's vessel, and the crew were shifting herring boxes. Before the child's astounded gaze, a young man, pale and exhausted, emerged from beneath the boxes in the hold and was helped into the rowboat. Minutes later it was lost in the darkness, heading for the Orkneys men. Another radio operator from the Resistance was on his way to England for training. His father made him promise never to mention what he had seen. A week later in Ålesund there was a rattle of rifle fire one evening, and his mother told him he should say his prayers extra hard because the schoolmaster was dead.

By the time he was in his early teens, growing out of clothes faster than his mother could make them, he, too, had become obsessed with radio and in two years had built his own transmitter-receiver. His father gazed at the apparatus in wonderment; it was beyond his comprehension. Thor was sixteen when, the day after Christmas of 1951, he picked up an SOS message from a ship in distress in the mid-Atlantic. She was the *Flying Enterprise*. Her cargo had shifted, and she was listing badly in heavy seas.

For sixteen days the world and a teenage Norwegian boy watched and listened with baited breath as the Danish-born American captain, Kurt Carlsen, refused to leave his sinking ship and nursed her painfully eastward through the gales toward the south of England. Sitting in his attic hour after hour with his headphones over his ears, looking out through the dormer window at the wild ocean beyond the mouth of the fjord, Thor Larsen had willed the old freighter to make it home to port. On January 10, 1952, she finally sank, just fifty-seven miles off Falmouth harbor.

Larsen heard her go down, listened to the shadowing tugs tell of her death and of the rescue of her indomitable captain. He took off his headphones, laid them down, and descended to his parents, who were at the table.

"I have decided," he told them, "what I am going to be. I am going to be a sea captain."

A month later he entered the merchant marine.

The plane touched down and rolled to a stop outside the small, neat terminal with its goose pond by the parking lot. His wife, Lisa, was waiting for him with the car; with her were Kristina, his sixteen-year-old daughter, and Kurt, his fourteen-year-old son. The pair chattered like magpies on the short drive across the island to the ferry, and across the sound to Ålesund, and all the way home to their comfortable ranch-style house in the secluded suburb of Bogneset.

It was good to be home. He would go fishing with Kurt out on the Borgund Fjord, as his father had taken him fishing there in his youth; they would picnic in the last days of the summer on their little cabin cruiser or on the knobby green islands that dotted the sound. He had three weeks of leave; then Japan, and in February the captaincy of the biggest ship the world had ever seen. He had come a long way from the wooden cottage in Buholmen, but Ålesund was still his home and for this descendant of Vikings there was nowhere in the world quite like it.

On the night of September 23, a Grumman Gulfstream in the livery of a well-known commercial corporation lifted off from Andrews Air Force Base and, carrying long-distance tanks, headed east across the Atlantic for the Irish airport of Shannon. It was phased into the Irish air-traffic-control network as a private charter flight. When it landed at Shannon it was shepherded in darkness to the side of the airfield away from the international terminal and surrounded by five black and curtained limousines.

Secretary of State David Lawrence and his party of six were greeted by the U.S. Ambassador and the deputy chief of mission, and all five limousines swept out of the airport perimeter fence by a side gate. They headed northeast through the sleeping countryside toward County Meath.

That same night a Tupolev-134 twin-jet of Aeroflot refueled at East Berlin's Schönefeld Airport and headed west over Germany and the Low Countries toward Britain and Ireland. It was slated as a special Aeroflot flight bringing a trade delegation to Dublin. As such, the British air-traffic controllers passed it over to their Irish colleagues as it left the coast of Wales. The Irish had their military air-traffic network take it over, and it landed two hours before dawn at the Irish Air Corps base at Baldonnel, outside Dublin.

Here the Tupolev was parked between two hangars out of sight of the main airfield buildings, and it was greeted by the Soviet Ambassador, the Irish Deputy Foreign Minister, and six limousines. Foreign Minister Rykov and his party entered the vehicles, were screened by the interior curtains, and left the air base.

High above the banks of the River Boyne, in an environment of great natural beauty and not far from the market town of Slane in County Meath, stands Slane Castle, ancestral home of the family Conyngham, earls of Mount Charles. The youthful earl had been quietly asked by the Irish government to accept a week's holiday in a luxury hotel in the west with his pretty countess, and to lend the castle to the government for a few days. He had agreed. The restaurant attached to the castle was marked as closed for repairs, the staff were given a week's leave, fresh government caterers moved in, and Irish police in plain clothes discreetly posted themselves at all points of the compass around the castle. When the two cavalcades of limousines had entered the grounds, the main gates were shut. If the local people noticed anything, they were courteous enough to make no mention of it.

In the Georgian private dining room before the marble fireplace by Adam, the two statesmen met for a sustaining breakfast.

"Dmitri, good to see you again," said David Lawrence, extending his hand.

Rykov shook it warmly. He glanced around him at the silver gifts from George IV, and the Conyngham portraits on the walls.

"So this is how you decadent bourgeois capitalists live," he said.

Lawrence roared with laughter. "I wish it were, Dmitri, I wish it were."

At eleven o'clock, surrounded by their aides in Johnston's magnificent Gothic circular library, the two men settled down to negotiate. The bantering was over.

"Mr. Foreign Minister," said Lawrence, "it seems we both have problems. Ours concern the continuing arms race between our two nations, which nothing seems able to halt or even slow down, and which worries us deeply. Yours seems to concern the forthcoming grain harvest in the Soviet Union. I hope we can find a means between us to lessen these, our mutual problems."

"I hope so, too, Mr. Secretary of State," said Rykov cautiously. "What have you in mind?"

There is only one direct flight a week between Athens and Istanbul, the Tuesday Sabena connection, leaving Athens's Ellinikon Airport at 1400 hours and landing at Istanbul at 1645. On Tuesday, September 28, Miroslav Kaminsky was on it, instructed to secure for Andrew Drake a consignment of sheepskin and suede coats and jackets for trading in Odessa.

That same afternoon, Secretary of State Lawrence finished reporting to the ad hoc committee of the National Security Council in the Oval Office.

"Mr. President, gentlemen, I think we have it. Providing Maxim Rudin can keep his hold on the Politburo and secure their agreement.

"The proposal is that we and the Soviets each send two teams of negotiators to a resumed arms-limitation conference. The suggested venue is Ireland again. The Irish government has agreed and will prepare a suitable conference hall and living accommodations, providing we and the Soviets signal our assent.

"One team from each side will face the other across the

table to discuss a broad range of arms limitations. This is the big one: I secured a concession from Dmitri Rykov that the ambit of the discussion need not exclude thermonuclear weapons, strategic weapons, inner space, international inspection, tactical nuclear weapons, conventional weapons and manpower levels, or disengagement of forces along the Iron Curtain line."

There was a murmur of approval and surprise from the other seven men present. No previous American-Soviet arms conference had ever had such widely drawn terms of reference. If all areas showed a move toward genuine and monitored détente, it would add up to a peace treaty.

"These talks will be what the conference is supposedly about, so far as the world is concerned, and the usual press bulletins will be necessary," resumed Secretary of State Lawrence. "Now, in back of the main conference, the secondary conference of technical experts will negotiate the sale by the U.S. to the Soviets at financial costs still to be worked out, but probably lower than world prices, of up to fifty-five million tons of grain, consumer-product technology, computers, and oil-extraction technology.

"At every stage there will be liaison between the up-front and the in-back teams of negotiators on each side. They make a concession on arms; we make a concession on low-cost goodies."

"When is this slated for?" asked Poklewski.

"That's the surprise element," said Lawrence. "Normally the Russians like to work very slowly. Now it seems they are in a hurry. They want to start in two weeks."

"Good God, we can't be ready for 'go' in two weeks!" exclaimed the Secretary of Defense, whose department was intimately involved.

"We have to be," said President Matthews. "There will never be another chance like this again. Besides, we have our SALT team ready and briefed. They have been ready for months. We have to bring in Agriculture, Trade, and Technology on this, and fast. We have to get together the team who can talk on the other—the trade and technology—side of the deal. Gentlemen, please see to it. At once."

Maxim Rudin did not put it to his Politburo quite like that, two days later.

"They have taken the bait," he said from his chair at the head of the table. "When they make a concession on wheat or technology in one of the conference rooms, we make the absolute minimum concession in the other conference room. We will get our grain, Comrades; we will feed our people, we will head off the famine, and at the minimum price. Americans, after all, have never been able to outnegotiate Russians."

There was a general buzz of agreement.

"What concessions?" snapped Vishnayev. "How far back will these concessions set the Soviet Union and the triumph of world Marxism-Leninism?"

"As to your first question," replied Rykov, "we cannot know until we are negotiating. As to your second, the answer must be substantially less than a famine would set us back."

"There are two points we should be clear on before we decide whether to talk or not," said Rudin. "One is that the Politburo will be kept fully informed at every stage, so if the moment comes when the price is too high, this council will have the right to abort the conference and I will defer to Comrade Vishnayev and his plan for a war in the spring. The second is that no concession we may make to secure the wheat need necessarily obtain for very long after the deliveries have taken place."

There were several grins around the table. This was the sort of realpolitik the Politburo was much more accustomed to, as they had shown in transforming the old Helsinki Agreement on détente into a farce.

"Very well," said Vishnayev, "but I think we should lay down the exact parameters of our negotiating teams' authority to concede points."

"I have no objection to that," said Rudin.

The meeting continued on this theme for an hour and a half. Rudin got his vote to proceed, by the same margin as before, seven against six.

On the last day of the month, Andrew Drake stood in the shade of a crane and watched the *Sanadria* battening down her hatches. Conspicuous on deck she had Vac-U-Vators for Odessa, powerful suction machines, like vacuum cleaners, for sucking wheat out of the hold of a ship and straight into a grain elevator. The Soviet Union must be trying to improve her grain-unloading capacity, he mused, though he did not know why. Below the weather deck were forklift trucks for Istanbul and agricultural machinery for Varna in Bulgaria, part of a transshipment cargo that had come in from America as far as Piraeus.

He watched the agent's water clerk leave the ship, giving Captain Thanos a last shake of the hand. Thanos scanned the pier and made out the figure of Drake loping toward him, his kit bag over one shoulder and his suitcase in the other hand.

In the captain's day cabin, Drake handed over his passport and vaccination certificates. He signed the ship's articles and became a member of the deck crew. While he was down below stowing his gear, Captain Thanos entered his name in the ship's crew list just before the Greek immigration officer came on board. The two men had the usual drink together.

"There's an extra crewman," said Thanos, as if in passing. The immigration officer scanned the list and the pile of seaman's books and passports in front of him. Most were Greek, but there were six others, non-Greek. Drake's British passport stood out. The immigration officer selected it and riffled through the pages. A fifty-dollar bill fell out.

"An out-of-work," said Thanos, "trying to get to Turkey and head for the East. Thought you'd be glad to be rid of him."

Five minutes later the crew's identity documents had been returned to their wooden tray and the vessel's papers stamped for outward clearance. Daylight was fading as her ropes were cast off, and *Sanadria* slipped away from her berth and headed south before turning northeast for the Dardanelles.

Below decks, the crew were grouping around the greasy messroom table. One of them was hoping no one would look under his mattress, where the Sako Hornet rifle was stored. In Moscow his target was sitting down to an excellent supper.

CHAPTER SEVEN

WHILE HIGH-RANKING and secret men launched themselves into a flurry of activity in Washington and Moscow, the old *Sanadria* thumped her way impassively northeast toward the Dardanelles and Istanbul.

On the second day, Drake watched the bare brown hills of Gallipoli slide by, and the sea dividing European and Asian

Turkey widen into the Sea of Marmara. Captain Thanos, who knew these waters like his own backyard on Chios, was doing his own pilotage.

Two Soviet cruisers steamed past them, heading from Sebastopol out to the Mediterranean to shadow the U.S. Sixth Fleet maneuvers. Just after sundown the twinkling lights of Istanbul and the Galata Bridge spanning the Bosporus came into view. The *Sanadria* anchored for the night and entered port at Istanbul the following morning.

While the forklift trucks were being unloaded, Andrew Drake secured his passport from Captain Thanos and slipped ashore. He met Miroslav Kaminsky at an agreed rendezvous in central Istanbul and took delivery of a large bundle of sheepskin and suede coats and jackets. When he returned to the ship, Captain Thanos raised an eyebrow.

"You aiming to keep your girl friend warm?" he asked.

Drake shook his head and smiled.

"The crew tell me half the seamen bring these ashore in Odessa," he said. "I thought it would be the best way to bring my own package."

The Greek captain was not surprised. He knew half a dozen of his own seamen would be bringing such luggage back to the ship with them, to trade the fashionable coats and blue jeans for five times their buying price to the black-marketeers of Odessa.

Thirty hours later the *Sanadria* cleared the Bosporus, watched the Golden Horn drop away astern, and chugged north for Bulgaria with her tractors.

Due west of Dublin lies County Kildare, site of the Irish horse-racing center at the Curragh and of the sleepy market town of Celbridge. On the outskirts of Celbridge stands the largest and finest Palladian stately home in the land, Castletown House. With the agreement of the American and Soviet ambassadors, the Irish government had proposed Castletown as the venue for the disarmament conference.

For a week, teams of painters, plasterers, electricians, and gardeners had been at work night and day putting the final touches to the two rooms that would hold the twin conferences, though no one knew what the second conference would be for.

The facade of the main house alone is 142 feet wide, and from each corner covered and pillared corridors lead away to further quarters. One of these wing blocks contains the kitchens and staff apartments, and it was here the American security force would be quartered; the other block contains the stables, with more apartments above them, and here the Russian bodyguards would live.

The principal house would act as both conference center and home for the subordinate diplomats, who would inhabit the numerous guest rooms and suites on the top floor. Only the two principal negotiators and their immediate aides would return each night to their respective embassies, equipped as they were with facilities for coded communications with Washington and Moscow.

This time there was to be no secrecy, save in the matter of the secondary conference. Before a blaze of world publicity the two foreign ministers, David Lawrence and Dmitri Rykov, arrived in Dublin and were greeted by the Irish President and Premier. After the habitual televised handshaking and toasting, they left Dublin in twin cavalcades for Castletown.

At midday on October 8, the two statesmen and their twenty advisers entered the vast Long Gallery, decorated in Wedgwood blue in the Pompeian manner and 140 feet long. Most of the center of the hall was taken up with the gleaming Georgian table, down each side of which the delegations seated themselves. Flanking each foreign minister were experts in defense, weapons systems, nuclear technology, inner space, and armored warfare.

The two statesmen knew they were there only to open the conference formally. After the opening and the agreement of agenda, each would fly home to leave the talks in the hands of the delegation leaders, Professor Ivan I. Sokolov for the Soviets and former Assistant Secretary of Defense Edwin J. Campbell for the Americans.

The remaining rooms on this floor were given over to the stenographers, typists, and researchers.

One floor below, at ground level, in the great dining room of Castletown, with drapes drawn to mute the autumn sunshine pouring onto the southeastern face of the mansion, the secondary conference quietly filed in to take their places. These were mainly technologists: experts in grain, oil, computers, and industrial plants.

Upstairs, Dmitri Rykov and David Lawrence each made a short address of welcome to the opposing delegation and expressed the hope and the confidence that the conference would succeed in diminishing the problems of a beleaguered and frightened world. Then they adjourned for lunch.

After lunch Professor Sokolov had a private conference with Rykov before the latter's departure for Moscow.

"You know our position, Comrade Professor," said Rykov. "Frankly, it is not a good one. The Americans will go for everything they can get. Your job is to fight every step of the way to minimize our concessions. But we must have that grain. Nevertheless, every concession on arms levels and deployment patterns in Eastern Europe must be referred back to Moscow. This is because the Politburo insists on being involved in approval or rejection in the sensitive areas."

He forbore to say that the sensitive areas were those that might impede a future Soviet strike into Western Europe, or that Maxim Rudin's political career hung by a thread.

In another drawing room at the opposite end of Castletown—a room that, like Rykov's, had been swept by his own electronics experts for possible "bugs"—David Lawrence was conferring with Edwin Campbell.

"It's all yours, Ed. This won't be like Geneva. The Soviet problems won't permit endless delays, adjournments, and referring back to Moscow for weeks on end. I estimate they have to have an agreement with us within six months. Either that or they don't get the grain.

"On the other hand, Sokolov will fight every inch of the way. We know each concession on arms will have to be referred to Moscow, but Moscow will have to decide fast one way or the other, or else the time will run out.

"One last thing. We know Maxim Rudin cannot be pushed too far. If he is, he could fall. But if he doesn't get the wheat, he could fall, too. The trick will be to find the balance; to get the maximum concessions without provoking a revolt in the Politburo."

Campbell removed his glasses and pinched the bridge of his nose. He had spent four years commuting from Washington to Geneva on the so-far-abortive SALT talks, and he was no newcomer to the problems of trying to negotiate with Russians.

"Hell, David, that sounds fine. But you know how they give nothing of their own inner position away. It would be a hell of a help to know just how far they can be pushed, and where the stop line lies."

David Lawrence opened his attaché case and withdrew a sheaf of papers. He proffered them to Campbell.

"What are these?" asked Campbell.

Lawrence chose his words carefully.

"Nine days ago in Moscow the full Politburo authorized Maxim Rudin and Dmitri Rykov to begin these talks. But only by a vote of seven against six. There's a dissident faction inside the Politburo that wishes to abort the talks and bring Rudin down. After the agreement the Politburo laid out the exact parameters of what Professor Sokolov could or could not concede, what the Politburo would or would not allow Rudin to grant. Go beyond the parameters and Rudin could be toppled. If that happened, we would have bad, very bad, problems."

"So what are the papers?" asked Campbell, holding the sheaf in his hands.

"They came in from London last night," said Lawrence. "They are the verbatim transcript of that Politburo meeting."

Campbell stared at them in amazement.

"Jesus," he breathed, "we can dictate our own terms."

"Not quite," corrected Lawrence. "We can require the maximum that the moderate faction inside the Politburo can get away with. Insist on more and we could be eating ashes."

The visit of the British Prime Minister and her Foreign Secretary to Washington two days later was described in the press as being informal. Ostensibly, Britain's first woman premier was to address a major meeting of the English-Speaking Union and take the opportunity of paying a courtesy call on the President of the United States.

But the crux of the latter came in the Oval Office, where President Bill Matthews, flanked by his national security adviser, Stanislaw Poklewski, and his Secretary of State, David Lawrence, gave the British visitors an exhaustive briefing on the hopeful start of the Castletown conference. The agenda, reported President Matthews, had been agreed to with unusual alacrity. At least three main areas for future discussion had been defined between the two teams, with a minimal presence of the usual Soviet objections to every dot and comma.

President Matthews expressed the hope that, after years of frustration, a comprehensive limitation of arms levels and troop deployments along the Iron Curtain from the Baltic to the Aegean could well emerge from Castletown.

The crunch came as the meeting between the two heads of government closed.

"We regard it as vital, ma'am, that the inside information of which we are in possession, and without which the conference could well fail, continue to reach us."

"You mean the Nightingale," said the British Premier crisply.

"Yes, ma'am, I do," said Matthews. "We regard it as indispensable that the Nightingale continue to operate."

"I understand your point, Mr. President," she answered calmly. "But I believe that the hazard levels of that operation are very high. I do not dictate to Sir Nigel Irvine what he shall or shall not do in the running of his service. I have too much respect for his judgment for that. But I will do what I can."

It was not until the traditional ceremony in front of the principal facade of the White House of seeing the British visitors into their limousines and smiling for the cameras was complete that Stanislaw Poklewski could give vent to his feelings.

"There's no hazard to a Russian agent in the world that compares with the success or failure of the Castletown talks," he said.

"I agree," said Bill Matthews, "but I understand from Bob Benson the hazard lies in the exposure of the Nightingale at this point. If that happened, and he were caught, the Politburo would learn what had been passed over. If that happened, they would shut off at Castletown. So the Nightingale either has to be silenced or brought out, but neither until we have a treaty sewn up and signed. And that could be six months yet."

That same evening, while the sun was still shining on Washington, it was setting over the port of Odessa as the *Sanadria* dropped anchor in the roads. When the clatter of the anchor cable had ceased, silence fell on the freighter, broken only by the low humming of the generators in the engine room and the hiss of escaping steam on deck. Andrew Drake leaned on the fo'c'sle rail, watching the lights of the port and city twinkle into life.

West of the ship, at the northern extremity of the port, lay the oil harbor and refinery, circled by chain-link fencing. To the south, the port was bounded by the protective arm of the great seaward mole. Ten miles beyond the mole the Dniester River flowed into the sea through the swampy marshes where, five months before, Miroslav Kaminsky had stolen his skiff and made a desperate bid for freedom. Now, thanks to him, Andrew Drake—Andriy Drach—had come home to the land of his ancestors. But this time he had come armed.

That evening, Captain Thanos was informed that he would be brought into port and moored alongside the following morning. Port health and customs officials visited the *Sanadria*, but they spent the hour on board closeted with Captain Thanos in his cabin, sampling his top-grade Scotch whisky, kept for the occasion. There was no search of the ship. Watching the launch leave the ship's side, Drake wondered if Thanos had betrayed him. It would have been easy enough: Drake would be arrested ashore; Thanos would sail with his five thousand dollars.

It all depended, he thought, on whether Thanos had accepted his story of bringing money to his fiancée. If he had, there was no motive to betray him, for the offense was routine enough; his own sailors brought contraband goods into Odessa on every voyage, and dollar bills were only another form of contraband. And if the rifle and pistols had been discovered, the simple thing would have been to throw the lot into the sea and sling Drake off the ship, once back in Piraeus. Still, he could neither eat nor sleep that night.

Just after dawn, the pilot boarded. The *Sanadria* weighed anchor, took a tug in attendance, and moved slowly between the breakwaters and into her berth. Often, Drake had learned, there was a berthing delay in this, the most congested of the Soviet Union's warm-water ports. They must want their Vac-U-Vators badly. He had no idea how badly. Once the shore cranes had started to unload the freighter, the watchkeepers among the crew were allowed to go ashore.

During the voyage Drake had become friendly with the *Sanadria's* carpenter, a middle-aged Greek seaman who had visited Liverpool and was keen to practice his twenty words of English. He had repeated them continuously to his intense delight whenever he met Drake during the voyage, and each time Drake had nodded furious encouragement and approval. He had explained to Constantine in English and sign language that he had a girl friend in Odessa and was bringing her presents. Constantine approved. With a dozen others, they trooped down the gangway and headed for the dock gates. Drake was wearing one of his best suede sheepskin coats, although the day was reasonably warm. Constantine carried a duffel shoulder bag with a brace of bottles of export-proof Scotch whisky.

The whole port area of Odessa is cordoned off from the city and its citizens by a high chain fence, topped with barbed wire and arc lights. The main dock gates habitually stand open in the daytime, the entrance being blocked only by a balanced red-and-white striped pole. This marks the passageway for lorries, with a customs official and two armed militiamen attending it.

Astride the entrance gate is a long, narrow shed, with one door inside the port area and one on the outside. The party from the *Sanadria* entered the first door, with Constantine in charge. There stood a long counter, attended by one customs man, and a passport desk, attended by an immigration officer and a militiaman. All three looked scruffy and exceptionally bored. Constantine approached the customs man and dumped his shoulder bag on the counter. The official opened it and extracted a bottle of whisky. Constantine gestured that it was a present from one to the other. The customs man managed a friendly nod and placed the bottle beneath his table.

Constantine clasped a brawny arm around Drake and pointed to him.

"Droog," he said, and beamed widely. The customs man nodded that he understood the newcomer was the Greek carpenter's friend and should be recognized as such. Drake smiled broadly. He stood back, eyeing the customs man as an outfitter eyes a customer. Then he stepped forward, slipped off the sheepskin coat and held it out, indicating that he and the customs man were about the same size. The official did not bother to try it on; it was a fine coat, worth a month's salary at least. He smiled his acknowledgment, placed the coat under the table, and waved the entire party through.

The immigration officer and militiaman showed no surprise. The second bottle of whisky was for the pair of them. The *Sanadria* crew members surrendered their seaman's books, and in the case of Drake his passport to the immigration officer, and each received in return a shore pass from a leather satchel the officer wore over his shoulder. Within a few minutes the *Sanadria* party emerged into the sunshine beyond the shed.

Drake's rendezvous was in a small café in the dockland area of old, cobbled streets, not far from the Pushkin Monument, where the ground rises from the docks to the main city.

He found it after thirty minutes of wandering, having separated himself from his fellow seamen on the grounds that he wanted to date his mythical girl friend. Constantine did not object; he had to contact his underworld friends to set up the delivery of his sackful of denim jeans.

It was Lev Mishkin who came, just after noon. He was wary, cautious, and sat alone, making no sign of recognition. When he had finished his coffee, he rose and left the café. Drake followed him. Only when the pair had reached the wide, sea-front highway of Primorsky Boulevard did he allow Drake to catch up. They spoke as they walked.

Drake agreed that he would make his first run, with the handguns stuck in his waistband and the image intensifier in a duffel bag with two clinking bottles of whisky, that evening. There would be plenty of Western ships' crews coming through for an evening in the dockland bars at the same time. He would be wearing another sheepskin coat to cover the handguns in his belt, and the chill of the evening air would justify his keeping the coat buttoned at the front. Mishkin and his friend David Lazareff would meet Drake in the darkness by the Pushkin Monument and take over the hardware.

Just after eight that evening, Drake came through with his first consignment. Jovially, he saluted the customs man, who waved him on and called to his colleague at the passport desk. The immigration man handed out a shore pass in exchange for his passport, jerked his chin toward the open door to the city of Odessa, and Drake was through. He was almost at the foot of the Pushkin Monument, seeing the writer's head raised against the stars above, when two figures joined him out of the darkness between the plane trees that crowd Odessa's open spaces.

"Any problems?" asked Lazareff.

"None," said Drake.

"Let's get it over with," said Mishkin. Both men were carrying the briefcases that everyone seems to carry in the Soviet Union. These cases, far from carrying documents, are the male version of the string bags the women carry, called "perhaps bags." They get their name from the hope that the women carry with them that perhaps they may spot a worthwhile consumer article on sale and snap it up before it is sold out or the queues form. Mishkin took the image intensifier and stuffed it into his larger briefcase; Lazareff took both the handguns, the spare ammunition slips, and the box of rifle shells and put them in his own.

"We're sailing tomorrow evening," said Drake. "I'll have to bring the rifle in the morning."

"Damn," said Mishkin, "daylight is bad. David, you know the port area best. Where is it to be?"

Lazareff considered. "There is an alley," he said, "between two crane-maintenance workshops."

He described the mud-colored workshops, not far from the docks.

"The alley is short, narrow. One end looks toward the sea, the other to a third blank wall. Enter the seaward end of the alley on the dot of eleven A.M. I will enter the other end. If there is anyone else in the alley, walk on, go around the block, and try again. If the alley is empty, we'll take delivery."

"How will you be carrying it?" asked Mishkin.

"Wrapped around with sheepskin coats," said Drake, "and stuffed in a kit bag about three feet long."

"Let's get out of here," said Lazareff. "Someone is coming."

When Drake returned to the *Sanadria*, the customs men had changed shifts and he was frisked. He was clean. The next morning he asked Captain Thanos for an extra spell ashore on the grounds that he wanted to spend the maximum time with his fiancée. Thanos excused him from deck duties and let him go. There was a nasty moment in the customs shed when Drake was asked to turn out his pockets. Placing his kit bag on the ground, he obeyed and revealed a wad of four ten-dollar bills. The customs man, who seemed to be in a bad mood, wagged an admonishing finger at Drake and confiscated the dollars. He ignored the kit bag. Sheepskin coats, it seemed, were respectable contraband; dollars were not.

The alley was empty, save for Mishkin and Lazareff walking down from one end and Drake walking up from the other. Mishkin gazed beyond Drake to the seaward end of the alley; when they were abreast he said, "Go," and Drake hefted the kit bag onto the shoulder of Lazareff. "Good luck," he said as he walked on, "see you in Israel."

Sir Nigel Irvine retained membership in three clubs in the west of London, but selected Brooks's for his dinner with Barry Ferndale and Adam Munro. By custom the serious business of the evening was left until they had quit the dining room and retired to the subscription room, where the coffee, port, and cigars were served.

Sir Nigel had asked the chief steward, called the dispense waiter, to reserve his favorite corner, near the windows looking down into St. James's Street, and four deep leather club chairs were waiting for them when they arrived. Munro selected brandy and water; Ferndale and Sir Nigel took a decanter of the club's vintage port and had it set on the table between them. Silence reigned while the cigars were lit, the coffee sipped. From the walls the Dilettantes, the eighteenth-century group of men-about-town, gazed down at them.

"Now, my dear Adam, what seems to be the problem?" asked Sir Nigel at last. Munro glanced to a nearby table where two senior civil servants conversed. For keen ears, they were within eavesdropping distance. Sir Nigel noticed the look.

"Unless we shout," he observed equably, "no one is going to hear us. Gentlemen do not listen to other gentlemen's conversations."

Munro thought this over.

"We do," he said simply.

"That's different," said Ferndale. "It's our job."

"All right," said Munro. "I want to bring the Nightingale out."

Sir Nigel studied the tip of his cigar.

"Ah, yes," he said. "Any particular reason?"

"Partly strain," said Munro. "The original tape recording in July had to be stolen, and a blank substituted in its place. That could be discovered, and it's preying on the Nightingale's mind. Secondly, the chances of discovery. Every abstraction of Politburo minutes heightens this. We now know Maxim Rudin is fighting for his political life, and the succession when he goes. If the Nightingale gets careless, or is even unlucky, he could get caught."

"Adam, that's one of the risks of defecting," said Ferndale. "It goes with the job. Penkovsky was caught."

"That's the point," pursued Munro. "Penkovsky had provided just about all he could. The Cuban missile crisis was over. There was nothing the Russians could do to undo the damage that Penkovsky had done to them."

"I would have thought that was a good reason for keeping the Nightingale in place," observed Sir Nigel. "There is still an awful lot more he can do for us."

"Or the reverse," said Munro. "If the Nightingale comes out, the Kremlin can never know what has been passed. If he is caught, they'll make him talk. What he can reveal now will be enough to bring Rudin down. This would seem to be the moment the West precisely would not wish Rudin to fall."

"Indeed it is," said Sir Nigel. "Your point is taken. It's a question of a balance of chances. If we bring the Nightingale out, the KGB will check back for months. The missing tape will presumably be discovered, and the supposition will be that even more was passed over before he left. If he is caught, it's even worse; a complete record of what he has passed over will be extracted from him. Rudin could well fall as a result. Even though Vishnayev would probably be disgraced also, the Castletown talks would abort. Thirdly, we keep the Nightingale in place until the Castletown talks are over and the arms-limitation agreement is signed. By then there will be nothing the war faction in the Politburo can do. It's a teasing choice."

"I'd like to bring him out," said Munro. "Failing that, let him lie low, cease transmitting."

"I'd like him to go on," said Ferndale, "at least until the end of Castletown."

Sir Nigel reflected on the alternative arguments.

"I spent the afternoon with the Prime Minister," he said at length. "The P.M. made a request, a very strong request, on behalf of herself and the President of the U.S.A. I cannot at this moment turn that request down unless it could be shown the Nightingale was on the very threshold of exposure. The Americans regard it as vital to their chances of securing an all-embracing treaty at Castletown that the Nightingale keep them abreast of the Soviet negotiating position. At least until the New Year.

"So I'll tell you what I'll do. Barry, prepare a plan to bring the Nightingale out. Something that can be activated at short notice. Adam, if the fuse begins to burn under the Nightingale's tail, we'll bring him out. Fast. But for the moment the Castletown talks and the frustration of the Vishnayev clique have to take first priority. Three or four more transmissions should see the Castletown talks in their final stages. The Soviets cannot delay some sort of a wheat agreement beyond February or March at the latest. After that, Adam, the Nightingale can come to the West, and I'm sure the Americans will show their gratitude in the habitual manner."

The dinner in Maxim Rudin's private suite in the Kremlin's inner sanctum was far more private than that at Brooks's in London. No confidence concerning the integrity of gentlemen where other gentlemen's conversations are concerned has ever marred the acute caution of the men of the Kremlin. There was no one within earshot but the silent Misha when Rudin took his place in his favorite chair of the study and gestured Ivanenko and Petrov to other seats.

"What did you make of today's meeting?" Rudin asked Petrov without preamble. The controller of the Party Organizations of the Soviet Union shrugged.

"We got away with it," he said. "Rykov's report was masterly. But we still have to make some pretty sweeping concessions if we want that wheat. And Vishnayev is still after his war."

Rudin grunted.

"Vishnayev is after my job," he said bluntly. "That's his ambition. It's Kerensky who wants the war. He wants to use his armed forces before he's too old."

"Surely it amounts to the same thing," said Ivanenko. "If Vishnayev can topple you, he will be so beholden to Kerensky he will neither be able, nor particularly wish, to oppose Kerensky's recipe for a solution to all the Soviet Union's problems. He will let Kerensky have his war next spring or early summer. Between them they'll devastate everything it has taken two generations to achieve."

"What is the news from your debriefing yesterday?" asked Rudin. He knew Ivanenko had recalled two of his most senior men from the Third World for consultations face-to-face. One was the controller of all subversive operations throughout Africa, the other his counterpart for the Middle East.

"Optimistic," said Ivanenko. "The capitalists have screwed up their African policies for so long now, their position is virtually irrecoverable. The liberals rule still in Washington and London, at least in foreign affairs. They are so totally absorbed with South Africa, they don't seem to notice Nigeria and Kenya at all. Both are on the verge of falling to us. The French in Senegal are proving more difficult. In the Middle East, I think we can count on Saudi Arabia's falling within three years. They're almost encircled."

"Time scale?" asked Rudin.

"Within a few years—say, by 1990 at the outside—we shall effectively control the oil and the sea routes. The euphoria campaign in Washington and London is being steadily increased, and it is working."

Rudin exhaled his smoke and stubbed the tube of his cigarette into an ashtray proffered by Misha.

"I won't see it," he said, "but you two will. Inside a decade the West will die of malnutrition, and we won't have to fire a shot. All the more reason why Vishnayev must be stopped while there is still time."

Four kilometers southwest of the Kremlin, inside a tight loop in the Moscow River and not far from the Lenin Stadium, stands the ancient monastery of Novodevichi. Its main entrance is right across the street from the principal Beriozka shop, where the rich and privileged, or foreigners, may buy for hard currency luxuries unobtainable by the common people.

The monastery grounds contain three lakes and a cemetery, and access to the cemetery is available to pedestrians. The gatekeeper will seldom bother to stop those bearing bunches of flowers.

Adam Munro parked his car in the Beriozka parking lot, among others whose number plates revealed them to belong to the privileged.

"Where do you hide a tree?" his instructor used to ask the class. "In a forest. And where do you hide a pebble? On the beach. Always keep it natural."

Munro crossed the road, traversed the cemetery with his bunch of carnations, and found Valentina waiting for him by one of the smaller lakes. Late October had brought the first bitter winds off the steppes to the east, and gray, scudding clouds across the sky. The surface of the water rippled and shivered in the wind.

"I asked them in London," he said gently. "They told me it is too risky at the moment. Their answer was that to bring you out now would reveal the missing tape, and thus the fact of the transcripts having been passed over. They feel if that happened, the Politburo would withdraw from the talks in Ireland and revert to the Vishnayev plan."

She shivered slightly, whether from the chill of the lakeside or from fear of her own masters he could not tell. He put an arm around her and held her to him.

"They may be right," she said quietly. "At least the Politburo is negotiating for food and peace, not preparing for war."

"Rudin and his group seem to be sincere in that," he suggested.

She snorted.

"They are as bad as the others," she said. "Without the pressure they would not be there at all."

"Well, the pressure is on," said Munro. "The grain is coming in. They know the alternatives now. I think the world will get its peace treaty."

"If it does, what I have done will have been worthwhile," said Valentina. "I don't want Sasha to grow up among the rubble as I did, nor live with a gun in his hand. That is what they would have for him, up there in the Kremlin."

"He won't," said Munro. "Believe me, my darling, he'll grow up in freedom, in the West, with you as his mother and me as his stepfather. My principals have agreed to bring you out in the spring."

She looked up at him with hope shining in her eyes.

"In the spring? Oh, Adam, when in the spring?"

"The talks cannot go on for too long. The Kremlin needs its grain by April at the latest. The last of the supplies and all the reserves will have run out by then. When the treaty is agreed upon, perhaps even before it is signed, you and Sasha will be brought out. Meanwhile, I want you to cut down on the risks you are taking. Only bring out the most vital material concerning the peace talks at Castletown."

"There's one in here," she said, nudging the bag over her shoulder. "It's from ten days ago. Most of it is so technical I can't understand it. It refers to permissible reductions of mobile SS-Twenties."

Munro nodded grimly.

"Tactical rockets with nuclear warheads, highly accurate and highly mobile, borne on the backs of tracked vehicles and parked in groves of trees and under netting all across Eastern Europe."

Twenty-four hours later, the package was on its way to London.

Three days before the end of the month, an old lady was heading down Sverdlov Street in central Kiev toward her apartment block. Though she was entitled to a car and a chauffeur, she had been born and brought up in the country, of strong peasant stock. Even in her mid-seventies she preferred to walk rather than drive for short distances. Her visit to spend the evening with a friend two blocks away was so short she had dismissed the car and chauffeur for the night. It was just after ten when she crossed the road in the direction of her own front door.

She didn't see the car, it came so fast. One minute she was in the middle of the road with no one about but two pedestrians a hundred yards away; the next, the vehicle was on her, lights blazing, tires squealing. She froze. The driver seemed to steer right at her, then swerved away. The wing of the vehicle crashed into her hip, bowling her over in the gutter. It failed to stop, roaring away toward Kreshchatik Boulevard at the end of the Sverdlov. She vaguely heard the crunch of feet running toward her as passersby came to her aid.

That evening, Edwin J. Campbell, the chief U.S. negotiator at the Castletown talks, arrived back, tired and frustrated, at the ambassadorial residence in Phoenix Park. It was an elegant mansion that America provided its envoy in Dublin, and fully modernized, with handsome guest suites, the finest of which Edwin Campbell had taken over. He was looking forward to a long, hot bath and a rest.

When he had dropped his coat and responded to his host's greeting, one of the messengers from the embassy handed him a fat manila envelope. As a result his sleep was curtailed that night, but it was worth it.

The next day, he took his place in the Long Gallery at Castletown and gazed impassively across the table at Professor Ivan I. Sokolov.

All right, Professor, he thought, I know what you can concede and what you cannot. So let's get on with it.

It took forty-eight hours for the Soviet delegate to agree to cut the Warsaw Pact presence of tracked tactical nuclear rockets in Eastern Europe by half. Six hours later, in the dining room, a protocol was agreed whereby the United States would sell the USSR $200 million worth of oil-drilling and -extraction technology at bargain-basement prices.

The old lady was unconscious when the ambulance brought her to the general hospital of Kiev, the October Hospital at 39 Karl Liebknecht Street. She remained so until the following morning. When she was able to explain who she was, panicked officials had her wheeled out of the general ward and into a private room, which rapidly filled with flowers. During that day the finest orthopedic surgeon in Kiev operated to set her broken femur.

In Moscow, Ivanenko took a call from his personal aide and listened intently.

"I understand," he said without hesitation. "Inform the authorities that I shall come at once. What? Well, then, when she has come out of the anesthetic. Tomorrow night? Very well, arrange it."

It was bitter cold on the evening of the last night of October. There was no one moving in Rosa Luxemburg Street, onto which the October Hospital backs. The two long black limousines stood unobserved at the curb by this back entrance which the KGB chief had chosen to use rather than the grand portico at the front.

The whole area stands on a slight rise of ground, amid trees, and farther down the street, on the opposite side, an annex to the hospital was under construction, its unfinished upper levels jutting above the greenery. The watchers among the frozen cement sacks rubbed their hands to keep the circulation going, and stared at the two cars by the door, dimly illuminated by a single bulb above the archway.

When he came down the stairs, the man with seven seconds to live was wearing a long, fur-collared overcoat and thick gloves, even for the short walk across the pavement to the warmth of the waiting car. He had spent two hours with his mother, comforting her and assuring her the culprits would be found, as the abandoned car had been found.

He was preceded by an aide, who ran ahead and flicked off the doorway light. The door and the pavement were plunged into darkness. Only then did Ivanenko advance to the door, held open by one of his six bodyguards, and pass through it. The knot of four others outside parted as his fur-coated figure emerged, merely a shadow among shadows.

He advanced quickly to the Zil, engine running, across the pavement. He paused for a second as the passenger door was swung open, and died, the bullet from the hunting rifle skewering through his forehead, splintering the parietal bone and exiting through the rear of the cranium to lodge in an aide's shoulder.

The crack of the rifle, the whack of the impacting bullet, and the first cry from Colonel Yevgeni Kukushkin, his senior bodyguard, took less than a second. Before the slumping man had hit the pavement, the plainclothes colonel had him under the armpits, dragging him into the recesses of the rear seat of the Zil. Before the door was closed, the colonel was screaming, "Drive! Drive!" to the shocked driver.

Colonel Kukushkin pillowed the bleeding head in his lap as the Zil screeched away from the curb. He thought fast. It was not merely a question of a hospital, but of which hospital for a man like this. As the Zil cleared the end of Rosa Luxemburg Street, the colonel flicked on the interior light. What he saw—and he had seen much in his career—was enough to tell him his master was beyond hospitals. His second reaction was programmed into his mind and his job: no one must know. The unthinkable had happened, and no one must know, save only those entitled to know. He had secured his promotion and his job by his presence of mind. Watching the second limousine, the bodyguards' Chaika, swing out of Rosa Luxemburg Street behind them, he ordered the driver to choose a quiet and darkened street not less than two miles away, and park.

Leaving the curtained and motionless Zil at the curb, with the bodyguards scattered in a screen around it, he took off his bloodsoaked coat and set off on foot. He finally made his phone call from a militia barracks, where his I.D. card and rank secured him instant access to the commandant's private office and phone. It also secured him a direct line. He was patched through in fifteen minutes.

"I must speak to Comrade Secretary-General Rudin urgently," he told the Kremlin switchboard operator. The woman knew from the line on which the call was coming that this was neither joke nor impertinence. She put it through to an aide inside the Armory Building, who held the call and spoke to Maxim Rudin on the internal phone. Rudin authorized the transfer of the call.

"Yes," he grunted on the line, "Rudin here."

Colonel Kukushkin had never spoken to him before, though he had seen him and heard him at close quarters many times. He knew it was Rudin. He swallowed hard, took a deep breath, and spoke.

At the other end, Rudin listened, asked two brief questions, rapped out a string of orders, and put the phone down. He turned to Vassili Petrov, who was with him, leaning forward, alert and worried.

"He's dead," said Rudin in disbelief. "Not a heart attack. Shot. Yuri Ivanenko. Someone has just assassinated the chairman of the KGB."

Beyond the windows the clock in the tower above Savior Gate chimed midnight, and a sleeping world began to move slowly toward war.

CHAPTER EIGHT

THE KGB has always ostensibly been answerable to the Soviet Council of Ministers. In practice, it answers to the Politburo.

The everyday working of the KGB, the appointment of every officer within it, every promotion, and the rigorous indoctrination of every staffer—all are supervised by the Politburo through the Party Organizations Section of the Central Committee. At every stage of the career of every KGB man, he is watched, informed on, and reported on; even the watchdogs of the Soviet Union are never themselves free of watching. Thus it is unlikely that this most pervasive and powerful of control machines can ever run out of control.

In the wake of the assassination of Yuri Ivanenko, it was Vassili Petrov who took command of the cover-up operation, which Maxim Rudin directly and personally ordered.

Over the telephone Rudin had ordered Colonel Kukushkin to bring the two-car cavalcade straight back to Moscow by road, stopping neither for food, drink, nor sleep, driving through the night, refueling the Zil bearing Ivanenko's corpse with jerry-cans, brought to the car by the Chaika and always out of sight of passersby.

On arrival at the outskirts of Moscow, the two cars were directed straight to the Politburo's own private clinic at Kuntsevo, where the corpse with the shattered head was quietly buried amid the pine forest within the clinic perimeter, in an unmarked grave. The burial party was of Ivanenko's own bodyguards, all of whom were then placed under house arrest at one of the Kremlin's own villas in the forest. The guard detail on these men was drawn not from the KGB but from the Kremlin palace guard.

Only Colonel Kukushkin was not held incommunicado. He was summoned to Petrov's private office in the Central Committee Building.

The colonel was a frightened man, and when he left Petrov's office he was little less so. Petrov gave him one chance to save his career and his life: he was put in charge of the cover-up operation.

At the Kuntsevo clinic he organized the closure of one entire ward and brought fresh KGB men from Dzerzhinsky Square to mount guard on it. Two KGB doctors were transferred to Kuntsevo and put in charge of the patient in the closed ward, a patient who was in fact an empty bed. No one else was allowed in, but the two doctors, knowing only enough to be badly frightened, ferried all the equipment and medicaments into the closed ward that would be needed for the treatment of a heart attack. Within twenty-four hours, save for the closed ward in the secret clinic off the road from Moscow to Minsk, Yuri Ivanenko had ceased to exist.

At this early stage, only one other man was let into the secret. Among Ivanenko's six deputies, all with their offices close to his on the third floor of KGB Center, one was his official deputy as chairman of the KGB. Petrov summoned General Konstantin Abrassov to his office and informed him of what had happened, a piece of information that shook the general as nothing in a thirty-year career in secret police work had done. Inevitably he agreed to continue the masquerade.

In the October Hospital in Kiev, the dead man's mother was surrounded by local KGB men and continued to receive daily written messages of comfort from her son.

Finally, the three workmen on the annex to the October Hospital who had discovered a hunting rifle and night-sight when they came to work the morning after the shooting were removed with their families to one of the camps in Mordovia, and two detectives were flown in from Moscow to investigate an act of hooliganism. Colonel Kukushkin was with them. The story they were given was that the shot had been fired at the moving car of a local Party official; it had passed through the windshield and been recovered from the upholstery. The real bullet, recovered from the KGB guard's shoulder and well washed, was presented to them. They were told to trace and identify the hooligans in conditions of complete secrecy. Somewhat perplexed and much frustrated, they proceeded to try. Work on the annex was stopped, the half-finished building sealed off, and all the forensic equipment they could ask for supplied. The only thing they did not get was a true explanation.

When the last piece of the jigsaw puzzle of deception was in place, Petrov reported personally to Rudin. To the old chief fell the worst task, that of informing the Politburo of what had really happened.

The private report of Dr. Myron Fletcher of the Agriculture Department to President William Matthews two days later was all and more than the ad hoc committee formed under the personal auspices of the President could have wished for. Not only had the benign weather brought North America a bumper crop in all areas of grain and cereals; it had broken existing records. Even with probable requirements for domestic consumption taken care of, even with existing aid levels to the poor countries of the world maintained, the surplus would nudge sixty million tons for the combined harvest of the United States and Canada.

"Mr. President, you've got it," said Stanislaw Poklewski. "You can buy that surplus any time you wish at July's price. Bearing in mind the progress at the Castletown talks, the House Appropriations Committee will not stand in your way."

"I should hope not," said the President. "If we succeed at Castletown, the reductions in defense expenditures will more than compensate for the commercial losses on the grains. What about the Soviet crop?"

"We're working on it," said Bob Benson. "The Condors are sweeping right across the Soviet Union, and our analysts are working out the yields of harvested grain, region by region. We should have a report for you in a week. We can correlate that with reports from our people on the ground over there, and give a pretty accurate figure—to within five percent, anyway."

"As soon as you can," said President Matthews. "I need to know the exact Soviet position in every area. That includes the Politburo reaction to their own grain harvest. I need to know their strengths and their weaknesses. Please get them for me, Bob."

No one in the Ukraine that winter would be likely to forget the sweeps by the KGB and militia against those in whom the slightest hint of nationalist sentiment could be detected.

While Colonel Kukushkin's two detectives carefully interviewed the pedestrians in Sverdlov Street the night Ivanenko's mother had been run down, meticulously took to pieces the stolen car that had performed the hit-and-run job on the old lady, and pored over the rifle, the image intensifier, and the area surrounding the hospital annex, General Abrassov went for the nationalists.

Hundreds were detained in Kiev, Ternopol, Lvov, Kanev, Rovno, Zhitomir, and Vinnitsa. The local KGB, supported by teams from Moscow, carried out the interrogations, ostensibly concerned with sporadic outbreaks of hooliganism such as the mugging of the KGB plainclothes man in August in Ternopol. Some of the senior interrogators were permitted to know their inquiries also concerned the firing of a shot in Kiev in late October, but no more.

In the seedy Lvov working-class district of Levandivka that November, David Lazareff and Lev Mishkin strolled through the snowy streets during one of their rare meetings. Because the fathers of both had been taken away to the camps, they knew time would run out for them eventually also. The word *Jew* was stamped on the identity card of each, as on those of every one of the Soviet Union's three million Jews. Sooner or later, the spotlight of the KGB must swing away from the nationalists to the Jews. Nothing ever changes that much in the Soviet Union.

"I posted the card to Andriy Drach yesterday, confirming the success of the first objective," said Mishkin. "How are things with you?"

"So far, so good," said Lazareff. "Perhaps things will ease off soon."

"Not this time, I think," said Mishkin. "We have to make our break soon if we are going to at all. The ports are out. It has to be by air. Same place next week. I'll see what I can discover about the airport."

Far away to the north of them an S.A.S. jumbo jet thundered on its polar route from Stockholm to Tokyo. Among its first-class passengers it bore Captain Thor Larsen toward his new command.

Maxim Rudin's report to the Politburo was delivered in his gravelly voice, without frills. But no histrionics in the world could have kept his audience more absorbed, nor their reaction more stunned. Since an Army officer had emptied a handgun at the limousine of Leonid Brezhnev as he passed through the Kremlin's Borovitsky Gate a decade before, the specter of the lone man with a gun penetrating the walls of security around the hierarchs had persisted. Now it had come out of conjecture to sit and stare at them from their own green baize table.

This time, the room was empty of secretaries. No tape recorders turned on the corner table. No aides, no stenographers were present. When he had finished, Rudin handed the floor to Petrov, who described the elaborate measures taken to mask the outrage, and the secret steps then in progress to identify and eliminate the killers after they had revealed all their accomplices.

"But you have not found them yet?" snapped Stepanov.

"It is only five days since the attack," said Petrov evenly. "No, not yet. They will be caught, of course. They cannot escape, whoever they are. When they are caught, they will reveal every last one of those who helped them. General Abrassov will see to that. Then every last person who knows what happened that night on Rosa Luxemburg Street, wherever they may be hiding, will be eliminated. There will be no trace left."

"And in the meantime?" asked Komarov.

"In the meantime," said Rudin, "it must be maintained with unbreakable solidarity that Comrade Yuri Ivanenko has sustained a massive heart attack and is under intensive care. Let us be clear on one thing. The Soviet Union cannot and will not tolerate the public humiliation of the world's ever being allowed to know what happened on Rosa Luxemburg Street. There are no Lee Harvey Oswald's in Russia, and never will be."

There was a murmur of assent. No one was prepared to disagree with Rudin's assessment.

"With respect, Comrade Secretary-General," Petrov cut in, "while the catastrophe of such news leaking abroad cannot be overestimated, there is another aspect, equally serious. If this news leaked out, the rumors would begin among our own population. Before long they would be more than rumors. The effect internally I leave to your imagination."

They all knew how closely the maintenance of public order

was linked to a belief in the impregnability and invincibility of the KGB.

"If this news leaked out," said Chavadze the Georgian slowly, "and even more so if the perpetrators escaped, the effect would be as bad as that of the grain famine."

"They cannot escape," said Petrov sharply. "They must not. They shall not."

"Then who are they?" growled Kerensky.

"We do not yet know, Comrade Marshal," replied Petrov, "but we will."

"But it was a Western gun," insisted Shushkin. "Could the West be behind this?"

"I think it almost impossible," said Rykov. "No Western government, no Third World government, would be crazy enough to support such an outrage, in the same way as we had nothing to do with the Kennedy assassination. Émigrés, possibly. Anti-Soviet fanatics, possibly. But not governments."

"Émigré groups abroad are also being investigated," said Petrov. "But discreetly. We have most of them penetrated. So far, nothing has come in. The rifle, ammunition, and nightsight are all of Western make. They are all commercially purchasable in the West. That they were smuggled in is beyond doubt. Which means either the users brought them in, or they had outside help. General Abrassov agrees with me that the primary requirement is to find the users, who will reveal their suppliers. Department V will take over from there."

Yefrem Vishnayev watched the proceedings with keen interest but took little part. Kerensky expressed the dissatisfaction of the dissident group instead. Neither sought a further vote on the choice of the Castletown talks or a war in 1983. Both knew that in the event of a tie, the Chairman's vote would prevail. Rudin had come one step nearer to falling but was not finished yet.

The meeting agreed that the announcement should be made, only within the KGB and the upper echelons of the Party machine, that Yuri Ivanenko had suffered a heart attack and been hospitalized. When the killers had been identified and they and their aides had been eliminated, Ivanenko would quietly expire from his illness.

Rudin was about to summon the secretaries to the chamber for the resumption of the usual Politburo meeting when Stepanov, who had originally voted for Rudin and negotiations with the United States, raised his hand.

"Comrades, I would regard it as a major defeat for our

country if the killers of Yuri Ivanenko were to escape and publish their action to the world. Should that happen, I would not be able to continue my support for the policy of negotiation and further concession in the matter of our armaments levels in exchange for American grain. I would switch my support to the proposal of Party theoretician Vishnayev."

There was dead silence.

"So would I," said Shushkin.

Eight against four, thought Rudin as he gazed impassively down the table. Eight against four if these two shits change sides now.

"Your point is taken, Comrades," said Rudin without a flicker of emotion. "There will be no publication of this deed. None at all."

Ten minutes later, the meeting reopened with a unanimous expression of regret at the sudden illness of Comrade Ivanenko. The subject then turned to the newly arrived figures of wheat and grain yields.

The Zil limousine of Yefrem Vishnayev erupted from the mouth of the Borovitsky Gate at the Kremlin's southwestern corner and straight across Manège Square. The policeman on duty in the square, forewarned by his bleeper that the Politburo cavalcade was leaving the Kremlin, had stopped all traffic. Within seconds the long, black, hand-tooled cars were scorching up Frunze Street, past the Defense Ministry, toward the homes of the privileged on Kutuzovsky Prospekt.

Marshal Kerensky sat beside Vishnayev in the latter's car, having accepted his invitation to drive together. The partition between the spacious rear area and the driver was closed and soundproof. The curtains shut out the gaze of the pedestrians.

"He's near to falling," growled Kerensky.

"No," said Vishnayev, "he's one step nearer and a lot weaker without Ivanenko, but he's not near to falling yet. Don't underestimate Maxim Rudin. He'll fight like a cornered bear on the taiga before he goes, but go he will because go he must."

"Well, there's not much time," said Kerensky.

"Less than you think," said Vishnayev. "There were food riots in Vilnius last week. Our friend Vitautas, who voted for our proposal in July, is getting nervous. He was on the verge of switching sides despite the very attractive villa I have offered him next to my own at Sochi. Now he is back in the fold, and Shushkin and Stepanov may change sides in our favor."

"But only if the killers escape, or the truth is published abroad," said Kerensky.

"Precisely. And that is what must happen."

Kerensky turned in the back seat, his florid face turning brick-red beneath his shock of white hair.

"Reveal the truth? To the whole world? We can't do that," he exploded.

"No, we can't. There are far too few people who know the truth, and mere rumors cannot succeed. They can be too easily discounted. An actor looking precisely like Ivanenko could be found, rehearsed, seen in public. So others must do it for us. With absolute proof. The guards who were present that night are in the hands of the Kremlin elite. That leaves only the killers themselves."

"But we don't have them," said Kerensky, "and are not likely to. The KGB will get them first."

"Probably, but we have to try," said Vishnayev. "Let's be plain about this, Nikolai. We are not fighting for the control of the Soviet Union anymore. We are fighting for our lives, like Rudin and Petrov. First the wheat, now Ivanenko. One more scandal, Nikolai, one more. Whoever is responsible—let me make that clear, whoever is responsible—Rudin will fall. There must be one more scandal. We must ensure that there is."

Thor Larsen, dressed in overalls and a safety helmet, stood on a gantry crane high above the dry dock at the center of the Ishikawajima-Harima shipyard and gazed down at the mass of the vessel that would one day be the *Freya*.

Even three days after his first sight, the size of her took his breath away. In his apprenticeship days, tankers had never gone beyond 30,000 tons, and it was not until 1956 that the world's first over that tonnage took the sea. They had to create a new class for such vessels, and called them supertankers. When someone broke the 50,000-ton ceiling, there was another new class, the VLCC, or Very Large Crude Carrier. As the 200,000-ton barrier was broken in the late sixties, the new class of Ultra Large Crude Carrier, or ULCC, came into being.

Once, at sea, Larsen had seen one of the French leviathans, weighing in at 550,000 tons, move past him. His crew had poured out on deck to watch her. What lay below him now was twice that size. As Wennerstrom had said, the world had never seen the like of her, nor ever would again.

She was 515 meters long, or 1,689 feet, or ten city blocks. She was 90 meters broad, or 295 feet from scupper to scupper, and her superstructure reared five stories into the air above her deck. Far below what he could see of her deck area, her keel plunged 36 meters, or 118 feet, toward the floor of the dry dock. Each of her sixty holds was bigger than a neighborhood cinema. Deep in her bowels below the superstructure, the four steam turbines mustering a total of 90,000 shaft horsepower were already installed, ready to drive her twin screws, whose 40-foot-diameter bronze propellers could be vaguely seen glinting below her stern.

From end to end she teemed with antlike figures, the workers preparing to leave her temporarily while the dock was filled. For twelve months, almost to the day, they had cut and burned, bolted, sawed, riveted, hacked, plated, and hammered the hull of her together. Great modules of high-tensile steel had swung in from the overhead gantries to drop into preassigned places and form her shape. As the men cleared away the ropes and chains, lines and cables that hung about her, she lay exposed at last, her sides clean of encumbrances, painted twenty coats of rustproof paint, waiting for the water.

At last, only the blocks that cradled her remained. The men who had built this, the biggest dry dock in the world, at Chita, near Nagoya on Ise Bay, had never thought to see their handiwork put to such use. It was the only dry dock that could take a million-tonner, and it was the first and last it would ever hold. Some of the veterans came to peer across the barriers to see the ceremony.

The religious ceremony took half an hour as the Shinto priest called down the blessings of the divine ones on those who had built her, those who would work on her yet, and those who would sail her one day, that they should enjoy safe labor and safe sailing. Thor Larsen attended, barefoot, with his chief engineer and first officer, the owner's chief superintendent (marine architect), who had been there from the start, and the yard's equivalent architect. The latter were the two men who had really designed and built her.

Shortly before noon the sluices were opened, and with a thundering roar the western Pacific began to flow in.

There was a formal lunch in the chairman's office, but when it was over, Thor Larsen went back to the dock. He was joined by his first officer, Stig Lundquist, and his chief engineer, Bjorn Erikson, both from Sweden.

"She's something else," said Lundquist as the water climbed her sides.

Shortly before sunset the *Freya* groaned like an awaking giant, moved half an inch, groaned again, then came free of her underwater supports and rode the tide. Around the dock, four thousand Japanese workers broke their studied silence and burst into cheering. Scores of white helmets were thrown into the air; the half-dozen Europeans from Scandinavia joined in, pumping hands and thumping backs. Below them the giant waited patiently, seemingly aware her turn would come.

The next day, she was towed out of the dock to the commissioning quay, where for three months she would once again play host to thousands of small figures working like demons to prepare her for the sea beyond the bay.

Sir Nigel Irvine read the last lines of the Nightingale transcript, closed the file, and leaned back.

"Well, Barry, what do you make of it?"

Barry Ferndale had spent most of his working life studying the Soviet Union, its masters and power structure. He breathed once more on his glasses and gave them a final rub.

"It's one more blow that Maxim Rudin's going to have to survive," he said. "Ivanenko was one of his staunchest supporters. And an exceptionally clever one. With him in hospital, Rudin has lost one of his ablest counselors."

"Will Ivanenko still retain his vote in the Politburo?" asked Sir Nigel.

"It's possible he can vote by proxy should another vote come," said Ferndale, "but that's not really the point. Even at a six-to-six tie on a major issue of policy at Politburo level, the Chairman's vote swings the issue. The danger is that one or two of the waverers might change sides. Ivanenko upright inspired a lot of fear, even that high up. Ivanenko in an oxygen tent, perhaps less so."

Sir Nigel handed the folder across the desk to Ferndale.

"Barry, I want you to go over to Washington with this one. Just a courtesy call, of course. But try to have a private dinner with Ben Kahn and compare notes with him. This exercise is becoming too damn much of a close-run thing."

"The way we see it, Ben," said Ferndale, two days later, after dinner in Kahn's Georgetown house, "is that Maxim Rudin is holding on by a thread in the face of a fifty-percent hostile Politburo, and that thread is getting extremely thin."

The Deputy Director (Intelligence) of the CIA stretched his feet toward the log fire in his redbrick grate and gazed at the brandy he twirled in his glass.

"I can't fault you on that, Barry," he said carefully.

"We also are of the view that if Rudin cannot persuade the Politburo to continue conceding the things he is yielding to you at Castletown, he could fall. That would leave a fight for the succession, to be decided by the full Central Committee. In which, alas, Yefrem Vishnayev has a powerful amount of influence and friends."

"True," said Kahn. "But then so does Vassili Petrov. Probably more than Vishnayev."

"No doubt," rejoined Ferndale, "and Petrov would probably swing the succession toward himself—if he had the backing of Rudin, who was retiring in his own time and on his own terms, and if he had the support of Ivanenko, whose KGB clout could help offset Marshal Kerensky's influence through the Red Army."

Kahn smiled across at his visitor.

"You're moving a lot of pawns forward, Barry. What's your gambit?"

"Just comparing notes," said Ferndale.

"All right, just comparing notes. Actually our own views at Langley go along pretty much with yours. David Lawrence at the State Department agrees. Stan Poklewski wants to ride the Soviets hard at Castletown. The President's in the middle—as usual."

"Castletown's pretty important to him, though?" suggested Ferndale.

"Very important. He has only two more years in office. In November 1984, there'll be a new President-elect. Bill Matthews would like to go out in style, leaving a comprehensive arms-limitation treaty behind him."

"We were just thinking . . ."

"Ah," said Kahn, "I think you are contemplating bringing your knight forward."

Ferndale smiled at the oblique reference to his "knight," the Director General of his service.

". . . that Castletown would certainly abort if Rudin fell from control at this juncture. And that he could use something from Castletown, from your side, to convince any waverers among his faction that he was achieving things there and that he was the man to back."

"Concessions?" asked Kahn. "We got the final analysis of the Soviet grain harvest last week. They're over a barrel. At least that's the way Poklewski put it."

"He's right," said Ferndale. "But the barrel's on the point of collapsing. And waiting inside it is dear Comrade Vishnayev, with his war plan. And we all know what that would entail."

"Point taken," said Kahn. "Actually, my own reading of the combined Nightingale file runs along very similar lines. I've got a paper in preparation for the President's eyes at the moment. He'll have it next week when he and Benson meet with Lawrence and Poklewski."

"These figures," asked President Matthews, "they represent the final aggregate grain crop the Soviet Union brought in a month ago?"

He glanced across at the four men seated in front of his desk. At the far end of the room a log fire crackled in the marble fireplace, adding a touch of visual warmth to the already high temperature assured by the central heating system. Beyond the bulletproof south windows, the sweeping lawns held their first dusting of November morning frost. Being from the South, William Matthews appreciated warmth.

Robert Benson and Dr. Myron Fletcher nodded in unison. David Lawrence and Stanislaw Poklewski studied the figures.

"All our sources have been called on for these figures, Mr. President, and all our information has been correlated extremely carefully," said Benson. "We could be out by five percent either way, no more."

"And according to the Nightingale, even the Politburo agrees with us," interposed the Secretary of State.

"One hundred million tons, total," mused the President. "It will last them till the end of March, with a lot of belt tightening."

"They'll be slaughtering the cattle by January," said Poklewski. "They have to start making sweeping concessions at Castletown next month if they want to survive."

The President laid down the Soviet grain report and picked up the presidential briefing prepared by Ben Kahn and presented by his Director of Central Intelligence. It had been read by all four in the room, as well as himself. Benson and Lawrence had agreed with it; Dr. Fletcher was not called upon for an opinion; the hawkish Poklewski dissented.

"We know—and they know—they are in desperate straits," said Matthews. "The question is, how far do we push them?"

"As you said weeks ago, Mr. President," said Lawrence, "if we don't push hard enough, we don't get the best deal we can for America and the free world. Push too hard and we force Rudin to abort the talks to save himself from his own hawks. It's a question of balance. At this point, I feel we should make them a gesture."

"Wheat?"

"Animal feed to help them keep some of their herds alive?" suggested Benson.

"Dr. Fletcher?" asked the President.

The man from the Agriculture Department shrugged.

"We have the feed available, Mr. President," he said. "The Soviets have a large proportion of their own merchant fleet, Sovfracht, standing by. We know that because with their subsidized freight rates they could all be busy, but they're not. They're positioned all over the warm-water ports of the Black Sea and down the Soviet Pacific coast. They'll sail for the United States if they're given the word from Moscow."

"What's the latest we need to give a decision on this one?" asked President Matthews.

"New Year's Day," said Benson. "If they know a respite is coming, they can hold off slaughtering the herds."

"I urge you not to ease up on them," pleaded Poklewski. "By March they'll be desperate."

"Desperate enough to concede enough disarmament to assure peace for a decade, or desperate enough to go to war?" asked Matthews rhetorically. "Gentlemen, you'll have my decision by Christmas Day. Unlike you, I have to take five chairmen of Senate subcommittees with me on this one: Defense, Agriculture, Foreign Relations, Trade, and Appropriations. And I can't tell them about the Nightingale, can I, Bob?"

The chief of the CIA shook his head.

"No, Mr. President. Not about the Nightingale. There are too many Senate aides, too many leaks. The effect of a leak of what we really know at this juncture could be disastrous."

"Very well, then. Christmas Day it is."

On December 15, Professor Ivan Sokolov rose to his feet at Castletown and began to read a prepared paper. The Soviet Union, he said, ever true to its traditions as a country devoted to the unswerving search for world peace, and mindful of its often-reiterated commitment to peaceful coexistence . . .

Edwin J. Campbell sat across the table and watched his Soviet opposite number with some fellow feeling. Over two months, working until fatigue overcame both of them, he had developed a fairly warm relationship with the man from Moscow—as much, at least, as their positions and their duties would allow.

In breaks between the talks, each had visited the other in the opposing delegation's suite. In the Soviet drawing room, with the Muscovite delegation present and its inevitable complement of KGB agents, the conversation had been agreeable but formal. In the American room, where Sokolov had arrived alone, he had relaxed to the point of showing Campbell pictures of his grandchildren on holiday on the Black Sea coast. As a leading member of the Academy of Sciences, the professor was rewarded for his loyalty to Party and cause with a limousine, chauffeur, city apartment, country dacha, seaside chalet, and access to the Academy's grocery store and commissary. Campbell had no illusions but that Sokolov was paid for his loyalty, for his ability to devote his talents to the service of a regime that committed tens of thousands to the labor camps of Mordovia; that he was one of the fat cats, the *nachalstvo*. But even the *nachalstvo* had grandchildren.

He sat and listened to the Russian with growing surprise.

You poor old man, he thought. What this must be costing you.

When the peroration was over, Edwin Campbell rose and gravely thanked the professor for his statement, which on behalf of the United States of America he had listened to with the utmost care and attention. He moved an adjournment while the U.S. government considered its position. Within an hour he was in the Dublin embassy to begin transmitting Sokolov's extraordinary speech to David Lawrence.

Some hours later in Washington's State Department, David Lawrence lifted one of his telephones and called President Matthews on his private line.

"I have to tell you, Mr. President, that six hours ago in Ireland the Soviet Union conceded six major points at issue. They concern total numbers of intercontinental ballistic missiles with hydrogen-bomb warheads, through conventional armor, to disengagement of forces along the Elbe River."

"Thanks, David," said Matthews. "That's great news. You were right. I think we should let them have something in return."

The area of birch and larch forest lying southwest of Moscow where the Soviet elite have their country dachas covers little more than a hundred square miles. They like to stick together. The roads in this area are bordered mile after mile by green-painted steel railings, enclosing the private estates of the men at the very top. The fences and the driveway gates seem largely abandoned, but anyone trying to scale the first or drive through the second will be intercepted within moments by guards who materialize out of the trees.

Lying beyond Uspenskoye Bridge, the area centers on a small village called Zhukovka, usually known as Zhukovka Village. This is because there are two other and newer settlements nearby: Sovmin Zhukovka, where the Party hierarchs have their weekend villas; and Akademik Zhukovka, which groups the writers, artists, musicians, and scientists who have found favor in Party eyes.

But across the river lies the ultimate, the even more exclusive, settlement of Usovo. Nearby, the General Secretary of the Communist Party of the Soviet Union, the Chairman of the Presidium of the Supreme Soviet, the Politburo, retires to a sumptuous mansion set in hundreds of acres of rigorously guarded forest.

Here on the night before Christmas, a feast he had not recognized in more than fifty years, Maxim Rudin sat in his favorite button-back leather chair, feet toward the enormous fireplace in rough-cut granite blocks where meter-long logs of split pine crackled. It was the same fireplace that had warmed Leonid Brezhnev and Nikita Khrushchev before him.

The bright yellow glare of the flames flickered on the paneled walls of the study and illuminated the face of Vassili Petrov, who faced him across the fire. By Rudin's chair arm, a small coffee table held an ashtray and half a tumbler of Armenian brandy, which Petrov eyed askance. He knew his aging protector was not supposed to drink. Rudin's inevitable cigarette was clipped between first finger and thumb.

"What news of the investigation?" asked Rudin.

"Slow," said Petrov. "That there was outside help is beyond doubt. We now know the night-sight was bought commercially in New York. The Finnish rifle was one of a consignment exported from Helsinki to Britain. We don't know which shop it came from, but the export order was for sporting rifles; therefore it was a private-sector commercial order, not an official one.

"The footprints at the building site have been checked out against the boots of all the workers at the place, and there are two sets of footprints that cannot be traced. There was damp in the air that night and a lot of cement dust lying around, so the prints are clear. We are reasonably certain there were two men."

"Dissidents?" asked Rudin.

"Almost certainly. And quite mad."

"No, Vassili, keep that for the Party meetings. Madmen take potshots, or sacrifice themselves. This was planned over months by someone. Someone out there, inside or outside Russia, who has got to be silenced, once and for all, with his secret untold. Whom are you concentrating on?"

"The Ukrainians," said Petrov. "We have all their groups in Germany, Britain, and America completely penetrated. No one has heard a rumor of such a plan. Personally, I still think they are in the Ukraine. That Ivanenko's mother was used as bait is undeniable. So who would have known she *was* Ivanenko's mother? Not some slogan-dauber in New York. Not some armchair nationalist in Frankfurt. Not some pamphleteer in London. Someone local, with contacts outside. We are concentrating on Kiev. Several hundred former detainees who were released and returned to the Kiev area are under interrogation."

"Find them, Vassili, find them and silence them." Maxim Rudin changed the subject, as he had a habit of doing without a change of tone. "Anything new from Ireland?"

"The Americans have resumed talking but have not responded to our initiative," said Petrov.

Rudin snorted. "That Matthews is a fool. How much further does he think we can go before we have to pull back?"

"He has those Soviet-hating senators to contend with," said Petrov, "and that Catholic fascist Poklewski. And of course he cannot know how close things are for us inside the Politburo."

Rudin grunted. "If he doesn't offer us something by the New Year, we won't carry the Politburo in the first week of January."

He reached out and took a draft of brandy, exhaling with a satisfied sigh.

"Are you sure you should be drinking?" asked Petrov. "The doctors forbade you five years ago."

"To hell with the doctors," said Rudin. "That's what I really called you here for. I can inform you beyond any doubt that I am not going to die of alcoholism or liver failure."

"I'm glad to hear it," said Petrov.

"There's more. On April thirtieth I am going to retire. Does that surprise you?"

Petrov sat motionless, alert. He had twice seen the supremos go down. Khrushchev in flames, ousted and disgraced, to become a nonperson. Brezhnev on his own terms. He had been close enough to feel the thunder when the most powerful tyrant in the world gives way to another. But never this close. This time he wore the mantle unless others could snatch it from him.

"Yes," he said carefully, "it does."

"In April I am calling a meeting of the full Central Committee," said Rudin. "To announce to them my decision to go on April thirtieth. On May Day there will be a new leader at the center of the line on the Mausoleum. I want it to be you. In June the plenary Party Congress is due. The leader will outline the policy from then on. I want it to be you. I told you that weeks ago."

Petrov knew he was Rudin's choice, since that meeting in the old leader's private suite in the Kremlin when the dead Ivanenko had been with them, cynical and watchful as ever. But he had not known it would be so fast.

"I won't get the Central Committee to accept your nomination unless I can give them something they want. Grain. They've all known the position for a long time. If Castletown fails, Vishnayev will have it all."

"Why so soon?" asked Petrov.

Rudin held up his glass. From the shadows the silent Misha appeared and poured brandy into it.

"I got the results of the tests from Kuntsevo yesterday," said Rudin. "They've been working on tests for months. Now they're certain. Not cigarettes and not Armenian brandy. Leukemia. Six to twelve months. Let's just say I won't see a Christmas after this one. And if we have a nuclear war, neither will you.

"In the next hundred days we have to secure a grain agreement from the Americans and wipe out the Ivanenko affair once and for all time. The sands are running out, and too damn fast. The cards are on the table, face up, and there are no more aces to play."

On December 28, the United States formally offered the Soviet Union a sale, for immediate delivery and at commercial rates, of ten million tons of animal feed grains, to be considered as being outside any terms still being negotiated at Castletown.

On New Year's Eve, an Aeroflot twin-jet Tupolev-134 took off from Lvov airport, bound for Minsk on an internal flight. Just north of the border between the Ukraine and White Russia, high over the Pripet Marshes, a nervous-looking young man rose from his seat and approached the stewardess, who was several rows back from the steel door leading to the flight deck, speaking with a passenger.

Knowing the toilets were at the other end of the cabin, she straightened as the young man approached her. As she did so, the young man spun her around, clamped his left forearm across her throat, drew a handgun, and jammed it into her ribs. She screamed. There was a chorus of shouts and yells from the passengers. The hijacker began to drag the girl backward to the locked door to the flight deck. On the bulkhead next to the door was the intercom enabling the stewardess to speak to the flight crew, who had orders to refuse to open the door in the event of a hijack.

From midway down the fuselage, one of the passengers rose, automatic in hand. He crouched in the aisle, both hands clasped around his gun, pointing it straight at the stewardess and the hijacker behind her.

"Hold it!" he shouted. "KGB. Hold it right there."

"Tell them to open the door," yelled the hijacker.

"Not a chance!" shouted the armed flight guard from the KGB back to the hijacker.

"If they don't, I'll kill the girl," screamed the man holding the stewardess.

The girl had a lot of courage. She lunged backward with her heel, caught the gunman in the shin, broke his grip, and made to run toward the police agent. The hijacker sprang after her, passing three rows of passengers. It was a mistake. From an aisle seat, one of them rose, turned, and slammed a fist into the nape of the hijacker's neck. The man fell, face downward; before he could move, his assailant had snatched the man's gun and was pointing it at him. The hijacker turned, sat up, looked at the gun, put his face in his hands, and began to moan softly.

From the rear the KGB agent stepped past the stewardess, gun still at the ready, and approached the rescuer.

"Who are you?" he asked. For answer, the rescuer reached into an inside pocket, produced a card, and flicked it open.

The agent looked at the KGB card.

"You're not from Lvov," he said.

"Ternopol," said the other. "I was going home on leave in Minsk, so I had no sidearm. But I have a good right fist." He grinned.

The agent from Lvov nodded.

"Thanks, Comrade. Keep him covered." He stepped to the intercom and talked rapidly into it. He was relating what had happened and asking for a police escort at Minsk.

"Is it safe to have a look?" asked a metallic voice from behind the door.

"Sure," said the KGB agent. "He's safe enough now."

There was a clicking behind the door, and it opened to show the head of the engineer, somewhat frightened and intensely curious.

The agent from Ternopol acted very strangely. He turned from the man on the floor, crashed the revolver into the base of his colleague's skull, shoved him aside, and thrust his foot in the space between the door and jamb before it could close. In a second he was through it, pushing the engineer backward onto the flight deck. The man on the floor behind him rose, grabbed the flight guard's own automatic, a standard KGB Tokarev nine-millimeter, followed through the steel door, and slammed it behind him. It locked automatically.

Two minutes later, under the guns of David Lazareff and Lev Mishkin, the Tupolev turned due west for Warsaw and Berlin, the latter being the ultimate limit of their fuel supply. At the controls Captain Mikhail Rudenko sat white-faced with rage; beside him his copilot, Sergei Vatutin, slowly answered the frantic requests from the Minsk control tower regarding the change of course.

By the time the airliner had crossed the border into Polish airspace, Minsk tower and four other airliners on the same wavelength knew the Tupolev was in the hands of hijackers. When it bored clean through the center of Warsaw's air-traffic-control zone, Moscow already knew. A hundred miles west of Warsaw, a flight of six Polish-based Soviet MIG-23 fighters swept in from starboard and formatted on the Tupolev. The flight leader was jabbering rapidly into his mask.

At his desk in the Defense Ministry on Frunze Street, Moscow, Marshal Nikolai Kerensky took an urgent call on the line linking him to Soviet Air Force headquarters.

"Where?" he barked.

"Passing over Poznán," was the answer. "Three hundred kilometers to Berlin. Fifty minutes' flying time."

The marshal considered carefully. This could be the scandal that Vishnayev had demanded. There was no doubt what should be done. The Tupolev should be shot down, with its entire passenger and crew complement. Later the version given out would be that the hijackers had fired within the fuselage, hitting a main fuel tank. It had happened twice in the past decade.

He gave his orders. A hundred meters off the airliner's wing tip, the commander of the MIG flight listened five minutes later.

"If you say so, Comrade Colonel," he told his base commander. Twenty minutes later, the airliner passed across the Oder–Niesse Line and began its descent into Berlin. As it did so, the MIGs peeled gracefully away and slipped down the sky toward their home base.

"I have to tell Berlin we're coming in," Captain Rudenko appealed to Mishkin. "If there's a plane on the runway, we'll end up as a ball of fire."

Mishkin stared ahead at the banks of steel-gray winter clouds. He had never been in an airplane before, but what the captain said made sense.

"Very well," he said, "break silence and tell Tempelhof you are coming in. No requests, just a flat statement."

Captain Rudenko was playing his last card. He leaned forward, adjusted the channel selection dial, and began to speak.

"Tempelhof, West Berlin. Tempelhof, West Berlin. This is Aeroflot flight three-five-one. . . ."

He was speaking in English, the international language of air traffic control. Mishkin and Lazareff knew almost none of it, apart from what they had picked up on broadcasts in Ukrainian from the West. Mishkin jabbed his gun into Rudenko's neck.

"No tricks," he said in Ukrainian.

In the control tower at East Berlin's Schönefeld Airport,

the two controllers looked at each other in amazement. They were being called on their own frequency but being addressed as Tempelhof. No Aeroflot plane would dream of landing in West Berlin—apart from which, Tempelhof had not been West Berlin's civil airport for ten years. Tempelhof had reverted to a U.S. Air Force base when Tegel took over as the civil airport. One of the East Germans, faster than the other, snatched the microphone.

"Tempelhof to Aeroflot three-five-one, you are cleared to land. Straight run-in," he said. In the airliner Captain Rudenko swallowed hard and lowered flaps and undercarriage. The Tupolev let down rapidly to the main airport of Communist East Germany. They broke cloud at a thousand feet and saw the landing lights ahead of them. At five hundred feet Mishkin peered suspiciously through the streaming perspex. He had heard of West Berlin, of brilliant lights, packed streets, teeming crowds of shoppers up the Kurfürstendamm, and Tempelhof Airport right in the heart of it all. This airport was right out in the countryside.

"It's a trick," he yelled at Lazareff, "it's the East!" He jabbed his gun into Captain Rudenko's neck. "Pull out," he screamed, "pull out or I'll shoot!"

The Ukrainian captain gritted his teeth and held course for the last hundred meters. Mishkin reached over his shoulder and tried to haul back on the control column. The twin booms, when they came, were so close together that it was impossible to tell which came first. Mishkin claimed the thump of the wheels hitting the tarmac caused the gun to go off; copilot Vatutin maintained Mishkin had fired first. It was too confused for a final and definitive version ever to be established.

The bullet tore a gaping hole in the neck of Captain Rudenko and killed him instantly. There was blue smoke in the flight deck, Vatutin hauling back on the stick, yelling to his engineer for more power. The jet engines screamed a mite louder than the passengers as the Tupelov, heavy as a wet loaf, bounced twice more on the tarmac, then lifted into the air, rolling, struggling for lift. Vatutin held her, nose high, wallowing, praying for more engine power, as the outer suburbs of East Berlin blurred past beneath them, followed by the Berlin Wall itself.

When the Tupolev came over the perimeter of Tempelhof, it cleared the nearest houses by six feet.

White-faced, the young copilot hammered the plane onto

the main runway with Lazareff's gun in his back. Mishkin held the red-soaked body of Captain Rudenko from falling across the control column. The Tupolev finally came to rest three quarters down the runway, still on all its wheels.

Staff Sergeant Leroy Coker was a patriotic man. He sat huddled against the cold at the wheel of his Security Police Jeep, his fur-trimmed parka drawn tight around the edges of his face, and he thought longingly of the warmth of Alabama. But he was on guard duty, and he took it seriously.

When the incoming airliner lurched over the houses beyond the perimeter fence, engines howling, undercarriage and flaps hanging, he let out a "What the sheee-yit!" and sat bolt upright. He had never been to Russia, nor even across to the East, but he had read all about them over there. He did not know much about the Cold War, but he well knew that an attack by the Communists was always imminent unless men like Leroy Coker kept on their guard. He also knew a red star when he saw one, and a hammer and sickle.

When the airliner slithered to a stop, he unslung his carbine, took a bead, and blew the nosewheel tires out.

Mishkin and Lazareff surrendered three hours later. Their intent had been to keep the crew, release the passengers, take on board three notables from West Berlin, and be flown to Tel Aviv. But a new nosewheel for a Tupolev was out of the question; the Russians would never supply one. And when the news of the killing of Rudenko was made known to the USAF base authorities, they refused to supply a plane of their own. Marksmen ringed the Tupolev; there was no way the two men could herd the others, even at gunpoint, to an alternative aircraft. The sharpshooters would have cut them down. After an hour's talk with the base commander, they walked out with their hands in the air.

That night, they were formally handed over to the West Berlin authorities for imprisonment and trial.

CHAPTER NINE

THE SOVIET AMBASSADOR to Washington was coldly angry when he faced David Lawrence at the State Department on January 2.

The American Secretary of State was receiving him at the Soviet government's request, though insistence would have been a better word.

The Ambassador read his formal protest in a flat monotone. When he had finished, he laid the text on the American's desk. Lawrence, who had known exactly what it would be, had an answer ready, prepared by his legal counselors, three of whom stood flanking him behind his chair.

He conceded that West Berlin was indeed not sovereign territory, but a city under Four Power occupation. Nevertheless, the Western Allies had long conceded that in matters of jurisprudence the West Berlin authorities should handle all criminal and civil offenses other than those falling within the ambit of the purely military laws of the Western Allies. The hijacking of the airliner, he continued, while a terrible offense, was not committed by U.S. citizens against U.S. citizens or within the U.S. air base of Tempelhof. It was therefore an affair within civil jurisprudence. In consequence, the United States government maintained, it could not legally have held non-U.S. nationals or non-U.S. material witnesses within the territory of West Berlin, even though the airliner had come to rest on a USAF air base.

He had no recourse, therefore, but to reject the Soviet protest.

The Ambassador heard him out in stony silence. He rejoined that he could not accept the American explanation, and rejected it. He would report back to his government in that vein. On this note, he left, to return to his embassy and report to Moscow.

In a small flat in Bayswater, London, three men sat that day and stared at the tangle of newspapers strewn on the floor around them.

"A disaster," snapped Andrew Drake, "a bloody disaster. By now they should have been in Israel. Within a month they'd have been released and could have given their press conference. What the hell did they have to shoot the captain for?"

"If he was landing at Schönefeld and refused to fly into West Berlin, they were finished, anyway," observed Azamat Krim.

"They could have clubbed him," snorted Drake.

"Heat of the moment," said Kaminsky. "What do we do now?"

"Can those handguns be traced?" asked Drake of Krim.

The small Tatar shook his head.

"To the shop that sold them, perhaps," he said. "Not to me. I didn't have to identify myself."

Drake paced the carpet, deep in thought.

"I don't think they'll be extradited back," he said at length. "The Soviets want them now for hijacking, shooting Rudenko, hitting the KGB man on board, and of course the other one they took the identity card from. But the killing of the captain is the serious offense. Still, I don't think a West German government will send two Jews back for execution. On the other hand, they'll be tried and convicted. Probably sentenced to life. Miroslav, will they open their mouths about Ivanenko?"

The Ukrainian refugee shook his head.

"Not if they've got any sense," he said. "Not in the heart of West Berlin. The Germans might have to change their minds and send them back after all. If they believed them, which they wouldn't because Moscow would deny Ivanenko is dead, and produce a look-alike as proof. But Moscow would believe them, and have them liquidated. The Germans, not believing them, would offer no special protection. They wouldn't stand a chance. They'll keep silent."

"That's no use to us," pointed out Krim. "The whole point of the exercise, of all we've gone through, was to deal a single massive humiliating blow to the whole Soviet state apparatus. *We* can't give that press conference; we don't have the tiny details that will convince the world. Only Mishkin and Lazareff can do that."

"Then they have to be got out of there," said Drake with

finality. "We have to mount a second operation to get them to Tel Aviv, with guarantees of their life and liberty. Otherwise it's all been for nothing."

"What happens now?" repeated Kaminsky.

"We think," said Drake. "We work out a way, we plan it, and we execute it. They are not going to sit and rot their lives away in Berlin, not with a secret like that in their heads. And we have little time; it won't take Moscow forever to put two and two together. They have their lead to follow now; they'll know who did the Kiev job pretty soon. Then they'll begin to plan their revenge. We have to beat them to it."

The chilly anger of the Soviet Ambassador to Washington paled into insignificance beside the outrage of his colleague in Bonn as the Russian diplomat faced the West German Foreign Minister two days later. The refusal of the government of the Federal Republic of Germany to hand the two criminals and murderers over to either the Soviet or the East German authorities was a flagrant breach of their hitherto friendly relations and could be construed only as a hostile act, he insisted.

The West German Foreign Minister was deeply uncomfortable. Privately he wished the Tupolev had stayed on the runway in East Germany. He refrained from pointing out that as the Russians had always insisted West Berlin was not a part of West Germany, they ought to be addressing themselves to the Senate in West Berlin.

The Ambassador repeated his case for the third time: the criminals were Soviet citizens; the victims were Soviet citizens; the airliner was Soviet territory; the outrage had taken place in Soviet airspace, and the murder either on or a few feet above the runway of East Germany's principal airport. The crime should therefore be tried under Soviet or at the very least under East German law.

The Foreign Minister pointed out as courteously as he could that all precedent indicated that hijackers could be tried under the law of the land in which they arrived, if that country wished to exercise the right. This was in no way an imputation of unfairness in the Soviet judicial procedure....

The hell it wasn't, he thought privately. No one in West Germany from the government to the press to the public had the slightest doubt that handing Mishkin and Lazareff back would mean KGB interrogation, a kangaroo court, and the firing squad. And they were Jewish—that was another problem.

The first few days of January are slack for the press, and the West German press was making a big story out of this. The conservative and powerful Axel Springer newspapers were insisting that whatever they had done, the two hijackers should receive a fair trial, and that could be guaranteed only in West Germany. The Bavarian Christian Social Union (CSU) Party, on which the governing coalition depended, was taking the same line. Certain quarters were giving the press a large amount of precise information and lurid details about the latest KGB crackdown in the Lvov area from which the hijackers came, suggesting that escape from the terror was a justifiable reaction, albeit a deplorable way of doing it. And lastly the recent exposure of yet another Communist agent high in the civil service would not increase the popularity of a government taking a conciliatory line toward Moscow. And with the state elections pending . . .

The Minister had his orders from the Chancellor. Mishkin and Lazareff, he told the Ambassador, would go on trial in West Berlin as soon as possible, and if—or rather when—convicted, would receive salutary sentences.

The Politburo meeting at the end of the week was stormy. Once again the tape recorders were off, the stenographers absent.

"This is an outrage," snapped Vishnayev. "Yet another scandal that diminishes the Soviet Union in the eyes of the world. It should never have happened."

He implied that it had happened only due to the ever-weakening leadership of Maxim Rudin.

"It would not have happened," retorted Petrov, "if the Comrade Marshal's fighters had shot the plane down over Poland, according to custom."

"There was a communications breakdown between ground control and the fighter leader," said Kerensky. "A chance in a thousand."

"Fortuitous, though," observed Rykov coldly. Through his ambassadors he knew the Mishkin and Lazareff trial would be public and would reveal exactly how the hijackers had first mugged a KGB officer in a park for his identity papers, then used the papers to penetrate to the flight deck.

"Is there any question," asked Petryanov, a supporter of Vishnayev, "that these two men could be the ones who killed Ivanenko?"

The atmosphere was electric.

"None at all," said Petrov firmly. "We know those two come from Lvov, not Kiev. They were Jews who had been refused permission to emigrate. We are investigating, of course, but so far there is no connection."

"Should such a connection emerge, we will of course be informed?" asked Vishnayev.

"That goes without saying, Comrade," growled Rudin.

The stenographers were recalled, and the meeting went on to discuss the progress at Castletown and the purchase of ten million tons of feed grain. Vishnayev did not press the issue. Rykov was at pains to show that the Soviet Union was gaining the quantities of wheat she would need to survive the winter and spring with minimal concessions of weapons levels, a point Marshal Kerensky disputed. But Komarov was forced to concede the imminent arrival of ten million tons of animal winter feed would enable him to release the same tonnage from hoarded stocks immediately, and prevent wholesale slaughter. The Maxim Rudin faction, with its hair-breadth supremacy, stayed intact.

As the meeting dispersed, the old Soviet chief drew Vassili Petrov aside.

"*Is* there any connection between the two Jews and the Ivanenko killing?" he inquired.

"There may be," conceded Petrov. "We know they did the mugging in Ternopol, of course, so they were evidently prepared to travel outside Lvov to prepare their escape. We have their fingerprints from the aircraft, and they match those in their living quarters in Lvov. We have found no shoes that match the prints at the Kiev murder site, but we are still searching for those shoes. One last thing. We have an area of palmprint taken from the car that knocked down Ivanenko's mother. We are trying to get a complete palmprint of both from inside Berlin. If they check . . ."

"Prepare a plan, a contingency plan, a feasibility study," said Rudin. "To have them liquidated inside their jail in West Berlin. Just in case. And another thing. If their identity as the killers of Ivanenko is proved, tell me, not the Politburo. We wipe them out first, then inform our comrades."

Petrov swallowed hard. Cheating the Politburo was playing for the highest stakes in Soviet Russia. One slip and there would be no safety net. He recalled what Rudin had told him by the fire out at Usovo a fortnight earlier. With the Politburo tied six against six, Ivanenko dead, and two of their own six about to change sides, there were no aces left.

"Very well," he said.

West German Chancellor Dietrich Busch received his Justice Minister in his private office in the Chancellery Building next to the old Palais Schaumberg just after the middle of the month. The government chief of West Germany was standing at his modern picture window, gazing out at the frozen snow. Inside the new, modern government headquarters overlooking Federal Chancellor Square, the temperature was warm enough for shirt sleeves, and nothing of the raw, bitter January of the riverside town penetrated.

"This Mishkin and Lazareff affair, how goes it?" asked Busch.

"It's strange," admitted his Justice Minister, Ludwig Fischer. "They are being more cooperative than one could hope for. They seem eager to achieve a quick trial with no delays."

"Excellent," said the Chancellor. "That's exactly what we want. A quick affair. Let's get it over with. In what way are they cooperating?"

"They were offered a star lawyer from the right wing, paid for by subscribed funds—possibly German contributions, possibly the Jewish Defense League from America. They turned him down. He wanted to make a major spectacle out of the trial, plenty of detail about the KGB terror against Jews in the Ukraine."

"A *right*-wing lawyer wanted that?"

"All grist to their mill. Bash the Russians, and so on," said Fischer. "Anyway, Mishkin and Lazareff want to go for an admission of guilt and plead mitigating circumstances. They insist on it. If they do so, and claim the gun went off by accident when the plane hit the runway at Schönefeld, they have a partial defense. Their new lawyer is asking for murder to be reduced to culpable homicide if they do."

"I think we can grant them that," said the Chancellor. "What would they get?"

"With the hijacking thrown in, fifteen to twenty years. Of course, they could be paroled after serving a third of the sentence. They're young—mid-twenties. They could be out by the time they're thirty."

"That's in five years," growled Busch. "I'm concerned about the next five months. Memories fade. In five years they'll be in the archives."

"Well, they admit everything, but they insist that the gun went off by accident. They claim they just wanted to reach Israel the only way they knew how. They'll plead guilty right down the line—to culpable homicide."

"Let them have it," said the Chancellor. "The Russians won't like it, but it's six of one, half a dozen of the other. They'd draw life for murder, but that's effectively twenty years nowadays."

"There's one other thing. They want to be transferred after the trial to a jail in West Germany."

"Why?"

"They seem terrified of revenge by the KGB. They think they'll be safer in West Germany than in West Berlin."

"Rubbish," snorted Busch. "They'll be tried and jailed in West Berlin. The Russians would not dream of trying to settle accounts inside a Berlin jail. They wouldn't dare. Still, we could do an internal transfer in a year or so. But not yet. Go ahead, Ludwig. Make it quick and clean, if they wish to co-operate. But get the press off my back before the elections, and the Russian Ambassador as well."

At Chita the morning sun glittered along the deck of the *Freya*, lying, as she had for two and a half months, by the commissioning quay. In those seventy-five days she had been transformed. Day and night she had lain docile while the tiny creatures who had made her swarmed into and out of every part of her. Hundreds of miles of lines had been laid the length and breadth of her—pipes, tubes, and electric cables. Her labyrinthine electrical networks had been connected and tested, her incredibly complex system of pumps installed and tried.

The computer-linked instruments that would fill her holds and empty them, thrust her forward or shut her down, hold her to any point of the compass for weeks on end without a hand on her helm, and observe the stars above her and the seabed below, had been set in their places.

The food lockers and deepfreezes to sustain her crew for months were fully installed; so, too, the furniture, doorknobs, lightbulbs, lavatories, galley stoves, central heating, air conditioning, cinema, sauna, three bars, two dining rooms, beds, bunks, carpets, and clothes hangers.

Her five-story superstructure had been converted from an empty shell into a luxury hotel; her bridge, radio room, and computer room from empty, echoing galleries to a low-humming complex of data banks, calculators, and control systems.

When the last of the workmen picked up their tools and left her alone, she was the ultimate in size, power, capacity, luxury, and technical refinement that man could ever have set to float on water.

The rest of her crew of thirty had arrived by air fourteen days earlier to familiarize themselves with every inch of her. Besides her master, Captain Thor Larsen, they were made up of the first officer, second mate, and third mate; the chief engineer, first engineer, second engineer, and electrical engineer (who ranked as a "first"); the radio officer and chief steward (also ranked as officers); and twenty others, to comprise the full complement: the first cook, four stewards, three firemen, one repairman, ten able seamen, and one pumpman.

Two weeks before she was due to sail, the tugs drew her away from the quay to the center of Ise Bay. There her great twin propellers bit into the waters to bring her out to the western Pacific for sea trials. For officers and crew, as well as for the dozen Japanese technicians who went with her, it would mean two weeks of grueling hard work, testing every single system against every known or possible contingency.

There was $170 million worth of her moving out to the mouth of the bay that morning, and the small ships standing off Nagoya watched her pass with awe.

Twenty kilometers outside Moscow lies the tourist village and estate of Arkhangelskoye, complete with museum and a restaurant noted for its genuine bear steaks. In the last week of that freezing January, Adam Munro had reserved a table there for himself and a date from the secretarial pool at the British Embassy.

He always varied his dinner companions so that no one girl should notice too much, and if the young hopeful of the evening wondered why he chose to drive the distance he did over icy roads in temperatures fifteen degrees below freezing, she made no comment on it.

The restaurant in any case was warm and snug, and when he excused himself to fetch extra cigarettes from his car, she thought nothing of it. In the parking lot, he shivered as the icy blast hit him, and hurried to where the twin headlights glowed briefly in the darkness.

He climbed into the car beside Valentina, put an arm around her, drew her close and kissed her.

"I hate the thought of you being in there with another woman, Adam," she whispered as she nuzzled his throat.

"It's nothing," he said. "Not important. An excuse for being able to drive out here to dine without being suspected. I have news for you."

"About us?" she asked.

"About us. I have asked my own people if they would help you to come out, and they have agreed. There is a plan. Do you know the port of Constanza on the Rumanian coast?"

She shook her head.

"I have heard of it, but never been there. I always holiday on the Soviet coast of the Black Sea."

"Could you arrange to holiday there with Sasha?"

"I suppose so," she said. "I can take my holidays virtually where I like. Rumania is within the Socialist bloc. It should not raise eyebrows."

"When does Sasha leave school for the spring holidays?"

"The last few days of March, I think. Is that important?"

"It has to be in mid-April," he told her. "My people think you could be brought off the beach to a freighter offshore. By speedboat. Can you make sure to arrange a spring holiday with Sasha at Constanza or the nearby Mamaia Beach in April?"

"I'll try," she said. "I'll try. April. Oh, Adam, it seems so close."

"It is close, my love. Less than ninety days. Be patient a little longer, as I have been, and we will make it. We'll start a whole new life."

Five minutes later she had given him the transcription of the early January Politburo meeting and driven off into the night. He stuffed the sheaf of papers inside his waistband beneath his shirt and jacket, and returned to the warmth of the Arkangelskoye Restaurant.

This time, he vowed, as he made polite conversation with

the secretary, there would be no mistakes, no drawing back, no letting her go, as there had been in 1961. This time it would be forever.

Edwin Campbell leaned back from the Georgian table in the Long Gallery at Castletown House and looked across at Professor Sokolov. The last point on the agenda had been covered, the last concession wrung. From the dining room below, a courier had reported that the secondary conference had matched the concessions of the upper floor with trade bargains from the United States to the Soviet Union.

"I think that's it, Ivan, my friend," said Campbell. "I don't think we can do any more at this stage."

The Russian raised his eyes from the pages of Cyrillic handwriting in front of him, his own notes. For over a hundred days he had fought tooth and claw to secure for his country the grain tonnages that could save her from disaster and yet retain the maximum in weapons levels from inner space to Eastern Europe. He knew he had had to make concessions that would have been unheard of four years earlier at Geneva, but he had done the best he could in the time scale allowed.

"I think you are right, Edwin," he replied. "Let us have the arms-reduction treaty prepared in draft form for our respective governments."

"And the trade protocol," said Campbell. "I imagine they will want that also."

Sokolov permitted himself a wry smile.

"I am sure they will want it very much," he said.

For the next week the twin teams of interpreters and stenographers prepared both the treaty and the trade protocol. Occasionally the two principal negotiators were needed to clarify a point at issue, but for the most part, the transcription and translation work was left to the aides. When the two bulky documents, each in duplicate, were finally ready, the two chief negotiators departed to their separate capitals to present them to their masters.

Andrew Drake threw down his magazine and leaned back.

"I wonder," he said.

"What?" asked Krim as he entered the small sitting room

with three mugs of coffee. Drake tossed the magazine to the Tatar.

"Read the first article," he said. Krim read in silence while Drake sipped his coffee. Kaminsky eyed them both.

"You're crazy," said Krim with finality.

"No," said Drake. "Without some audacity we'll be sitting here for the next ten years. It could work. Look, Mishkin and Lazareff come up for trial in a fortnight. The outcome is a foregone conclusion. We might as well start planning now. We know we're going to have to do it, anyway, if they are ever to come out of that jail. So let's start planning. Azamat, you were in the paratroops in Canada?"

"Sure," said Krim. "Five years."

"Did you ever do an explosives course?"

"Yep. Demolition and sabotage. I was assigned for training to the Engineers for three months."

"And years ago I used to have a passion for electronics and radio," said Drake. "Probably because my dad had a radio repair shop before he died. We could do it. We'd need help, but we could do it."

"How many more men?" asked Krim.

"We'd need one on the outside, just to recognize Mishkin and Lazareff on their release. That would have to be Miroslav, here. For the job, us two, plus five to stand guard."

"Such a thing has never been done before," observed the Tatar doubtfully.

"All the more reason why it will be unexpected, therefore unprepared for."

"We'd get caught at the end of it," said Krim.

"Not necessarily. I'd cover the pullout if I had to. And anyway, the trial would be the sensation of the decade. With Mishkin and Lazareff free in Israel, half the Western world would applaud. The whole issue of a free Ukraine would be blazoned across every newspaper and magazine outside the Soviet bloc."

"Do you know five more who would come in on it?"

"For years I've been collecting names," said Drake. "Men who are sick and tired of talking. If they knew what we'd done already, yes, I could get five before the end of the month."

"All right," said Krim, "if we're into this thing, let's do it. Where do you want me to go?"

"Belgium," said Drake. "I want a large apartment in Brussels. We'll bring the men there and make the apartment the group's base."

On the other side of the world while Drake was talking, the sun rose over Chita and the Ishikawajima-Harima shipyard. The *Freya* lay alongside her commissioning quay, her engines throbbing.

The previous evening had seen a lengthy conference in the office of the IHI chairman, attended by both the yard's and the company's chief superintendents, the accountants, Harry Wennerstrom, and Thor Larsen. The two technical experts had agreed that every one of the giant tanker's systems was in perfect working order. Wennerstrom had signed the final release document, conceding that the *Freya* was all he had paid for.

In fact, he had paid five percent of her on the signature of the original contract to build her, five percent at the keel-laying ceremony, five percent when she rode water, and five percent at official handover. The remaining eighty percent plus interest was payable over the succeeding eight years. But to all intents and purposes, she was his. The yard's company flag had been ceremoniously hauled down, and the silver-on-blue winged Viking helmet emblem of the Nordia Line now fluttered in the dawn breeze.

High on the bridge, towering over the vast spread of her deck, Harry Wennerstrom drew Thor Larsen by the arm into the radio room and closed the door behind him. The room was completely soundproof with the door closed.

"She's all yours, Thor," he said. "By the way, there's been a slight change of plan regarding your arrival in Europe. I'm not lightening her offshore. Not for her maiden voyage. Just this once, you're going to bring her into the Europoort at Rotterdam fully laden."

Larsen stared at his employer in disbelief. He knew as well as Wennerstrom that fully loaded ULCCs never entered ports; they stood well offshore and lightened themselves by disgorging most of their cargo into other, smaller tankers in order to reduce their draft for the shallow seas. Or they berthed at "sea islands"—networks of pipes on stilts, well out to sea—from which their oil could be pumped ashore. The idea of a girl in every port was a hollow joke for the crews of the supertankers; they often did not berth anywhere near a city from year's end to year's end, but were flown off their ships for periodic leave periods. That was why the crew quarters had to be a real home away from home.

"The English Channel will never take her," said Larsen.

"You're not going up the Channel," said Wennerstrom. "You're going west of Ireland, west of the Hebrides, north of the Pentland Firth, between the Orkneys and the Shetlands, then south down the North Sea, following the twenty-fathom line, to moor at the deep-water anchorage. From there the pilots will bring you down the main channel toward the Mass Estuary. The tugs will bring you in from the Hook of Holland to the Europoort."

"The Inner Channel from K.I. Buoy to the Mass won't take her, fully laden," protested Larsen.

"Yes, it will," said Wennerstrom calmly. "They have dredged this channel to one hundred fifteen feet over the past four years. You'll be drawing ninety-eight feet. Thor, if I were asked to name any mariner in the world who could bring a million-tonner into the Europoort, it would be you. It'll be tight as all hell, but let me have this one last triumph. I want the world to see her, Thor. My *Freya*. I'll have them all there waiting for her. The Dutch government, the world's press. They'll be my guests, and they'll be dumbfounded. Otherwise, no one will ever see her; she'll spend her whole life out of sight of land."

"All right," said Larsen slowly. "Just this once. I'll be ten years older when it's over."

Wennerstrom grinned like a small boy.

"Just wait till they see her," he said. "The first of April. See you in Rotterdam, Thor Larsen."

Ten minutes later he was gone. At noon, with the Japanese workers lining the quayside to cheer her on her way, the mighty *Freya* eased away from the shore and headed for the mouth of the bay. At two P.M. on February 2, she came out again into the Pacific and swung her bow south toward the Philippines, Borneo, and Sumatra at the start of her maiden voyage.

On February 10, the Politburo in Moscow met to consider, approve, or reject the draft treaty and accompanying trade protocol negotiated at Castletown. Rudin and those who supported him knew that if they could carry the terms of the treaty at this meeting, then, barring accidents thereafter, it could be ratified and signed. Yefrem Vishnayev and his faction of hawks were no less aware. The meeting was lengthy and exceptionally hard fought.

It is often assumed that world statesmen, even in private conclave, use moderate language and courteous address to their colleagues and advisers. This has not been true of several recent U.S. presidents and is completely untrue of the Politburo in closed session. The Russian equivalent of four-letter words flew thick and fast. Only the fastidious Vishnayev kept his language restrained, though his tone was acid as he and his allies fought every concession, line by line.

It was the Foreign Minister, Dmitri Rykov, who carried the others in the moderate faction.

"What we have gained," he said, "is the assured sale to us, at last July's reasonable prices, of fifty-five million tons of grains. Without them we face disaster on a national scale. Besides, we have nearly three billion dollars' worth of the most modern technology, in consumer industries, computers, and oil production. With these we can master the problems that have beset us for two decades, and conquer them within five years.

"Against this we have to offset certain minimal concessions in arms levels and states of preparedness, which, I stress, will in no way at all hinder or retard our capacity to dominate the Third World and its raw-material resources inside the same five years. From the disaster that faced us last May, we have emerged triumphant, thanks to the inspired leadership of Comrade Maxim Rudin. To reject this treaty now would bring us back to last May, but worse: the last of our 1982 harvest grains will run out in sixty days."

When the meeting voted on the treaty terms, which was in fact a vote on the continuing leadership of Maxim Rudin, the six-to-six tie remained intact.

"There's only one thing that can bring him down now," said Vishnayev with quiet finality to Marshal Kerensky in the former's limousine as they drove home that evening. "If something serious happens to sway one or two of his faction before the treaty is ratified. If not, the Central Committee will approve the treaty on the Politburo's recommendation, and it will go through. If only it could be proved that those two damned Jews in Berlin killed Ivanenko. . . ."

Kerensky was less than his blustering self. Privately he was beginning to wonder if he had chosen the wrong side. Three months ago it had looked so certain that Rudin would be pushed too far, too fast, by the Americans and would lose his crucial support at the green baize table. But Kerensky was committed to Vishnayev now; there would be no massive Soviet maneuvers in East Germany in two months, and he had to swallow that.

"One other thing," said Vishnayev. "If it had appeared six months ago, the power struggle would be over by now. I heard news from a contact out at the Kuntsevo clinic. Maxim Rudin is dying."

"Dying?" repeated the Defense Minister. "When?"

"Not soon enough," said the Party theoretician. "He'll live to carry the day over this treaty, my friend. Time is running out for us, and there is nothing we can do about it. Unless the Ivanenko affair can yet blow up in his face."

As he was speaking, the *Freya* was steaming through the Sunda Strait. To her port side lay Java Head, and far to starboard the great mass of the volcano Krakatau reared toward the night sky. On the darkened bridge a battery of dimly lit instruments told Thor Larsen, the senior officer of the watch, and the junior officer all they needed to know. Three separate navigational systems correlated their findings into the computer, set in the small room aft of the bridge, and those findings were dead accurate. Constant compass readings, true to within half a second of a degree, cross-checked themselves with the stars above, unchanging and unchangeable. Man's artificial stars, the all-weather satellites, were also monitored and the resultant findings fed into the computer. Here the memory banks had absorbed tide, wind, undercurrents, temperatures, and humidity levels. From the computer, endless messages were flashed automatically to the gigantic rudder, which, far below the stern transom, flickered with the sensitivity of a fish's tail.

High above the bridge, the two radar scanners whirled unceasingly, picking up coasts and mountains, ships and buoys, feeding them all into the computer, which processed this information, too, ready to activate its hazard-alarm device at the first hint of danger. Beneath the water, the echo sounders relayed a three-dimensional map of the seabed far below, while from the bulbous bow section the forward sonar scanner looked ahead and down into the black waters. For the *Freya*, elapsed time from full-ahead to crash-stop would be thirty minutes, and she would cover three to four kilometers. She was that big.

Before dawn she had cleared the narrows of Sunda and her computers had turned her northwest along the hundred-fathom line to cut south of Sri Lanka for the Arabian Sea.

Two days later, on February 12, eight men grouped themselves in the apartment Azamat Krim had rented in a suburb of Brussels. The five newcomers had been summoned by Drake, who long ago had noted them all, met and spoken with them long into the night, before deciding that they, too, shared his dream of striking a blow against Moscow. Two of the five were German-born Ukrainians, scions of the large Ukrainian community in the Federal Republic. One was an American from New York, also of a Ukrainian father, and the other two were Ukrainian-British.

When they heard what Mishkin and Lazareff had done to the head of the KGB, there was a babble of excited comment. When Drake proposed that the operation could not be completed until the two partisans were free and safe, no one dissented. They talked through the night, and by dawn they had split into four teams of two.

Drake and Kaminsky would return to England to buy the necessary electronic equipment that Drake estimated he required. One of the Germans would partner one of the Englishmen and return to Germany to seek out the explosives they needed. The other German, who had contacts in Paris, would take the other Englishman to find and buy, or steal, the weaponry. Azamat Krim took his fellow North American to seek a motor launch. The American, who had worked in a boatyard in upper New York State, reckoned he knew what he wanted.

Eight days later in the tightly guarded courtroom attached to Moabit Prison in West Berlin, the trial of Mishkin and Lazareff started. Both men were silent and subdued in the dock as, within concentric walls of security from the barbed-wire entanglements atop the perimeter walls to the armed guards scattered all over the courtroom, they listened to the charges. The list took ten minutes to read. There was an audible gasp from the packed press benches when both men pleaded guilty to all charges. The state prosecutor rose to begin his narration of the events of New Year's Eve to the panel of judges. When he had finished, the judges adjourned to discuss the sentence.

The *Freya* moved slowly and sedately through the Strait of Hormuz and into the Persian Gulf. The breeze had freshened with the sunrise into the chilly shamal wind coming into her nose from the northwest, sand-laden, causing the horizon to be hazy and vague. Her crew all knew this landscape well enough, having passed many times on their way to collect crude oil from the Gulf. They were all experienced tanker-men.

To one side of the *Freya,* barren, arid Qeshm Island slid by, barely two cables away; to the other, the officers on the bridge could make out the bleak moonscape of Cape Musandam, with its sheer rocky mountains. The *Freya* was riding high, and the depth in the channel presented no problems. On the return, when she was laden with crude oil, it would be different. She would be almost shut down, moving slowly, watch officer's eyes riveted on her depth sounder, watching the map of the seabed pass barely a few feet beneath her keel, ninety-eight feet below the waterline.

She was still in ballast, as she had been all the way from Chita. She had sixty giant tanks or holds, three abreast in lines of twenty, fore to aft. One of these was the slop tank, to be used for nothing else but gathering the slops from her fifty crude-carrying cargo tanks. Nine were permanent ballast tanks, to be used for nothing but pure seawater to give her stability when she was empty of cargo.

But her remaining fifty crude-oil tanks were sufficient. Each held 20,000 tons of crude oil. It was with complete confidence in the impossibility of her causing accidental oil pollution that she steamed on to Abu Dhabi to load her first cargo.

There is a modest bar on the rue Miollin in Paris where the small fry of the world of mercenaries and arms sellers are wont to forgather and take a drink together. It was here the German-Ukrainian and his English colleague were brought by the German's French contact man.

There were several hours of low-voiced negotiation between the Frenchman and another French friend of his.

Eventually the contact man came across to the two Ukrainians.

"My friend says it is possible," he told the Ukrainian from Germany. "Five hundred dollars each, American dollars, cash. One magazine per unit included."

"We'll take it if he'll throw in one handgun with full magazine," said the man from Germany.

Three hours later in the garage of a private house near Neuilly, six submachine carbines and one MAB automatic nine-millimeter handgun were wrapped in blankets and stowed in the trunk of the Ukrainians' car. The money changed hands. In twelve hours, just before midnight of February 24, the two men arrived at their apartment in Brussels and stored their equipment at the back of a closet.

As the sun rose on February 25, the *Freya* eased her way back through the Strait of Hormuz, and on the bridge there was a sigh of relief as the officers gazing at the depth sounder saw the seabed drop away from in front of their eyes to the deep of the ocean. On the digital display, the figures ran rapidly from twenty to one hundred fathoms. The *Freya* moved steadily back to her full-load service speed of fifteen knots as she went southeast back down the Gulf of Oman.

She was heavy-laden now, doing what she had been designed and built for—carrying a million tons of crude oil to the thirsty refineries of Europe and the millions of family cars that would drink it. Her draft was now at her designed ninety-eight feet, and her hazard-alarm devices had ingested the knowledge and knew what to do if the seabed ever approached too close.

Her nine ballast tanks were now empty, acting as buoyancy tanks. Far away in the forepart, the first row of three tanks contained a full crude tank on port and starboard, with the single slop tank in the center. One row back were the first three empty ballast tanks. The second row of three was amidships, and the third row of three was at the foot of the superstructure, on the fifth floor of which Captain Thor Larsen handed the *Freya* to the senior officer of the watch and went down to his handsome day cabin for breakfast and a short sleep.

On the morning of February 26, after an adjournment of several days, the presiding judge in the Moabit courtroom in West Berlin began to read the judgment of himself and his two colleagues. It took several hours.

In their walled dock, Mishkin and Lazareff listened impassively. From time to time each sipped water from the glasses placed on the tables in front of them. From the packed booths reserved for the international press they were under scrutiny, as were the figures of the judges, while the findings were read. But one magazine journalist representing a leftist German monthly magazine seemed more interested in the glasses they drank from than in the prisoners themselves.

The court adjourned for lunch, and when it resumed, the journalist was missing from his seat. He was phoning from one of the kiosks outside the hearing room. Shortly after three, the judge reached his conclusion. Both men were required to rise, to hear themselves sentenced to fifteen years' imprisonment.

They were led away to begin their sentences at Tegel Jail in the northern part of the city, and within minutes the courtroom had emptied. The cleaners took over, removing the brimming wastepaper baskets, carafes, and glasses. One of the middle-aged ladies occupied herself with cleaning the interior of the dock. Unobserved by her colleagues, she quietly picked up the prisoners' two drinking glasses, wrapped each in a dustcloth, and placed them in her shopping bag beneath the empty wrappers of her sandwiches. No one noticed, and no one cared.

On the last day of the month, Vassili Petrov sought and received a private audience with Maxim Rudin in the latter's Kremlin suite.

"Mishkin and Lazareff," he said without preamble.

"What about them? They got fifteen years. It should have been the firing squad."

"One of our people in West Berlin abstracted the glasses they used for water during the trial. The palmprint on one matches that from the car used in the hit-and-run affair in Kiev in October."

"So it was them," said Rudin grimly. "Damn them to hell! Vassili, wipe them out. Liquidate them as fast as you can. Give it to 'Wet Affairs.' "

The KGB, vast and complex in its scope and organization,

consists basically of four chief directorates, seven independent directorates, and six independent departments.

But the four chief directorates comprise the bulk of the KGB. One of these, the First, concerns itself exclusively with clandestine activities outside the USSR.

Deep within the heart of it is a section known simply as Department V (as in Victor), or the Executive Action Department. This is the one the KGB would most like to keep hidden from the rest of the world, inside and outside the USSR. For its tasks include sabotage, extortion, kidnapping, and assassination. Within the jargon of the KGB itself, it usually has yet another name: the department of *mokrie dyela*, or "Wet Affairs," so called because its operations not infrequently involve someone's getting wet with blood. It was to this Department V of the First Chief Directorate of the KGB that Maxim Rudin ordered Petrov to hand the elimination of Mishkin and Lazareff.

"I have already done as much," said Petrov. "I thought of giving the affair to Colonel Kukushkin, Ivanenko's head of security. He has a personal reason to wish to succeed—to save his own skin, apart from avenging Ivanenko and his own humiliation. He's already served his time in Wet Affairs—ten years ago. Inevitably he is already aware of the secret of what happened in Rosa Luxemburg Street—he was there. And he speaks German. He would report back only to General Abrassov or to me."

Rudin nodded grimly.

"All right, let him have the job. He can pick his own team. Abrassov will give him everything he needs. The apparent reason will be to avenge the death of Flight Captain Rudenko. And Vassili, he had better succeed the first time. If he tries and fails, Mishkin and Lazareff could open their mouths. After a failed attempt to kill them, someone might believe them. Certainly Vishnayev would, and you know what that would mean."

"I know," said Petrov quietly. "He will not fail. He'll do it himself."

CHAPTER TEN

"IT'S THE BEST we'll get, Mr. President," said Secretary of State David Lawrence. "Personally, I believe Edwin Campbell has done us proud at Castletown."

Grouped before the President's desk in the Oval Office were the secretaries of State, Defense, and the Treasury, with Stanislaw Poklewski, and Robert Benson of the CIA. Beyond the French windows the Rose Garden was whipped by a bitter wind. The snows had gone, but March 1 was bleak and uninviting.

President William Matthews laid his hand on the bulky folder in front of him, the draft agreement wrung out of the Castletown talks.

"A lot of it is too technical for me," he confessed, "but the digest from the Defense Department impresses me. The way I see it is this: if we reject the agreement now, after the Soviet Politburo has accepted it, there'll be no renegotiation, anyway. The matter of grain deliveries will become academic to Russia in three months in any case. By then they'll be starving and Rudin will be gone. Yefrem Vishnayev will get his war. Right?"

"That seems to be the unavoidable conclusion," said David Lawrence.

"How about the other side of it—the concessions we have made?" asked the President.

"The secret trade protocol in the separate document," said the Secretary of the Treasury, "requires us to deliver fifty-five million tons of mixed grains at production costs and nearly three billion dollars' worth of oil, computer, and consumer industry technology, rather heavily subsidized. The total cost to the United States runs to almost four billion dollars. On the other hand, the sweeping arms reductions should enable us to claw back that much and more by reduced defense expenditures."

"If the Soviets abide by their undertakings," said the Secretary of Defense hastily.

"But if they do, and we have to believe they will," countered Lawrence, "by our own experts' calculations they could not launch a successful conventional or tactical nuclear war across the face of Europe for at least five years."

President Matthews knew that the presidential election of 1984 would not see his candidacy. But if he could step down in January 1985, leaving behind him peace for even half a decade, with the burdensome arms race of the seventies halted in its tracks, he would take his place among the great U.S. presidents. He wanted that more than anything else this spring of 1983.

"Gentlemen," he said, "we have to approve this treaty as it stands, and for once I'm confident the Senate will see it the same way. David, inform Moscow we join them in agreeing to the terms, and propose that our negotiators reconvene at Castletown to draw up the formal treaty ready for signing. While this is going on, we will permit the loading of the grain ships, ready to sail on the day of signature. That is all."

On March 3, Azamat Krim and his Ukrainian-American collaborator clinched the deal that acquired them a sturdy and powerful launch. She was the kind of craft much favored by enthusiastic sea anglers on both the British and European coasts of the North Sea, steel-hulled, forty feet long, tough, and secondhand. She had Belgian registration, and they had found her near Ostende.

Up front, she had a cabin whose roof extended the forward third of her length. A companionway led down to a cramped four-berth resting area, with a tiny toilet and galley. Aft of the rear bulkhead she was open to the elements, and beneath the deck lay a powerful engine capable of taking her through the wild North Sea to the fishing grounds and back.

Krim and his companion brought her from Ostende to Blankenberge, farther up the Belgian coast, and when she was moored in the marina, she attracted no attention. Spring always brings its crop of hardy sea anglers to the coasts with their boats and tackle. The American chose to live on board and work on the engine. Krim returned to Brussels to find that Andrew Drake had taken over the kitchen table as a workbench and was deeply engrossed in preparations of his own.

For the third time on her maiden voyage, the *Freya* had crossed the Equator, and March 7 found her entering the Mozambique Channel, heading south by southwest toward the Cape of Good Hope. She was still following her hundred-fathom line, leaving six hundred feet of clear ocean beneath her keel, a course that took her to seaward of the main shipping lanes. She had not seen land since coming out of the Gulf of Oman, but on the afternoon of the seventh she passed through the Comoro Islands at the north end of the Mozambique Channel. To starboard, her crew, taking advantage of the moderate winds and seas to stroll the quarter mile of forward deck or lounge beside the screened swimming pool up on C deck, saw Great Comoro Island, the peak of its densely wooded mountain hidden in clouds, the smoke from the burning undergrowth on its flanks drifting across the green water. By nightfall the skies had overcast with gray cloud, the wind turned squally. Ahead lay the heaving seas of the Cape and the final northward run to Europe and her welcome.

The following day, Moscow replied formally to the proposal of President Matthews, welcoming his agreement, with the concurrence of the United States Senate, to the terms of the draft treaty and agreeing that the chief negotiators of Castletown should reconvene jointly to draft the formal treaty while remaining in constant contact with their respective governments.

The bulk of the Soviet merchant marine fleet, Sovfracht, along with the numerous other vessels already chartered by the Soviet Union, had already sailed at the American government's invitation for the grain ports of North America. In Moscow the first reports were coming in of excessive quantities of meat appearing in the peasant markets, indicating livestock slaughter was taking place even on the state and collective farms, where it was forbidden. The last reserves of grain for animals and humans alike were running out.

In a private message to President Matthews, Maxim Rudin regretted that for health reasons he would not personally be able to sign the treaty on behalf of the Soviet Union unless the ceremony were held in Moscow; he therefore proposed a formal signature by foreign ministers in Dublin on April 10.

The winds of the Cape were hellish; the South African summer was over, and the autumn gales thundered up from the Antarctic to batter Table Mountain. The *Freya* by March 12 was in the heart of the Agulhas Current, pushing westward through mountainous green seas, taking the gales from the southwest on her port beam.

It was bitter cold out on deck, but no one was there. Behind the double-glazing of the bridge, Captain Thor Larsen and his two officers of the watch stood with the helmsman, radio officer, and two others in shirt sleeves. Warm, safe, protected by the aura of her invincible technology, they gazed forward to where forty-foot waves impelled by the force 10 winds out of the southwest reared above the *Freya*'s port side, hovered for a moment, then crashed down to obscure her gigantic deck and its myriad pipes and valves in a swirling maelstrom of white foam. While the waves burst, only the fo'c'sle, far ahead, was discernible, like a separate entity. As the foam receded, defeated, through the scuppers, the *Freya* shook herself and buried her bulk in another oncoming mountain. A hundred feet beneath the men, ninety thousand shaft horsepower pushed a million tons of crude oil another few yards toward Rotterdam. High above, the Cape albatrosses wheeled and glided, their lost cries unheard behind the Plexiglas. Coffee was served by one of the stewards.

Two days later, on Monday the fourteenth, Adam Munro drove out of the courtyard of the Commercial Section of the British Embassy and turned sharp right into Kutuzovsky Prospekt toward the city center. His destination was the main embassy building, where he had been summoned by the head of Chancery. The telephone call, certainly tapped by the KGB, had referred to the clarification of minor details for a forthcoming trade delegation visit from London. In fact it meant that there was a message awaiting him in the cipher room.

The cipher room in the embassy building on Maurice Thorez Embankment is in the basement, a secure room regularly checked by the "sweepers," who are not looking for dust, but for listening devices. The cipher clerks are diplomatic personnel and security-checked to the highest level. Nevertheless, sometimes messages come in that bear a coding to indicate they will not and cannot be decoded by the normal decoding machines. The tag on these messages will indicate that they have to be passed to one particular cipher clerk, a man who has the right to know because he has a need to know. Occasionally a message for Adam Munro bore such a coding, as today. The clerk in question knew Munro's real job because he needed to—if for no other reason, to protect him from those who did not.

Munro entered the cipher room, and the clerk spotted him. They withdrew to a small annex where the clerk, a precise, methodical man with bifocal glasses, used a key from his waistband to unlock a separate decoding machine. He passed the London message into it, and the machine spat out the translation. The clerk took no notice, averting his gaze as Munro moved away.

Munro read the message and smiled. He memorized it within seconds and passed it straight into a shredder, which reduced the thin paper to fragments hardly bigger than dust. He thanked the clerk and left, with a song in his heart. Barry Ferndale had informed him that with the Russian-American treaty on the threshold of signature, the Nightingale could be brought out, to a discreet but extremely generous welcome, from the coast of Rumania near Constanza, during the week of April 16–23. There were further details for the exact pickup. He was asked to consult with the Nightingale and confirm acceptance and agreement.

After receiving Maxim Rudin's personal message, President Matthews had remarked to David Lawrence:

"Since this is more than a mere arms-limitation agreement, I suppose it really can be called a treaty. And since it seems destined to be signed in Dublin, no doubt history will call it the Treaty of Dublin."

Lawrence had consulted with the government of the Republic of Ireland, whose officials had agreed with barely hidden delight that they would be pleased to host the formal signing ceremony between David Lawrence for the United States and Dmitri Rykov for the USSR in St. Patrick's Hall, Dublin Castle, on April 10.

On March 16, therefore, President Matthews replied to Maxim Rudin, agreeing to the proposed place and date.

There are two fairly large rock quarries in the mountains outside Ingolstadt in Bavaria. During the night of March 18, the night watchman in one of these was attacked and tied up by two masked men, at least one of them armed with a handgun, he later told police. The men, who seemed to know what they were looking for, broke into the dynamite store, using the night watchman's keys, and stole 250 kilograms of rock-blasting explosives and a number of electric detonators. Long before morning they were gone, and as the following day was Saturday the nineteenth, it was almost noon before the trussed night watchman was rescued and the theft discovered. Subsequent police investigations were intensive, and in view of the apparent knowledge of the layout of the quarry by the robbers, concentrated on the area of former employees. But the search was for extreme left-wingers, and the name Klimchuk, which belonged to a man who had been employed three years earlier at the quarry, attracted no particular attention, being assumed to be of Polish extraction. Actually it is a Ukrainian name. By that Saturday evening the two cars bearing the explosives had arrived back in Brussels, penetrating the German–Belgian border on the Aachen–Liège motorway. They were not stopped, weekend traffic being especially heavy.

By the evening of the twentieth the *Freya* was well past Senegal, having made good time from the Cape with the aid of the southeast trade winds and a helpful current. Though it was early in the year for Northern Europe, there were vacationers on the beaches of the Canary Islands.

The *Freya* was far to the west of the islands, but just after dawn on the twenty-first her bridge officers could make out the volcanic Pico de Monte Teide on Tenerife, their first landfall since they had glimpsed the rugged coastline of Cape Province. As the mountains of the Canaries dropped away, they knew that apart from the chance of seeing Madeira's summit they would next see the lights warning them to stay clear of the wild coasts of Mayo and Donegal.

Adam Munro had waited impatiently for a week to see the woman he loved, but there was no way he could get through to her before their prearranged meet on Monday the twenty-first. For the site he had returned to the Exhibition of Economic Achievements, whose 238 hectares of parks and grounds merged with the main Botanical Gardens of the

USSR Academy of Sciences. Here, in a sheltered arboretum in the open air, he found her waiting just before noon. Because of the chance of a casual glance from a passerby, he could not take the risk of kissing her as he wanted to.

Instead he told her with controlled excitement of the news from London. She was overjoyed.

"I have news for you," she told him. "There will be a Central Committee fraternal delegation to the Rumanian Party Congress during the first half of April, and I have been asked to accompany it. Sasha's school breaks for vacation on March twenty-ninth, and we will leave for Bucharest on April fifth. After ten days it will be perfectly normal for me to take a bored little boy to the resort beaches for a week."

"Then I'll fix it for the night of Monday, the eighteenth of April. That will give you several days in Constanza to find your way around. You must hire or borrow a car, and acquire a powerful torch. Now, Valentina my love, these are the details. Memorize them, for there can be no mistakes:

"North of Constanza lies the resort of Mamaia, where the western package tourists go. Drive north from Constanza through Mamaia on the evening of the eighteenth. Exactly six miles north of Mamaia a track leads right from the coast highway to the beach. On the headland at the junction you will see a short stone tower with its lower half painted white. It is a coast marker for fishermen. Leave the car well off the road and descend the bluff to the beach. At two A.M. you will see a light from the sea: three long dashes and three short ones. Take your own torch with its beam cut down by a tube of cardboard and point it straight at where the light came from. Flash back the reverse signal: three shorts and three longs. A speedboat will come out of the sea for you and Sasha. There will be one Russian-speaker and two Marines. Identify yourself with the phrase 'The Nightingale sings in Berkeley Square.' Have you got that?"

"Yes. Adam, where is Berkeley Square?"

"In London. It is very beautiful, like you. It has many trees."

"And do nightingales sing there?"

"According to the words of the song, one used to. Darling, it seems so short. Four weeks today. When we get to London I'll show you Berkeley Square."

"Adam, tell me something. Have I betrayed my own people—the Russian people?"

"No," he said with finality, "you have not. The leaders

nearly did. If you had not done what you did, Vishnayev and your uncle might have got their war. In it, Russia would have been destroyed, most of America, my country, and Western Europe. You have not betrayed the people of your country."

"But they would never understand, never forgive me," she said. There was a hint of tears in her dark eyes. "They will call me a traitor. I shall be an exile."

"One day, perhaps, this madness will end. One day, perhaps, you can come back. Listen, my love, we cannot stay longer. It's too risky. There is one last thing. I need your private phone number. No, I know we agreed that I would never ring. But I will not see you again until you are in the West in safety. If there should by any remote chance be a change of plan or date, I may have to contact you as a matter of emergency. If I do, I will pretend to be a friend called Gregor, explaining that I cannot attend your dinner party. If that happens, leave at once and meet me in the park of the Mojarsky Hotel at the top of Kutuzovsky Prospekt."

She nodded meekly and gave him her number. He kissed her on the cheek.

"I'll see you in London, my darling," he told her, and was gone through the trees. Privately he knew he would have to resign and take the icy anger of Sir Nigel Irvine when it became plain the Nightingale was not Anatoly Krivoi but a woman, and his wife-to-be. But by then it would be too late for even the service to do anything about it.

Ludwig Jahn stared at the two men who occupied the available chairs of his tidy bachelor flat in Wedding, the working-class district of West Berlin, with growing fear. They bore the stamp of men he had seen once, long before, and whom he had hoped never to see again.

The one who was talking was undoubtedly German; Jahn had no doubt about that. What he did not know was that the man was Major Gerhard Schulz, of the East German secret police, the dreaded Staatssicherheitsdienst, known simply as the SSD. He would never know the name, but he could guess the occupation.

He could also guess that the SSD had copious files on every East German who had ever quit to come to the West, and that was his problem. Thirty years earlier, as an eighteen-year-old, Jahn had taken part in the building workers' riots in East Berlin that had become the East German uprising.

He had been lucky. Although he had been picked up in one of the sweeps by the Russian police and their East German Communist acolytes, he had not been held. But he recalled the smell of the detention cells, and the stamp of the men who ruled them. His visitors this March 22, three decades later, bore the same stamp.

He had kept his head low for eight years after the 1953 riots; then in 1961, before the Wall was completed, he quietly walked into the West. For the past fifteen years he had had a good job with the West Berlin civil service, starting as a guard in the prison service and rising to Oberwachmeister, chief officer of Two Block, Tegel Jail.

The other man in his room that evening kept silent. Jahn would never know that he was a Soviet colonel named Kukushkin, present on behalf of the "Wet Affairs" department of the KGB.

Jahn stared in horror at the photographs the German eased from a large envelope and placed before him slowly, one by one. They showed his widowed mother in a cell, terrified, aged nearly eighty, staring at the camera obediently, hopeful of release. There were his two younger brothers, handcuffs on wrists, in different cells, the masonry of the walls showing up clearly in the high-definition prints.

"Then there are your sisters-in-law and your three delightful little nieces. Oh, yes, we know about the Christmas presents. What is it they call you? Uncle Ludo? How very charming. Tell me, have you ever seen places like these?"

There were more photographs—pictures that made the comfortably plump Jahn close his eyes for several seconds. Strange, zombielike figures, clad in rags, moved through the pictures, shaven, skull-like faces peering dully at the camera. They huddled; they shuffled; they wrapped their withered feet in rags to keep out the Arctic cold. They were stubbled, shriveled, subhuman. They were some of the inhabitants of the slave labor camps of the Kolyma complex, far away at the eastern end of Siberia, north of the Kamchatka Peninsula, where gold is mined deep in the Arctic Circle.

"Life sentences in these . . . resorts . . . are only for the worst enemies of the state, Herr Jahn. But my colleague here can ensure such life sentences for all your family—yes, even your dear old mother—with just one single telephone call. Now, tell me, do you want him to make that call?"

Jahn gazed across into the eyes of the man who had not spoken. The eyes were as bleak as the Kolyma camps.

"*Nein,*" he whispered. "No, please. What do you want?"

It was the German who answered.

"In Tegel Jail are two hijackers, Mishkin and Lazareff. Do you know them?"

Jahn nodded dumbly.

"Yes. They arrived four weeks ago. There was much publicity."

"Where, exactly, are they?"

"Number Two Block. Top floor, east wing. Solitary confinement, at their own request. They fear the other prisoners. Or so they say. There is no reason. For child rapists there is a reason, but not for these two. Yet they insist."

"But you can visit them, Herr Jahn? You have access?"

Jahn remained silent. He began to fear what the visitors wanted with the hijackers. They came from the East; the hijackers had escaped from there. It could not be to bring them birthday gifts.

"Have another look at the pictures, Jahn. Have a good look before you think of obstructing us."

"Yes, I can visit them. On my rounds. But only at night. During the day shift there are three guards in that corridor. One or two would always accompany me if I wished to visit them. But in the day shift there would be no reason for me to visit them. Only to check on them during the night shift."

"Are you on the night shift at the moment?"

"No. Day shift."

"What are the hours of the night shift?"

"Midnight to eight A.M. Lights are out at ten P.M. Shift changes at midnight. Relief is at eight A.M. During the night shift I would patrol the block three times, accompanied by the duty officer of each floor."

The unnamed German thought for a while.

"My friend here wishes to visit them. When do you return to the night shift?"

"Monday, April fourth," said Jahn.

"Very well," said the East German. "This is what you will do."

Jahn was instructed to acquire from the locker of a vacationing colleague the necessary uniform and pass card. At two A.M. on the morning of Monday, April 4, he would descend to the ground floor and admit the Russian by the staff entrance from the street. He would accompany him to the top floor and hide him in the staff dayroom, to which he would acquire a duplicate key. He would cause the night duty officer on the top floor to absent himself on an errand, and take over the watch from him while he was away. During the man's absence he would allow the Russian into the solitary-confinement corridor, lending him his passkey to both cells. When the Russian had "visited" Mishkin and Lazareff, the process would be reversed. The Russian would hide again until the duty officer returned to his post. Then Jahn would escort the Russian back to the staff entrance and let him out.

"It won't work," whispered Jahn, well aware that it probably would.

The Russian spoke at last, in German.

"It had better," he said. "If it does not, I will personally ensure that your entire family begins a regime in Kolyma that will make the 'extrastrict' regime operating there seem like the honeymoon suite at the Kempinski Hotel."

Jahn felt as if his bowels were being sprayed with liquid ice. None of the hard men in the "special wing" could compare with this man. He swallowed.

"I'll do it," he whispered.

"My friend will return here at six in the evening of Sunday, April third," said the East German. "No reception committees from the police, if you please. It will do no good. We both have diplomatic passes in false names. We will deny everything and walk away quite freely. Just have the uniform and pass card awaiting him."

Two minutes later they were gone. They took their photos with them. There was no evidence left. It did not matter. Jahn could see every detail in his nightmares.

By March 23 over two hundred fifty ships, the first wave of the waiting merchant fleet, were docked in the major grain ports from Lake Superior to the Gulf of Mexico. There was still ice in the St. Lawrence, but it was shattered to mosaic by the icebreakers, aware of its defeat as the grain ships moved through it to berth by the grain elevators.

A fair proportion of these ships were of the Russian Sovfracht fleet, but the next largest numbers were flying the U.S. flag, for one of the conditions of the sale had been that American carriers take the prime contracts to move the grain.

Within ten days they would begin moving east across the Atlantic, bound for Arkhangelsk and Murmansk in the Soviet Arctic, Leningrad at the head of the Gulf of Finland, and the warm-water ports of Odessa, Sevastopol, and Novorossisk on the Black Sea. Flags of ten other nations mingled with them to effect the biggest single dry-cargo movement since the Second World War. Elevators from Duluth to Houston spewed a golden tide of wheat, barley, oats, rye, and corn into their bellies, all destined within a month for the hungry millions of Russia.

On the twenty-sixth, Andrew Drake rose from his work at the kitchen table of an apartment in the suburbs of Brussels and pronounced that he was ready.

The explosives had been packed into ten fiber suitcases, the submachine guns rolled in towels and stuffed into haversacks. Azamat Krim kept the detonators bedded in cotton in a cigar box that never left him. When darkness fell, the cargo was carried in relays down to the group's secondhand, Belgian-registered panel van, and they set off for Blankenberge.

The little seaside resort facing the North Sea was quiet, the harbor virtually deserted, when they transferred their equipment under cover of darkness to the bilges of the fishing launch. It was a Saturday, and though a man walking his dog along the quay noticed them at work, he thought no more of it. Parties of sea anglers stocking up for a weekend's fishing were common enough, even though it was a mite early in the year and still chilly.

On Sunday the twenty-seventh, Miroslav Kaminsky bade them good-bye, took the van, and drove back to Brussels. His job was to clean the Brussels flat from top to bottom and end to end, to abandon it, and to drive the van to a prearranged rendezvous in the polders of Holland. There he would leave it, with its ignition key in an agreed place, then take the ferry from the Hook back to Harwich and London. He had his itinerary well rehearsed and was confident he could carry out his part of the plan.

The remaining seven men left port and cruised sedately up the coast to lose themselves in the islands of Walcheren and North Beveland, just across the border with Holland. There, with their fishing rods much in evidence, they hove to and waited. On a powerful radio down in the cabin, Andrew Drake sat hunched, listening to the wavelength of Maas Estuary Control and the endless calls of the ships heading into or out of the Europoort and Rotterdam.

"Colonel Kukushkin is going into Tegel Jail to do the job early in the morning of April fourth," Vassili Petrov told Maxim Rudin in the Kremlin that same Sunday morning. "There is a senior guard who will let him in, bring him to the cells of Mishkin and Lazareff, and let him out of the jail by the staff doorway when it is over."

"The guard is reliable? One of our people?" asked Rudin.

"No, but he has family in East Germany. He has been persuaded to do as he is told. Kukushkin reports that he will not contact the police. He is too frightened."

"Then he knows already whom he is working for. Which means he knows too much."

"Kukushkin will silence him also, just as he steps out of the doorway. There will be no trace," said Petrov.

"Eight days," grunted Rudin. "He had better get it right."

"He will," said Petrov. "He, too, has a family. By a week from tomorrow Mishkin and Lazareff will be dead, and their secret with them. Those who helped them will keep silent to save their own lives. Even if they talk, it will be disbelieved. Mere hysterical allegations. No one will believe them."

When the sun rose on the morning of the twenty-ninth, its first rays picked up the mass of the *Freya* twenty miles west of Ireland, cutting north by northeast through the eleven-degree longitude on a course to skirt the Outer Hebrides.

Her powerful radar scanners had picked up the fishing fleet in the darkness an hour before, and her officer of the watch noted them carefully. The nearest to her was well to the east, or landward side, of the tanker.

The sun glittered over the rocks of Donegal, a thin line on the eastward horizon to the men on the bridge with their advantage of eighty feet of altitude. It caught the small fishing smacks of the men from Killybegs, drifting out in the western seas for mackerel, herring, and whiting. And it caught the bulk of the *Freya* herself, like a moving landmass, steaming out of the south past the drifters and their gently bobbing nets.

Christy O'Byrne was in the tiny wheelhouse of the smack he and his brother owned, the *Bernadette*. He blinked several times, put down his cocoa mug, and stepped the three feet from the wheelhouse to the rail. His vessel was the nearest to the passing tanker.

From behind him, when they saw the *Freya*, the fishermen

tugged on the horn lanyards, and a chorus of thin whoops disturbed the dawn. On the bridge of the *Freya,* Thor Larsen nodded to his junior officer; seconds later the bellowing bull roar of the *Freya* answered the Killybegs fleet.

Christy O'Byrne leaned on the rail and watched the *Freya* fill the horizon, heard the throb of her power beneath the sea, and felt the *Bernadette* begin to roll in the widening wake of the tanker.

"Holy Mary," he whispered, "would you look at the size of her."

On the eastern shore of Ireland, compatriots of Christy O'Byrne were at work that morning in Dublin Castle, for seven hundred years the seat of power of the British. As a tiny boy perched on his father's shoulder, Martin Donahue had watched from outside as the last British troops marched out of the castle forever, following the signing of a peace treaty. Sixty-one years later, on the verge of retirement from government service, he was a cleaner, pushing a Hoover back and forth over the electric-blue carpet of St. Patrick's Hall.

He had not been present when any of Ireland's successive presidents had been inaugurated beneath Vincent Waldré's magnificent 1778 painted ceiling, nor would he be present in twelve days when two superpowers signed the Treaty of Dublin below the motionless heraldic banners of the long-gone Knights of St. Patrick. For forty years he had just kept it dusted for them.

Rotterdan, too, was preparing, but for a different ceremony. Harry Wennerstrom arrived on the thirtieth and installed himself in the best suite at the Hilton Hotel.

He had come by his private executive jet, now parked at Schiedam municipal airport just outside the city. Throughout the day four secretaries fussed around him, preparing for the Scandinavian and Dutch dignitaries, the tycoons from the worlds of oil and shipping, and the scores of press people who would attend his reception on the evening of April 1 for Captain Thor Larsen and his officers.

A select party of notables and members of the press would be his guests on the flat roof of the modern Maas Control building, situated on the very tip of the sandy shore at the Hook of Holland. Well protected against the stiff spring breeze, they would watch from the north shore of the Maas Estuary as the six tugs pulled and pushed the *Freya* those last few kilometers from the estuary into the Caland Kanaal, from there to the Beer Kanaal, and finally to rest by Clint Blake's new oil refinery in the heart of the Europoort.

While the *Freya* closed down her systems during the afternoon, the group would come back by cavalcade of limousines to central Rotterdam, forty kilometers up the river, for an evening reception. A press conference would precede this, during which Wennerstrom would present Thor Larsen to the world's press.

Already, he knew, newspapers and television had leased helicopters to give the last few miles of the *Freya* and her berthing complete camera coverage.

Harry Wennerstrom was a contented old man.

By the early hours of March 30 the *Freya* was well through the channel between the Orkneys and the Shetlands. She had turned south, heading down the North Sea. As soon as she entered the crowded lanes of the North Sea, the *Freya* had reported in, contacting the first of the shore-based area traffic-control officers at Wick on the coast of Caithness in the far north of Scotland.

Because of her size and draft, she was a "hampered vessel." She had reduced speed to ten knots and was following the instructions fed to her from Wick by VHF radiotelephone. All around her, unseen, the various control centers had her marked on their high-definition radars, manned by qualified pilot operators. These centers are equipped with computerized support systems capable of rapid assimilation of weather, tide, and traffic-density information.

Ahead of the *Freya* as she crawled down the southbound traffic lane, smaller ships were crisply informed to get out of her way. At midnight she passed Flamborough Head on the coast of Yorkshire, now moving farther east, away from the British coast and toward Holland. Throughout her passage she had followed the deepwater channel, a minimum of twenty fathoms. On her bridge, despite the constant instructions from ashore, her officers watched the echo-sounder readings, observing the banks and sandbars that make up the floor of the North Sea slide past on either side of her.

Just before sundown of March 31, at a point exactly fifteen sea miles due east of the Outer Gabbard Light, now down to her bare steerage speed of five knots, the giant swung gently eastward and moved to her overnight position, the deep-draft anchorage located at fifty-two degrees north. She was twenty-seven sea miles due west of the Maas Estuary, twenty-seven miles from home and glory.

It was midnight in Moscow. Adam Munro had decided to walk home from the diplomatic reception at the embassy. He had been driven there by the commercial counselor, so his own car was parked by his flat off Kutuzovsky Prospekt.

Halfway over the Serafimov Bridge, he paused to gaze down at the Moscow River. To his right he could see the illuminated cream-and-white stucco facade of the embassy; to his left the dark red walls of the Kremlin loomed above him, and above them the upper floor and dome of the Great Kremlin Palace.

It had been roughly ten months since he had flown from London to take up his new appointment. In that time he had pulled off the greatest espionage coup for decades, running the only spy the West had ever operated inside the heart of the Kremlin. They would savage him for breaking training, for not telling them all along who she was, but they could not diminish the value of what he had brought out.

Three weeks more and she would be out of this place, safe in London. He would be out, too, resigning from the service to start a new life somewhere else with the only person in the world he loved, ever had loved, or ever would.

He would be glad to leave Moscow, with its secrecy, its endless furtiveness, its mind-numbing drabness. In ten days the Americans would have their arms-reduction treaty, the Kremlin its grain and technology, the service its thanks and gratitude from Downing Street and the White House alike. A week more and he would have his wife-to-be, and she her freedom. He shrugged deeper into his thick, fur-collared coat and walked on across the bridge.

Midnight in Moscow is ten P.M. in the North Sea. By 2200 hours the *Freya* was motionless at last. She had steamed 7,085 miles from Chita to Abu Dhabi and a further 12,015 miles from there to where she now lay. She lay motionless along the line of the tide; from her stem a single anchor chain streamed out and down to the seabed, with five shackles on deck. Each link of the chain needed to hold her was nearly a yard long, and the steel thicker than a man's thigh.

Because of her "hampered" state, Captain Larsen had brought her down from the Orkneys himself, with two navigating officers to assist him, as well as the helmsman. Even at the overnight anchorage he left his first officer, Stig Lundquist, his third mate, Tom Keller (a Danish-American), and an able seaman on the bridge through the night. The officers would maintain constant anchor watch; the seaman would carry out periodic deck inspection.

Though the *Freya*'s engines were closed down, her turbines and generators hummed rhythmically, churning out the power to keep her systems functioning.

Among these were constant input of tide and weather, of which the latest reports were heartening.

He could have had March gales; instead, an unseasonal area of high pressure almost stationary over the North Sea and the English Channel had brought a mild early spring to the coasts. The sea was almost a flat calm; a one-knot tide ran northeastward from the vessel toward the West Frisians. The sky had been a near-cloudless blue all day, and despite a touch of frost that night, bade fair to be so again on the morrow.

Bidding his officers goodnight, Captain Larsen left the bridge and descended one floor to D deck. Here, on the extreme starboard side, he had his suite. The spacious and well-appointed day cabin carried four windows looking forward down the length of the vessel, and two looking out to starboard. Aft of the day cabin were his bedroom and bathroom. The sleeping cabin also had two windows, both to starboard. All the windows were sealed, save one in the day cabin that was closed but with screw bolts that could be manually undone.

Outside his sealed windows to forward, the facade of the superstructure fell sheer to the deck; to starboard the windows gave onto ten feet of steel landing, beyond which was the starboard rail, and beyond it the sea. Five flights of steel ladders ran from the lowest A deck up five floors to the bridge-wing above his head, each stage of the ladders debouching onto a steel landing. All these sets of ladders and landings were open to the sky, exposed to the elements. They were seldom used, for the interior stairwells were heated and warm.

Thor Larsen lifted the napkin off the plate of chicken and

salad the chief steward had left him, looked longingly at the bottle of Scotch in his liquor cabinet, and settled for coffee from the percolator. After eating he decided to work the night away on a final run-through of the channel charts for the morning's berthing. It was going to be tight, and he wanted to know that channel as well as the two Dutch pilots who would arrive by helicopter from Amsterdam's Schiphol Airport at seven-thirty to take her over. Prior to that, he knew, a gang of ten men from ashore, the extra hands, called "riggers," who were needed for the berthing operation, would arrive by launch at 0700.

As midnight struck, he settled at the broad table in his day cabin, spread his charts, and began to study.

At ten minutes before three in the morning, it was frosty but clear outside. A half-moon caused the rippling sea to glitter. Inside the bridge Stig Lundquist and Tom Keller shared a companionable mug of coffee. The able seaman prowled the flowing screens along the bridge console.

"Sir," he called, "there's a launch approaching."

Tom Keller rose and crossed to where the seaman pointed at the radar screen. There were a score of blips—some stationary, some moving, but all well away from the *Freya*. One tiny blip seemed to be approaching from the southeast.

"Probably a fishing boat making sure of being ready on the fishing grounds by sunrise," said Keller.

Lundquist was looking over his shoulder. He flicked to a lower range.

"She's coming very close," he said.

Out at sea, the launch had to be aware of the mass of the *Freya*. The tanker carried anchor lights above the fo'c'sle and at the stern. Besides, her deck was floodlit and her superstructure was lit like a Christmas tree by the lights in the accommodation. The launch, instead of veering away, began to curve in toward the stern of the *Freya*.

"She looks as if she's going to come alongside," said Keller.

"She can't be the berthing crew," said Lundquist. "They're not due till seven."

"Perhaps they couldn't sleep, wanted to be well on time," said Keller.

"Go down to the head of the ladder," Lundquist told the

seaman, "and tell me what you see. Put on the headset when you get there, and stay in touch."

The accommodation ladder on the ship was amidships. On a big vessel it is so heavy that steel cables powered by an electric motor either lower it from the ship's rail to the sea level or raise it to lie parallel to the rail. On the *Freya,* even full-laden, the rail was nine meters above the sea, an impossible jump, and the ladder was fully raised.

Seconds later the two officers saw the seaman leave the superstructure below them and begin to stroll down the deck. When he reached the ladder head, he mounted a small platform that jutted over the sea, and looked down. As he did so, he took a headset from a weatherproof box and fitted the earphones over his head. From the bridge Lundquist pressed a switch and a powerful light came on, illuminating the seaman far away along the deck as he peered down to the black sea. The launch had vanished from the radar screen; she was too close to be observed.

"What do you see?" asked Lundquist into a stick microphone.

The seaman's voice came back into the bridge. "Nothing, sir."

Meanwhile the launch had passed around the rear of the *Freya,* under the very overhang of her stern. For seconds it was out of sight. At either side of the stern, the guardrail of A deck was at its nearest point to the sea, just six meters above the water. The two men standing on the cabin roof of the launch had reduced this to three meters. As the launch emerged from the transom shadow, both men slung the three-point grapnels they held, the hooks sheathed in black rubber hose.

Each grapnel, trailing rope, rose twelve feet, dropped over the guardrail, and caught fast. As the launch moved on, both men were swept off the cabin roof to hang by the ropes, ankles in the sea. Then each began to climb rapidly, hand over hand, unheeding of the submachine carbines strapped to their backs. In two seconds the launch emerged into the light and began to run down the side of the *Freya* toward the courtesy ladder.

"I can see it now," said the seaman high above. "It looks like a fishing launch."

"Keep the ladder up until they identify themselves," ordered Lundquist from the bridge.

Far behind and below him the two boarders were over the

rail. Each unhooked his grapnel and heaved it into the sea, where it sank, trailing rope. The two men set off at a fast lope, around to the starboard side and straight for the steel ladders. On soundless rubber-soled shoes they began to race upward.

The launch came to rest beneath the ladder, eight meters above the cramped cabin. Inside, four men crouched. At the wheel, the helmsman stared silently up at the seaman above him.

"Who are you?" called the seaman. "Identify yourself."

There was no answer. Far below, in the glare of the spotlight, the man in the black woolen helmet just stared back.

"He won't answer," said the seaman into his mouthpiece.

"Keep the spotlight on them," ordered Lundquist. "I'm coming to have a look."

Throughout the interchange the attention of both Lundquist and Keller had been to the port side and forward of the bridge. On the starboard side the door leading from the bridgewing into the bridge suddenly opened, bringing a gust of icy air. Both officers spun around. The door closed. Facing them were two men in black balaclava helmets, black crewneck sweaters, black track-suit trousers, and rubber deck shoes. Each pointed a submachine carbine at the officers.

"Order your seaman to lower the ladder," said one in English. The two officers stared at them unbelievingly. This was impossible. The gunman raised his weapon and squinted down the sight at Keller.

"I'll give you three seconds," he said to Lundquist. "Then I'm blowing the head off your colleague."

Brick-red with anger, Lundquist leaned to the stick mike.

"Lower the ladder," he told the seaman.

The disembodied voice came back into the bridge. "But sir . . ."

"It's all right, lad," said Lundquist. "Do as I say."

With a shrug the seaman pressed a button on the small console at the ladder head. There was a hum of motors and the ladder slowly lowered to the sea. Two minutes later four other men, all in black, were herding the seaman back along the deck to the superstructure while the fifth man made the launch fast. Two more minutes and the six of them entered the bridge from the port side, the seaman's eyes wide with fright. When he entered the bridge he saw the other two gunmen holding his officers.

"How on earth . . . ?" asked the seaman.

"Take it easy," ordered Lundquist. To the only gunman who had spoken so far, he asked in English, "What do you want?"

"We want to speak to your captain," said the man behind the mask. "Where is he?"

The door from the wheelhouse to the inner stairwell opened, and Thor Larsen stepped onto the bridge. His gaze took in his three crewmen with their hands behind their heads, and seven black-clad terrorists. His eyes, when he turned to the man who had asked the question, were blue and friendly as a cracking glacier.

"I am Captain Thor Larsen, master of the *Freya,*" he said slowly, "and who the hell are you?"

"Never mind who we are," said the terrorist leader. "We have just taken over your ship. Unless your officers and men do as they are told, we shall start by making an example of your seaman. Which is it to be?"

Larsen looked slowly around him. Three of the submachine guns were pointing straight at the eighteen-year-old deckhand. He was white as chalk.

"Mr. Lundquist," said Larsen formally, "do as these men say." Turning back to the leader he asked, "What exactly is it you want with the *Freya?*"

"That is easy," said the terrorist without hesitation. "We wish you no harm personally, but unless our requirements are carried out—to the letter—we shall not hesitate to do what we have to in order to secure compliance."

"And then?" asked Larsen.

"Within thirty hours the West German government is going to release two of our friends from a West Berlin jail and fly them to safety. If they do not, I am going to blast you, your crew, your ship, and one million tons of crude oil all over the North Sea."

CHAPTER ELEVEN

0300 to 0900

THE LEADER of the seven masked terrorists set his men to work with a methodical precision that he had evidently rehearsed over many hours in his own mind. He issued a rapid stream of orders in a language neither Captain Larsen nor his own officers and the young seaman could understand.

Five of the masked men herded the two officers and seaman to the rear of the bridge, well away from the instrument panels, and surrounded them. The leader jerked his handgun at Captain Larsen and said in English:

"Your cabin, if you please, Captain."

In single file, Larsen leading, the leader of the terrorists next, and one of his henchmen with a submachine carbine bringing up the rear, the three men descended the stairs from the bridge to D deck, one flight below. Halfway down the stairs, at the turn, Larsen turned to look back and up at his two captors, measuring the distances, calculating whether he could overcome them both.

"Don't even try it," said the voice behind the mask at his shoulder. "No one in his right mind argues with a submachine gun at a range of ten feet."

Larsen led them onward down the stairs. D deck was the senior officers' living quarters. The captain's suite was in the extreme starboard corner of the great sweep of superstructure. Moving to port, next came a small chart library, the door open to reveal locker after locker of high-quality sea charts, enough to take him into any ocean, any bay, any suitable anchorage in the world. They were all copies of originals made by the British Admiralty, and the best in the world.

Next was the conference suite, a spacious cabin where the captain or owner could, if he wished, receive a sizable number of visitors all at one time. Next to this were the owner's staterooms, closed and empty, reserved for the chairman, should he ever wish to sail with his ship. At the port end was another suite of cabins identical but in reverse to the captain's quarters. Here the chief engineer lived.

Aft of the captain's cabins was the smaller suite for the first officer, and aft of the chief engineer dwelt the chief steward. The whole complex formed a hollow square, whose center was taken up by the flight of stairs going around and around and downward to A deck, three levels below.

Thor Larsen led his captors to his own cabin and stepped into the dayroom. The terrorist leader followed him in and quickly ran through the other rooms, bedroom and bathroom. There was no one else present.

"Sit down, Captain," he said, the voice slightly muffled by the mask. "You will remain here until I return. Please do not move. Place your hands on the table and keep them there, palms downward."

There was another stream of orders in a foreign language, and the machine gunner took up a position with his back to the far bulkhead of the cabin, facing Thor Larsen but twelve feet away, the barrel of his gun pointing straight at the white crew-neck sweater Thor Larsen wore. The leader checked to see that all the curtains were well drawn, then left, closing the door behind him. The other two inhabitants of the deck were asleep in their respective cabins and heard nothing. Within minutes the leader was back on the bridge.

"You"—he pointed his gun at the boyish seaman—"come with me."

The lad looked imploringly at First Officer Stig Lundquist.

"You harm that boy and I'll personally hang you out to dry," said Tom Keller in his American accent. Two submachine-gun barrels moved slightly in the hands of the ring of men around him.

"Your chivalry is admirable, your sense of reality deplorable," said the voice behind the leader's mask. "No one gets hurt unless you try something stupid. Then there'll be a bloodbath, and you'll be right under the taps."

Lundquist nodded to the seaman.

"Go with him," he said. "Do what he wants."

The seaman was escorted back down the stairs. At the D deck level, the terrorist stopped him.

"Apart from the captain, who lives on this deck?" he asked.

"The chief engineer, over there," said the seaman. "The

first officer, over there, but he's up on the bridge now. And the chief steward, there."

There was no sign of life behind any of the doors.

"The paint locker, where is it?" asked the terrorist. Without a word the seaman turned and headed down the stairs. They went through C deck and B deck. Once a murmur of voices came to them, from behind the door of the seamen's mess-room, where four men who could not sleep were apparently playing cards over coffee.

At A deck they had reached the level of the base of the superstructure. The seaman opened an exterior door and stepped outside. The terrorist followed him. The cold night air made them both shiver after the warmth of the interior. They found themselves aft of the superstructure on the poop. To one side of the door from which they emerged, the bulk of the funnel towered a hundred feet up toward the stars.

The seaman led the way across the poop to where a small steel structure stood. It was six feet by six and about the same in height. In one side of it there was a steel door, closed by two great screw bolts with butterfly nuts on the outside.

"Down there," said the seaman.

"Go on down," said the terrorist. The boy spun the twin butterfly handles, unscrewing the cleats, and pulled them back. Seizing the door handle, he swung it open. There was a light inside, showing a tiny platform and a steel stairway running down to the bowels of the *Freya.* At a jerk from the gun, the seaman stepped inside and began to head downward, the terrorist behind him.

Over seventy feet of the stairs led down, past several galleries from which steel doors led off. When they reached the bottom they were well below waterline, only the keel beneath the deck plating under their feet. They were in an enclosure with four steel doors. The terrorist nodded to the one facing aft.

"What's that lead to?"

"Steering-gear housing."

"Let's have a look."

When the door was open, it showed a great vaulted hall all in metal and painted pale green. It was well lit. Most of the center of the deck space was taken up by a mountain of encased machinery, the device which, receiving its orders from the computers of the bridge, would move the rudder. The walls of the cavity were curved to the nethermost part of the ship's hull. Aft of the chamber, beyond the steel, the great rudder of the *Freya* would be hanging inert in the black waters of the North Sea. The terrorist ordered the door closed again and bolted shut.

Port and starboard of the steering-gear chamber were, respectively, a chemical store and a paint store. The chemical store the terrorist ignored; he was not going to make men prisoners where there was acid to play with. The paint store was better. It was quite large, airy, well ventilated, and its outer wall was the hull of the ship.

"What's the fourth door?" asked the terrorist. The fourth was the only door with no handles.

"It leads to the rear of the engine room," said the seaman. "It is bolted on the other side."

The terrorist pushed against the steel door. It was rock-solid. He seemed satisfied.

"How many men on this ship?" he asked. "Or women. No tricks. If there is one more than the figure you give, we'll shoot them."

The boy ran his tongue over dry lips.

"There are no women," he said. "There might be wives next trip, but not on the maiden voyage. There are thirty men, including Captain Larsen."

Knowing what he needed to know, the terrorist pushed the frightened young man into the paint locker, swung the door closed, and threw one of the twin bolts into its socket. Then he returned back up the ladder.

Emerging on the poop deck, he avoided the interior stairs and raced back up the outside ladders to the bridge, stepping in from outside where they reached the bridgewing.

He nodded to his five companions, who still held the two officers at gunpoint, and issued a stream of further orders. Minutes later the two bridge officers, joined by the chief steward and chief engineer, roused from their beds on D deck below the bridge, were marched down to the paint locker. Most of the crew were asleep on B deck, where the bulk of the cabins were situated, much smaller than the officers' accommodations above their heads, on C and D.

There were protests, exclamations, bitter language, as they were herded out and down. But at every stage the leader of the terrorists, the only one who spoke at all, informed them in English that their captain was held in his own cabin and would die in the event of any resistance. The officers and men obeyed their orders.

Down in the paint locker the crew was finally counted:

twenty-nine. The first cook and two of the four stewards were allowed to return to the galley on A deck and ferry down to the paint store trays of buns and rolls, along with crates of bottled lemonade and canned beer. Two buckets were provided for toilets.

"Make yourselves comfortable," the terrorist leader told the twenty-nine angry men who stared back at him from inside the paint locker. "You won't be here long. Thirty hours at most. One last thing. Your captain wants the pumpman. Who is he?"

A Swede called Martinsson stepped forward.

"I'm the pumpman," he said.

"Come with me." It was four-thirty.

A deck, the ground floor of the superstructure, was entirely devoted to the rooms containing the services of the marine giant. Located there were the main galley, deepfreeze chamber, cool room, other assorted food stores, liquor store, soiled-linen store, automatic laundry, cargo-control room, including the inert-gas cntrol, and the firefighting-control room, also called the foam room.

Above it was B deck, with all nonofficer accommodations, cinema, library, four recreation rooms, and three bars.

C deck held the officer cabins apart from the four on the level above, plus the officers' dining salon and smoking room, and the crew's club, with swimming pool, sauna, and gymnasium.

It was the cargo-control room on A deck that interested the terrorist, and he ordered the pumpman to bring him to it. There were no windows; it was centrally heated, air-conditioned, silent, and well lit. Behind his mask the eyes of the terrorist chief flickered over the banks of switches and settled on the rear bulkhead. Here behind the control console where the pumpman now sat, a visual display board, nine feet wide and four feet tall, occupied the wall. It showed in map form the crude-tank layout of the *Freya*'s cargo capacity.

"If you try to trick me," he told the pumpman, "it may cost me the life of one of my men, but I shall surely find out. If I do, I shall not shoot you, my friend, I shall shoot your Captain Larsen. Now, point out to me where the ballast holds are, and where the cargo holds."

Martinsson was not going to argue, with his captain's life at stake. He was in his mid-twenties, and Thor Larsen was a generation older. He had sailed with Larsen twice before, including his first-ever voyage as pumpman, and like all the crew he had enormous respect and liking for the towering Norwegian, who had a reputation for unflagging consideration for his crew and for being the best mariner in the Nordia fleet. He pointed at the diagram in front of him.

The sixty holds were laid out in sets of three across the beam of the *Freya*; twenty such sets.

"Up here in the forepart," said Martinsson, "the port and starboard tanks are full of crude. The center is the slop tank, empty now, like a buoyancy tank, because we are on our maiden voyage and have not discharged cargo yet. So there has been no need to scour the cargo tanks and pump the slops in here. One row back, all three are ballast tanks. They were full of seawater from Japan to the Gulf; now they are full of air."

"Open the valves," said the terrorist, "between all three ballast tanks and the slop tank." Martinsson hesitated. "Go on, do it."

Martinsson pressed three square plastic controls on the console in front of him. There was a low humming from behind the console. A quarter of a mile in front of them, down below the steel deck, great valves the size of normal garage doors swung open, forming a single, linked unit out of the four tanks, each capable of holding twenty thousand tons of liquid. Not only air but any liquid now entering one of the tanks would flow freely to the other three.

"Where are the next ballast tanks?" asked the terrorist. With his forefinger Martinsson pointed halfway down the ship.

"Here, amidships, there are three in a row, side by side," he said.

"Leave them alone," said the terrorist. "Where are the others?"

"There are nine ballast tanks in all," said Martinsson. "The last three are here, side by side as usual, right up close to the superstructure."

"Open the valves so they communicate with each other."

Martinsson did as he was bid.

"Good," said the terrorist. "Now, can the ballast tanks be linked straight through to the cargo tanks?"

"No," said Martinsson, "it's not possible. The ballast tanks are permanent for ballast—that is, seawater or air—but never oil. The cargo tanks are the reverse. The two systems do not interconnect."

"Fine," said the masked man. "We can change all that. One

last thing. Open all the valves between all the cargo tanks, laterally and longitudinally, so that all fifty communicate with each other."

It took fifteen seconds for all the necessary control buttons to be pushed. Far down in the treacly blackness of the crude oil, scores of gigantic valves swung open, forming one enormous, single tank containing a million tons of crude. Martinsson stared at his handiwork in horror.

"If she sinks with one tank ruptured," he whispered, "the whole million tons will flow out."

"Then the authorities had better make sure she doesn't sink," said the terrorist. "Where is the master power source from this control panel to the hydraulic pumps that control the valves?"

Martinsson gestured to an electrical junction box on the wall near the ceiling. The terrorist reached up, opened the box, and pulled the contact breaker downward. With the box dead, he removed the ten fuses and pocketed them. The pumpman looked on with fear in his eyes. The valve-opening process had become irreversible. There were spare fuses, and he knew where they were stored. But he would be in the paint locker. No stranger entering his sanctum could find them in time to close those vital valves.

Bengt Martinsson knew, because it was his job to know, that a tanker cannot simply be loaded or unloaded haphazardly. If all the starboard cargo tanks are filled on their own, with the others left empty, the ship will roll over and sink. If the port tanks are filled alone, she will roll the other way. If the forward tanks are filled but not balanced at the stern, she will dive by the nose, her stern high in the air; and the reverse if the stern half is full of liquid and the for'ard empty.

But if the stem and stern ballast tanks are allowed to flood with water while the center section is buoyant with air, she will arch like an acrobat doing a backspring. Tankers are not designed for such strains; the *Freya*'s massive spine would break at the midsection.

"One last thing," said the terrorist. "What would happen if we opened all the fifty inspection hatches to the cargo tanks?"

Martinsson was tempted, sorely tempted, to let them try it. He thought of Captain Larsen sitting high above him, facing a submachine carbine. He swallowed.

"You'd die," he said, "unless you had breathing apparatus."

He explained to the masked man beside him that when a tanker's holds are full, the liquid crude is never quite up to the ceilings of the holds. In the gap between the slopping surface of the oil and the ceiling of the hold, gases form, given off by the crude oil. They are volatile gases, highly explosive. If they were not bled off, they would turn the ship into a bomb.

Years earlier, the system for bleeding them off was by way of gas lines fitted with pressure valves so that the gases could escape to the atmosphere above deck, where, being very light, they would go straight upward. More recently, a far safer system had been devised: inert gases from the main engine exhaust flue were fed into the holds to expel oxygen and seal the surface of the crude oil; carbon monoxide was the principal constituent of these inert gases.

Because the inert gases created a completely oxygen-free atmosphere, fire or spark, which requires oxygen, was banished. But every tank had a one-meter circular inspection hatch let into the main deck; if a hatch were opened by an incautious visitor, he would immediately be enveloped in a carpet of inert gas reaching to above his head. He would die choking, asphyxiated in an atmosphere containing no oxygen.

"Thank you," said the terrorist. "Who handles the breathing apparatus?"

"The first officer is in charge of it," said Martinsson. "But we are all trained to use it."

Two minutes later he was back in the paint store with the rest of the crew. It was five o'clock.

While the leader of the masked men had been in the cargo-control room with Martinsson, and another held Thor Larsen prisoner in his own cabin, the remaining five had unloaded their launch. The ten suitcases of explosive stood on the deck amidships at the top of the courtesy ladder, awaiting the leader's instructions for placing. These orders he gave with crisp precision. Far away on the foredeck the inspection hatches of the port and starboard ballast tanks were unscrewed and removed, revealing the single steel ladder descending eighty feet into the black depths of musty air.

Azamat Krim took off his mask, stuffed it in his pocket, took his flashlight, and descended into the first. Two suitcases were lowered after him on long cords. Working in the base of the hold by lamplight, he placed one entire suitcase against the outer hull of the *Freya* and lashed it to one of the vertical ribs with cord. He opened the other case and extracted its contents in two halves. One half went against the forward bulkhead, beyond which lay twenty thousand tons of oil; the other half went against the aft bulkhead, behind which was another twenty thousand tons of crude. Sandbags, also brought from the launch, were packed around the charges to concentrate the blast. When he was satisfied that the detonators were in place and linked to the triggering device, he came back to the starlight on deck.

The same process was repeated on the other side of the *Freya,* and then twice again in the port and starboard ballast tanks close up to the superstructure. He had used eight of his suitcases in four ballast holds. The ninth he placed in the center ballast tank amidships, not to blast a hole for the waiting sea, but to help crack the spine.

The tenth was brought down to the engine room. Here in the curvature of the *Freya*'s hull, close up against the bulkhead to the paint locker, strong enough to break both open simultaneously, it was laid and primed. If it went off, those men in the paint locker a half-inch of steel away who survived the blast would drown when the sea, under immense pressure at eighty feet below the waves, came pounding through. It was six-fifteen and dawn was breaking over the *Freya*'s silent decks when he reported to Andrew Drake.

"The charges are laid and primed, Andriy," he said. "I pray to God we never set them off."

"We won't have to," said Drake. "But I have to convince Captain Larsen. Only when he has seen and believed, will he convince the authorities. Then they'll have to do as we want. They'll have no alternative."

Two of the crew were brought from the paint locker, made to don protective clothing, face masks, and oxygen bottles, and proceed down the deck from the fo'c'sle to the housing, opening every one of the fifty inspection hatches to the oil-cargo tanks. When the job was done, the men were returned to the paint locker. The steel door was closed and the two bolts screwed shut on the outside, not to be opened again until two prisoners were safe in Israel.

At six-thirty, Andrew Drake, still masked, returned to the captain's day cabin. Wearily he sat down, facing Thor Larsen, and told him from start to finish what had been done. The Norwegian stared back at him impassively, held in check by the submachine gun pointing at him from the corner of the room.

When he had finished, Drake held up a black plastic instrument and showed it to Larsen. It was no larger than two king-size cigarette packs bound together; there was a single red button on the face of it, and a four-inch steel aerial sticking from the top.

"Do you know what this is, Captain?" asked the masked Drake. Larsen shrugged. He knew enough about radio to recognize a small transistorized transmitter.

"It's an oscillator," said Drake. "If that red button is pressed, it will emit a single VHF note, rising steadily in tone and pitch to a scream that our ears could not begin to listen to. But attached to every single charge on this ship is a receiver that can and will listen. As the tonal pitch rises, a dial on the receivers will show the pitch, the needles moving around the dials until they can go no further. When that happens, the devices will blow their fuses and a current will be cut. The cutting of that current in each receiver will convey its message to the detonators, which will then operate. You know what that would mean?"

Thor Larsen stared back at the masked face across the table from him. His ship, his beloved *Freya*, was being raped, and there was nothing he could do about it. His crew was crowded into a steel coffin inches away through a steel bulkhead from a charge that would crush them all, and cover them in seconds with freezing seawater.

His mind's eye conjured a picture of hell. If the charges blew, great holes would be torn in the port and starboard sides of four of his ballast tanks. Roaring mountains of sea would rush in, filling both the outer and the center ballast tanks in minutes. Being heavier than the crude oil, the seawater would have the greater pressure; it would push through the other gaping holes inside the tanks to the neighboring cargo holds, spewing the crude oil upward through the inspection hatches, so that six more holds would fill with water. This would happen right up in the forepeak, and right aft, beneath his feet. In minutes the engine room would be flooded with tens of thousands of tons of green water. The stern and the bow would drop at least ten feet, but the buoyant midsection would ride high, its ballast tanks untouched. The *Freya*, most beautiful of all the Norse goddesses, would arch her back once, in pain, and split in two. Both sections would drop straight, without rolling, twenty-five feet to the seabed beneath, to sit there with fifty inspection hatches open and facing upward. A million tons of crude would gurgle out to the surface of the North Sea.

It might take an hour for the mighty goddess to sink completely, but the process would be irreversible. In such shallow water, part of her bridge might still be above the tide, but she could never be refloated. It might take three days for the last of her cargo to reach the surface, but no diver could work among fifty columns of vertically rising crude oil. No one would close the hatches again. The escape of the oil, like the destruction of his ship, would be irreversible.

He stared back at the masked face but made no reply. There was a deep, seething anger inside him, growing with each passing minute, but he gave no sign of it.

"What do you want?" he growled. The terrorist glanced at the digital display clock on the wall. It read a quarter to seven.

"We're going to the radio room," he said. "We talk to Rotterdam. Or rather, you talk to Rotterdam."

Twenty-seven miles to the east, the rising sun had dimmed the great yellow flames that spout day and night from the oil refineries of the Europoort. Through the night, from the bridge of the *Freya*, it had been possible to see these flames in the dark sky above Chevron, Shell, British Petroleum, and even, far beyond them, the cool blue glow of Rotterdam's streetlighting.

The refineries and the labyrinthine complexity of the Europoort, the greatest oil terminal in the world, lie on the south shore of the Maas Estuary. On the north shore in the Hook of Holland, with its ferry terminal and the Maas Control building, squatting beneath its whirling radar antennae.

Here at six-forty-five on the morning of April 1, duty officer Bernhard Dijkstra yawned and stretched. He would be going home in fifteen minutes for a well-earned breakfast. Later, after a sleep, he would motor back from his home at Gravenzande in his spare time to see the new supergiant tanker pass through the estuary. It should be quite a day. As if to answer his thoughts, the speaker in front of him came to life.

"Pilot Maas, Pilot Mass, this is the *Freya.*"

The supertanker was on Channel 20, the usual channel for a tanker out at sea to call up Mass Control by radiotelephone. Dijkstra leaned forward and flicked a switch.

"*Freya*, this is Pilot Maas. Go ahead."

"Pilot Maas, this is the *Freya.* Captain Thor Larsen speaking. Where is the launch with my berthing crew?"

Dijkstra consulted a clipboard to the left of his console.

"*Freya*, this is Pilot Maas. They left the Hook over an hour ago. They should be with you in twenty minutes."

What followed caused Dijkstra to shoot bolt-upright in his chair.

"*Freya* to Pilot Maas. Contact the launch immediately and tell them to return to port. We cannot accept them on board. Inform the Maas pilots not to take off—repeat, not to take off. We cannot accept them on board. We have an emergency —I repeat, we have an emergency."

Dijkstra covered the speaker with his hand and yelled to his fellow duty officer to throw the switch on the tape recorder. When it was spinning to record the conversation, Dijkstra removed his hand and said carefully:

"*Freya*, this is Pilot Maas. Understand you do not wish the berthing crew to come alongside. Understand you do not wish the pilots to take off. Please confirm."

"Pilot Maas, this is *Freya*. Confirm. Confirm."

"*Freya*, please give details of your emergency."

There was silence for ten seconds, as if a consultation were taking place on the *Freya*'s bridge far out at sea. Then Larsen's voice boomed out again in the control room.

"Pilot Maas, *Freya*. I cannot give the nature of the emergency. But if any attempt is made by anyone to approach the *Freya*, people will get killed. Please stay away. Do not make any further attempt to contact the *Freya* by radio or telephone. Finally, the *Freya* will contact you again at oh-nine-hundred hours exactly. Have the chairman of the Rotterdam Port Authority present in the control room. That is all."

The voice ended, and there was a loud click. Dijkstra tried to call back two or three times. Then he looked across at his colleague.

"What the hell did that mean?"

Officer Wilhelm Schipper shrugged in perplexity. "I didn't like the sound of it," he said. "Captain Larsen sounded as if he might be in danger."

"He spoke of men getting killed," said Dijkstra. "How killed? What's he got, a mutiny? Someone run amok?"

"We'd better do what he says until this is sorted out," said Schipper.

"Right," said Dijkstra. "You get on to the chairman. I'll contact the launch and the two pilots up at Schiphol."

The launch bearing the berthing crew was chugging at a

steady ten knots across the flat calm toward the *Freya,* with three miles still to go. It was developing into a beautiful spring morning, warm for the time of year. At three miles the bulk of the giant tanker was already looming large, and the ten Dutchmen who would help her berth, but who had never seen her before, were craning their necks as they came closer.

No one thought anything when the ship-to-shore radio by the helmsman's side crackled and squawked. He took the handset off its cradle and held it to his ear. With a frown he cut the engine to idling, and asked for a repeat. When he got it, he put the helm hard a-starboard and brought the launch around in a semicircle.

"We're going back," he told the men, who looked at him with puzzlement. "There's something wrong. Captain Larsen's not ready for you yet."

Behind them the *Freya* receded again toward the horizon as they headed back to the Hook.

Up at Schiphol Airport, south of Amsterdam, the two estuary pilots were walking toward the Port Authority helicopter that would airlift them out to the deck of the tanker. It was routine procedure; they always went out to waiting ships by whirlybird.

The senior pilot, a grizzled veteran with twenty years at sea, a master's ticket, and fifteen years as a Maas Pilot, carried his "brown box," the instrument that would help him steer her to within a yard of seawater if he wished to be so precise. With the *Freya* clearing twenty feet only from the shoals and the Inner Channel barely fifty feet wider than the *Freya* herself, he would need it this morning.

As they ducked underneath the whirling blades, the helicopter pilot leaned out and wagged a warning finger at them.

"Something seems to be wrong," he yelled above the roar of the engine. "We have to wait. I'm closing her down."

The engine cut, the blades swished to a stop.

"What the hell's all that about?" asked the second pilot.

The helicopter flier shrugged.

"Don't ask me," he said. "Just came through from Maas Control. The ship isn't ready for you yet."

At his handsome country house outside Vlaardingen, Dirk Van Gelder, chairman of the Port Authority, was at breakfast a few minutes before eight when the phone rang. His wife answered it.

"It's for you," she called, and went back to the kitchen, where the coffee was perking. Van Gelder rose from the breakfast table, dropped his newspaper on the chair, and shuffled in carpet slippers out to the hallway.

"Van Gelder," he said into the telephone. As he listened, he stiffened, his brow furrowed.

"What did he mean, killed?" he asked.

There was another stream of words into his ear.

"Right," said Van Gelder. "Stay there. I'll be with you in fifteen minutes."

He slammed the phone down, kicked off the slippers, and put on his shoes and jacket. Two minutes later he was at his garage doors. As he climbed into his Mercedes and backed out to the gravel driveway, he was fighting back thoughts of his personal and abiding nightmare.

"Dear God, not a hijack. Please, not a hijack."

After replacing the VHF radiotelephone on the bridge of the *Freya,* Captain Thor Larsen had been taken at gunpoint on a tour of his own ship, peering with flashlight into the forward ballast holds to note the big packages strapped far down below the waterline.

Returning down the deck, he had seen the launch with the berthing crew turn, three miles out, and head back for the shore. To seaward a small freighter had passed, heading south, and had greeted the leviathan at anchor with a cheery hoot. It was not returned.

He had seen the single charge in the center ballast tank amidships, and the further charges in the after ballast tanks close by the superstructure. He did not need to see the paint locker. He knew where it was, and could imagine how close the charges were placed.

At half past eight, while Dirk Van Gelder was striding into the Maas Control Building to listen to the tape recording, Thor Larsen was being escorted back to his day cabin. He had noted one of the terrorists, muffled against the chill, perched right up in the fo'c'sle apron of the *Freya,* watching the arc of the sea out in front of the vessel. Another was high on the top of the funnel casing, over a hundred feet up, with a commanding view of the sea around him. A third was on the bridge, patrolling the radar screens, able, thanks to the

Freya's own technology, to see a circle of ocean with a radius of forty-eight miles, and most of the sea beneath her.

Of the remaining four, two, the leader and another, were with him; the other two must be below decks somewhere.

The terrorist leader forced him to sit at his own table in his own cabin. The man tapped the oscillator, which was clipped to his belt.

"Captain, please don't force me to press this red button. And please don't think that I will not—either if there is any attempt at heroics on this ship or if my demands are not met. Now, please read this."

He handed Captain Larsen a sheaf of three sheets of foolscap paper covered with typed writing in English. Larsen went rapidly through it.

"At nine o'clock you are going to read that message over the ship-to-shore radio to the chairman of the Port Authority of Rotterdam. No more, and no less. No breaking into Dutch or Norwegian. No supplementary questions. Just the message. Understand?"

Larsen nodded grimly. The door opened, and a masked terrorist came in. He had apparently been in the galley. He bore a tray with fried eggs, butter, jam, and coffee, which he placed on the table between them.

"Breakfast," said the terrorist leader. He gestured toward Larsen. "You might as well eat."

Larsen shook his head, but drank the coffee. He had been awake all night, and had risen from his bed the previous morning at seven. Twenty-six hours awake, and many more to go. He needed to stay alert, and guessed the black coffee might help. He calculated also that the terrorist across the table from him had been awake the same amount of time.

The terrorist signaled the remaining gunman to leave. As the door closed they were alone, but the broad expanse of table put the terrorist well out of Larsen's reach. The gun lay within inches of the man's right hand; the oscillator was at his waist.

"I don't think we shall have to abuse your hospitality for more than thirty hours, maybe forty," said the masked man. "But if I wear this mask during that time, I shall suffocate. You have never seen me before, and after tomorrow you will never see me again."

With his left hand, the man pulled the black balaclava helmet from his head. Larsen found himself staring at a man in his early thirties, with brown eyes and medium-brown hair.

He puzzled Larsen. The man spoke like an Englishman, behaved like one. But Englishmen did not hijack tankers, surely. Irish, perhaps? IRA? But he had referred to friends of his in prison in Germany. Arab, perhaps? There were PLO terrorists in prison in Germany. And he spoke a strange language to his companions. Not Arabic by the sound of it, yet there were scores of different dialects in Arabic, and Larsen knew only the Gulf Arabs. Again, Irish perhaps.

"What do I call you?" he asked the man whom he would never know as Andriy Drach or Andrew Drake. The man thought for a moment as he ate.

"You can call me 'Svoboda,'" he said at length. "It is a common name in my language. But it is also a word. It means 'freedom.'"

"That's not Arabic," said Larsen.

The man smiled for the first time.

"Certainly not. We are not Arabs. We are Ukrainian freedom fighters, and proud of it."

"And you think the authorities will free your friends in prison?" asked Larsen.

"They will have to," said Drake confidently. "They have no alternative. Come, it is almost nine o'clock."

CHAPTER TWELVE

0900 to 1300

"PILOT MAAS, Pilot Maas, this is the *Freya*."

Captain Thor Larsen's baritone voice echoed into the main control room at the squat building on the tip of the Hook of Holland. In the first-floor office with its sweeping picture windows gazing out over the North Sea, now curtained against the bright morning sun to give clarity to the radar screens, five men sat waiting.

Dijkstra and Schipper were still on duty, thoughts of breakfast forgotten. Dirk Van Gelder stood behind Dijkstra, ready to take over when the call came through. At another console, one of the day-shift men was taking care of the rest of the estuary traffic, bringing ships in and out, but keeping them away from the *Freya,* whose blip on the radar screen was at the limit of vision but still larger than all the others. The senior maritime safety officer of Maas Control was also present.

When the call came, Dijkstra slipped out of his chair before the speaker, and Van Gelder sat down. He gripped the stem of the table microphone, cleared his throat, and threw the "transmit" switch.

"*Freya,* this is Pilot Maas. Go ahead, please."

Beyond the confines of the building, which looked for all the world like a chopped-off air-traffic control tower sitting on the sand, other ears were listening. During the earlier transmission, two other ships had caught part of the conversation, and there had been a bit of chitchat between ships' radio officers in the intervening two hours. Now a dozen were listening keenly.

On the *Freya,* Larsen knew he could switch to Channel 16, speak to Scheveningen Radio, and ask for a patch-through to Maas Control for greater privacy, but the listeners would soon join him on that channel. So he stayed with Channel 20.

"*Freya* to Pilot Maas, I wish to speak personally to the chairman of the Port Authority."

"This is Pilot Maas. This is Dirk Van Gelder speaking. I am the chairman of the Port Authority."

"This is Captain Thor Larsen, master of the *Freya.*"

"Yes, Captain Larsen, your voice is recognized. What is your problem?"

At the other end, on the bridge of the *Freya,* Drake gestured with the tip of his gun to the written statement in Larsen's hand. Larsen nodded, flicked his "transmit" switch, and began to read into the telephone.

"I am reading a prepared statement. Please do not interrupt and do not pose questions.

" 'At three o'clock this morning, the *Freya* was taken over by armed men. I have already been given ample reason to believe they are in deadly earnest and prepared to carry out all their threats unless their demands are met.' "

In the control tower on the sand, there was a hiss of indrawn breath from behind Van Gelder. He closed his eyes wearily. For years he had been urging that some security measures be taken to protect these floating bombs from a hijacking. He had been ignored, and now it had happened at last. The voice from the speaker went on; the tape recorder revolved impassively.

" 'My entire crew is presently locked in the lowest portion of the ship, behind steel doors, and cannot escape. So far, no harm has come to them. I myself am held at gunpoint on my own bridge.

" 'During the night, explosive charges have been placed at strategic positions at various points inside the *Freya*'s hull. I have examined these myself, and can corroborate that if exploded they would blast the *Freya* apart, kill her crew instantly, and vent one million tons of crude oil into the North Sea.' "

"Oh, my God," said a voice behind Van Gelder. He waved an impatient hand for the speaker to shut up.

" 'These are the immediate demands of the men who hold the *Freya* prisoner. One: all sea traffic is to be cleared at once from the area inside the arc from a line forty-five degrees south of a bearing due east of the *Freya*, and forty-five degrees north of the same bearing—that is, inside a ninety-degree arc between the *Freya* and the Dutch coast. Two: no vessel, surface or submarine, is to attempt to approach the *Freya* on any other bearing to within five miles. Three: no aircraft is to pass overhead the *Freya* within a circle of five miles' radius of her, and below a height of ten thousand feet.' Is that clear? You may answer."

Van Gelder gripped the microphone hard.

"*Freya*, this is Pilot Maas. Dirk Van Gelder speaking. Yes, that is clear. I will have all surface traffic cleared from the area enclosed by a ninety-degree arc between the *Freya* and the Dutch coast, and from an area five sea miles from the *Freya* on all other sides. I will instruct Schiphol Airport traffic control to ban all air movements within the five-mile-radius area below ten thousand feet. Over."

There was a pause, and Larsen's voice came back.

"I am informed that if there is any attempt to breach these orders, there will be an immediate riposte without further consultation. Either the *Freya* will vent twenty thousand tons of crude oil immediately, or one of my seamen will be . . . executed. Is that understood? You may answer."

Dirk Van Gelder turned to his traffic officers.

"Jesus, get the shipping out of that area, fast. Get on to Schiphol and tell them. No commercial flights, no private aircraft, no choppers taking pictures—nothing. Now move."

To the microphone he said, "Understood, Captain Larsen. Is there anything else?"

"Yes," said the disembodied voice. "There will be no further radio contact with the *Freya* until twelve hundred hours. At that time the *Freya* will call you again. I will wish to speak directly and personally to the Prime Minister of the Netherlands and the West German Ambassador. Both must be present. That is all."

The microphone went dead. On the bridge of the *Freya*, Drake removed the handset from Larsen's hand and replaced it. Then he gestured the Norwegian to return to the day cabin. When they were seated with the seven-foot table between them, Drake laid down his gun and leaned back. As his sweater rode up, Larsen saw the lethal oscillator clipped at his waistband.

"What do we do now?" asked Larsen.

"We wait," said Drake. "While Europe goes quietly mad."

"They'll kill you, you know," said Larsen. "You've got on board, but you'll never get off. They may have to do what you say, but when they have done it, they'll be waiting for you."

"I know," said Drake. "But you see, I don't mind if I die. I'll fight to live, of course, but I'll die, and I'll kill, before I'll see them kill off my project."

"You want these two men in Germany free, that much?" asked Larsen.

"Yes, that much. I can't explain why, and if I did, you wouldn't understand. But for years my land, my people, have been occupied, persecuted, imprisoned, killed. And no one cared a shit. Now I threaten to kill one single man, or hit Western Europe in the pocket, and you'll see what they do. Suddenly it's a disaster. But for me, the slavery of my land, that is the disaster."

"This dream of yours, what is it, exactly?" asked Larsen.

"A free Ukraine," said Drake simply. "Which cannot be achieved short of a popular uprising by millions of people."

"In the Soviet Union?" said Larsen. "That's impossible. That will never happen."

"It could," countered Drake. "It could. It happened in East Germany, in Hungary, in Czechoslovakia. But first, the conviction by those millions that they could never win, that their oppressors are invincible, must be broken. If it once were, the floodgates could open wide."

"No one will ever believe that," said Larsen.

"Not in the West, no. But there's the strange thing. Here in the West, people would say I cannot be right in that calculation. But in the Kremlin they know I am."

"And for this . . . popular uprising, you are prepared to die?" asked Larsen.

"If I must. That is my dream. That land, that people, I love more than life itself. That's my advantage: within a hundred-mile radius of us here, there is no one else who loves something more than his life."

A day earlier Thor Larsen might have agreed with the fanatic. But something was happening inside the big, slow-moving Norwegian that surprised him. For the first time in his life he hated a man enough to kill him. Inside his head a private voice said, "I don't care about your Ukrainian dream, Mr. Svoboda. You are not going to kill my crew and my ship."

At Felixstowe on the coast of Suffolk, the English Coastguard officer walked quickly away from his coastal radio set and picked up the telephone.

"Get me the Department of the Environment in London," he told the operator.

"By God, those Dutchies have got themselves a problem this time," said his deputy, who had heard the conversation between the *Freya* and Maas Control also.

"It's not just the Dutch," said the senior coastguardsman. "Look at the map."

On the wall was a map of the entire southern portion of the North Sea and the northern end of the English Channel. It showed the coast of Suffolk right across to the Maas Estuary. In chinagraph pencil the coastguardsman had marked the *Freya* at her overnight position. It was a little more than two-thirds of the way from England to Holland.

"If she blows, lad, our coasts will also be under a foot of oil from Hull round to Southampton."

Minutes later he was talking to a civil servant in London, one of the men in the department of the ministry specifically concerned with oil-slick hazards. What he said caused the morning's first cup of tea in London to go quite cold.

Dirk Van Gelder managed to catch the Prime Minister at his residence, just about to leave for his office. The urgency of the Port Authority chairman finally persuaded the young aide from the Cabinet Office to pass the phone to the Premier.

"Jan Grayling," he said into the speaker. As he listened to Van Gelder his face tightened.

"Who are they?" he asked.

"We don't know," said Van Gelder. "Captain Larsen was reading from a prepared statement. He was not allowed to deviate from it, nor answer questions."

"If he was under duress, perhaps he had no choice but to confirm the placing of the explosives. Perhaps that's a bluff," said Grayling.

"I don't think so, sir," said Van Gelder. "Would you like me to bring the tape to you?"

"Yes, at once, in your own car," said the Premier. "Straight to the Cabinet Office."

He put the phone down and walked to his limousine, his mind racing. If what was threatened was indeed true, the bright summer morning had brought the worst crisis of his term of office. As his car left the curb, followed by the inevitable police vehicle, he leaned back and tried to think out some of the first priorities. An immediate emergency cabinet meeting, of course. The press—they would not be long. Many ears must have listened to the ship-to-shore conversation; someone would tell the press before noon.

He would have to inform a variety of foreign governments through their embassies. And authorize the setting up of an immediate crisis management committee of experts. Fortunately he had access to a number of such experts since the hijacks by the South Moluccans several years earlier. As he drew up in front of the prime ministerial office building, he glanced at his watch. It was half past nine.

The phrase "crisis management committee" was already being thought, albeit as yet unspoken, in London. Sir Rupert Mossbank, Permanent Under Secretary to the Department of the Environment, was on the phone to the Cabinet Secretary, Sir Julian Flannery.

"It's early days yet, of course," said Sir Rupert. "We don't know who they are, how many, if they're serious, or whether there are really any bombs on board. But if that amount of crude oil did get spilt, it really would be rather messy."

Sir Julian thought for a moment, gazing out through his first-floor windows onto Whitehall.

"Good of you to call so promptly, Rupert," he said. "I think I'd better inform the P.M. at once. In the meantime, just as a precaution, could you ask a couple of your best minds to put together a memo on the prospective consequences if she does blow up? Question of spillage, area of ocean covered, tide flow, speed, area of our coastline likely to be affected. That sort of thing. I'm pretty sure she'll ask for it."

"I have it in hand all ready, old boy."

"Good," said Sir Julian. "Excellent. Fast as possible. I suspect she'll want to know. She always does."

He had worked under three prime ministers, and the latest was far and away the toughest and most decisive. For years it had been a standing joke that the government party was full of old women of both sexes, but fortunately was led by a real man. The name of the latter was Joan Carpenter. The Cabinet Secretary had his appointment within minutes and walked through the bright morning sunshine across the lawn to No. 10, with purpose but without hurry, as was his wont.

When he entered the Prime Minister's private office she was at her desk, where she had been since eight o'clock. A coffee set of bone china lay on a side table, and three red dispatch boxes lay open on the floor. Sir Julian was admiring; the woman went through documentation like a paper shredder, and the papers were already finished by ten A.M., either agreed to, rejected, or bearing a crisp request for further information, or a series of pertinent questions.

"Good morning, Prime Minister."

"Good morning, Sir Julian, a beautiful day."

"Indeed, ma'am. Unfortunately it has brought a piece of unpleasantness with it."

He took a seat at her gesture and accurately sketched in the details of the affair in the North Sea, as well as he knew them. She was alert, absorbed.

"If it is true, then this ship, the *Freya,* could cause an environmental disaster," she said flatly.

"Indeed, though we do not know yet the exact feasibility of sinking such a gigantic vessel with what are presumably industrial explosives. There are men who would be able to give an assessment, of course."

"In the event that it is true," said the Prime Minister, "I believe we should form a crisis management committee to consider the implications. If it is not, then we have the opportunity for a realistic exercise."

Sir Julian raised an eyebrow. The idea of putting a thunderflash down the trousers of a dozen ministerial departments as an exercise had not occurred to him. He supposed it had a certain charm.

For thirty minutes the Prime Minister and her Cabinet Secretary listed the areas in which they would need professional expertise if they were to be accurately informed of the options in a major tanker hijacking in the North Sea.

In the matter of the supertanker herself, she was insured by Lloyd's, which would be in possession of a complete plan of her layout. Concerning the structure of tankers, British Petroleum's Marine Division would have an expert in tanker construction who could study those plans and give a precise judgment on feasibility.

In spillage control, they agreed to call on the senior research analyst at the Warren Springs Laboratory at Stevenage, close to London, run jointly by the Department of Trade and Industry and the Ministry of Agriculture, Fisheries, and Food.

The Ministry of Defense would be called on for a serving officer in the Royal Engineers, an expert in explosives, to estimate that side of things, and the Department of the Environment itself had people who could calculate the scope of the catastrophe to the ecology of the North Sea. Trinity House, head authority of the pilotage services around Britain's coasts, would be asked to inform on tide flows and speeds. Relations and liaison with foreign governments would fall to the Foreign Office, which would send an observer. By ten-thirty the list seemed complete. Sir Julian prepared to leave.

"Do you think the Dutch government will handle this affair?" asked the Prime Minister.

"It's early days to say, ma'am. At the moment the terrorists wish to put their demands to Mr. Grayling personally at noon, in ninety minutes. I have no doubt The Hague will feel able to handle the matter. But if the demands cannot be met, or if the ship blows up anyway, then as a coastal nation we are involved in any case.

"Furthermore, our capacity to cope with oil spillage is the most advanced in Europe, so we may be called on to help by our allies across the North Sea."

"Then all the sooner we are ready, the better," said the Prime Minister. "One last thing, Sir Julian. It will probably never come to it, but if the demands cannot be met, the contingency may have to be considered of storming the vessel to liberate the crew and defuse the charges."

For the first time Sir Julian was not comfortable. He had

been a professional civil servant all his life, since leaving Oxford with a Double First. He believed the word, written and spoken, could solve most problems, given time. He abhorred violence.

"Ah, yes, Prime Minister. That would of course be a last resort. I understand it is called 'the hard option.' "

"The Israelis stormed the airliner at Entebbe," mused the Prime Minister. "The Germans stormed the one at Mogadisho. The Dutch stormed the train at Assen. When they were left with no alternative. Supposing it were to happen again."

"Well, ma'am, perhaps they would."

"Could the Dutch Marines carry out such a mission?"

Sir Julian chose his words carefully. He had a vision of burly Marines clumping all over Whitehall. Far better to keep those people playing their lethal games well out of the way on Exmoor.

"If it came to storming a vessel at sea," he said, "I believe a helicopter landing would not be feasible. It would be spotted by the deck watch, and of course the ship has a radar scanner. Similarly, an approach by surface vessel would also be observed. This is not an airliner on a concrete runway, nor a stationary train, ma'am. This is a ship over twenty-five miles from land."

That, he hoped, would put a stop to it.

"What about an approach by armed divers or frogmen?" she asked.

Sir Julian closed his eyes. Armed frogmen indeed. He was convinced politicians read too many novels for their own good.

"Armed frogmen, Prime Minister?" The blue eyes across the desk did not leave him.

"I understand," she said clearly, "that our capacity in this regard is among the most advanced in Europe."

"I believe it may well be so, ma'am."

"And who are these underwater experts?"

"The Special Boat Service, Prime Minister."

"Who, in Whitehall, liaises with our special services?" she asked.

"There is a Royal Marine colonel in Defense," he conceded, "called Holmes."

It was going to be bad; he could see it coming. They had used the land-based counterpart of the SBS, the better-known Special Air Service, or SAS, to help the Germans at Mogadisho, and in the Balcombe Street siege. Harold Wilson had always wanted to hear all the details of the lethal games these roughnecks played with their opponents. Now they were going to start another James Bond–style fantasy.

"Ask Colonel Holmes to attend the crisis management committee—in a consultative capacity only, of course."

"Of course, ma'am."

"And prepare UNICORNE. I shall expect you to take the chair at noon, when the terrorists' demands are known."

Three hundred miles across the North Sea, the activity in Holland was already, by midmorning, becoming frenetic.

From his office in the seaside capital of The Hague, the Premier, Jan Grayling, and his staff were putting together the same sort of crisis management committee that Mrs. Carpenter in London had in mind. The first requirement was to know the exact perspectives of any conceivable human or environmental tragedy stemming from the damage at sea to a ship like the *Freya*, and the various options the Dutch government faced.

To secure this information the same kinds of experts were being called upon for their specialized knowledge: in shipping, oil slicks, tides, speeds, directions, future weather prospects, and even the military option.

Dirk Van Gelder, having delivered the tape recording of the nine o'clock message from the *Freya*, drove back to Maas Control on the instructions of Jan Grayling to sit by the VHF radiotelephone set in case the *Freya* called up again before twelve noon.

It was he who at ten-thirty took the call from Harry Wennerstrom. Having finished breakfast in his penthouse suite at the Rotterdam Hilton, the old shipping magnate was still in ignorance of the disaster to his ship. Quite simply, no one had thought to call him.

Wennerstrom was calling to inquire about the progress of the *Freya*, which by this time, he thought, would be well into the Outer Channel, moving slowly and carefully toward the Inner Channel, several kilometers past Euro Buoy 1 and moving along a precise course of 080.5 degrees. He expected to leave Rotterdam with his convoy of notables to witness the *Freya*'s coming into sight about lunchtime, as the ride rose to its peak.

Van Gelder apologized for not having called him at the

Hilton, and carefully explained what had happened at 0645 and 0900 hours. There was silence from the Hilton end of the line. Wennerstrom's first reaction could have been to mention that there was $170 million worth of ship being held prisoner out beyond the western horizon, carrying $140 million worth of crude oil. It was a reflection on the man that he said, at length:

"There are thirty of my seamen out there, Mr. Van Gelder. And starting right now, let me tell you that if anything happens to any one of them because the terrorists' demands are not met, I shall hold the Dutch authorities personally responsible."

"Mr. Wennerstrom," said Van Gelder, who had also commanded a ship in his career, "we are doing everything we can. The requirements of the terrorists regarding the distance of clear water around the *Freya* are being met, to the letter. Their primary demands have not yet been stated. The Prime Minister is in his office now in The Hague doing what he can, and he will be here at noon for the next message from the *Freya*."

Harry Wennerstrom replaced the receiver and stared through the picture windows of the sitting room in the sky toward the west, where his dream ship was lying at anchor on the open sea with armed terrorists aboard her.

"Cancel the convoy to Maas Control," he said suddenly to one of his secretaries. "Cancel the champagne lunch. Cancel the reception this evening. Cancel the press conference. I'm going."

"Where, Mr. Wennerstrom?" asked the amazed young woman.

"To Maas Control. Alone. Have my car waiting by the time I reach the garage."

With that, the old man stumped from the suite and headed for the elevator.

Around the *Freya* the sea was emptying. Working closely with their British colleagues at Flamborough Head and Felixstowe, the Dutch marine-traffic-control officers diverted shipping into fresh sea-lanes west of the *Freya*, the nearest being over five miles west of her.

Eastward of the stricken ship, coastal traffic was ordered to stop or turn back, and movements into and out of the Europoort and Rotterdam were halted. Angry sea captains, whose voices poured into Maas Control demanding explanations were told simply that an emergency had arisen and they were to avoid at all costs the sea area whose coordinates were read out to them.

It was impossible to keep the press in the dark. A group of several-score journalists from technical and marine publications, as well as the shipping correspondents of the major daily papers from the neighboring countries, were already in Rotterdam for the reception arranged for the *Freya*'s triumphal entry that afternoon. By eleven A.M. their curiosity was aroused, partly by the cancellation of the journey to the Hook to witness the *Freya* come over the horizon into the Inner Channel, and partly by tips reaching their head offices from those numerous radio hams who like to listen to maritime radio talk.

Shortly after eleven, calls began to flood into the penthouse suite of their host, Harry Wennerstrom, but he was not there and his secretaries knew nothing. Other calls came to Maas Control, and were referred to The Hague. In the Dutch capital the switchboard operators put the calls through to the Prime Minister's private press secretary, on Grayling's orders, and the harassed young man fended them off as best he could.

The lack of information simply intrigued the press corps more than ever, so they reported to their editors that something serious was afoot with the *Freya.* The editors dispatched other reporters, who forgathered through the morning outside the Maas Control Building at the Hook where they were firmly kept outside the chain-link fence that surrounds the building. Others grouped in The Hague to pester the various ministries, but most of all the Prime Minister's office.

The editor of *De Telegraaf* received a tip from a radio ham that there were terrorists on board the *Freya* and that they would issue their demands at noon. He at once ordered a radio monitor to be placed on Channel 20 with a tape recorder to catch the whole message.

Jan Grayling personally telephoned the West German Ambassador, Konrad Voss, and told him in confidence what had happened. Voss called Bonn at once, and within thirty minutes replied to the Dutch Premier that he would of course accompany him to the Hook for the twelve o'clock contact as the terrorists had demanded. The government of the Federal

Republic of Germany, he assured the Dutchman, would do everything it could to help.

The Dutch Foreign Ministry as a matter of courtesy informed the ambassadors of all the nations concerned: Sweden, whose flag the *Freya* flew and whose seamen were on board; Norway, Finland, and Denmark, which also had seamen on board; the United States, because four of those seamen were Scandinavian-Americans with U.S. passports and dual nationality; Britain, as a coastal nation and whose institution, Lloyd's, was insuring both ship and cargo; and Belgium and France as coastal nations.

In nine European capitals the telephones rang between ministry and department, from call box to editorial room, in insurance offices, shipping agencies, and private homes. For those in government, banking, shipping, insurance, the armed forces, and the press, the prospect of a quiet weekend that Friday morning receded into the flat blue ocean, where under a warm spring sun a million-ton bomb called the *Freya* lay silent and still.

Harry Wennerstrom was halfway from Rotterdam to the Hook when an idea occurred to him. The limousine was passing out of Schiedam on the motorway toward Vlaardingen when he recalled that his private jet was at Schiedam municipal airport. He reached for the telephone and called his principal secretary, still trying to fend off calls from the press in his suite at the Hilton. When he got through to her at the third attempt, he gave her a string of orders for his pilot.

"One last thing," he said. "I want the name and office phone number of the police chief of Ålesund. Yes, Ålesund, in Norway. As soon as you have it, call him up and tell him to stay where he is and await my call back to him."

Lloyd's Intelligence Unit had been informed shortly after ten o'clock. A British dry-cargo vessel had been preparing to enter the Maas Estuary for Rotterdam when the 0900 call was made from the *Freya* to Maas Control. The radio officer had heard the whole conversation, noted it verbatim in shorthand, and shown it to his captain. Minutes later, he was dictating it to the ship's agent in Rotterdam, who passed it to the head office in London. The office had called Colchester, Essex, and repeated the news to Lloyd's. One of the chairmen of twenty-five separate firms of underwriters had been contacted and informed. The consortium that had put together the $170-million hull insurance on the *Freya* had to be big; so also was the group of firms covering the million-ton cargo for Clint Blake in his office in Texas. But despite the size of the *Freya* and her cargo, the biggest single policy was the protection and indemnity insurance, for the persons of the crew and pollution compensation. The P and I policy would be the one to cost the biggest bundle of money if the *Freya* were blown apart.

Shortly before noon, the chairman of Lloyd's, in his office high above the City, stared at a few calculations on his jotting pad.

"We're talking about a billion-dollar loss if worse comes to worst," he remarked to his personal aide. "Who the hell *are* these people?"

The leader of "these people" sat at the epicenter of the growing storm and faced a bearded Norwegian captain in the day cabin beneath the starboard wing of the *Freya*'s bridge. The curtains were drawn back, and the sun shone warmly. From the windows stretched a panoramic view of the silent foredecks, running away a quarter of a mile to the tine fo'c'sle.

The miniature, shrouded figure of a man sat high on the bow apron above the stern, looking out from his perch at the glittering blue sea. On either side of the vessel, the same blue water lay flat and calm, a mild zephyr ruffling its surface. During the morning that breeze had gently blown away the invisible clouds of poisonous inert gases that had welled out from the holds when the inspection hatches were lifted; it was now safe to walk along the deck, or the man on the fo'c'sle would not have been there.

The temperature in the cabin was still stabilized, the air conditioning having taken over from the central heating when the sun became hotter through the double-glazed windows.

Thor Larsen sat where he had sat all morning, at one end of his main table, with Andrew Drake at the other.

Since the argument between the 0900 radio call and ten o'clock, there had been mainly silence between them. The tension of waiting was beginning to make itself felt. Each knew that across the water in both directions frantic preparations would be taking place: firstly to try to estimate exactly what had happened aboard the *Freya* during the night, and secondly to estimate what, if anything, could be done about it.

Larsen knew no one would do anything, take any initiative, until the noon broadcast of demands. In that sense the intense young man facing him was not stupid. He had elected to keep the authorities guessing. By forcing Larsen to speak in his stead, he had given no clue to his identity or his origins. Even his motivations were unknown outside the cabin in which they sat. And the authorities would want to know more, to analyze the tapes of the broadcasts, identify the speech patterns and ethnic origins of the speaker, before taking action. The man who called himself Svoboda was denying them that information, undermining the self-confidence of the men he had challenged to defy him.

He was also giving the press ample time to learn of the disaster, but not the terms; letting them evaluate the scale of the catastrophe if the *Freya* blew up, so that their head of steam, their capacity to pressure the authorities, would be well prepared ahead of the demands. When the demands came, they would appear mild compared to the alternative, thus subjecting the authorities to press pressure before they had considered the demands.

Larsen, who knew what the demands would be, could not see how the authorities would refuse. The alternative was too terrible for all of them. If Svoboda had simply kidnapped an industrialist or a politician, as the Baader-Meinhof people had kidnapped Hanns-Martin Schleyer, or the Red Brigades Aldo Moro, he might have been refused his friends' release. But he had elected to destroy five national coastlines, one sea, thirty lives, and hundreds of millions of dollars in property.

"Why are these two men so important to you?" asked Larsen suddenly.

The younger man stared back.

"They're friends," he said.

"No," said Larsen. "I recall from last January reading that they were two Jews from Lvov who had been refused permission to emigrate, so they hijacked a Russian airliner and forced it to land in West Berlin. How does that produce your popular uprising?"

"Never mind," said his captor. "It is five to twelve. We return to the bridge."

Nothing had changed on the bridge, except that there was an extra terrorist there, curled up asleep in the corner, his gun still clutched in his hand. He was masked, like the one who patrolled the radar and sonar screens. Svoboda asked the man something in the language Larsen now knew to be Ukrainian. The man shook his head and replied in the same language. At a word from Svoboda the masked man turned his gun on Larsen.

Svoboda walked over to the scanners and read them. There was a peripheral ring of clear water around the *Freya* at least to five miles on the western, southern, and northern sides. To the east, the sea was clear to the Dutch coast. He strode out through the door leading to the bridgewing, turned, and called upward. From high above, Larsen heard the man atop the funnel assembly shout back. Svoboda returned to the bridge.

"Come," he said to the captain, "your audience is waiting. One attempt at a trick, and I shoot one of your seamen, as promised."

Larsen took the handset and pressed for transmit.

"Maas Control, Maas Control, this is the *Freya.*"

Though he could not know it, over fifty different offices received that call. Five major intelligence services were listening, plucking Channel 20 out of the ether with their sophisticated listeners. The words were heard simultaneously by the National Security Agency in Washington, by the British SIS, the French SDECE, the West German BND, the Soviet KGB, and the various services of Holland, Belgium, and Sweden. There were ships' radio officers listening, radio hams and journalists as well.

A voice came back from the Hook of Holland.

"*Freya,* this is Maas Control. Go ahead, please."

Thor Larsen read from his sheet of paper.

"This is Captain Thor Larsen. I wish to speak personally to the Prime Minister of the Netherlands."

A new voice, speaking in English, came on the radio from the Hook.

"Captain Larsen, this is Jan Grayling. I am the Prime Minister of the Kingdom of the Netherlands. Are you all right?"

On the *Freya,* Svoboda clapped his hand over the mouthpiece of the telephone.

"No questions," he said to Larsen. "Just ask if the West German Ambassador is present, and get his name."

"Please ask no questions, Prime Minister. I am not permitted to answer them. Is the West German Ambassador with you?"

At Maas Control, the microphone was passed to Konrad Voss.

On the bridge of the *Freya*, Svoboda nodded at Larsen. "That's right," he said, "go ahead and read it out."

The six men grouped around the console in Maas Control listened in silence. One premier, one ambassador, one psychiatrist, a radio engineer in case of a transmission breakdown, Van Gelder of the Port Authority, and the duty officer. All other shipping traffic had now been diverted to a spare channel. The two tape recorders whirled silently. Volume was switched high; Thor Larsen's voice echoed in the room.

" 'I repeat what I told you at nine this morning. The *Freya* is in the hands of partisans. Explosive devices have been placed that would, if detonated, blow her apart. These devices can be detonated at the touch of a button. I repeat, at the touch of a button. No attempt whatever must be made to approach her, board her, or attack her in any way. In such an event the detonator button will be pressed instantly. The men concerned have convinced me they are prepared to die rather than give in.'

"I continue. 'If any approach at all is made, by surface craft or light aircraft, one of my seamen will be executed, or twenty thousand tons of crude oil vented, or both. Here are the demands of the partisans:

" 'The two prisoners of conscience, David Lazareff and Lev Mishkin, presently in jail at Tegel in West Berlin, are to be liberated. They are to be flown by a West German civilian jet from West Berlin to Israel. Prior to this, the Prime Minister of the State of Israel is to give a public guarantee that they will be neither repatriated to the Soviet Union, nor extradited back to West Germany, nor reimprisoned in Israel.

" 'Their liberation must take place at dawn tomorrow. The Israeli guarantee of safe conduct and freedom must be given by midnight tonight. Failure to comply will place the entire responsibility for the outcome on the shoulders of West Germany and Israel. That is all. There will be no more contact until the demands have been met.' "

The radiotelephone went dead with a click. The silence persisted inside the control building. Jan Grayling looked at Konrad Voss. The West German envoy shrugged.

"I must contact Bonn urgently," Voss said.

"I can tell you that Captain Larsen is under some strain," said the psychiatrist.

"Thank you very much," said Grayling. "So am I. Gentlemen, what has just been said cannot fail to be made public within the hour. I suggest we return to our offices. I shall prepare a statement for the one o'clock news. Mr. Ambassador, I fear the pressure will now begin to swing toward Bonn."

"Indeed it will," said Voss. "I must be back inside the embassy as soon as possible."

"Then accompany me to The Hague," said Grayling. "I have police outriders, and we can talk in the car."

Aides brought the two tapes, and the group left for The Hague, fifteen minutes up the coast. When they were gone, Dirk Van Gelder walked up to the flat roof where Harry Wennerstrom would have held his lunch with Van Gelder's permission, the other guests looking eagerly to seaward, as they supped on champagne and salmon sandwiches, to catch the first glimpse of the leviathan.

Now perhaps she would never come, thought Van Gelder, staring out at the blue water. He, too, had his master's ticket, having served as a Dutch merchant navy captain until he was offered the shore job with the promise of a regular life with his wife and children. As a seaman he thought of the *Freya*'s crew, locked far beneath the waves, waiting helplessly for rescue or death. But as a seaman he would not be in charge of negotiations. It was out of his hands now. Smoother men, calculating in political rather than human terms, would take over.

He thought of the towering Norwegian skipper, whose picture he had seen but whom he had never met, now facing madmen armed with guns and dynamite, and wondered how he would have reacted had it ever happened to him. He had warned that this could happen one day, that the supertankers were too unprotected and highly dangerous. But money had spoken louder; the more powerful argument had been the extra cost of installing the necessary devices to make tankers like banks and explosive stores, both of which in a way they were. No one had listened, and no one ever would. People were concerned about airliners because they could crash on houses, but not about tankers, which traveled out of sight of land. So the politicians had not insisted, and the merchants had not volunteered. Now, because supertankers could be taken as easily as piggy banks, a captain and his crew of twenty-nine might die like rats in a swirl of oil and water.

He ground a cigarette under his heel into the tar of the roof, and looked again at the empty horizon.

"You poor bastards," he said, "you poor bloody bastards. If only they'd listened."

CHAPTER THIRTEEN

1300 to 1900

IF THE REACTION of the media to the 0900 transmission had been muted and speculative, due to the uncertainty of the reliability of their informants, the reaction to the 1200 broadcast was frantic.

From twelve o'clock onward there was no doubt whatever what had happened to the *Freya*, or what had been said by Captain Larsen on his radiotelephone to Maas Control. Too many people had been listening.

Banner headlines that had been available for the noon editions of the evening papers, prepared at ten A.M., were swept away. Those that went to press at twelve-thirty were stronger in tone and size. There were no more question marks at the ends of sentences. Editorial columns were hastily prepared, specialist correspondents in matters of shipping and the environment required to produce instant assessments within the hour.

Radio and television programs were interrupted throughout Europe's Friday lunch hour to beam the news to listeners and viewers.

On the dot of five past twelve, a man in a motorcyclist's helmet, with goggles and scarf drawn around the lower part of the face, had walked calmly into the lobby of 85 Fleet Street and deposited an envelope addressed to the news editor of the Press Association. No one later recalled the man; dozens of such messengers walk into that lobby every day.

By twelve-fifteen the news editor was opening the envelope. It contained a transcript of the statement read by Captain Larsen fifteen minutes earlier, though it must have been prepared well before that. The news editor reported the delivery to his editor in chief, who told the Metropolitan Police. That did not stop the text from going straight onto the wires, both of the PA and their cousins upstairs, Reuters, who put out the text across the world.

Leaving Fleet Street, Miroslav Kaminsky dumped his helmet, goggles, and scarf in a garbage can, took a taxi to Heathrow Airport, and boarded the two-fifteen plane for Tel Aviv.

By two P.M. the editorial pressure on both the Dutch and West German governments was beginning to build up. Neither had had any time to consider in peace and quiet the reactions they should make to the demands. Both governments began to receive a flood of phone calls urging them to agree to release Mishkin and Lazareff rather than face the disaster promised by the destruction of the *Freya* off their coasts.

By one o'clock the West German Ambassador to The Hague was speaking directly to his Foreign Minister in Bonn, Klaus Hagowitz, who interrupted the Chancellor at his desk lunch. The text of the 1200 broadcast was already in Bonn, once from the BND intelligence service and once on the Reuters teleprinter. Every newspaper office in Germany also had the text from Reuters, and the telephone lines to the Chancellery Press Office were jammed with calls.

At one-forty-five the Chancellery put out a statement to the effect that an emergency cabinet meeting had been called for three o'clock to consider the entire situation. Ministers canceled their plans to leave Bonn for the weekend. Lunches were ill-digested.

The governor of Tegel Jail put down his telephone at two minutes past two with a certain deference. It was not often the Federal Republic's Justice Minister cut clean through the protocol of communicating with the Governing Mayor of West Berlin and called him personally.

He picked up the internal phone and gave an order to his secretary. Doubtless the Berlin Senate would be in contact in due course with the same request, but so long as the Governing Mayor was out of touch at lunch somewhere, he would not refuse the Minister from Bonn.

Three minutes later, one of his senior prison officers entered the office.

"Have you heard the two o'clock news?" asked the governor.

It was only five past two. The officer pointed out that he had been on his rounds when the bleeper in his breast pocket buzzed, requiring him to go straight to a wall phone and check in. No, he had not heard the news. The governor told him of the noon demand of the terrorists on board the *Freya.* The officer's jaw dropped open.

"One for the book, isn't it?" said the governor. "It looks as if we shall be in the news within minutes. So, batten down the hatches. I've given orders to the main gate: no admissions by anyone other than staff. All press inquiries to the authorities at City Hall.

"Now, as regards Mishkin and Lazareff. I want the guard on that floor, and particularly in that corridor, trebled. Cancel free periods to raise enough staff. Transfer all other prisoners in that corridor to other cells or other levels. Seal the place. A group of intelligence people are flying in from Bonn to ask them who their friends in the North Sea are. Any questions?"

The prison officer swallowed and shook his head.

"Now," resumed the governor, "we don't know how long this emergency will last. When were you due off duty?"

"Six o'clock tonight, sir."

"Returning on Monday morning at eight?"

"No, sir. On Sunday night at midnight. I go on the night shift next week."

"I'll have to ask you to work right on through," said the governor. "Of course, we'll make up the time to you later with a generous bonus. But I'd like you right on top of the job from here on. Agreed?"

"Yes, sir. Whatever you say. I'll get on with it now."

The governor, who liked to adopt a comradely attitude with his staff, came around the desk and clapped the man on the shoulder.

"You're a good fellow, Jahn. I don't know what we'd do without you."

Squadron Leader Mark Latham stared down the runway, heard his takeoff clearance from the control tower, and nodded to his copilot. The younger man's gloved hand eased the four throttles slowly open; in the wing roots, four Rolls-Royce Spey engines rose in pitch to push out forty-five thousand pounds of thrust, and the Nimrod Mark 2 climbed away from the RAF station at Kinross and turned southeast from Scotland toward the North Sea and the Channel.

What the thirty-one-year-old squadron leader of Coastal Command was flying he knew to be about the best aircraft for submarine and shipping surveillance in the world. With its crew of twelve, improved power plants, performance, and surveillance aids, the Nimrod could either skim the waves at low level, slow and steady, listening on electronic ears to the sounds of underwater movement, or cruise at altitude, hour after hour, two engines shut down for fuel economy, observing an enormous area of ocean beneath it.

Its radars would pick up the slightest movement of a metallic substance down there on the water's surface; its cameras could photograph by day and night; it was unaffected by storm or snow, hail or sleet, fog or wind, light or dark. Its Data Link computers could process the received information, identify what it saw for what it was, and transmit the whole picture, in visual or electronic terms, back to base or to a Royal Navy vessel tapped into the Data Link.

His orders, that sunny spring Friday, were to take up station fifteen thousand feet above the *Freya* and keep circling until relieved.

"She's coming on screen, skipper," Latham's radar operator called on the intercom. Back in the hull of the Nimrod, the operator was gazing at his scanner screen, picking out the area of traffic-free water around the *Freya* on its northern side, watching the large blip move from the periphery toward the center of the screen as they aproached.

"Cameras on," said Latham calmly. In the belly of the Nimrod the *f*/126 daytime camera swiveled like a gun, spotted the *Freya*, and locked on. Automatically it adjusted range and focus for maximum definition. Like moles in their blind hull, the crew behind him saw the *Freya* come onto their picture screen. From now on, the aircraft could fly all over the sky, but the cameras would stay locked on the *Freya*, adjusting for distance and light changes, swiveling in their housings to compensate for the circling of the Nimrod. Even if the *Freya* began to move, they would still stay on her, like an unblinking eye, until given fresh orders.

"And transmit," said Latham.

The Data Link began to send the pictures back to Britain, and thence to London. When the Nimrod was over the *Freya*, she banked to port, and from his left-hand seat Squadron Leader Latham looked down visually. Behind him and below him, the camera zoomed closer, beating the human eye. It picked out the lone figure of the terrorist in the forepeak, masked face staring upward at the silver swallow three miles above him. It picked out the second terrorist on top of the funnel, and zoomed until his black balaclava filled the screen. The man cradled a submachine carbine in his arms in the sunshine far below.

"There they are, the bastards," called the camera operator. The Nimrod established a gentle, rate 1 turn above the *Freya,* went over to automatic pilot, closed down the engine, reduced power to maximum endurance setting on the other two, and began to do its job. It circled, watched and waited, reporting everything back to base. Mark Latham ordered his copilot to take over, unbuckled, and left the flight deck. He went aft to the four-man dining area, visited the toilet, washed his hands, and sat down with a vacuum-heated lunch-box. It was, he reflected, really rather a comfortable way to go to war.

The gleaming Volvo of the police chief of Ålesund ground up the gravel drive of the timber-construction, ranch-style house at Bogneset, twenty minutes out from the town center, and halted by the rough-stone porch.

Trygve Dahl was a contemporary of Thor Larsen. They had grown up together in Ålesund, and Dahl had entered the force as a police cadet about the time Larsen had joined the merchant marine. He had known Lisa Larsen since his friend had brought the young bride back from Oslo after their marriage. His own children knew Kurt and Kristina, played with them at school, sailed with them in the long summer holidays.

Damn it, he thought as he climbed out of the Volvo, what the hell do I tell her?

There had been no reply on the telephone, which meant she must be out. The children would be at school. If she was shopping, perhaps she had met someone who had told her already. He rang the bell, and when no one answered, walked around to the back.

Lisa Larsen liked to keep a large vegetable garden, and he found her feeding carrot tops to Kristina's pet rabbit. She looked up and smiled when she saw him coming around the house.

She doesn't know, he thought. She pushed the remainder of the carrots through the wire of the cage and came over to him, pulling off her gardening gloves.

"Trygve, how nice to see you. What brings you out of town?"

"Lisa, have you listened to the news this morning on the radio?"

She considered the question.

"I listened to the eight o'clock broadcast over breakfast. I've been out here since then, in the garden."

"You didn't answer the telephone?"

For the first time a shadow came into her bright brown eyes. The smile faded.

"No. I wouldn't hear it. Has it been ringing?"

"Look, Lisa, be calm. Something has happened. No, not to the children. To Thor."

She went pale beneath the honey-colored outdoor tan. Carefully, Trygve Dahl told her what had happened since the small hours of the morning, far to the south off Rotterdam.

"So far as we know, he's perfectly all right. Nothing has happened to him, and nothing will. The Germans are bound to release these two men, and all will be well."

She did not cry. She stood quite calmly amid the spring lettuce and said, "I want to go to him."

The police chief was relieved. He could have expected it of her, but he was relieved. Now he could organize things. He was better at that.

"Harald Wennerstrom's private jet is due at the airport in twenty minutes," he said. "I'll run you there. He called me an hour ago. He thought you might want to go to Rotterdam, to be close. Now, don't worry about the children. I'm having them picked up from school before they hear from the teachers. We'll look after them; they can stay with us, of course."

Twenty minutes later she was in the front seat of the car with Dahl, heading quickly back toward Ålesund. The police chief used his radio to hold the ferry across to the airfield. Just after three-thirty the Jetstream in the silver and ice-blue livery of the Nordia Line howled down the runway, swept out over the waters of the bay, and climbed toward the south.

Since the sixties, and particularly through the seventies, the growing outbreaks of terrorism had caused the formation of a routine procedure on the part of the British government to facilitate the handling of them. The principal procedure is called the crisis management committee.

When the crisis is serious enough to involve numerous departments and sections, the committee, grouping liaison officers from all these departments, meets at a central point close to the heart of government to pool information and correlate decisions and actions. This central point is a well-protected chamber two floors below the parquet of the Cabinet Office on Whitehall and a few steps across the lawn from 10 Downing Street. In this room meets the United Cabinet Office Review Group (National Emergency), or UNICORNE.

Surrounding the main meeting room are smaller offices; a separate telephone switchboard, linking UNICORNE with every department of state through direct lines that cannot be interfered with; a teleprinter room fitted with the printers of the main news agencies; a telex room and radio room; and a room for secretaries with typewriters and copiers. There is even a small kitchen where a trusted attendant prepares coffee and light snacks.

The men who grouped under the chairmanship of Cabinet Secretary Sir Julian Flannery just after noon that Friday represented all the departments he adjudged might conceivably be involved.

At this stage, no cabinet ministers were present, though each had sent a representative of at least assistant under secretary level. These included the Foreign Office, Home Office, Defense Ministry, and the departments of the Environment, Trade and Industry, Agriculture and Fisheries, and Energy.

Assisting them were a bevy of specialist experts, including three scientists in various disciplines, notably explosives, ships, and pollution; the Vice Chief of Defense Staff (a vice admiral), someone from Defense Intelligence, from MI5, from the SIS, a Royal Air Force group captain, and a senior Royal Marine colonel named Timothy Holmes.

"Well now, gentlemen," Sir Julian Flannery began, "we have all had the time to read the transcript of the noon broadcast from Captain Larsen. First I think we ought to have a few indisputable facts. May we begin with this ship, the . . . er . . . *Freya*. What do we know about her?"

The shipping expert, coming under the Trade and Industry people, found all eyes on him.

"I've been to Lloyd's this morning and secured the plan of the *Freya*," he said briefly. "I have it here. It's detailed down to the last nut and bolt."

He went on for ten minutes, the plan spread on the table, describing the size, cargo capacity, and construction of the *Freya* in clear, layman's language.

When he had finished, the expert from the Department of

Energy was called on. He had an aide bring to the table a five-foot-long model of a supertanker.

"I borrowed this, this morning," he said, "from British Petroleum. It's a model of their supertanker *British Princess,* quarter of a million tons. But the design differences are few; the *Freya* is just bigger, really."

With the aid of the model of the *Princess* he went on to point out where the bridge was, where the captain's cabin would be, where the cargo holds and ballast holds would probably be, adding that the exact locations of these holds would be known when the Nordia Line could pass them over to London.

The surrounding men watched the demonstration and listened with attention. None more than Colonel Holmes; of all those present, he would be the one whose fellow Marines might have to storm the vessel and wipe out her captors. He knew those men would want to know every nook and cranny of the real *Freya* before they went on board.

"There is one last thing," said the scientist from Energy. "She's full of Mubarraq."

"God!" said one of the other men at the table.

Sir Julian Flannery regarded the speaker benignly.

"Yes, Dr. Henderson?"

The man who had spoken was the scientist from Warren Springs Laboratory who had accompanied the representative of Agriculture and Fisheries.

"What I mean," said Henderson in his unrecycled Scottish accent, "is that Mubarraq, which is a crude oil from Abu Dhabi, has some of the properties of diesel fuel."

He went on to explain that when crude oil is spilled on the sea, it contains both "lighter fractions" which evaporate into the air, and "heavier fractions" which cannot evaporate and which are what viewers see washed onto the beaches as thick black sludge.

"What I mean is," he concluded, "it'll spread all over the bloody place. It'll spread from coast to coast before the lighter fractions evaporate. It'll poison the whole North Sea for weeks, denying the marine life the oxygen it needs to live."

"I see," said Sir Julian gravely. "Thank you, Doctor."

There followed information from other experts. The explosives man from the Royal Engineers explained that, placed in the right areas, industrial dynamite could destroy a ship this size.

"It's also a question of the sheer latent strength contained in the weight represented by a million tons of oil—or anything. If the holes are made in the right places, the unbalanced mass of her will pull her apart. There's one last thing; the message read out by Captain Larsen mentioned the phrase 'at the touch of a button.' He then repeated that phrase. It seems to me there must be nearly a dozen charges placed. That phrase 'the touch of a button,' seems to indicate triggering by radio impulse."

"Is that possible?" asked Sir Julian.

"Perfectly possible," said the sapper, and explained how an oscillator worked.

"Surely they could have wires to each charge, linked to a plunger?" asked Sir Julian.

"It's a question of the weight again," said the engineer. "The wires would have to be waterproof, plastic-coated. The weight of that number of miles of electric cable would nearly sink the launch on which these terrorists arrived."

There was more information about the destructive capacity of the oil by pollution, the few chances of rescuing the trapped crewmen, and the SIS admitted they had no information that might help identify the terrorists from among foreign groups of such people.

The man from MI5, who was actually the deputy chief of C4 Department within that body, the section dealing exclusively with terrorism as it affected Britain, underlined the strange nature of the demands of the captors of the *Freya*.

"These men, Mishkin and Lazareff," he pointed out, "are Jewish. Hijackers who tried to escape from the USSR and ended up shooting a flight captain. One has to assume that those seeking to free them are their friends or admirers. That tends to indicate fellow Jews. The only ones who fit into that category are those of the Jewish Defense League. But so far they've just demonstrated and thrown things. In our files we haven't had Jews threatening to blow people to pieces to free their friends since the Irgun and the Stern Gang."

"Oh dear, one hopes they don't start that again," observed Sir Julian. "If not them, then who else?"

The man from C4 shrugged.

"We don't know," he admitted. "We can notice no one in our files conspicuous by being missing, nor do we have a trace from what Captain Larsen has broadcast to indicate their origins. This morning I thought of Arabs, even Irish.

But neither would lift a finger for imprisoned Jews. It's a blank wall."

Still photographs were brought in, taken by the Nimrod an hour earlier, some showing the masked men on lookout. They were keenly examined.

"MAT-forty-nine," said Colonel Holmes briefly, studying the submachine gun one of the men cradled in his arms. "It's French."

"Ah," said Sir Julian, "now perhaps we have something. These blighters could be French?"

"Not necessarily," said Holmes. "You can buy these things in the underworld. The Paris underworld is famous for its taste for submachine guns."

At three-thirty, Sir Julian Flannery brought the meeting into recess. It was agreed to keep the Nimrod circling above the *Freya* until further notice. The Vice Chief of Defense Staff put forward and had accepted his proposal to divert a naval warship to take up station just over five miles west of the *Freya* to watch her also, in case of an attempt by the terrorists to leave under cover of darkness. The Nimrod would spot them and pass their position to the Navy. The warship would easily overhaul the fishing launch still tied by the *Freya*'s side.

The Foreign Office agreed to ask to be informed of any decision by West Germany and Israel on the terrorists' demands.

"There does not, after all, appear much that Her Majesty's government can do at the present moment," Sir Julian pointed out. "The decision is up to the Israeli Prime Minister and the West German Chancellor. Personally I cannot see what else they can do except to let these wretched young men go to Israel, repugnant though the idea of yielding to blackmail must be."

When the men left the room, only Colonel Holmes of the Royal Marines stayed behind. He sat down again and stared at the model of the quarter-million-ton British Petroleum tanker in front of him.

"Supposing they don't?" he said to himself.

Carefully he began to measure the distance in feet from the sea to the stern taffrail.

The Swedish pilot of the Jetstream was at fifteen thousand feet off the West Frisian Islands, preparing to let down into

Schiedam airfield outside Rotterdam. He turned around and called something to the petite woman who was his passenger. She unbuckled and came forward to where he sat.

"I asked if you wanted to see the *Freya*," the pilot repeated. The woman nodded.

The Jetstream banked away to the sea, and five minutes later tilted gently onto one wing. From her seat, face pressed to the tiny porthole, Lisa Larsen looked down. Far below in a blue sea, like a gray sardine nailed to the water, the *Freya* lay at anchor. There were no ships around her; she was quite alone in her captivity.

Even from fifteen thousand feet, through the clear spring air, Lisa Larsen could make out where the bridge would be, where the starboard side of that bridge was; below it she knew her husband was facing a man with a gun pointed straight at his chest, with explosive beneath his feet. She did not know whether the man with the gun was mad, brutal, or reckless. That he must be a fanatic, she knew.

Two tears welled out of her eyes and ran down her cheeks. When she whispered, her breath misted the perspex disk in front of her.

"Thor, my darling, please come out of there alive."

The Jetstream banked again and began its long drop toward Schiedam. The Nimrod, miles away across the sky, watched it go.

"Who was that?" asked the radar operator of no one in particular.

"Who was what?" replied a sonar operator, having nothing to do.

"Small executive jet just banked over the *Freya*, had a look, and went off to Rotterdam," said the radarman.

"Probably the owner checking on his property," said the crew's wit from the radio console.

On the *Freya* the two lookouts gazed through eyeslits after the tiny sliver of metal high above as it headed east toward the Dutch coast. They did not report it to their leader; it was well above ten thousand feet.

The West German cabinet meeting began just after three P.M. in the Chancellery Office, with Dietrich Busch in the chair as usual. He went straight to the point, as he had a habit of doing.

"Let's be clear about one thing: this is not Mogadisho all

over again. This time we do not have a German plane with a German crew and mainly German passengers on an airstrip whose authorities are prepared to be collaborative toward us. This is a Swedish vessel with a Norwegian captain in international waters; she has crewmen from five countries including the United States, an American-owned cargo insured by a British company, and her destruction would affect at least five coastal nations, including ourselves. Foreign Minister?"

Hagowitz informed his colleagues he had already received polite queries from Finland, Norway, Sweden, Denmark, Holland, Belgium, France, and Britain regarding the kind of decision the government of the Federal Republic might come to. After all, they held Mishkin and Lazareff.

"They are being courteous enough not to exert any pressure to influence our decision, but I have no doubt they would view a refusal on our part to send Mishkin and Lazareff to Israel with the deepest misgivings," he said.

"Once you start giving in to this terrorist blackmail, it never ends," put in the Defense Minister.

"Dietrich, we gave in over the Peter Lorenz affair years ago and paid for it. The very terrorists we freed came back and operated again. We stood up to them over Mogadisho and won; we stood up again over Schleyer and had a corpse on our hands. But at least those were pretty well all-German affairs. This isn't. The lives at stake aren't German; the property isn't German. Moreover, the hijackers in Berlin aren't from a German terrorist group. They're Jews who tried to get away from Russia the only way they knew how. Frankly, it puts us in the devil of a spot," Hagowitz concluded.

"Any chance that it's a bluff, a confidence trick, that they really can't destroy the *Freya* or kill her crew?" someone asked.

The Interior Minister shook his head.

"We can't bank on that. These pictures the British have just transmitted to us show the armed and masked men are real enough. I've sent them along to the leader of GSG-nine to see what he thinks. But the trouble is, approaching a ship with all-around, over-and-under radar and sonar cover is not their area of expertise. It would mean divers or frogmen."

He was referring by GSG-nine to the ultratough unit of West German commandos drawn from the Border Troops who had stormed the hijacked aircraft at Mogadisho five years earlier.

The argument continued for an hour: whether to accede to the terrorists' demands in view of the several nationalities of the probable victims of a refusal, and accept the inevitable protests from Moscow; or whether to refuse and call their bluff; or whether to consult with the British allies about the idea of storming the *Freya*. A compromise view of adopting delaying tactics, stalling for time, testing the determination of the *Freya*'s captors, seemed to be gaining ground. At four-fifteen, there was a quiet knock on the door. Chancellor Busch frowned; he did not like interruptions.

"Herein," he called. An aide entered the room and whispered urgently in the Chancellor's ear. The head of the Federal Republic's government paled.

"Du lieber Gott," he breathed.

When the light aircraft, later traced as a privately owned Cessna on charter from Le Touquet airfield on the northern French coast, began to approach, she was spotted by three different air-traffic-control zones: at Heathrow, Brussels, and Amsterdam. She was flying due north, and the radars put her at five thousand feet, on track for the *Freya*. The ether began to crackle furiously.

"Unidentified light aircraft . . . identify yourself and turn back. You are entering a prohibited area. . . ."

French and English were used; later, Dutch. They had no effect. Either the pilot had switched off his radio or he was on the wrong channel. The operators on the ground began to weep through the wave bands.

The circling Nimrod picked the aircraft up on radar and tried to contact her.

On board the Cessna, the pilot turned to his passenger in despair.

"They'll have my license," he yelled. "They're going mad down there."

"Switch off," the passenger shouted back. "Don't worry, nothing will happen. You never heard them, okay?"

The passenger gripped his camera and adjusted the telephoto lens. He began to sight up on the approaching supertanker. In the forepeak, the masked lookout stiffened and squinted against the sun, now in the southwest. The plane was coming from due south. After watching for several seconds, he took a walkie-talkie from his anorak and spoke sharply into it.

On the bridge, one of his colleagues heard the message, peered forward through the panoramic screen, and walked hurriedly outside onto the wing. Here he, too, could hear the engine note. He reentered the bridge and shook his sleeping colleague awake, snapping several orders in Ukrainian. The man ran downstairs to the door of the day cabin and knocked.

Inside the cabin, Thor Larsen and Andrew Drake, both looking unshaven and more haggard than twelve hours earlier, were still at the table, the gun by the Ukrainian's right hand. A foot away from him was his powerful transistor radio, picking up the latest news. The masked man entered on his command and spoke in Ukrainian. His leader scowled and ordered the man to take over in the cabin.

Drake left the cabin quickly, raced up to the bridge and out onto the wing. As he did so, he pulled on his black mask. From the bridge he gazed up as the Cessna, banking at a thousand feet, performed one orbit of the *Freya* and flew back to the south, climbing steadily. While it turned he had seen the great zoom lens poking down at him.

Inside the aircraft, the free-lance cameraman was exultant.

"Fantastic!" he shouted at the pilot. "Completely exclusive. The magazines will pay their right arms for this."

Drake returned to the bridge and issued a rapid stream of orders. Over the walkie-talkie he told the man up front to continue his watch. The bridge lookout was sent below to summon two men who were catching sleep. When all three returned, he gave them further instructions. When he returned to the day cabin, he did not dismiss the extra guard.

"I think it's time I told those stupid bastards over there in Europe that I am not joking," he told Thor Larsen.

Five minutes later the camera operator on the Nimrod called over the intercom to his captain.

"There's something happening down there, skipper."

Squadron Leader Latham left the flight deck and walked back to the center section of the hull, where the visual image of what the cameras were photographing was on display. Two men were walking down the deck of the *Freya*, the great wall of superstructure behind them, the long, lonely deck ahead. One of the men, the one at the rear, was in black from head to foot, with a submachine gun. The one ahead wore sneakers, casual slacks, and a nylon-type anorak with three horizontal black stripes across its back. The hood was up against the chill afternoon breeze.

"Looks like a terrorist at the back, but a seaman in front," said the camera operator. Latham nodded. He could not see the colors; his pictures were monochrome.

"Give me a closer look," he said, "and transmit."

The camera zoomed down until the frame occupied forty feet of foredeck, both men walking in the center of the picture.

Captain Thor Larsen could see the colors. He gazed through the wide forward windows of his cabin beneath the bridge in disbelief. Behind him the guard with the machine gun stood well back, muzzle trained on the middle of the Norwegian's white sweater.

Halfway down the foredeck, reduced by distance to matchstick figures, the second man, in black, stopped, raised his machine gun, and aimed at the back in front of him. Even through the glazing the crackle of the one-second burst could be heard. The figure in the pillar-box red anorak arched as if kicked in the spine, threw up its arms, pitched forward, rolled once, and came to rest, half-obscured beneath the inspection catwalk.

Thor Larsen slowly closed his eyes. When the ship had been taken over, his third mate, Danish-American Tom Keller, had been wearing fawn slacks and a light nylon windbreaker in bright red with three black stripes across the back. Larsen leaned his forehead against the back of his hand on the glass. Then he straightened, turned to the man he knew as Svoboda, and stared at him.

Drake stared back.

"I warned them," he said angrily. "I told them exactly what would happen, and they thought they could play games. Now they know they can't."

Twenty minutes later the still pictures showing the sequence of what had happened on the deck of the *Freya* were coming out of a machine in the heart of London. Twenty minutes after that, the details in verbal terms were rattling off a teleprinter in the Federal Chancellery in Bonn. It was four-thirty P.M.

Chancellor Busch looked at his cabinet.

"I regret to have to inform you," he said, "that one hour ago a private plane apparently sought to take pictures of the *Freya* from close range, about a thousand feet. Ten minutes later the terrorists walked one of the crew halfway down the deck and, under the cameras of the British Nimrod above them, executed him. His body now lies half under the catwalk, half under the sky."

There was dead silence in the room.

"Can he be identified?" asked one of the ministers in a low voice.

"No, his face was partly covered by the hood of his anorak."

"Bastards," said the Defense Minister. "Now thirty families all over Scandinavia will be in anguish, instead of one. They're really turning the knife."

"In the wake of this, so will the four governments of Scandinavia, and I shall have to answer their ambassadors," said Hagowitz. "I really don't think we have any alternative."

When the hands were raised, the majority were for Hagowitz's proposal: that he instruct the German Ambassador to Israel to seek an urgent interview with the Israeli Premier and ask from him, at Germany's request, the guarantee the terrorists had demanded. Following which, if it was given, the Federal Republic would announce that with regret it had no alternative, in order to spare further misery to innocent men and women outside West Germany, but to release Mishkin and Lazareff to Israel.

"The terrorists have given the Israeli Prime Minister until midnight to offer that guarantee," said Chancellor Busch. "And ourselves until dawn to put these hijackers on a plane. We'll hold our announcement until Jerusalem agrees. Without that, there is nothing we can do, anyway."

By agreement among the NATO allies concerned, the RAF Nimrod remained the only aircraft in the sky above the *Freya*, circling endlessly, watching and noting, sending pictures back to base whenever there was anything to show—pictures that went immediately to London and to the capitals of the concerned countries.

At five P.M. the lookouts were changed, the men from the fo'c'sle and funnel top, who had been there for ten hours, being allowed to return, chilled and stiff, to the crew's quarters for food, warmth, and sleep. For the night watch, they were replaced by others, equipped with walkie-talkies and powerful flashlights.

But the allied agreement on the Nimrod did not extend to surface ships. Each coastal nation wanted an on-site observer from its own Navy. During the late afternoon the French light cruiser *Montcalm* stole quietly out of the south and hove to, just over five nautical miles from the *Freya.* Out of the north, where she had been cruising off the Frisians, came the Dutch missile frigate *Breda,* which stopped six nautical miles to the north of the helpless tanker.

She was joined by the German missle frigate *Brunner,* and the frigates lay five cable lengths away from each other, both watching the dim shape on the southern horizon. From the Scottish port of Leith, where she had been on a courtesy visit, H.M.S. *Argyll* put to sea, and as the first evening star appeared in the cloudless sky, she took up her station due west of the *Freya.*

She was a guided-missile light cruiser, known as a DLG, of just under six thousand tons, armed with batteries of Exocet missiles. Her modern gas-turbine and steam engines had enabled her to put to sea at a moment's notice, and deep in her hull the Data Link computer she carried was tapped into the Data Link of the Nimrod circling fifteen thousand feet above in the darkening sky. Toward her stern, one step up from the afterdeck, she carried her own Westland Wessex helicopter.

Beneath the water, the sonar ears of the warships surrounded the *Freya* on three sides; above the water, the radar scanners swept the ocean constantly. With the Nimrod above, *Freya* was cocooned in an invisible shroud of electronic surveillance. She lay silent and inert as the sun prepared to fall over the English coast.

It was five o'clock in Western Europe but seven in Israel when the West German Ambassador asked for a personal audience with Premier Benyamin Golen. It was pointed out to him at once that the Sabbath had started one hour before and that as a devout Jew the Premier was at rest in his own home. Nevertheless, the message was relayed because neither the Prime Minister's private office nor he himself was unaware of what was happening in the North Sea. Indeed, since the 0900 broadcast from Thor Larsen, the Israeli intelligence service, Mossad, had been keeping Jerusalem informed, and following the demands made at noon concerning Israel, the most copious position papers had been prepared. Before the official start of the Sabbath at six o'clock, Premier Golen had read them all.

"I am not prepared to break *Shabbat* and drive to the office," he told his aide, who telephoned him with the news, "even though I am now answering this telephone. And it is rather a long way to walk. Ask the Ambassador to call on me personally."

Ten minutes later the German Embassy car drew up outside the Premier's ascetically modest house in the suburbs of Jerusalem. When the envoy was shown in, he was apologetic.

After the traditional greetings of "Shabbat Shalom," the Ambassador said:

"Prime Minister, I would not have disturbed you for all the world during the hours of the Sabbath, but I understand it is permitted to break the Sabbath if human life is at stake."

Premier Golen inclined his head.

"It is permitted if human life is at stake or in danger," he conceded.

"In this case, that is very much so," said the Ambassador. "You will be aware, sir, of what has been happening on board the supertanker *Freya* in the North Sea these past twelve hours."

The Premier was more than aware; he was deeply concerned, for since the noon demands, it had become plain that the terrorists, whoever they were, could not be Palestinian Arabs, and might even be Jewish fanatics. But his own agencies, the external Mossad and the internal Sherut Bitachon, called from its initials Shin Bet, had not been able to find any trace of such fanatics being missing from their usual haunts.

"I am aware, Ambassador, and I join in sorrow for the murdered seaman. What is it that the Federal Republic wants of Israel?"

"Prime Minister, my country's cabinet has considered all the issues for several hours. Though it regards the prospect of acceding to terrorist blackmail with utter repugnance, and though if the affair were a completely internal German matter it might be prepared to resist, in the present case it feels it must yield.

"My government's request is therefore that the State of Israel agree to accept Lev Mishkin and David Lazareff, with the guarantees of nonprosecution and nonextradition that the terrorists demand."

Premier Golen had in fact been considering the reply he would make to such a request for several hours. It came as no surprise to him. He had prepared his position. His government was a finely balanced coalition, and privately he was aware that many if not most of his own people were so incensed by the continuing persecution of Jews and the Jewish religion inside the USSR that for them Mishkin and Lazareff were hardly to be considered terrorists in the same class as the Baader-Meinhof gang or the PLO. Indeed, some sympathized with them for seeking to escape by hijacking a Soviet airliner, and accepted that the gun in the cockpit had gone off by accident.

"You have to understand two things, Ambassador. One is that although Mishkin and Lazareff may be Jews, the State of Israel had nothing to do with their original offenses, nor with the demand for their freedom now made."

If the terrorists themselves turn out to be Jewish, how many people are going to believe that? he thought.

"The second thing is that the State of Israel is not directly affected by the plight of the *Freya*'s crew, nor by the effects of her possible destruction. It is not the State of Israel that is under pressure here, or being blackmailed."

"That is understood, Prime Minister," said the German.

"If, therefore, Israel agrees to receive these two men, it must be clearly and publicly understood that she does so at the express and earnest request of the government of the Federal Republic of Germany."

"That request is being made, sir, by me, now, on behalf of my government."

Fifteen minutes later the format was arranged. West Germany would publicly announce that it had made the request to Israel on its own behalf. Immediately afterward, Israel would announce that she had reluctantly agreed to the request. Following that, West Germany could announce the release of the prisoners at 0800 hours the following morning, European time. The announcements would come from Bonn and Jerusalem, and would be synchronized at ten-minute intervals, starting one hour hence. It was seven-thirty in Israel, five-thirty in Europe.

Across the continent the last editions of the afternoon newspapers whirled onto the streets, to be snapped up by a public of three hundred million who had followed the drama since midmorning. The latest headlines gave details of the murder of the unidentified seaman and the arrest of a free-lance French photographer and a pilot at Le Touquet.

Radio bulletins carried the news that the West German Ambassador to Israel had visited Premier Golen in his private house during the Sabbath, and had left thirty-five minutes later. There was no news from the meeting, and speculation was rife. Television had pictures of anyone who would pose for them, and quite a few who preferred not to. The latter were the ones who knew what was going on. No pictures taken by the Nimrod of the seaman's body were released by the authorities.

The daily papers, preparing for issue starting at midnight, were holding front pages for the chance of a statement from Jerusalem or Bonn, or another transmission from the *Freya*. The learned articles on the inside pages about the *Freya* herself, her cargo, the effects of its spillage, speculation on the identity of the terrorists, and editorials urging the release of the two hijackers, covered many columns of copy.

A mild and balmy dusk was ending a glorious spring day when Sir Julian Flannery completed his report to the Prime Minister in her office at 10 Downing Street. It was comprehensive and yet succinct, a masterpiece of draftsmanship.

"We have to assume, then, Sir Julian," she said at length, "that they certainly exist, that they have undoubtedly taken complete possession of the *Freya*, that they could well be in a position to blow her apart and sink her, that they would not stop at doing so, and that the financial, environmental, and human consequences would constitute a catastrophe of appalling dimensions."

"That, ma'am, might seem to be the most pessimistic interpretation, yet the crisis management committee feels it would be rash to assume a more hopeful tone," the Secretary to the Cabinet replied. "Only four have been seen: the two lookouts and their replacements. We feel we must assume another on the bridge, one watching the prisoners, and a leader; that makes a minimum of seven. They might be too few to stop an armed boarding party, but we cannot assume so. They might have no dynamite on board, or too little, or have placed it wrongly, but we cannot assume so. Their triggering device might fail, they might have no second device, but we cannot assume so. They might not be prepared to kill any more seamen, but we cannot assume so. Finally, they might not be prepared actually to blow the *Freya* apart and die with her, but we cannot assume so. Your committee feels it would be wrong to assume less than the possible, which is the worst."

The telephone from her private staff tinkled, and she answered it. When she replaced the receiver, she gave Sir Julian a fleeting smile.

"It looks as if we may not face the catastrophe after all," she said. "The West German government has just announced it has made the request to Israel. Israel has replied that she accedes to the German request. Bonn countered by announcing the release of these two men at eight tomorrow morning."

It was twenty to seven.

The same news came over the transistor radio in the day cabin of Captain Thor Larsen. Keeping him covered all the time, Drake had switched the cabin lights on an hour earlier and drawn the curtains. The cabin was well-lit, warm, almost cheery. The percolator of coffee had been exhausted and replenished five times. It was still bubbling. Both men, the mariner and the fanatic, were stubbled and tired. But one was filled with grief for the death of a friend, and anger; the other triumphant.

"They've agreed," said Drake. "I knew they would. The odds were too long, the consequences too bad."

Thor Larsen might have been relieved at the news of the pending reprieve of his ship. But the controlled anger was burning too hot even for this comfort.

"It's not over yet," he growled.

"It will be. Soon. If my friends are released at eight, they will be in Tel Aviv by one P.M., or two at the latest. With an hour for identification and the publication of the news by radio, we should know by three or four o'clock tomorrow. After dark, we will leave you safe and sound."

"Except Tom Keller out there," snapped the Norwegian.

"I'm sorry about that. The demonstration of our seriousness was necessary. They left me no alternative."

The Soviet Ambassador's request was unusual, highly so, in that it was repeated, tough, and insistent. Although representing a supposedly revolutionary country, Soviet ambassadors are usually meticulous in their observance of diplomatic procedures, originally devised by Western capitalist nations.

David Lawrence repeatedly asked over the telephone whether Ambassador Konstantin Kirov could not talk to him, as U.S. Secretary of State. Kirov replied that his message was for President Matthews personally, extremely urgent, and finally that it concerned matters Chairman Maxim Rudin personally wished to bring to President Matthews's attention.

The President granted Kirov his face-to-face, and the long black limousine with the hammer-and-sickle emblem swept into the White House grounds during the lunch hour.

It was a quarter to seven in Europe, but only a quarter to two in Washington. The envoy was shown straight to the Oval Room by the Secretary of State, to face a President who was puzzled, intrigued, and curious. The formalities were observed, but neither party's mind was on them.

"Mr. President," said Kirov, "I am instructed by a personal order from Chairman Maxim Rudin to seek this urgent interview with you. I am instructed to relay to you his personal message, without variation. It is:

"In the event that the hijackers and murderers Lev Mishkin and David Lazareff are freed from jail and released from their just deserts, the USSR will not be able to sign the Treaty of Dublin in the week after next, or at any time at all. The Soviet Union will reject the treaty permanently."

President Matthews stared at the Soviet envoy in stunned amazement. It was several seconds before he spoke.

"You mean, Maxim Rudin will just tear it up?"

Kirov was ramrod-stiff, formal, unbending.

"Mr. President, that is the first part of the message I have been instructed to deliver to you. It goes on to say that if the nature or contents of this message are revealed, the same reaction from the USSR will apply."

When he was gone, William Matthews turned helplessly to Lawrence.

"David, what the hell is going on? We can't just bully the West German government into reversing its decision without explaining why."

"Mr. President, I think you are going to have to. With respect, Maxim Rudin has just left you no alternative."

CHAPTER FOURTEEN

1900 to Midnight

PRESIDENT WILLIAM MATTHEWS sat stunned by the suddenness, the unexpectedness, and the brutality of the Soviet reaction. He waited while his CIA Director, Robert Benson, and his national security adviser, Stanislaw Poklewski, were sent for.

When the pair joined the Secretary of State in the Oval Office, Matthews explained the burden of the visit from Ambassador Kirov.

"What the hell are they up to?" demanded the President.

None of his three principal advisers could come up with an answer. Various suggestions were put forward, notably that Maxim Rudin had suffered a reverse within his own Politburo and could not proceed with the Treaty of Dublin, and the *Freya* affair was simply his excuse for getting out of signing.

The idea was rejected by mutual consent. Without the treaty the Soviet Union would receive no grain, and they were at their last few truckloads. It was suggested the dead Aeroflot pilot, Captain Rudenko, represented the sort of loss of face the Kremlin could not stomach. This, too, was rejected. International treaties are not torn up because of dead pilots.

The Director of Central Intelligence summed up the feelings of everybody after an hour.

"It just doesn't make sense, and yet it must. Maxim Rudin would not react like a madman unless he had a reason, a reason we don't know."

"That still doesn't get us out from between two appalling alternatives," said President Matthews. "Either we let the release of Mishkin and Lazareff go through, and lose the most important disarmament treaty of our generation, and witness war within a year, or we use our clout to block that release, and subject Western Europe to the biggest ecological disaster of this generation."

"We have to find a third choice," said David Lawrence. "But in God's name, where?"

"There is only one place to look," replied Poklewski. "Inside Moscow. The answer lies inside Moscow somewhere. I do not believe we can formulate a policy aimed at avoiding both the alternative disasters unless we know why Maxim Rudin has reacted in this way."

"I think you're referring to the Nightingale," Benson cut in. "There just isn't the time. We're not talking about weeks, or even days. We have only hours. I believe, Mr. President, that you should seek to speak personally with Maxim Rudin on the direct line. Ask him, as President to President, why he is taking this attitude over two Jewish hijackers."

"And if he declines to give his reason?" asked Lawrence. "He could have given a reason through Kirov. Or sent a personal letter. . . ."

President Matthews made up his mind.

"I am calling Maxim Rudin," he said. "But if he will not take my call or declines to give me an explanation, we will have to assume he is himself under intolerable pressures of some kind within his own circle. So while I am waiting for the call, I am going to entrust Mrs. Carpenter with the secret of what has just happened here and ask for her help through Sir Nigel Irvine and the Nightingale. In the last resort I will call Chancellor Busch in Bonn and ask him to give me more time."

When the caller asked for Ludwig Jahn personally, the switchboard operator at Tegel Jail was prepared to cut him off. There had been numerous press calls seeking to speak with specific officers on the staff in order to elicit details on Mishkin and Lazareff. The operator had her orders: no calls.

But when the caller explained he was Jahn's cousin and that Jahn was to have attended his daughter's wedding the following day at noon, the operator softened. Family was different. She put the call through; Jahn took it from his office.

"I think you remember me," the voice told Jahn.

The officer remembered him well—the Russian with the labor-camp eyes.

"You shouldn't have called me here," he whispered hoarsely. "I can't help you. The guards have been trebled, the shifts changed. I am on shift permanently now, sleeping here in the office until further notice—those are the orders. They are unapproachable now, those two men."

"You had better make an excuse to get out for an hour," said the voice of Colonel Kukushkin. "There's a bar four hundred meters from the staff gate." He named the bar and gave its address. Jahn did not know it, but he knew the street. "In one hour," said the voice. There was a click.

It was eight P.M. in Berlin, and quite dark.

The British Prime Minister had been taking a quiet supper with her husband in the private apartments atop 10 Downing Street when she was summoned to accept a personal call from President Matthews. She was back at her desk when the call came through. The two government leaders knew each other well, and had met a dozen times since Britain's first woman premier came to office. Face-to-face they used Christian names, but even though the super-secure call across the Atlantic could not be eavesdropped, there was an official record made, so they stayed with formalities.

In careful, succinct terms, President Matthews explained the message he had received from Maxim Rudin via his Ambassador in Washington. Joan Carpenter was stunned.

"In heaven's name, why?" she asked.

"That's my problem, ma'am," came the Southern drawl from across the Atlantic. "There is no explanation. None at all. Two more things. Ambassador Kirov advised me that if the content of Rudin's message ever became public knowledge, the same consequences to the Treaty of Dublin would still apply. I may count on your discretion?"

"Implicitly," she replied. "The second thing?"

"I've tried to call Maxim Rudin on the hot line. He is unavailable. Now, from that, I have to assume he has his problems right in the heart of the Kremlin and he can't talk about them. Frankly, that has put me in an impossible position. But about one thing I am absolutely determined. I cannot let that treaty be destroyed. It is far too important to the whole of the Western world. I have to fight for it. I cannot let two hijackers in a Berlin jail destroy it; I cannot let a bunch of terrorists on a tanker in the North Sea unleash an armed conflict between East and West such as would ensue."

"I entirely agree with you, Mr. President," said the Premier from her London desk. "What do you want from me? I imagine you would have more influence with Chancellor Busch than I."

"It's not that, ma'am. Two things. We have a certain amount of information about the consequences to Europe of the *Freya*'s blowing up, but I assume you have more. I need to know every conceivable possible consequence and option in the event the terrorists aboard do their worst."

"Yes," said Mrs. Carpenter, "during the whole of today our people have put together an in-depth study of the ship, her cargo, the chances of containing the spillage, and so on. So far, we haven't examined the idea of storming her. Now we may have to. I will have all our information on those aspects on their way to you within the hour. What else?"

"This is the hard one, and I scarcely know how to ask it," said William Matthews. "We believe there has to be an explanation of Rudin's behavior, and until we know it, we are groping in the dark. If I am to handle this crisis, I have to see some daylight. I have to have that explanation. I need to know if there is a third option. I would like you to ask your people to activate the Nightingale one last time and get that answer for me."

Joan Carpenter was pensive. She had always made it a policy not to interfere with the way Sir Nigel Irvine ran his service. Unlike several of her predecessors, she had steadily declined to poke around in the intelligence services to satisfy her curiosity. Since coming to office she had doubled the budgets of both her directors, of SIS and MI5, had chosen hard-core professionals for the posts, and had been rewarded by their unswerving loyalty. Secure in that loyalty, she trusted them not to let her down. And neither had.

"I will do what I can," she said at length. "But we are talking about something in the very heart of the Kremlin, and a matter of hours. If it is possible, it will be done. You have my word on it."

When the telephone was back in its cradle, she called her husband to tell him not to wait for her, she would be at her desk all night. From the kitchen she ordered a pot of coffee. The practical side of things arranged, she called Sir Julian Flannery at his home, told him simply over the line that a fresh crisis had arisen, and asked him to return at once to the Cabinet Office. Her last call was not on an open line; it was to the duty officer at the head office of the Firm. She asked for Sir Nigel Irvine to be contacted wherever he was, and to be asked to come immediately to No. 10. While waiting, she switched on the office television and caught the start of the nine o'clock BBC news. The long night had begun.

Ludwig Jahn slipped into the booth and sat down, sweating gently. From across the table the Russian regarded him coldly. The plump prison guard could not know that the fearsome Russian was fighting for his own life; the man gave no hint.

He listened impassively as Jahn explained the new procedures, instituted since two that afternoon. In point of fact, Kukushkin had no diplomatic cover; he was hiding out in an SSD safe house in West Berlin as a guest of his East German colleagues.

"So you see," concluded Jahn, "there is nothing I can do. I could not possibly get you into that corridor. There are three on duty, as a minimum figure, night and day. Passes have to be shown every time one enters the corridor, even by me, and we all know each other. We have worked together for years. No new face would be admitted without a check call to the governor."

Kukushkin nodded slowly. Jahn felt relief rising in his chest. They would let him go; they would leave him alone; they would not hurt his family. It was over.

"You enter the corridor, of course," said the Russian. "You may enter the cells."

"Well, yes, I am the Oberachmeister. At periodic intervals I have to check that they are all right."

"At night they sleep?"

"Maybe. They have heard about the matter in the North Sea. They lost their radios just after the noon broadcasts, but one of the other prisoners in solitary shouted the news across to them before the corridor was cleared of all other prisoners. Perhaps they will sleep, perhaps not."

The Russian nodded somberly.

"Then," he said, "you will do the job yourself."

Jahn's jaw dropped.

"No, no," he babbled. "You don't understand. I couldn't use a gun. I couldn't kill anyone."

For answer the Russian laid two slim tubes like fountain pens on the table between them.

"Not guns," he said. "These. Place the open end, here, a few centimeters from the mouth and nose of the sleeping man. Press the button on the side, here. Death occurs within three seconds. Inhalation of hydrogen cyanide gas causes instantaneous death. Within an hour the effects are identical to those of cardiac arrest. When it is done, close the cells, return to the staff area, wipe the tubes clean, and place them in the locker of another guard with access to the same pair of cells. Very simple, very clean. And it leaves you in the clear."

What Kukushkin had laid before the horrified gaze of the senior officer was an updated version of the same sort of poison-gas pistols with which the "Wet Affairs" department of the KGB had assassinated the two Ukrainian nationalist leaders Stepan Bandera and Lev Rebet in Germany two decades earlier. The principle was still simple, the efficiency of the gas increased by further research. Inside the tubes, glass globules of prussic acid rested. The trigger impelled a spring, which worked on a hammer, which crushed the glass. Simultaneously the acid was vaporized by a compressed-air canister, activated in the same motion of pressing the trigger button. Impelled by the compressed air, the gas vapor shot out of the tube into the breathing passages in an invisible cloud. An hour later the telltale bitter almond smell of prussic acid was gone, the muscles of the corpse relaxed again; the symptoms were those of heart attack.

No one would believe two simultaneous heart attacks in two young men; a search would be made. The gas guns, found in the locker of a guard, would incriminate the man almost completely.

"I . . . I can't do that," whispered Jahn.

"But I can, and will, see your entire family in an Arctic labor camp for the rest of their lives," murmured the Russian. "A simple choice, Herr Jahn. The overcoming of your scruples for a brief ten minutes, against all their lives. Think about it."

Kukushkin took Jahn's hand, turned it over, and placed the tubes in the palm.

"Think about it," he said, "but not too long. Then walk into those cells and do it. That's all."

He slid out of the booth and left. Minutes later Jahn closed his hand around the gas guns, slipped them in his raincoat pocket, and went back to Tegel Jail. At midnight, in three hours, he would relieve the evening-shift supervisor. At one A.M. he would enter the cells and do it. He knew he had no alternative.

As the last rays of the sun left the sky, the Nimrod over the *Freya* had switched from her daytime *f*/126 camera to her nighttime *f*/135 version. Otherwise, nothing had changed. The night-vision camera, peering downward with its infrared sights, could pick out most of what was happening fifteen thousand feet beneath. If the Nimrod's captain wanted, he could take still pictures with the aid of the *f*/135's electronic flash, or throw the switch on his aircraft's million-candle-power searchlight.

The night camera failed to notice the figure in the anorak, lying prostrate since midafternoon, slowly begin to move, crawling under the inspection catwalk, and from there inching its way back toward the superstructure. When the figure finally crawled over the sill of the half-open doorway and stood up in the interior, no one noticed. At dawn it was supposed the body had been thrown into the sea.

The man in the anorak went below to the galley, rubbing hands and shivering repeatedly. In the galley he found one of his colleagues and helped himself to a piping mug of coffee. When he had finished he returned to the bridge and sought out his own clothes, the black tracksuit and sweater he had come aboard with.

"Jeez," he told the man on the bridge in his American accent, "you sure didn't miss. I could feel the wadding from those blanks slapping into the back of the windbreaker."

The bridge watch grinned.

"Andriy said to make it good," he replied. "It worked. Mishkin and Lazareff are coming out at eight tomorrow morning. By afternoon they'll be in Tel Aviv."

"Great," said the Ukrainian-American. "Let's hope Andriy's plan to get us off this ship works as well as the rest."

"It will," said the other. "You better get your mask on and give those clothes back to that Yankee in the paint locker. Then grab some sleep. You're on watch at six in the morning."

Sir Julian Flannery reconvened the crisis management committee within an hour of his private talk with the Prime Minister. She had told him the reason why the situation had changed, but he and Sir Nigel Irvine would be the only ones to know, and they would not talk. The members of the committee would simply need to know that, for reasons of state, the release of Mishkin and Lazareff at dawn might be delayed or canceled, depending on the reaction of the German Chancellor.

Elsewhere in Whitehall, page after page of data about the *Freya,* her crew, cargo, and hazard potential were being photographically transmitted direct to Washington.

Sir Julian had been lucky; most of the principal experts from the committee lived within a sixty-minute fast-drive radius of Whitehall. Most were caught over dinner at home, none had left for the countryside; two were traced to restaurants, one to the theater. By nine-thirty the bulk of UNICORNE were seated in conference once again.

Sir Julian explained that their duty now was to assume that the whole affair had passed from the realm of a form of exercise and into the major-crisis category.

"We have to assume that Chancellor Busch will agree to delay the release, pending the clarification of certain other matters. If he does, we have to assume the chance that the terrorists will at least activate their first threat, to vent oil cargo from the *Freya.* Now we have to plan to contain and destroy a possible first slick of twenty thousand tons of crude oil; secondly, to envisage that figure being multiplied fiftyfold."

The picture that emerged was gloomy. Public indifference over years had led to political neglect; nevertheless, the amounts of crude-oil emulsifier in the hands of the British, and the vehicles for their delivery onto an oil slick, were still greater than those of the rest of Europe combined.

"We have to assume that the main burden of containing the ecological damage will fall to us," said the man from Warren Springs. "In the *Amoco Cadiz* affair in 1978, the French refused to accept our help, even though we had better emulsifiers and better delivery systems than they did. Their fishermen paid bitterly for that particular stupidity. The old-fashioned detergent they used instead of our emulsifier concentrates caused as much toxic damage as the oil itself. And they had neither enough of it nor the right delivery systems. It was like trying to kill an octopus with a peashooter."

"I have no doubt the Germans, Dutch, and Belgians will not hesitate to ask for a joint allied operation in this matter," said the man from the Foreign Office.

"Then we must be ready," said Sir Julian. "How much have we got?"

Dr. Henderson from Warren Springs continued.

"The best emulsifier, in concentrated form, will emulsify—that is, break down into minuscule globules that permit natural bacteria to complete the destruction—twenty times its own volume. One gallon of emulsifier for twenty gallons of crude oil. We have one thousand tons in stock."

"Enough for one slick of twenty thousand tons of crude oil," observed Sir Julian. "What about a million tons?"

"Not a chance," said Henderson grimly. "Not a chance in hell. If we start to produce more now, we can manufacture a thousand tons every four days. For a million tons, we'd need fifty thousand tons of emulsifier. Frankly, those maniacs in the black helmets could wipe out most marine life in the North Sea and English Channel, and foul up the beaches from Hull to Cornwall on our side, and Bremen to Ushant on the other."

There was silence for a while.

"Let's assume the first slick," said Sir Julian quietly. "The other is beyond belief."

The committee agreed to issue immediate orders for the procurement during the night of every ton of emulsifier from the store in Hampshire; to commandeer tanker lorries from the petroleum companies through the Energy Ministry; to bring the whole consignment to the esplanade parking lot at Lowestoft on the east coast; and to get under way and divert to Lowestoft every single marine tug with spray equipment, including the Port of London firefighting vessels and the Royal Navy equivalents. By late morning it was hoped to have the entire flotilla in Lowestoft port, tanking up with emulsifier.

"If the sea remains calm," said Dr. Henderson, "the slick will drift gently northeast of the *Freya* on the tide, heading for North Holland, at about two knots. That gives us time. When the tide changes, it should drift back again. But if the wind rises, it might move faster, in any direction, according to the wind, which will overcome the tide at surface level. We should be able to cope with a twenty-thousand ton slick."

"We can't move ships into the area five miles round the *Freya* on three sides, or anywhere between her and the Dutch coast," the Vice Chief of Defense Staff pointed out.

"But we can watch the slick from the Nimrod," said the group captain from the RAF. "If it moves out of range of the *Freya,* your Navy chaps can start squirting."

"So far, so good, for the threatened twenty-thousand-ton spillage," said the Foreign Office man. "What happens after that?"

"Nothing," said Dr. Henderson. "After that, we're finished, expended."

"Well, that's it, then. An enormous administrative task awaits us," said Sir Julian.

"There is one other option," said Colonel Holmes of the Royal Marines. " The hard option."

There was an uncomfortable silence around the table. The vice admiral and the group captain did not share the discomfort; they were interested. The scientists and bureaucrats were accustomed to technical and administrative problems, their countermeasures and solutions. Each suspected the rawboned colonel in civilian clothes was talking about shooting holes in people.

"You may not like the option," said Holmes reasonably, "but these terrorists have killed one sailor in cold blood. They may well kill another twenty-nine. The ship costs one hundred seventy million dollars, the cargo one hundred forty million dollars, the clean-up operation treble that. If, for whatever reason, Chancellor Busch cannot or will not release the men in Berlin, we may be left with no alternative but to try to storm the ship and knock off the man with the detonator before he can use it."

"What exactly do you propose, Colonel Holmes?" asked Sir Julian.

"I propose that we ask Major Fallon to drive up from Dorset and that we listen to him," said Holmes.

It was agreed, and on that note the meeting adjourned until three A.M. It was ten minutes before ten o'clock.

During the meeting, not far away from the Cabinet Office, the Prime Minister had received Sir Nigel Irvine.

"That, then, is the position, Sir Nigel," she concluded. "If we cannot come up with a third alternative, either the men go free and Maxim Rudin tears up the Treaty of Dublin, or they stay in jail and their friends tear up the *Freya*. In the second case, they might stay their hand and not do it, but we can entertain no hopes of that. It might be possible to storm it, but chances of success are slim. In order to have a chance of perceiving the third alternative, we have to know why Maxim Rudin is taking this course. Is he, for example, overplaying his hand? Is he trying to bluff the West into sustaining enormous economic damage in order to offset his own embarrassment over his grain problems? Will he really go through with his threat? We have to know."

"How long have you got, Prime Minister? How long has President Matthews got?" asked the Director General of the SIS.

"One must assume, if the hijackers are not released at dawn, we will have to stall the terrorists, play for time. But I would hope to have something for the President by afternoon tomorrow."

"As a rather long-serving officer, I would have thought that was impossible, ma'am. It is the middle of the night in Moscow. The Nightingale is virtually unapproachable, except at meetings planned well ahead. To attempt an instant rendezvous might well blow that agent sky-high."

"I know your rules, Sir Nigel, and I understand them. The safety of the agent out in the cold is paramount. But so are matters of state. The destruction of the treaty, or the destruction of the *Freya,* is a matter of state. The first could jeopardize peace for years, perhaps put Yefrem Vishnayev in power, with all its consequences. The financial losses alone sustained by Lloyd's, and through Lloyd's the British economy, if the *Freya* destroyed herself and the North Sea, would be disastrous, not to mention the deaths of the remaining twenty-nine seamen. I make no flat order, Sir Nigel. I ask you to put the certain alternatives against the putative hazard to one single Russian agent."

"Ma'am, I will do what I can. You have my word on it," said Sir Nigel, and left to return to his headquarters.

From an office in the Defense Ministry, Colonel Holmes was on the telephone to Poole, Dorset, headquarters of the Special Boat Service, or SBS. Major Simon Fallon was found befriending a pint of beer in the officers' mess and brought to the telephone. The two Marines knew each other well.

"You've been following the *Freya* affair?" asked Holmes from London.

There was a dry chuckle from the other end.

"I thought you'd come shopping here eventually," said Fallon. "What do they want?"

"Things are turning sour," said Holmes. "The Germans may have to change their minds and keep those two jokers in Berlin after all. I've just spent an hour with the reconvened

CMC. They don't like it, but they may have to consider our way. Got any ideas?"

"Sure," said Fallon. "Been thinking about it all day. Need a model, though, and a plan. And the gear."

"Right," said Holmes. "I have the plan here, and a pretty good model of another but similar ship. Get the boys together. Get all the gear out of stores: underwater magnets, all the types of hardware, stun grenades—you name it. The lot. What you don't need can be returned. I'm asking the Navy to come round from Portland and pick up the lot: the gear and the team. When you've left a good man in charge, jump into the car and get up to London. Report at my office as soon as you can."

"Don't worry," said Fallon. "I've got the gear sorted and bagged already. Get the transport here as fast as you can. I'm on my way."

When the hard, chunky major returned to the bar, there was silence. His men knew he had taken a call from London. Within minutes they were rousing the NCOs and Marines from their barracks, changing rapidly out of the plain clothes they had been wearing in the mess into the black webbing and green berets of their unit. Before midnight they were waiting on the stone jetty tucked away in their cordoned section of the Marine base; waiting for the arrival of the Navy to take their equipment to where it was needed.

There was a bright moon rising over Portland Bill to the west of them as the three fast patrol boats *Sabre*, *Cutlass* and *Scimitar* came out of the harbor, heading east for Poole. When the throttles were open, the three prows rose, the sterns buried in the foaming water, and the thunder echoed across the bay.

The same moon illuminated the long track of the Hampshire motorway as Major Fallon's Rover sedan burned up the miles to London.

"Now, what the hell do I tell Chancellor Busch?" President Matthews asked his advisers.

It was five in the afternoon in Washington; though night had long settled on Europe, the late-afternoon sun was still on the Rose Garden beyond the French windows where the first buds were responding to the spring warmth.

"I don't believe you can reveal to him the real message received from Kirov," said Robert Benson.

"Why the devil not? I told Joan Carpenter, and no doubt she'll have had to tell Nigel Irvine."

"There's a difference," pointed out the CIA chief. "The British can take the necessary precautions to cope with an ecological problem in the sea off their coasts by calling on their technical experts. It's a technical problem; Joan Carpenter did not need to call a full cabinet meeting. Dietrich Busch is going to be asked to hold onto Mishkin and Lazareff at the risk of provoking a catastrophe for his European neighbors. For that he'll almost certainly consult his cabinet—"

"He's an honorable man," cut in Lawrence. "If he knows that the price is the Treaty of Dublin, he'll feel bound to share that knowledge with his cabinet."

"And there's the problem," concluded Benson. "That a minimum of fifteen more people would learn of it. Some of them would confide in their wives, their aides. We still haven't forgotten the Günter Guillaume affair. There are just too damn many leaks in Bonn. If it got out, the Dublin Treaty would be finished in any case, regardless of what happened in the North Sea."

His call went through in a minute. "What the hell do I tell him?" repeated Matthews.

"Tell him you have information that simply cannot be divulged on any telephone line, even a secure transatlantic line," suggested Poklewski. "Tell him the release of Mishkin and Lazareff would provoke a greater disaster than even frustrating the terrorists on the *Freya* for a few more hours. Ask him at this stage simply to give you a little time."

"How long?" asked the President.

"As long as possible," said Benson.

"And when the time runs out?" asked the President.

The call to Bonn came through. Chancellor Busch had been contacted at his home. The top-security call was patched through to him there. There was no need of translators on the line; Dietrich Busch spoke fluent English. President Matthews spoke to him for ten minutes while the Bonn government chief listened with growing amazement.

"But why?" he asked at length. "Surely the matter hardly affects the United States."

Matthews was tempted. At the Washington end, Robert Benson wagged a warning finger.

"Mr. Chancellor, please. Believe me. I'm asking you to trust me. On this line, on any line across the Atlantic, I can't be as frank as I'd like to be. Something has cropped up, something of enormous dimensions. Look, I'll be as plain as I can. Over here we have discovered something about these two men; their release would be disastrous at this stage, for the next few hours. I'm asking for time, my friend, just time. A delay until certain things can be taken care of."

The German Chancellor was standing in his study with the strains of Beethoven drifting through the door from the sitting room where he had been enjoying a cigar and a concert on the stereo. To say that he was suspicious would be putting it mildly. So far as he was concerned, the transatlantic line, established years before to link the NATO government heads, and checked regularly, was perfectly safe. Moreover, he reasoned, the United States had perfectly good communications with their Bonn Embassy and could send him a personal message on that route if desired. It did not occur to him that Washington would simply not trust his cabinet with a secret of this magnitude after the repeated exposure of East German agents close to the seat of power on the Rhine.

On the other hand, the President of the United States was not given to making late-night calls or crazy appeals. He had to have his reasons, Busch knew. But what he was being asked was not something he could decide without consultation.

"It is just past ten P.M. over here," he told Matthews. "We have until dawn to decide. Nothing fresh ought to happen until then. I shall reconvene my cabinet during the night and consult with them. I cannot promise you more."

President William Matthews had to be satisfied with that.

When the phone was replaced, Dietrich Busch stayed for long minutes in thought. There was something going on, he reasoned, and it concerned Mishkin and Lazareff, sitting in their separate cells in Tegel Jail in West Berlin. If anything happened to them, there was no way in which the Federal Republic's government would escape a howl of censure from within Germany, by the combined media and the political opposition. And with the state elections coming up . . .

His first call was to Ludwig Fischer, his Minister of Justice, also at home in the capital. None of his ministers would be weekending in the country, by prior agreement. His suggestion was met with immediate agreement by the Justice Minister. To transfer the pair from the old-fashioned prison of Tegel to the much newer and super-secure jail of Moabit was an obvious precaution. No CIA operatives would ever get at them inside Moabit. Fischer telephoned the instruction to Berlin immediately.

There are certain phrases, innocent enough, which when used by the senior cipher clerk at the British Embassy in Moscow to the man he knows to be the SIS resident on the embassy staff, mean, in effect, "Get the hell down here fast. Something urgent is coming through from London." Such was the phrase that brought Adam Munro from his bed at midnight Moscow time, ten P.M. London time, across town to Maurice Thorez Embankment.

Driving back from Downing Street to his office, Sir Nigel Irvine had realized the Prime Minister was absolutely right. Compared to the destruction of the Treaty of Dublin on the one hand or the destruction of the *Freya*, her crew, and her cargo on the other, putting a Russian agent at risk of exposure was the lesser evil. What he was going to ask Munro in Moscow to do, and the way he would have to demand it, gave him no pleasure. But before he arrived at the SIS building he knew it would have to be done.

Deep in the basement, the communications room was handling the usual routine traffic when he entered and startled the night duty staff. But the scrambler telex raised Moscow in less than five minutes. No one queried the right of the Master to talk directly to his Moscow resident in the middle of the night. It was thirty minutes later that the telex from the Moscow cipher room chattered its message that Munro was there and waiting.

The operators at both ends, senior men of a lifetime's experience, could be trusted with the whereabouts of Christ's bones, if necessary—they had to be, they handled, as routine, messages that could bring down governments. From London the telex would send its scrambled, uninterceptible message down to a forest of aerials outside Cheltenham, better known for its horse races and woman's college. From there the words would be converted automatically into an unbreakable one-off code and beamed out over a sleeping Europe to an aerial on the embassy roof. Four seconds after they were typed in London, they would emerge, in clear, on the telex in the basement of the old sugar magnate's house in Moscow.

There, the cipher clerk turned to Munro, standing by his side.

"It's the Master himself," he said, reading the code tag on the incoming message. "There must be a flap on."

Sir Nigel had to tell Munro the burden of Kirov's message to President Matthews of only three hours earlier. Without that knowledge, Munro could not ask the Nightingale for the answer to Matthews's question: Why?

The telex rattled for several minutes. Munro read the message that spewed out, with horror.

"I can't do that," he told the impassive clerk over whose shoulder he was reading. When the message from London was ended, he told the clerk:

"Reply as follows: 'Not repeat not possible obtain this sort of answer in time scale.' Send it."

The interchange between Sir Nigel Irvine and Adam Munro went on for fifteen minutes. There is a method of contacting N at short notice, suggested London. Yes, but only in case of dire emergency, replied Munro. This qualifies one hundred times as emergency, chattered the machine from London. But N could not begin to inquire in less than several days, pointed out Munro. Next regular Politburo meeting not due until Thursday following. What about records of last Thursday's meeting? asked London. *Freya* was not hijacked last Thursday, retorted Munro. Finally Sir Nigel did what he hoped he would not have to do.

"Regret," tapped the machine, "prime ministerial order not refusable. Unless attempt made avert this disaster, operation to bring out N to West cannot proceed."

Munro looked down at the stream of paper coming out of the telex with disbelief. For the first time he was caught in the net of his own attempts to keep his love for the agent he ran from his superiors in London. Sir Nigel Irvine thought the Nightingale was an embittered Russian turncoat called Anatoly Krivoi, right-hand man to the warmonger Vishnayev.

"Make to London," he told the clerk dully, "the following: 'Will try this night stop decline to accept responsibility if N refuses or is unmasked during attempt stop.' "

The reply from the Master was brief: "Agree. Proceed." It was half past one in Moscow, and very cold.

Half past six in Washington, and the dusk was settling over the sweep of lawns beyond the bulletproof windows behind the President's chair, causing the lamps to be switched on. The group in the Oval Office was waiting: waiting for

Chancellor Busch, waiting for an unknown agent in Moscow, waiting for a masked terrorist of unknown origins sitting on a million-ton bomb off Europe with a detonator in his hand. Waiting for the chance of a third alternative.

The phone rang and it was for Stanislaw Poklewski. He listened, held a hand over the mouthpiece, and told the President it was from the Navy Department in answer to his query of an hour earlier.

There was one U.S. Navy vessel in the area of the *Freya*. She had been paying a courtesy visit to the Danish coastal city of Esbjerg, and was on her way back to join her squadron of the Standing Naval Force Atlantic, or STANFORLANT, then cruising on patrol west of Norway. She was well off the Danish coast, steaming north by west to rejoin her NATO allies.

"Divert to *Freya*'s area," said the President.

Poklewski passed the Commander in Chief's order back to the Navy Department, which soon began to make signals via STANFORLANT headquarters to the American warship.

Just after one in the morning, the U.S.S. *Moran*, halfway between Denmark and the Orkney Islands, put her helm about, opened her engines to full power, and then began racing through the moonlight southward for the English Channel. She was a guided-missle ship of almost eight thousand tons, which, although heavier than the British light cruiser *Argyll*, was classified as a destroyer, or DD. Moving at full power in a calm sea, she was making close to thirty knots to bring her to her station five miles from the *Freya* at eight A.M.

There were few cars in the parking lot of the Mojarsky Hotel, just off the roundabout at the far end of Kutuzovsky Prospekt. Those that were there were dark, uninhabited, save two.

Munro watched the lights of the other car flicker and dim, then climbed from his own vehicle and walked across to it. When he climbed into the passenger seat beside her, Valentina was alarmed and trembling.

"What is it, Adam? Why did you call me at the apartment? The call must have been recorded."

He put his arm around her, feeling the trembling through her coat.

"It was from a call box," he said, "and only concerned

Gregor's inability to attend your dinner party. No one will suspect anything."

"At two in the morning?" she remonstrated. "No one makes calls like that at two in the morning. I was seen to leave the apartment compound by the night watchman. He will report it."

"Darling, I'm sorry. Listen."

He told her of the visit by Ambassador Kirov to President Matthews the previous evening; of the news being passed to London; of the demand to him that he try to find out why the Kremlin was taking such an attitude over Mishkin and Lazareff.

"I don't know," she said simply. "I haven't the faintest idea. Perhaps because those animals murdered Captain Rudenko, a man with a wife and children."

"Valentina, we have listened to the Politburo these past nine months. The Treaty of Dublin is vital to your people. Why would Rudin put it in jeopardy over these two men?"

"He has not done so," answered Valentina. "It is possible for the West to control the oil slick if the ship blows up. The costs can be met. The West is rich."

"Darling, there are twenty-nine seamen aboard that ship. They, too, have wives and children. Twenty-nine men's lives against the imprisonment of two. There has to be another and more serious reason."

"I don't know," she repeated. "It has not been mentioned in Politburo meetings. You know that also."

Munro stared miserably through the windshield. He had hoped against hope she might have an answer for Washington, something she had heard inside the Central Committee building. Finally he decided he had to tell her.

When he had finished, she stared through the darkness with round eyes. He caught a hint of tears in the dying light of the moon.

"They promised," she whispered. "They promised they would bring me and Sasha out, in a fortnight, from Rumania."

"They've gone back on their word," he confessed. "They want this last favor."

She placed her forehead on her gloved hands, supported by the steering wheel.

"They will catch me," she mumbled. "I am so frightened."

"They won't catch you." He tried to reassure her. "The KGB acts much more slowly than people think, and the higher their suspect is placed, the more slowly they have to act. If you can get this piece of information for President Matthews, I think I can persuade them to get you out in a few days, you and Sasha, instead of two weeks. Please try, my love. It's our only chance left of ever being together."

Valentina stared through the glass.

"There was a Politburo meeting this evening," she said finally. "I was not there. It was a special meeting, out of sequence. Normally on Friday evenings they are all going to the country. Transcription begins tomorrow—that is, today—at ten in the morning. The staff have to give up their weekend to get it ready for Monday. Perhaps they mentioned the matter."

"Could you get in to see the notes, listen to the tapes?" he asked."

"In the middle of the night? There would be questions asked."

"Make an excuse, darling. Any excuse. You want to start and finish your work early, so as to get away."

"I will try," she said eventually. "I will try—for you, Adam, not for those men in London."

"I know those men in London," said Adam Munro. "They will bring you and Sasha out if you help them now. This will be the last risk, truly the last."

She seemed not to have heard him, and to have overcome, for a while, her fear of the KGB, exposure as a spy, the awful consequences of capture unless she could escape in time. When she spoke, her voice was quite level.

"You know Detsky Mir? The soft-toys counter. At ten o'clock this morning."

He stood on the black tarmac and watched her taillights vanish. It was done. They had asked him to do it, demanded that he do it, and he had done it. He had diplomatic protection to keep him out of Lubyanka. The worst that could happen would be his Ambassador's summons to the Foreign Ministry on Monday morning to receive Dmitri Rykov's icy protest and demand for his removal. But Valentina was walking right into the secret archives, without even the disguise of normal, accustomed, justified behavior to protect her. He looked at his watch. Seven hours, seven hours to go, seven hours of knotted stomach muscles and ragged nerve ends. He walked back to his car.

Ludwig Jahn stood in the open gateway of Tegel Jail and watched the taillights of the armored van bearing Mishkin and Lazareff disappear down the street.

For him, unlike for Munro, there would be no more waiting, no tension stretching through the dawn and into the morning. For him the waiting was over.

He walked carefully to his office on the first floor and closed the door. For a few moments he stood by the open window, then drew back one hand and hurled the first of the cyanide pistols far into the night. He was fat, overweight, unfit. A heart attack would be accepted as possible, provided no evidence was found.

Leaning far out of the window, he thought of his nieces over the Wall in the East, their laughing faces when Uncle Ludo had brought the presents four months ago at Christmas. He closed his eyes, held the other tube beneath his nostrils, and pressed the trigger button.

The pain slammed across his chest like a giant hammer. The loosened fingers dropped the tube, which fell with a tinkle to the street below. Jahn slumped, hit the windowsill, and caved backward into his office, already dead. When they found him, they would assume he had opened the window for air when the first pain came. Kukushkin would not have his triumph. The chimes of midnight were drowned by the roar of a truck that crushed the tube in the gutter to fragments.

The hijacking of the *Freya* had claimed its first victim.

CHAPTER FIFTEEN

Midnight to 0800

THE RESUMED West German cabinet meeting assembled in the Chancellery at one A.M., and the mood when the ministers heard from Dietrich Busch the plea from Washington varied between exasperation and truculence.

"Well, why the hell won't he give a reason?" asked the Defense Minister. "Doesn't he trust us?"

"He claims he has a reason of paramount importance, but cannot divulge it even over the hot line," replied Chancellor Busch. "That gives us the opportunity of either believing him or calling him a liar. At this stage I cannot do the latter."

"Has he any idea what the terrorists will do when they learn Mishkin and Lazareff are not to be released at dawn?" queried another.

"Yes, I think he has. At least the texts of all the exchanges between the *Freya* and Maas Control are in his hands. As we all know, they have threatened either to kill another seaman, or to vent twenty thousand tons of crude, or both."

"Well, then, let him carry the responsibility," urged the Interior Minister. "Why should we take the blame if that happens?"

"I haven't the slightest intention that we should," replied Busch, "but that doesn't answer the question. Do we grant President Matthews's request or not?"

There was silence for a while. The Foreign Minister broke it.

"How long is he asking for?"

"As long as possible," said the Chancellor. "He seems to have some plan afoot to break the deadlock, to find a third alternative. But what the plan is, or what the alternative could be, he alone knows. He and a few people he evidently trusts with the secret," he added with some bitterness. "But that doesn't include us, for the moment."

"Well, personally I think it is stretching the friendship between us a bit far," said the Foreign Minister, "but I think we ought to grant him an extension, while making plain, at least unofficially, that it is at his request, not ours."

"Perhaps he has an idea to storm the *Freya*," suggested Defense.

"Our own people say that would be extremely risky," replied the Interior Minister. "It would require an underwater approach for at least the last two miles, a sheer climb up smooth steel from the sea to the deck, a penetration of the superstructure without being observed from atop the funnel, and the selection of the right cabin with the leader of the terrorists in it. If, as we suspect, the man holds a remote-control detonating mechanism in his hand, he'd have to be shot and killed before he could press the button."

"In any case, it is too late to do it before dawn," said the Defense Minister. "It would have to be in darkness, and that means ten P.M. at the earliest, twenty-one hours from now."

At a quarter to three the German cabinet finally agreed to grant President Matthews his request: an indefinite delay on the release of Mishkin and Lazareff, while reserving the right to keep the consequences under constant review and to reverse that decision if it became regarded in Western Europe as impossible to continue to hold the pair.

At the same time the government spokesman was quietly asked to leak the news to two of his most reliable media contacts that only massive pressure from Washington had caused the about-face in Bonn.

It was eleven P.M. in Washington, four A.M. in Europe, when the news from Bonn reached President Matthews. He sent back his heartfelt thanks to Chancellor Busch and asked David Lawrence:

"Any reply from Jerusalem yet?"

"None," said Lawrence. "We know only that our Ambassador there has been granted a personal interview with Benyamin Golen."

When the Israeli Premier was disturbed for the second time during the Sabbath night, his tetchy capacity for patience was wearing distinctly thin. He received the U.S. Ambassador in his dressing gown, and the reception was frosty. It was three A.M. in Europe, but five in Jerusalem, and the first thin light of Saturday morning was on the hills of Judea.

He listened without reaction to the Ambassador's personal plea from President Matthews. His private fear was for the identity of the terrorists aboard the *Freya*. No terrorist action aimed at delivering Jews from a prison cell had been mounted since the days of his own youth, fighting right on the soil where he stood. Then it had been to free condemned Jewish partisans from a British jail at Acre, and he had been a part of that fight. Now it was Israel that roundly condemned terrorism, the taking of hostages, the blackmail of regimes. And yet . . .

And yet, hundreds of thousands of his own people would secretly sympathize with two youths who had sought to escape the terror of the KGB in the only way left open to them. The same voters would not openly hail the youths as heroes, but they would not condemn them as murderers, either. As to the masked men on the *Freya*, there was a chance that they, too, were Jewish—possibly (heaven forbid) Israelis. He had hoped the previous evening that the affair would be over by sundown of the Sabbath, the prisoners from Berlin inside Israel, the terrorists on the *Freya* captured or dead. There would be a fuss, but it would die down.

Now he was learning that there would be no release. The news hardly inclined him to the American request, which was in any case impossible. When he had heard the Ambassador out, he shook his head.

"Please convey to my good friend William Matthews my heartfelt wish that this appalling affair can be concluded without further loss of life," he replied. "But on the matter of Mishkin and Lazareff my position is this: if on behalf of the government and the people of Israel, and at the urgent request of West Germany, I give a solemn public pledge not to imprison them here or return them to Berlin, then I shall have to abide by that pledge. I'm sorry, but I cannot do as you ask and return them to jail in Germany as soon as the *Freya* has been released."

He did not need to explain what the American Ambassador already knew: that apart from any question of national honor, even the explanation that promises extracted under duress were not binding would not work in this case. The outrage from the National Religious Party, the Gush Emunim extremists, the Jewish Defense League, and the hundred thousand Israeli voters who had come from the USSR in the past decade—all these alone would prevent any Israeli premier from reneging on an international pledge to set Mishkin and Lazareff free.

"Well, it was worth a try," said President Matthews when the cable reached Washington an hour later.

"It now ranks as one possible 'third alternative' that no longer exists," remarked David Lawrence, "even if Maxim Rudin had accepted it, which I doubt."

It was one hour to midnight; lights were burning in five government departments scattered across the capital, as they burned in the Oval Office and a score of other rooms throughout the White House where men and women sat at telephones and teleprinters awaiting the news from Europe. The four men in the Oval Office settled to await the reaction from the *Freya*.

Doctors say three in the morning is the time when the human spirit is at its lowest ebb; it is the hour of deepest weariness, slowest reactions, and gloomiest depression. Three A.M. marked one complete cycle of the sun and moon for the two men who faced each other in the captain's cabin of the *Freya*.

Neither had slept that night or the previous one; each had been forty-four hours without rest; each was drawn and red-eyed.

Thor Larsen, at the epicenter of a whirling storm of international activity, of cabinets and councils, embassies and meetings, plottings and consultations that kept the lights burning on three continents from Jerusalem to Washington, was playing his own game. He was pitting his own capacity to stay awake against the will of the fanatic who faced him, knowing that at stake if he failed were the lives of his crew and his ship.

Larsen knew that the man who called himself Svoboda, younger and consumed by his own inner fire, nerves tightened by a combination of black coffee and the tension of his gamble against the world, could have ordered the Norwegian captain to be tied up while he himself sought rest. So the bearded mariner sat facing the barrel of a gun and played on his captor's pride, hoping that the man would take his challenge, refuse to back down, and concede defeat in the game of beating sleep.

It was Larsen who proposed the endless cups of strong black coffee, a drink he usually took with milk and sugar only two or three times a day. It was he who talked through the day and the night, provoking the Ukrainian with suggestions of eventual failure, then backing off when the man became too irritable for safety. Long years of experience, nights of yawning, gritty-mouthed training as a sea captain, had taught the bearded giant to stay awake and alert through the night watches, when the cadets drowsed and the deckhands dozed.

So he played his own solitary game, without guns or ammunition, without teleprinters or night-sight cameras, without support and without company. All the superb technology the Japanese had built into his new command was as much use as rusty nails to him now. If he pushed the man across the table too far, he might lose his temper and shoot to kill. If he were provoked too far, he could order the execution of another crewman. If he felt himself becoming too drowsy, he might have himself relieved by another, fitter terrorist while he himself took sleep and undid all that Larsen was trying to do to him.

That Mishkin and Lazareff would be released at dawn, Larsen still had reason to believe. After their safe arrival in Tel Aviv, the terrorists would prepare to quit the *Freya*. Or would they? Could they? Would the surrounding warships let them go so easily? Even away from the *Freya*, attacked by the NATO navies, Svoboda could press his button and blow the *Freya* apart.

But that was not all of it. This man in black had killed one of the crew. Thor Larsen wanted him for that, and he wanted him dead. So he talked the night away to the man opposite him, denying them both sleep.

Whitehall was not sleeping, either. The crisis management committee had been in session since three A.M., and by four, the progress reports were complete.

Across southern England the bulk tanker lorries, commandeered from Shell, British Petroleum, and a dozen other sources, were filling up with emulsifier concentrate at the Hampshire depot. Bleary-eyed drivers rumbled through the night, empty toward Hampshire or loaded toward Lowestoft, moving hundreds of tons of the concentrate to the Suffolk port. By four A.M. the stocks were empty; all one thousand tons of the national supply were headed east to the coast.

So also were inflatable booms to try to hold the vented oil away from the coast until the chemicals could do their work. The factory that made the emulsifier had been geared for maximum output until further notice.

At half past three the news had come from Washington that the Bonn cabinet had agreed to hold Mishkin and Lazareff for a while longer.

"Does Matthews know what he's doing?" someone asked.

Sir Julian Flannery's face was impassive.

"We must assume that he does," he said smoothly. "We must also assume that a venting by the *Freya* will probably now take place. The efforts of the night have not been in vain. At least we are now almost ready."

"We must also assume," said the civil servant from the Foreign Ministry, "that when the announcement becomes public, France, Belgium, and Holland are going to ask for assistance in fighting any oil slick that may result."

"Then we shall be ready to do what we can," said Sir Julian. "Now, what about the spraying and firefighting vessels?"

The report in the UNICORNE room mirrored what was happening at sea. From the Humber estuary, tugs were churning south toward Lowestoft harbor, while from the Thames and even as far around as the Navy base at Lee, other tugs capable of spraying liquid onto the surface of the sea were moving to the rendezvous point on the Suffolk coast. They were not the only things moving around the south coast that night.

Off the towering cliffs of Beachy Head, the *Cutlass, Scimitar,* and *Sabre,* carrying the assorted, complex, and lethal hardware of the world's toughest team of assault frogmen, were pointing their noses north of east to bring them past Sussex and Kent toward where the cruiser *Argyll* lay at anchor in the North Sea.

The boom of their engines echoed off the chalk battlements of the southern coast, and light sleepers in Eastbourne heard the rumble out to sea.

Twelve Royal Marines of the Special Boat Service clung to the rails of the bucking craft, watching over their precious kayaks and the crates of diving gear, weapons, and unusual explosives that made up the props of their trade. It was all being carried as deck cargo.

"I hope," shouted the young lieutenant commander who skippered the *Cutlass* to the Marine beside him, the second-in-command of the team, "that those whizz-bangs you're carrying back there don't go off."

"They won't," said the Marine captain with confidence, "not until we use them."

In a room adjoining the main conference center beneath the Cabinet Office, their commanding officer was poring over photographs of the *Freya,* taken by night and day. He was comparing the configuration shown by the Nimrod's pictures with the scale plan provided by Lloyd's and the model of the supertanker *British Princess* lent by British Petroleum.

"Gentlemen," said Colonel Holmes, joining the assembled men next door, "I think it's time we considered one of the less palatable choices we may have to face."

"Ah, yes," said Sir Julian regretfully, "the hard option."

"If," pursued Holmes, "President Matthews continues to

object to the release of Mishkin and Lazareff, and West Germany continues to accede to that demand, the moment may well come when the terrorists will realize the game is up, that their blackmail is not going to work. At that moment they may well refuse to have their bluff called, and blow the *Freya* to pieces. Personally, it seems to me this will not happen before nightfall, which gives us about sixteen hours."

"Why nightfall, Colonel?" asked Sir Julian.

"Because, sir, unless they are all suicide candidates, which they may be, one must assume that they will seek their own escape in the confusion. Now, if they wish to try to live, they may well leave the ship and operate their remote-control detonator at a certain distance from the ship's side."

"And your proposal, Colonel?"

"Twofold, sir. Firstly, their launch. It is still moored beside the courtesy ladder. As soon as darkness falls, a diver could approach that launch and attach a delayed-action explosive device to it. If the *Freya* were to blow up, nothing within a half-mile radius would be safe. Therefore I propose a charge detonated by a mechanism operated by water pressure. As the launch moves away from the ship's side, the forward thrust of the launch will cause water to enter a funnel beneath the keel. This water will operate a trigger, and sixty seconds later the launch will blow up, before the terrorists have reached a point half a mile from the *Freya*, and therefore before they can operate their own detonator."

"Would the exploding of their launch not detonate the charges on the *Freya?*" asked someone.

"No. If they have a remote-control detonator, it must be electronically operated. The charge would blow the launch carrying the terrorists to smithereens. No one would survive."

"But if the detonator sank, would not the water pressure depress the button?" asked one of the scientists.

"No. Once under the water, the remote-control detonator would be safe. It could not beam its radio message to the larger charges in the ship's tanks."

"Excellent," said Sir Julian. "Can this plan not operate before darkness falls?"

"No, it cannot," answered Holmes. "A frogman diver leaves a trail of bubbles. In stormy weather this might not be noticed, but on a flat sea it would be too obvious. One of the lookouts could spot the bubbles rising. It would provoke what we are trying to avoid."

"After dark it is, then," said Sir Julian.

"Except for one thing, which is why I oppose the idea of sabotaging their escape launch as the only ploy. If, as may well happen, the leader of the terrorists is prepared to die with the *Freya*, he may not leave the ship with the rest of his team. So I believe we may have to storm the ship during a night attack and get to him before he can use his device."

The Cabinet Secretary sighed.

"I see. Doubtless you have a plan for that as well?"

"Personally, I do not. But I would like you to meet Major Simon Fallon, commanding the Special Boat Service."

It was all the stuff of Sir Julian Flannery's nightmares. The Marine major was barely five feet eight inches tall, but he seemed about the same across the shoulders and was evidently of that breed of men who talk about reducing other humans to their component parts with the same ease that Lady Flannery talked of dicing vegetables for one of her famous Provençal salads.

In at least three encounters the peace-loving Cabinet Secretary had had occasion to meet officers from the SAS, but this was the first time he had seen the commander of the other, smaller specialist unit, the SBS. They were, he observed to himself, of the same breed.

The SBS had originally been formed for conventional war, to act as specialists in attacks from the sea on coastal installations. That was why they were drawn from the Marine commandos. As a basic requirement they were physically fit to a revolting degree, experts in swimming, canoeing, diving, climbing, marching, and fighting.

From there they went on to become proficient in parachuting, explosives, demolition, and the seemingly limitless techniques of cutting throats or breaking necks with knife, wire loop, or simply bare hands. In this, and in their capacity for living in self-sufficiency on, or rather off, the countryside for extended periods and leaving no trace of their presence, they simply shared the skills of their cousins in the SAS.

It was in their underwater skills that the SBS men were different. In frogman gear they could swim prodigious distances and lay explosive charges, or drop their swimming gear while treading water without a ripple and emerge from the sea with their arsenal of special weapons wrapped about them.

Some of their weaponry was fairly routine: knives and cheese wire. But since the start of that rash of outbreaks of terrorism in the late sixties, they had acquired fresh toys that delighted them.

All were expert marksmen with their high-precision, hand-tooled Finlanda rifle, a Norwegian-made piece that had been evaluated as perhaps the best rifle in the world. It could be, and usually was, fitted with an image intensifier, a sniperscope as long as a bazooka, and a completely effective silencer and flash guard.

For taking doors away in half a second, they tended, like the SAS, toward short-barreled pump-action shotguns firing solid charges. These they never aimed at the lock, for there could be other bolts behind the door; they fired two simultaneously to take off both hinges, kicked the door down, and opened fire with the silenced Ingram machine pistols.

Also in the arsenal that had helped the SAS assist the Germans at Mogadisho were their flash-bang-crash grenades, a sophisticated development of the "stun" grenades. These do more than just stun; they paralyze. With a half-second delay after pulling the pin, these grenades, thrown into a confined space containing both terrorists and hostages, have three effects. The flash blinds anyone looking in that direction for at least thirty seconds, the bang blows the eardrums out, causing instant pain and a certain loss of concentration, and the crash is a tonal sound that enters the middle ear and causes a ten-second paralysis of all muscles. (During tests, one of their own men once tried to pull the trigger of a gun pressed into a companion's side while the grenade went off. It was impossible. Both "terrorist" and "hostage" lost their eardrums. But eardrums can grow again; dead hostages cannot.)

While the paralytic effect lasts, the rescuers spray bullets four inches over head height while their colleagues dive for the hostages, dragging them to the floor. At this point, the firers drop their aim by six inches.

The exact position of hostage and terrorist in a closed room can be determined by the application of an electronic stethoscope to the outside of the door. Speech inside the room is not necessary; breathing can be heard and located accurately. The rescuers communicate in an elaborate sign language that permits of no misunderstanding.

Major Fallon placed the model of the *Princess* on the conference table, aware he had the attention of everyone present.

"I propose," he began, "to ask the cruiser *Argyll* to turn herself broadside on to the *Freya,* and then before dawn park the assault boats containing my men and equipment close up in the lee of the *Arygll*, where the lookout, here, on top of the *Freya*'s funnel, cannot see them, even with binoculars. That will enable us to make our preparations, unobserved, through the afternoon. In case of airplanes hired by the press, I would like the sky cleared, and any emulsifier-spraying tugs within visual range of what we are doing to keep silent."

There was no dissent to that. Sir Julian made two notes.

"I would approach the *Freya* with four two-man kayaks, halting at a range of three miles, in darkness, before the rising of the moon. Her radar will not spot kayaks. They are too small, too low in the water; they are of wood and canvas construction, which does not effectively register on radar. The paddlers will be in rubber, leather, wool undervests, and so on, and all buckles will be plastic. Nothing should register on the *Freya*'s radar.

"The men in the rear seats will be frogmen; their oxygen bottles have to be of metal, but at three miles will not register larger than a floating oil drum, not enough to cause alarm on the *Freya*'s bridge. At a range of three miles the divers take a compass bearing on the *Freya*'s stern, which they can see because it is illuminated, and drop overboard. They have luminescent wrist compasses, and swim by these."

"Why not go for the bow?" asked the RAF group captain. "It's darker there."

"Partly because it would mean eliminating the man on lookout high up on the fo'c'sle, and he may be in walkie-talkie contact with the bridge," said Fallon. "Partly because it's a hell of a long walk down that deck, and they have a spotlight operable from the bridge. Partly because the superstructure, approached from the front, is a steel wall five stories high. We would climb it, but it has windows to cabins, some of which may be occupied.

"The four divers, one of whom will be me, rendezvous at the stern of the *Freya*. There should be a tiny overhang of a few feet. Now, there's a man on top of the funnel, a hundred feet up. But people a hundred feet up tend to look outward rather than straight down. To help him in this, I want the *Argyll* to start flashing her searchlight to another nearby vessel, creating a spectacle for the man to watch. We will come up the stern from the water, having shed flippers, masks, oxygen bottles, and weighted belts. We will be bareheaded, barefoot, in rubber wet suits only. All weaponry carried in wide webbing belts round the waist."

"How do you get up the side of the *Freya* carrying forty

pounds of metal after a three-mile swim?" asked one of the ministry men.

Fallon smiled.

"It's only thirty feet at most to the taffrail," he said. "While practicing on the North Sea oil rigs, we've climbed a hundred sixty feet of vertical steel in four minutes."

He saw no point in explaining the details of the fitness necessary for such a feat, nor of the equipment that made it possible.

The boffins had long ago developed for the SBS some remarkable climbing gear. Included among it were magnetic climbing clamps. These were like dinner plates, fringed with rubber so that they could be applied to metal without making a sound. The plate itself was rimmed with steel beneath the rubber, and this steel ring could be magnetized to enormous strength.

The magnetic force could be turned on or off by a thumb switch pressed by the man holding the grip on the back of the plate. The electrical charge came from a small but reliable nickel-cadmium battery inside the climbing plate.

The divers were trained to come out of the sea, reach upward and affix the first plate, then turn on the current. The magnet jammed the plate to the steel structure. Hanging on this, they reached higher and hung the second plate. Only when it was secure did they unlock the first disk, reach higher still, and reaffix it. Hand over hand, hanging on by fist grip, wrist, and forearm, they climbed out of the sea and upward—body, legs, feet, and equipment swinging free, pulling against the hands and wrists.

So strong were the magnets, so strong also the arms and shoulders, that the commandoes could climb an overhang of forty-five degrees if they had to.

"The first man goes up with the special clamps," said Fallon, "trailing a rope behind him. If it is quiet on the poop deck, he fixes the rope, and the other three can be on deck inside ten seconds. Now, here, in the lee of the funnel assembly, this turbine housing should cast a shadow in the light thrown by the lamp above the door to the superstructure at A deck level. We group in this shadow. We'll have black wet suits; black hands, feet, and faces.

"The first major hazard is getting across this patch of illuminated afterdeck from the shadow of the turbine housing to the main superstructure with all its living quarters."

"So how do you do it?" asked the vice admiral, fascinated by this return from technology to the days of Nelson.

"We don't, sir," said Fallon. "We will be on the side of the funnel assembly away from where the *Argyll* is stationed. We hope the lookout atop the funnel will be looking at the *Argyll,* away from us. We move across from the shadow of the turbine housing, round the corner of the superstructure to this point here, outside the window of the dirty-linen store. We cut the plate-glass window in silence with a miniature blowtorch working off a small gas bottle, and go in through the window. The chances of the door of such a store being locked are pretty slim. No one pinches dirty linen, so no one locks such doors. By this time we will be inside the superstructure, emerging to a passage a few yards from the main stairway leading up to B, C, and D decks, and the bridge."

"Where do you find the terrorist leader," asked Sir Julian Flannery, "the man with the detonator?"

"On the way up the stairs we listen at every door for sounds of voices," said Fallon. "If there are any, we open the door and eliminate everyone in the room with silenced automatics. Two men entering the cabin; two men outside on guard. All the way up the structure. Anyone met on the stairs, the same thing. That should bring us to D deck unobserved. Here we have to take a calculated gamble. One choice is the captain's cabin; one man will take that choice. Open the door, step inside, and shoot without any question. Another man will take the chief engineer's cabin on the same floor, other side of the ship. Same procedure. The last two men will cover the first officer's and chief steward's cabins and take the bridge itself; one man with grenades, the second with an Ingram. It's too big an area, that bridge, to pick targets. We'll just have to sweep it with the Ingram and take everybody in the place after the grenades have paralyzed them."

"What if one of them is Captain Larsen?" asked a ministry man.

Fallon studied the table.

"I'm sorry, there's no way of identifying targets," he said.

"Suppose none of the cabins or the bridge contains the leader? Suppose the man with the remote-control detonator is somewhere else? Out on deck taking the air? In the lavatory? Asleep in another cabin?"

Simon Fallon shrugged. "Bang," he said, "big bang."

"There are twenty-eight crewmen locked down below,"

protested a scientist. "Can't you get them out? Or at least up on deck where they could have a chance to swim for it?"

"No, sir. I've tried every way of getting down to the paint locker, if they are indeed in the paint locker. To attempt to get down through the deck housing would give the game away: the bolts could well squeak; the opening of the steel door would flood the poop deck with light. To go down through the main superstructure to the engine room and try to get them that way would split my force. Moreover, the engine room is vast: three levels of it, vaulted like a cathedral. One single man down there, in communication with his leader before we could silence him, and everything would be lost. I believe getting the man with the detonator is our best chance."

"If she does blow up with you and your men topside, I suppose you can dive over the side and swim for the *Argyll?*" suggested another of the ministry civil servants.

Major Fallon looked at the man with anger in his suntanned face.

"Sir, if she blows up, any swimmer within two hundred yards of her will be sucked down into the currents of water pouring into her holes."

"I'm sorry, Major Fallon," interposed the Cabinet Secretary hurriedly. "I am sure my colleague was simply concerned for your own safety. Now the question is this. The percentage chance of your hitting the holder of the detonator is a highly problematical figure. Failure to stop the man from setting off his charges would provoke the very disaster we are trying to avoid—"

"With the greatest respect, Sir Julian," cut in Colonel Holmes, "if the terrorists threaten during the course of the day to blow up the *Freya* at a certain hour tonight, and Chancellor Busch will not weaken in the matter of releasing Mishkin and Lazareff, surely we will have to try Major Fallon's way. We'll be in a no-win situation then, anyway. We'll have no alternative."

The meeting murmured assent. Sir Julian conceded.

"Very well. Defense Ministry will please make to *Argyll*: she should turn herself broadside to the *Freya* and provide a lee shelter for Major Fallon's assault boats when they arrive. Environment will instruct air-traffic controllers to spot and turn back all aircraft trying to approach the *Argyll* at any altitude; various responsible departments will instruct the tugs and other vessels near the *Argyll* not to betray Major Fallon's preparations to anyone. What about you personally, Major Fallon?"

The Marine commando glanced at his watch. It was five-fifteen.

"The Navy is lending me a helicopter from the Battersea Heliport to the afterdeck of the *Argyll*," he said. "I'll be there when my men and equipment arrive by sea if I leave now. . . ."

"Then be on your way, and good luck to you, young man."

The men at the meeting stood up in tribute as a somewhat embarrassed major gathered his model ship, his plans and photographs, and left with Colonel Holmes for the helicopter pad beside the Thames Embankment.

A weary Sir Julian Flannery left the smoke-charged room to ascend to the chill of the predawn of another spring day and report to his Prime Minister.

At six A.M. a simple statement from Bonn was issued to the effect that after due consideration of all the factors involved, the government of the Federal Republic of Germany had come to the conclusion that it would after all be wrong to accede to blackmail and that therefore the policy of releasing Mishkin and Lazareff at eight A.M. had been reconsidered.

Instead, the statement continued, the Federal Republic's government would do all in its power to enter into negotiations with the captors of the *Freya*, with a view to seeking the release of the ship and its crew by alternative proposals.

The European allies of West Germany were informed of this statement just one hour before it was issued. Each and every premier privately asked the same question:

"What the hell is Bonn up to?"

The exception was Joan Carpenter in London, who knew already. But unofficially, each government was informed that the reversal of position stemmed from urgent American pressure on Bonn during the night, and informed, moreover, that Bonn had agreed to delay the release only pending further and, it was hoped, more optimistic developments.

With the breaking of the news, the Bonn government spokesman had a brief and very private working breakfast with two influential German journalists, during which the newsmen were given to understand in oblique terms that the change of policy stemmed only from brutal pressure from Washington.

The first radio newscasts of the day carried the fresh statement out of Bonn even as the listeners were picking up their newspapers, which confidently announced the release at breakfast time of the two hijackers. The newspaper editors were not amused and bombarded the government's press office for an explanation. None was forthcoming that satisfied anyone. The Sunday papers, due for preparation that Saturday, geared themselves for an explosive issue the following morning.

On the *Freya*, the news from Bonn came over the BBC World Service, to which Drake had tuned his portable radio, at six-thirty. Like many another interested party in Europe that morning, the Ukrainian listened to the news in silence, then burst out:

"What the hell do they think they're up to?"

"Something has gone wrong," said Thor Larsen flatly. "They've changed their minds. It's not going to work."

For answer, Drake leaned far across the table and pointed his handgun straight at the Norwegian's face.

"Don't you gloat!" he shouted. "It's not just my friends in Berlin they're playing silly games with. It's not just me. It's your precious ship and crew they're playing with. And don't you forget it."

He went into deep thought for several minutes, then used the captain's intercom to summon one of his men from the bridge. The man, when he came to the cabin, was still masked, and spoke to his chief in Ukrainian, but the tone sounded worried. Drake left him to guard Captain Larsen and was away for fifteen minutes. When he returned, he brusquely beckoned the *Freya*'s skipper to accompany him to the bridge.

The call came in to Maas Control just a minute before seven. Channel 20 was still reserved for the *Freya* alone, and the duty operator was expecting something, for he, too, had heard the news from Bonn. When the *Freya* called, he had the tape spinning.

Larsen's voice sounded tired, but he read the statement from his captors in an unemotional tone.

" 'Following the stupid decision of the government in Bonn to reverse its decision to release Lev Mishkin and David Lazareff at oh-eight-hundred hours this morning, those who presently hold the *Freya* announce the following: in the event that Mishkin and Lazareff are not released and airborne on their way to Tel Aviv by noon today, the *Freya* will, on the stroke of noon, vent twenty thousand tons of crude oil into the North Sea. Any attempt to prevent this, or interfere with the process, and any attempt by ships or aircraft to enter the area of clear water around the *Freya*, will result in the immediate destruction of the ship, her crew, and her cargo.' "

The transmission ceased, and the channel was cut off. No questions were asked. Almost a hundred listening posts heard the message, and it was contained in news flashes on the breakfast radio shows across Europe within fifteen minutes.

President Matthews's Oval Office was beginning to adopt the aspect of a council of war by the small hours of the morning.

All four men in it had taken their jackets off and loosened ties. Aides came and went with messages from the communications room for one or another of the presidential advisers. The corresponding communication rooms at Langley and the State Department had been patched through to the White House. It was seven-fifteen European time but two-fifteen in the small hours when the news of Drake's ultimatum was brought into the office and handed to Robert Benson. He passed it without a word to President Matthews.

"I suppose we should have expected it," said the President wearily, "but that makes it no easier to take."

"Do you think he'll really do it, whoever he is?" asked Secretary of State David Lawrence.

"He's done everything else he's promised so far, damn him," replied Stanislaw Poklewski.

"I assume Mishkin and Lazareff are under extra-heavy guard in Tegel," said Lawrence.

"They're not in Tegel anymore," replied Benson. "They were moved just before midnight, Berlin time, to Moabit. It's more modern and more secure."

"How do you know, Bob?" asked Poklewski.

"I've had Tegel and Moabit under surveillance since the *Freya*'s noon broadcast," said Benson.

Lawrence, the old-style diplomat, looked exasperated.

"Is it the new policy to spy even on our allies?" he snapped.

"Not quite," replied Benson. "We've always done it."

"Why the change of jail, Bob?" asked Matthews. "Does

Dietrich Busch think the Russians would try to get at Mishkin and Lazareff?"

"No, Mr. President. He thinks I will," said Benson.

"There seems to me a possibility here that maybe we hadn't thought of," interposed Poklewski. "If the terrorists on the *Freya* go ahead and vent twenty thousand tons of crude, and, say, threaten to vent a further fifty thousand tons later in the day, the pressures on Busch could become overwhelming. . . ."

"No doubt they will," observed Lawrence.

"What I mean is, Busch might simply decide to go it alone and release the hijackers unilaterally. Remember, he doesn't know that the price of such an action would be the destruction of the Treaty of Dublin."

There was silence for several seconds.

"There's nothing I can do to stop him," said President Matthews quietly.

"There is, actually," said Benson. He had the instant attention of the other three. When he described what it was, the faces of Matthews, Lawrence, and Poklewski showed disgust.

"I couldn't give that order," said the President.

"It's a pretty terrible thing to do," agreed Benson, "but it's the only way to preempt Chancellor Busch. And we will know if he tries to make secret plans to release the pair prematurely. Never mind how; we *will* know. Let's face it; the alternative would be the destruction of the treaty, and the consequences in terms of a resumed arms race that this must bring. If the treaty is destroyed, presumably we will not go ahead with the grain shipments to Russia. In that event, Rudin may fall. . . ."

"Which makes his reaction over this business so crazy," Lawrence pointed out.

"Maybe so, but that *is* his reaction, and until we know why, we can't judge how crazy he is," Benson resumed. "Until we do know, Chancellor Busch's private knowledge of the proposal I have just made should hold him in check awhile longer."

"You mean we could just use it as something to hold over Busch's head?" asked Matthews hopefully. "We might never actually have to do it?"

At that moment a personal message arrived for the President from Prime Minister Carpenter in London.

"That's some woman," he said when he had read it. "The British think they can cope with the first oil slick of twenty thousand tons, but no more. They're preparing a plan to storm the *Freya* with specialist frogmen after sundown and silence the man with the detonator. They give themselves a better than even chance."

"So we only have to hold the German Chancellor in line for another twelve hours," said Benson. "Mr. President, I urge you to order what I have just proposed. The chances are it will never have to be activated."

"But if it must be, Bob? If it must be?"

"Then it must be."

William Matthews placed the palms of his hands over his face and rubbed tired eyes with his fingertips.

"Dear God, no man should be asked to give orders like that," he said. "But if it must . . . Bob, give the order."

The sun was just clear of the horizon, away to the east over the Dutch coast. On the afterdeck of the cruiser *Argyll*, now turned broadside to where the *Freya* lay, Major Fallon stood and looked down at the three fast assault craft tethered to her lee side. From the lookout on the *Freya*'s funnel top, all three would be out of vision. So, too, the activity on their decks, where Fallon's team of Marine commandos were preparing their kayaks and unpacking their unusual pieces of equipment. It was a bright, clear sunrise, giving promise of another warm and sunny day. The sea was a flat calm. Fallon was joined by the *Argyll*'s skipper, Captain Richard Preston.

They stood side by side, looking down at the three sleek sea greyhounds that had brought the men and equipment from Poole in eight hours. The boats rocked in the swell of a warship passing several cables to the west of them. Fallon looked up.

"Who's that?" he asked, nodding toward the gray warship flying the Stars and Stripes that was moving to the south.

"The American Navy has sent an observer," said Captain Preston. "The U.S.S. *Moran*. She'll take up station between us and the *Montcalm*." He glanced at his watch. "Seven-thirty. Breakfast is being served in the wardroom, if you'd care to join us."

It was seven-fifty when there was a knock at the door of the cabin of Captain Michael Manning, commanding the *Moran*.

She was at anchor after her race through the night, and

Manning, who'd been on the bridge throughout the night, was running a razor over the stubble on his chin. When the radioman entered, Manning took the proffered message and gave it a glance, still shaving. He stopped and turned to the sailor.

"It's still in code," he said.

"Yes, sir. It's tagged for your eyes only, sir."

Manning dismissed the man, went to his wall safe and took out his personal decoder. Such an occurrence was unusual, but not unheard of. He began to run a pencil down columns of figures, seeking the groups on the message in front of him and their corresponding letter combinations. When he had finished decoding, he just sat at his table and stared at the message, searching for any error. He rechecked the beginning of the message, hoping it was a practical joke. But there was no joke. It was for him, via STANFORLANT through the Navy Department, Washington. And it was a presidential order, personal to him from the Commander in Chief, U.S. Armed Forces, White House, Washington.

"He can't ask me to do that," he breathed. "No man can ask a sailor to do that."

But the message did, and it was unequivocal: "In the event the West German government seeks to release the hijackers in Berlin unilaterally, the U.S.S. *Moran* is to sink the supertanker *Freya* by shellfire, using all possible measures to ignite cargo and minimize environmental damage. This action will be taken on receipt by U.S.S. *Moran* of the signal THUNDERBOLT repeat THUNDERBOLT. Destroy message."

Mike Manning was forty-three years old, married, with four children who lived with their mother outside Norfolk, Virginia. He had been an officer in the United States Navy for twenty-one years and had never yet thought to question a superior's order.

He walked to the porthole and looked across the five miles of ocean to the low outline between himself and the climbing sun. He thought of his magnesium-based starshells slamming into her unprotected skin, penetrating the volatile crude oil beneath. He thought of twenty-eight men, crouched deep beneath the waterline, eighty feet beneath the waves, in a steel coffin, waiting for rescue, thinking of their own families. He crumpled the paper in his hand.

"Mr. President," he whispered, "I don't know if I can do that."

CHAPTER SIXTEEN

0800 to 1500

DETSKY MIR means "Children's World" and is Moscow's premier toyshop—four stories of dolls and playthings, puppets and games. Compared to a Western equivalent, the layout is drab and the stock shabby, but it is the best the Soviet capital has, apart from the hard-currency Beriozka shops, where mainly foreigners go.

By an unintended irony it is across Dzerzhinsky Square from the KGB headquarters, which is definitely not a children's world. Adam Munro was at the ground-floor soft-toys counter just before ten A.M. Moscow time, two hours later than North Sea time. He began to examine a nylon bear as if debating whether to buy it for his offspring.

Two minutes after ten, someone moved to the counter beside him. Out of the corner of his eye he saw that she was pale, her normally full lips drawn, tight, the color of cigarette ash.

She nodded. Her voice was pitched, like his own, low, conversational, uninvolved.

"I managed to see the transcript, Adam. It's serious."

She picked up a hand puppet shaped like a small monkey in artificial fur, and told him quietly what she had discovered.

"That's impossible," he muttered. "He's still convalescing from a heart attack."

"No. He was shot dead last October thirty-first in the middle of the night on a street in Kiev."

Two salesgirls leaning against the wall twenty feet away eyed them without curiosity and returned to their gossip. One of the few advantages of shopping in Moscow is that one is guaranteed complete privacy from assistance by the sales staff.

"And those two in Berlin were the ones?" asked Munro.

"It seems so," she said dully. "The fear is that if they escape to Israel they will hold a press conference and inflict an intolerable humiliation on the Soviet Union."

"Causing Maxim Rudin to fall," breathed Munro. "No wonder he will not countenance their release. He cannot. He, too, has no alternative. And you—are you safe, darling?"

"I don't know. I don't think so. There were suspicions. Unspoken, but they were there. Soon there will be a report from the man on the telephone switchboard about your call; the gateman will report about my drive in the small hours. It will come together."

"Listen, Valentina, I will get you out of here. Quickly, in the next few days."

For the first time, she turned and faced him. He saw that her eyes were brimming.

"It's over, Adam. I've done what you asked of me, and now it's too late." She reached up and kissed him briefly, before the astonished gaze of the salesgirls. "Good-bye, Adam, my love. I'm sorry."

She turned, paused for a moment to collect herself, and walked away, through the glass doors to the street, back through the gap in the Wall into the East. From where he stood with a plastic-faced milkmaid doll in his hand, he saw her reach the pavement and turn out of sight. A man in a gray trench coat, who had been wiping the windshield of a car, straightened, nodded to a colleague behind the windshield, and strolled after her.

Adam Munro felt the grief and the anger rising in his throat like a ball of sticky acid. The sounds of the shop muted as a roaring invaded his ears. His hand closed around the head of the doll, crushing, cracking, splintering the smiling pink face beneath the lace cap. A salesgirl appeared rapidly at his side.

"You've broken it," she said. "That will be four rubles."

Compared with the whirlwind of public and media concern that had concentrated on the West German Chancellor the previous afternoon, the recriminations that poured upon Bonn that Saturday morning were more like a hurricane.

The Foreign Ministry received a continual stream of requests couched in the most urgent terms from the embassies of Finland, Norway, Sweden, Denmark, France, Holland, and Belgium, asking that their ambassadors be received. Each wish was granted, and each ambassador asked in the courteous phraseology of diplomacy the same question: What the hell is going on?

Newspapers, television, and radio operations called in all their staffers from weekend leave and tried to give the affair saturation coverage, which was not easy. There were no pictures of the *Freya* since the hijacking, save those taken by the French free-lance, who was under arrest and his pictures confiscated. In fact the same pictures were under study in Paris, but the shots from the successive Nimrods were just as good, and the French government was receiving them, anyway.

For lack of hard news, the papers hunted anything they could go for. Two enterprising Englishmen bribed the Hilton Hotel staff in Rotterdam to lend them their uniforms, and tried to reach the penthouse suite where Harry Wennerstrom and Lisa Larsen were under siege.

Others sought out former prime ministers, cabinet officeholders, and tanker captains for their views. Extraordinary sums were waved in the faces of the wives of the crewmen, almost all of whom had been traced, to be photographed praying for their husbands' deliverance.

One former mercenary commander offered to storm the *Freya* alone for a million-dollar fee; four archbishops and seventeen parliamentarians of varying persuasions and ambitions offered themselves as hostages in exchange for Captain Larsen and his crew.

"Separately, or in job lots?" snapped Dietrich Busch when he was informed. "I wish William Matthews were on board instead of those good sailors. I'd hold out till Christmas."

By midmorning, the leaks to the two German stars of press and radio were beginning to have their effect. Their respective comments on German radio and television were picked up by the news agencies and Germany-based correspondents and given wider coverage. The view began to percolate that Dietrich Busch had in fact been acting in the hours before dawn under massive American pressure.

Bonn declined to confirm this, but refused to deny it, either. The sheer evasiveness of the government spokesman there told the press its own story.

As dawn broke over Washington, five hours behind Europe, the emphasis switched to the White House. By six A.M. in Washington the White House press corps was clamoring for an interview with the President himself. They had to be satisfied, but were not, with a harrassed and evasive official spokesman. The spokesman was evasive only because he did not know what to say; his repeated appeals to the Oval Office brought only further instructions that he tell the newshounds the matter was a European affair and the Europeans must do as they thought best. Which threw the affair back into the lap of an increasingly outraged German Chancellor.

"How much longer can this go on?" shouted a thoroughly shaken William Matthews to his advisers as he pushed away a plate of scrambled eggs just after six A.M. Washington time.

The same question was being asked, but not answered, in a score of offices across America and Europe that unquiet Saturday morning.

From his office in Texas, the owner of the one million tons of Mubarraq crude lying dormant but dangerous beneath the *Freya*'s deck was on the line to Washington.

"I don't care what the hell time of the morning it is," he shouted to the party campaign manager's secretary. "You get him on the line and tell him this is Clint Blake, you hear?"

When the campaign manager of the political party to which the President belonged finally came on the line, he was not a happy man. When he put the receiver back in its cradle, he was downright morose. A man who all but controls more than a hundred delegates to the national convention is no small potatoes, and Clint Blake's threat to do a John Connally and switch parties was no joke.

It seemed to matter little to Blake that the cargo was fully insured against loss by Lloyd's. He was one very angry Texan that morning.

Harry Wennerstrom was on the line most of the morning to Stockholm, calling every one of his friends and contacts in shipping, banking, and government to bring pressure on the Swedish Premier. The pressure was effective, and it was passed on to Bonn.

In London, the chairman of Lloyd's, Sir Murray Kelso, found the Permanent Under Secretary to the Department of the Environment still at his desk in Whitehall. Saturday is not normally a day when the senior members of Britain's civil service are to be found at their desks, but this was no normal Saturday. Sir Rupert Mossbank had driven hastily back from his country home before dawn when the news came from Downing Street that Mishkin and Lazareff were not to be released. He showed his visitor to a chair.

"Damnable business," said Sir Murray.

"Perfectly appalling," agreed Sir Rupert.

He proferred the Butter Osbornes, and the two knights sipped their tea.

"The thing is," said Sir Murray at length, "the sums involved are really quite vast. Close to a billion dollars. Even if the victim countries of the oil spillage if the *Freya* blows up were to sue West Germany rather than us, we'd still have to carry the loss of the ship, cargo, and crew. That's about four hundred million dollars."

"You'd be able to cover it, of course," said Sir Rupert anxiously. Lloyd's was more than just a company, it was an institution, and as Sir Rupert's department covered merchant shipping, he was concerned.

"Oh, yes, we would cover it. Have to," said Sir Murray. "Thing is, it's such a sum it would have to be reflected in the country's invisible earnings for the year. Probably tip the balance, actually. And what with the new application for another International Monetary Fund Loan . . ."

"It's a German question, you know," said Mossbank. "Not really up to us."

"Nevertheless, one might press the Germans a bit over this one. Hijackers are bastards, of course, but in this case, why not just let those two blighters in Berlin go? Good riddance to them."

"Leave it to me," said Mossbank. "I'll see what I can do."

Privately, he knew he could do nothing. The confidential file locked in his safe told him Major Fallon was going in by kayak in eleven hours, and until then the Prime Minister's orders were that the line had to hold.

Chancellor Dietrich Busch received the news of the intended underwater attack in a midmorning face-to-face interview with the British Ambassador. He was slightly mollified.

"So that's what it's all about," he said when he had examined the plan unfolded before him. "Why could I not have been told of this before?"

"We were not sure whether it would work before," said the Ambassador smoothly. Those were his instructions. "We were working on it through the afternoon of yesterday and last night. By dawn we were certain it was perfectly feasible."

"What chance of success do you give yourselves?" asked Dietrich Busch.

The Ambassador cleared his throat.

"We estimate the odds at three to one in our favor," he

said. "The sun sets at seven-thirty. Darkness is complete by nine. The men are going in at ten tonight."

The Chancellor looked at his watch. Twelve hours to go. If the British tried and succeeded, much of the credit would go to their frogmen, but much also to him for keeping his nerve. If they failed, theirs would be the responsibility.

"So it all depends now on this Major Fallon. Very well, Ambassador, I will continue to play my part until ten tonight."

Apart from her batteries of guided missiles, the U.S.S. *Moran* was armed with two five-inch Mark 45 naval guns, one forward, one aft. They were of the most modern type available, radar-aimed and computer-controlled.

Each could fire a complete magazine of twenty shells in rapid succession without reloading, and the sequence of various types of shell could be preset on the computer.

The old days when naval guns' ammunition had to be manually hauled out of the deep magazine, hoisted up to the gun turret by steam power, and rammed into the breech by sweating gunners, were long gone. On the *Moran* the shells would be selected by type and performance from the stock in the magazine by the computer, the shells brought to the firing turret automatically, the five-inch guns loaded, fired, voided, reloaded, and fired again, without a human hand.

The aiming was by radar; the invisible eyes of the ship would seek out the target according to the programmed instructions, adjust for wind, range, and the movement of either target or firing platform, and once locked on, hold that aim until given fresh orders. The computer would work together with the eyes of radar, absorbing within fractions of a second any tiny shift of the *Moran* herself, the target, or the wind strength between them. Once locked on, the target could begin to move, the *Moran* could go anywhere she liked; the guns would simply move on silent bearings, keeping their deadly muzzles pointed to just where the shells should go. Wild seas could force the *Moran* to pitch and roll; the target could yaw and swing; it made no difference, the computer compensated. Even the pattern in which the homing shells should fall could be preset.

As a backup, the gunnery officer could scan the target visually with the aid of a camera mounted high aloft, and issue fresh instructions to both radar and computer when he wished to change target.

With grim concentration, Captain Mike Manning surveyed the *Freya* from where he stood by the rail. Whoever had advised the President must have done his homework well. The environmental hazard in the death of the *Freya* lay in the escape in crude-oil form of her million-ton cargo. But if that cargo were ignited while still in the holds, or within a few seconds of the ship's rupture, it would burn. In fact it would more than burn—it would explode.

Normally, crude oil is exceptionally difficult to burn, but if heated enough, it will inevitably reach its flashpoint and take fire. The Mubarraq crude the *Freya* carried was the lightest of them all, and to plunge lumps of blazing magnesium, burning at more than a thousand degrees Centigrade, into her hull would do the trick with margin to spare. Up to ninety percent of her cargo would never reach the ocean in crude-oil form; it would flame, making a fireball over ten thousand feet high.

What would be left of the cargo would be scum, drifting on the sea's surface, and a black pall of smoke as big as the cloud that once hung over Hiroshima. Of the ship herself, there would be nothing left, but the environmental problem would have been reduced to manageable proportions. Mike Manning summoned his gunnery officer, Lieutenant Commander Chuck Olsen, to join him by the rail.

"I want you to load and lay the forward gun," he said flatly. Olsen began to note the commands.

"Ordnance: three semi-armor-piercing, five magnesium starshell, two high explosive. Total: ten. Then repeat that sequence. Total: Twenty."

"Yes, sir. Three SAP, five star, two HE. Fall pattern?"

"First shell on target; next shell two hundred meters farther; third shell two hundred meters farther still. Backtrack in forty-meter drops with the five starshells. Then forward again with the high explosive, one hundred meters each."

Lieutenant Commander Olsen noted the fall pattern his captain required. Manning stared over the rail. Five miles away, the bow of the *Freya* was pointing straight at the *Moran*. The fall pattern he had dictated would cause the shells to drop in a line from the forepeak of the *Freya* to the base of her superstructure, then back to the bow, then back again with the explosive toward the superstructure. The semi-armor-piercing shells would cut open her tanks through the deck metal as a scalpel opens skin; the starshells would drop in a line of five down the cuts; the high explosive would push the blazing crude oil outward into all the port and starboard holds.

"Got it, Captain. Fall point for first shell?"

"Ten meters over the bow of the *Freya.*"

Olsen's pen halted above the paper of his clipboard. He started at what he had written, then raised his eyes to the *Freya,* five miles away.

"Captain," he said slowly, "if you do that, she won't just sink; she won't just burn; she won't just explode. She'll vaporize."

"Those are my orders, Mr. Olsen," said Manning stonily. The young Swedish-American by his side was pale.

"For Christ's sake, there are twenty-nine Scandinavian seamen on that ship."

"Mr. Olsen, I am aware of the facts. You will either carry out my orders and lay that gun, or announce to me that you refuse."

The gunnery officer stiffened to attention.

"I'll load and lay your gun for you, Captain Manning," he said, "but I will not fire it. If the fire button has to be pressed, you must press it yourself."

He snapped a perfect salute and marched away to the fire-control station below decks.

You won't have to, thought Manning, and I couldn't charge you with mutiny. If the President himself orders me, I will fire it. Then I will resign my commission.

An hour later the Westland Wessex from the *Argyll* came overhead and winched a Royal Navy officer to the deck of the *Moran.* He asked to speak to Captain Manning in private and was shown to the American's cabin.

"Compliments of Captain Preston, sir," said the ensign, and handed Manning a letter from Preston. When he had finished reading it, Manning sat back like a man reprieved from the gallows. It told him that the British were sending in a team of armed frogmen at ten that night, and all governments had agreed to undertake no independent action in the meantime.

While Manning was thinking the unthinkable aboard the U.S.S. *Moran,* the airliner bearing Adam Munro back to the West was clearing the Soviet-Polish border.

From the toyshop on Dzerzhinsky Square, Munro had gone to a public call box and telephoned the head of Chancery at his embassy. He had told the amazed diplomat in coded language that he had discovered what his masters wanted to know, but would not be returning to the embassy. Instead, he was heading straight for the airport to catch the noon plane.

By the time the diplomat had informed the Foreign Office of this, and the FO had told the SIS, the message back to the effect that Munro should cable his news was too late. Munro was boarding.

"What the devil's he doing?" asked Sir Nigel Irvine of Barry Ferndale in the SIS head office in London when he learned his stormy petrel was flying home.

"No idea," replied the controller of Soviet Section. "Perhaps the Nightingale's been blown and he needs to get back urgently before the diplomatic incident blows up. Shall I meet him?"

"When does he land?"

"One-forty-five London time," said Ferndale. "I think I ought to meet him. It seems he has the answer to President Matthews's question. Frankly, I'm curious to find out what the devil it can be."

"So am I," said Sir Nigel. "Take a car with a scrambler phone and stay in touch with me personally."

At a quarter to twelve, Drake sent one of his men to bring the *Freya*'s pumpman back to the cargo-control room on A deck. Leaving Thor Larsen under the guard of another terrorist, Drake descended to cargo control, took the fuses from his pocket, and replaced them. Power was restored to the cargo pumps.

"When you discharge cargo, what do you do?" he asked the crewman. "I've still got a submachine gun pointing at your captain, and I'll order it to be used if you play any tricks."

"The ship's pipeline system terminates at a single point, a cluster of pipes that we call the manifold," said the pumpman. "Hoses from the shore installation are coupled to the manifold. After that, the main gate valves are opened at the manifold, and the ship begins to pump."

"What's your rate of discharge?"

"Twenty thousand tons per hour," said the man. "During

discharge, the ship's balance is maintained by venting several tanks at different points on the ship simultaneously."

Drake had noted that there was a slight, one-knot tide flowing past the *Freya*, northeast toward the West Frisian Islands. He pointed to a tank amidships on the *Freya*'s starboard side.

"Open the master valve on that one," he said. The man paused for a second, then obeyed.

"Right," said Drake. "When I give the word, switch on the cargo pumps and vent the entire tank."

"Into the sea?" asked the pumpman incredulously.

"Into the sea," said Drake grimly. "Chancellor Busch is about to learn what international pressure really means."

As the minutes ticked away to midday of Saturday, April 2, Europe held its breath. So far as anyone knew, the terrorists had already executed one seaman for a breach of the airspace above them, and had threatened to do it again, or vent crude oil, on the stroke of noon.

The Nimrod that had replaced Squadron Leader Latham's aircraft the previous midnight had run short of fuel by eleven A.M., so Latham was back on duty, cameras whirring as the minutes to noon ticked away.

Many miles above him, a Condor spy satellite was on station, bouncing its continuous stream of picture images across the globe to where a haggard American President sat in the Oval Office watching a television screen. On the TV the *Freya* inched gently into the frame from the bottom rim, like a pointing finger.

In London, men of rank and influence in the Cabinet Office briefing room grouped around a screen on which was presented what the Nimrod was seeing. The Nimrod was on continuous camera roll from five minutes before twelve, her pictures passing to the Data Link on the *Argyll* beneath her, and from there to Whitehall.

Along the rails of the *Montcalm*, *Breda*, *Brunner*, *Argyll*, and *Moran*, sailors of five nations passed binoculars from hand to hand. Their officers stood as high aloft as they could get, with telescopes to eye.

On the BBC World Service, the bell of Big Ben struck noon. In the Cabinet Office two hundred yards from Big Ben and two floors beneath the street, someone shouted, "Christ, she's venting!" Three thousand miles away, four shirt-sleeved Americans in the Oval Office watched the same spectacle.

From the side of the *Freya,* midships to starboard, a column of sticky, ocher-red crude oil erupted.

It was thick as a man's torso. Impelled by the power of the *Freya*'s mighty pumps, the oil leaped the starboard rail, dropped twenty-five feet, and thundered into the sea. Within seconds, the blue-green water was discolored, putrefied. As the oil bubbled back to the surface, a stain began to spread, moving out and away from the ship's hull on the tide.

For sixty minutes the venting went on, until the single tank was dry. The great stain formed the shape of an egg, broad nearest the Dutch coast and tapering near to the ship. Finally the mass of oil parted company with the *Freya* and began to drift. The sea being calm, the oil slick stayed in one piece, but it began to expand as the light crude ran across the surface of the water. At two P.M., an hour after the venting ended, the slick was ten miles long and seven miles wide at its broadest.

The Condor passed on, and the slick moved off the screen in Washington. Stanislaw Poklewski switched off the set.

"That's just one fiftieth of what she carries," he said. "Those Europeans will go mad."

Robert Benson took a telephone call and turned to President Matthews.

"London just checked in with Langley," he said. "Their man from Moscow has cabled that he has the answer to our question. He claims he knows why Maxim Rudin is threatening to tear up the Treaty of Dublin if Mishkin and Lazareff go free. He's flying personally with the news from Moscow to London, and he should land in one hour."

Matthews shrugged.

"With this man Major Fallon going in with his divers in nine hours, maybe it doesn't matter anymore," he said, "but I'd sure be interested to know."

"He'll report to Sir Nigel Irvine, who will tell Mrs. Carpenter. Maybe you could ask her to use the hot line the moment she knows," suggested Benson.

"I'll do that thing," said the President.

It was just after eight A.M. in Washington but past one P.M. in Europe when Andrew Drake, who had been pensive and withdrawn while the oil was being vented, decided to make contact again.

By twenty past one, Captain Thor Larsen was speaking again to Maas Control, from whom he asked at once to be patched through to the Dutch Premier, Jan Grayling. The patch-through to The Hague took no time; the possibility had been foreseen that sooner or later the Premier might get a chance to talk to the leader of the terrorists personally and appeal for negotiations on behalf of Holland and Germany.

"I am listening to you, Captain Larsen," said the Dutchman to the Norwegian in English. "This is Jan Grayling speaking."

"Prime Minister, you have seen the venting of twenty thousand tons of crude oil from my ship?" asked Larsen, the gun barrel an inch from his ear.

"With great regret, yes," said Grayling.

"The leader of the partisans proposes a conference."

The captain's voice boomed through the Premier's office in The Hague. Grayling looked up sharply at the two senior civil servants who had joined him. The tape recorder rolled impassively.

"I see," said Grayling, who did not see at all but was stalling for time. "What kind of conference?"

" 'A face-to-face conference with the representatives of the coastal nations and other interested parties,' " said Larsen, reading from the paper in front of him.

Jan Grayling clapped his hand over the mouthpiece.

"The bastard wants to talk," he said excitedly. And then, into the telephone, he said, "On behalf of the Dutch government, I agree to be host to such a conference. Please inform the partisan leader of this."

On the bridge of the *Freya*, Drake shook his head and placed his hand over the mouthpiece. He had a hurried discussion with Larsen.

"Not on land," said Larsen into the phone. "Here at sea. What is the name of that British cruiser?"

"She's called the *Argyll*," said Grayling.

"She has a helicopter," said Larsen at Drake's instruction. "The conference will be aboard the *Argyll*. At three P.M. Those present should include yourself, the West German Ambassador, and the captains of the five NATO warships. No one else."

"That is understood," said Grayling. "Will the leader of the partisans attend in person? I would need to consult the British about a guarantee of safe-conduct."

There was silence as another conference took place on the bridge of the *Freya*. Captain Larsen's voice came back.

"No, the leader will not attend. He will send a representative. At five minutes before three, the helicopter from the *Argyll* will be permitted to hover over the helipad of the *Freya*. There must be no soldiers or Marines on board. Only the pilot and the winchman, both unarmed. The scene will be observed from the bridge. There will be no cameras. The helicopter will not descend lower than twenty feet. The winchman will lower a harness, and the emissary will be lifted off the main deck and across to the *Argyll*. Is that understood?"

"Perfectly," said Grayling. "May I ask who the representative will be?"

"One moment," said Larsen, and the line went dead. On the *Freya*, Larsen turned to Drake and asked:

"Well, Mr. Svoboda, if not yourself, whom are you sending?"

Drake smiled briefly.

"You," he said. "You will represent me. You are the best person I can think of to convince them I am not joking—not about the ship, or the crew, or the cargo. And that my patience is running short."

The phone in Premier Grayling's hand crackled to life.

"I am informed it will be me," said Larsen, and the line was cut.

Jan Grayling glanced at his watch.

"One-forty-five," he said. "Seventy-five minutes to go. Get Konrad Voss over here. Prepare a helicopter to take off from the nearest point to this office. And I want a direct line to Mrs. Carpenter in London."

He had hardly finished speaking before his private secretary told him Harry Wennerstrom was on the line. The old millionaire in the penthouse above the Hilton in Rotterdam had acquired his own radio receiver during the night and had mounted a permanent watch on Channel 20.

"You'll be going out to the *Argyll* by helicopter," he told the Dutch Premier without preamble. "I'd be grateful if you would take Mrs. Lisa Larsen with you."

"Well, I don't know—" began Grayling.

"For pity's sake, man," boomed the Swede, "the terrorists will never know. And if this business isn't handled right, it may be the last time she ever sees him."

"Get her here in forty minutes," said Grayling. "We take off at half past two."

The conversation on Channel 20 had been heard by every intelligence network and most of the media. Lines were already buzzing between Rotterdam and nine European capitals. The National Security Agency in Washington had a transcript clattering off the White House teleprinter for President Matthews. An aide was darting across the lawn from the Cabinet Office to Mrs. Carpenter's study at 10 Downing Street. The Israeli Ambassador in Bonn was urgently asking Chancellor Busch to ascertain for Prime Minister Golen from Captain Larsen whether the terrorists were Jews or not, and the West German government chief promised to do this.

The afternoon newspapers and radio and TV shows across Europe had their headlines for the five P.M. edition, and frantic calls were made to four Navy ministries for a report on the conference if and when it took place.

As Jan Grayling put down the telephone after speaking to Thor Larsen, the jet airliner carrying Adam Munro from Moscow touched the tarmac of Runway 1 at London's Heathrow Airport.

Barry Ferndale's Foreign Office pass had brought him to the foot of the aircraft steps, and he ushered his bleak-faced colleague from Moscow into the back seat. The car was better than most that the Firm used; it had a screen between driver and passengers, and a telephone linked to the head office.

As they swept down the tunnel from the airport to the M4 motorway, Ferndale broke the silence.

"Rough trip, old boy?" He was not referring to the airplane journey.

"Disastrous," snapped Munro. "I think the Nightingale is blown. Certainly followed by the Opposition. May have been picked up by now."

Ferndale clucked sympathy.

"Bloody bad luck," he said. "Always terrible to lose an agent. Damned upsetting. Lost a couple myself, you know. One died damned unpleasantly. But that's the trade we're in, Adam. That's part of what Kipling used to call the Great Game."

"Except this is no game," said Munro, "and what the KGB will do to the Nightingale is no joke."

"Absolutely not. Sorry. Shouldn't have said that." Ferndale paused expectantly as their car joined the M4 traffic stream. "But you did get the answer to our question: Why is Rudin so pathologically opposed to the release of Mishkin and Lazareff?"

"The answer to *Mrs. Carpenter's* question," said Munro grimly. "Yes, I got it."

"And it is?"

"She asked it," said Munro. "She'll get the answer. I hope she'll like it. It cost a life to get it."

"That might not be wise, Adam old son," said Ferndale. "You can't just walk in on the P.M., you know. Even the Master has to make an appointment."

"Then ask him to make one," said Munro, gesturing to the telephone.

"I'm afraid I'll have to," said Ferndale quietly. It was a pity to see a talented man blow his career to bits, but Munro had evidently reached the end of his tether. Ferndale was not going to stand in his way; the Master had told him to stay in touch. He did exactly that.

Ten minutes later, Mrs. Joan Carpenter listened carefully to the voice of Sir Nigel Irvine on the scrambler telephone.

"To give the answer to me personally, Sir Nigel?" she asked. "Isn't that rather unusual?"

"Extremely so, ma'am. In fact, it's unheard of. I fear it has to mean Mr. Munro and the service's parting company. But short of asking the specialists to require the information out of him, I can hardly force him to tell me. You see, he's lost an agent who seems to have become a personal friend over the past nine months, and he's just about at the end of his tether."

Joan Carpenter thought for several moments.

"I am deeply sorry to have been the cause of so much distress," she said. "I would like to apologize to your Mr. Munro for what I had to ask him to do. Please ask his driver to bring him to Number Ten. And join me yourself, immediately."

The line went dead. Sir Nigel Irvine stared at the receiver for a while. That woman never ceases to surprise me, he thought. All right, Adam, you want your moment of glory, son, you'll have it. But it'll be your last. After that, it's pastures new for you. Can't have prima donnas in the Firm.

As he descended to his car, Sir Nigel reflected that however interesting the explanation might be, it was academic, or soon would be. In seven hours Major Simon Fallon would steal aboard the *Freya* with three companions and wipe out the terrorists. After that, Mishkin and Lazareff would stay where they were for fifteen years.

At two o'clock, back in the day cabin, Drake leaned forward toward Thor Larsen and told him:

"You're probably wondering why I set up this conference on the *Argyll*. I know that while you are there you will tell them who we are and how many we are. What we are armed with and where the charges are placed. Now listen carefully because this is what you must also tell them if you want to save your crew and ship from instant destruction."

He talked for over thirty minutes. Thor Larsen listened impassively, drinking in the words and their implications.

When he had finished, the Norwegian captain said, "I'll tell them. Not because I aim to save your skin, Mr. Svoboda, but because you are not going to kill my crew and my ship."

There was a trill from the intercom in the soundproof cabin. Drake answered it and looked out through the windows to the distant fo'c'sle. Approaching from the seaward side, very slowly and carefully, was the Wessex helicopter from the *Argyll*, the Royal Navy markings clear along her tail.

Five minutes later, under the eyes of cameras that beamed their images across the world, watched by men and women in subterranean offices hundreds and even thousands of miles away, Captain Thor Larsen, master of the biggest ship ever built, stepped out of her superstructure into the open air. He had insisted on donning his black trousers, and over his white sweater had buttoned his merchant navy jacket with the four gold rings of a sea captain. On his head was the braided cap with the Viking helmet emblem of the Nordia Line. He was in the uniform he would have worn the previous evening to meet the world's press for the first time. Squaring his broad shoulders, he began the long, lonely walk down the vast expanse of his ship to where the harness and cable dangled from the helicopter a third of a mile in front of him.

CHAPTER SEVENTEEN

1500 to 2100

SIR NIGEL IRVINE'S personal limousine, bearing Barry Ferndale and Adam Munro, arrived at 10 Downing Street a few seconds before three o'clock. When the pair were shown into the anteroom leading to the Prime Minister's study, Sir Nigel himself was already there. He greeted Munro coolly.

"I do hope this insistence on delivering your report to the P.M. personally will have been worth all the effort, Munro," he said.

"I think it will, Sir Nigel," replied Munro.

The Director General of the SIS regarded his staffer quizzically. The man was evidently exhausted, and had had a rough deal over the Nightingale affair. Still, that was no excuse for breaking discipline. The door to the private study opened and Sir Julian Flannery appeared.

"Do come in, gentlemen," he said.

Adam Munro had never met the Prime Minister personally. Despite not having slept for two days, she appeared fresh and poised. She greeted Sir Nigel first, then shook hands with the two men she had not met before, Barry Ferndale and Adam Munro.

"Mr. Munro," she said, "let me state at the outset my deep regret that I had to cause you both personal hazard and possible exposure to your agent in Moscow. I had no wish to do so, but the answer to President Matthews's question was of truly international importance, and I do not use that phrase lightly."

"Thank you for saying so, ma'am," replied Munro.

She went on to explain that, even as they talked, the captain of the *Freya*, Thor Larsen, was landing on the afterdeck of the cruiser *Argyll* for a conference; and that, scheduled for ten that evening, a team of SBS frogmen was going to attack the *Freya* in an attempt to wipe out the terrorists and their detonator.

Munro's face was set like granite when he heard.

"If, ma'am," he said clearly, "these commandos are successful, then the hijacking will be over, the two prisoners in Berlin will stay where they are, and the probable exposure of my agent will have been in vain."

She had the grace to look thoroughly uncomfortable.

"I can only repeat my apology, Mr. Munro. The plan to storm the *Freya* was only devised in the small hours of this morning, ten hours after Maxim Rudin delivered his ultimatum to President Matthews. By then you were already consulting the Nightingale. It was impossible to call that agent back."

Sir Julian entered the room and told the Premier, "They're coming on patch-through now, ma'am."

The Prime Minister asked her three guests to be seated. A box speaker had been placed in the corner of her office, and wires led from it to a neighboring anteroom.

"Gentlemen, the conference on the *Argyll* is beginning. Let us listen to it, and then we will learn from Mr. Munro the reason for Maxim Rudin's extraordinary ultimatum."

As Thor Larsen stepped from the harness onto the afterdeck of the British cruiser at the end of his dizzying five-mile ride through the sky beneath the Wessex, the roar of the engines above his head was penetrated by the shrill welcome of the bosun's pipes.

The *Argyll*'s captain stepped forward, saluted, and held out his hand.

"Richard Preston," said the Royal Navy captain. Larsen returned the salute and shook hands.

"Welcome aboard, Captain," said Preston.

"Thank you," said Larsen.

"Would you care to step down to the wardroom?"

The two captains descended from the fresh air into the largest cabin in the cruiser, the officers' wardroom. There Captain Preston made the formal introductions.

"The Right Honorable Jan Grayling, Prime Minister of the Netherlands. You have spoken on the telephone already, I believe. . . . His Excellency Konrad Voss, Ambassador of the Federal Republic of Germany. Captain Desmoulins of the

French Navy, de Jong of the Dutch Navy, Hasselmann of the German Navy, and Manning of the United States Navy."

Mike Manning put out his hand and stared into the eyes of the bearded Norwegian.

"Good to meet you, Captain." The words stuck in his throat. Thor Larsen looked into his eyes a fraction longer than he had into those of the other naval commanders, and passed on.

"Finally," said Captain Preston, "may I present Major Simon Fallon of the Royal Marine commandos."

Larsen looked down at the short, burly Marine and felt the man's hard fist in his own. So, he thought, Svoboda was right after all.

At Captain Preston's invitation they all seated themselves at the expansive dining table.

"Captain Larsen, I should make plain that our conversation has to be recorded, and will be transmitted in uninterceptible form directly from this cabin to Whitehall, where the British Prime Minister will be listening."

Larsen nodded. His gaze kept wandering to the American; everyone else was looking at him with interest; the U.S. Navy man was studying the mahogany table.

"Before we begin, may I offer you anything?" asked Preston. "A drink, perhaps? Food? Tea or coffee?"

"Just a coffee, thank you. Black, no sugar."

Captain Preston nodded to a steward by the door, who disappeared.

"It has been agreed that, to begin with, I shall ask the questions that interest and concern all our governments," continued Captain Preston. "Mr. Grayling and Mr. Voss have graciously conceded to this. Of course, anyone may pose a question that I may have overlooked. Firstly, may we ask you, Captain Larsen, what happened in the small hours of yesterday morning."

Was it only yesterday? Larsen thought. Yes, three A.M. in the small hours of Friday morning; and it was now five past three on Saturday afternoon. Just thirty-six hours. It seemed like a week.

Briefly and clearly he described the takeover of the *Freya* during the night watch, how the attackers came so effortlessly aboard and herded the crew down to the paint locker.

"So there are seven of them?" asked the Marine major. "You are quite certain there are no more?"

"Quite certain," said Larsen. "Just seven."

"And do you know who they are?" asked Preston. "Jews? Arabs? Red Brigades?"

Larsen stared at the ring of faces in surprise. He had forgotten that outside the *Freya* no one knew who the hijackers were.

"No," he said. "They're Ukrainians. Ukrainian nationalists. The leader calls himself simply Svoboda. He said it means 'freedom' in Ukrainian. They always talk to each other in what must be Ukrainian. Certainly, it's Slavic."

"Then why the hell are they seeking the liberation of two Russian Jews in Berlin?" asked Jan Grayling in exasperation.

"I don't know," said Larsen. "The leader claims they are friends of his."

"One moment," said Ambassador Voss. "We have all been mesmerized by the fact that Mishkin and Lazareff are Jews and wish to go to Israel. But of course they both come from the Ukraine, the city of Lvov. It did not occur to my government that they could be Ukrainian partisan fighters as well."

"Why do they think the liberation of Mishkin and Lazareff will help their Ukrainian nationalist cause?" asked Preston.

"I don't know," said Larsen. "Svoboda won't say. I asked him; he nearly told me, but then shut up. He would say only that the liberation of those two men would cause such a blow to the Kremlin, it could start a widespread popular uprising."

There was blank incomprehension on the faces of the men around him. The final questions about the layout of the ship, where Svoboda and Larsen stayed, the deployment of the terrorists, took a further ten minutes. Finally, Preston looked around at the other captains and the representatives of Holland and Germany. The men nodded. Preston leaned forward.

"Now, Captain Larsen, I think it is time to tell you. Tonight, Major Fallon here and a group of his colleagues are going to approach the *Freya* underwater, scale her sides, and wipe out Svoboda and his men."

He sat back to watch the effect.

"No," said Thor Larsen slowly, "they are not."

"I beg your pardon."

"There will be no underwater attack unless you wish to have the *Freya* blown up and sunk. That is what Svoboda sent me here to tell you."

Item by item, Captain Larsen spelled out Svoboda's message to the West. Before sundown every single floodlight on the *Freya* would be switched on. The man in the fo'c'sle would be withdrawn; the entire foredeck from the bow to the base of the superstructure would be bathed in light.

Inside the superstructure, every door leading outside would be locked and bolted on the inside. Every interior door would also be locked, to prevent access via a window.

Svoboda himself, with his detonator, would remain inside the superstructure, but would select one of the more than fifty cabins to occupy. Every light in every cabin would be switched on, and every curtain drawn.

One terrorist would remain on the bridge, in walkie-talkie contact with the man atop the funnel. The other four men would ceaselessly patrol the taffrail around the entire stern area of the *Freya* with powerful flashlights, scanning the surface of the sea. At the first trace of a stream of bubbles, or someone climbing the vessel's side, the patrol would fire a shot. The man atop the funnel would alert the bridge watch, who would shout a warning on the telephone to the cabin where Svoboda hid. This telephone line would be kept open all night. On hearing the word of alarm, Svoboda would press his red button.

When Larsen had finished, there was silence around the table.

"Bastard," said Captain Preston with feeling. The group's eyes swiveled to Major Fallon, who stared unblinkingly at Larsen.

"Well, Major?" asked Grayling.

"We could come aboard at the bow instead," said Fallon.

Larsen shook his head.

"The bridge watch would see you in the floodlights," he said. "You wouldn't get halfway down the foredeck."

"We'll have to booby-trap their escape launch, anyway," said Fallon.

"Svoboda thought of that, too," said Larsen. "They are going to pull it around to the stern, where it will be in the glare of the deck lights."

Fallon shrugged.

"That just leaves a frontal assault," he said. "Come out of the water firing, use more men, come aboard against the opposition, beat in the door, and move through the cabins one by one."

"Not a chance," said Larsen firmly. "You wouldn't be over the rail before Svoboda had heard you and blown us all to kingdom come."

"I'm afraid I have to agree with Captain Larsen," said Jan

Grayling. "I don't believe the Dutch government would agree to a suicide mission."

"Nor the West German government," said Voss.

Fallon tried one last move.

"You are alone with Svoboda for much of the time, Captain Larsen. Would you kill him?"

"Willingly," said Larsen, "but if you are thinking of giving me a weapon, don't bother. On my return I am to be skin-searched, well out of Svoboda's reach. Any weapon found, and another of my seamen is executed. I'm not taking anything back on board. Not weapons, not poison."

"I'm afraid it's over, Major Fallon," said Captain Preston gently. "The hard option won't work."

He rose from the table.

"Well, gentlemen, barring further questions to Captain Larsen, I believe there is little more we can do. It now has to be passed back to the concerned governments. Captain Larsen, thank you for your time and your patience. In my personal cabin there is someone who would like to speak with you."

Thor Larsen was shown from the silent wardroom by a steward. An anguished Mike Manning watched him leave. The destruction of the plan of attack by Major Fallon's party now brought back to terrible possibility the order he had been given that morning from Washington.

The steward showed the Norwegian captain through the door of Preston's personal living quarters. Lisa Larsen rose from the edge of the bed where she had been sitting, staring out of the porthole at the dim outline of the *Freya.*

"Thor," she said. Larsen kicked back and slammed the door shut. He opened his arms and caught the running woman in a hug.

"Hello, little snow mouse."

In the Prime Minister's private office on Downing Street, the transmission from the *Argyll* was switched off.

"Blast!" said Sir Nigel, expressing the views of them all.

The Prime Minister turned to Munro.

"Now, Mr. Munro, it seems that your news is not so academic after all. If the explanation can in any way assist us to solve this impasse, your risks will not have been run in vain. So, in a sentence, why is Maxim Rudin behaving in this way?"

"Because, ma'am, as we all know, his supremacy in the Politburo hangs by a thread and has done so for months. . . ."

"But on the question of arms concessions to the Americans, surely," said Mrs. Carpenter. "That is the issue on which Vishnayev wishes to bring him down."

"Ma'am, Yefrem Vishnayev has made his play for supreme power in the Soviet Union and cannot go back now. He will bring Rudin down any way he can, for if he does not, then following the signature of the Treaty of Dublin in eight days' time, Rudin will destroy him. These two men in Berlin can deliver to Vishnayev the instrument he needs to swing one or two more members of the Politburo to change their votes and join his faction of hawks."

"How?" asked Sir Nigel.

"By speaking. By opening their mouths. By reaching Israel alive and holding an international press conference. By inflicting on the Soviet Union a massive public and international humiliation."

"Not for killing an airline captain no one had ever heard of?" asked the Prime Minister.

"No. Not for that. The killing of Captain Rudenko in that cockpit was almost certainly an accident. The escape to the West was indispensable if they were to give their real achievement the worldwide publicity it needed. You see, ma'am, on the thirty-first of October last, during the night, in a street in Kiev, Mishkin and Lazareff assassinated Yuri Ivanenko, the head of the KGB."

Sir Nigel Irvine and Barry Ferndale sat bolt-upright, as if stung.

"So that's what happened to him," breathed Ferndale, the Soviet expert. "I thought he must be in disgrace."

"Not disgrace, a grave," said Munro. "The Politburo knows it, of course, and at least one, maybe two, of Rudin's faction have threatened they will change sides if the assassins escape scot-free and humiliate the Soviet Union."

"Does that make sense in Russian psychology, Mr. Ferndale?" the Prime Minister asked.

Ferndale's handkerchief whirled in circles across the lenses of his glasses as he polished them furiously.

"Perfect sense, ma'am," he said excitedly. "Internally and externally. In times of crisis, such as food shortages, it is imperative that the KGB inspire awe in the people, especially the non-Russian nationalities, to hold them in check. If that awe were to vanish, if the terrible KGB were to become a laughingstock, the repercussions could be appalling—seen from the Kremlin, of course.

"Externally, and especially in the Third World, the impression that the power of the Kremlin is an impenetrable fortress is of paramount importance to Moscow in maintaining its hold and its steady advance.

"Yes, those two men are a time bomb for Maxim Rudin. The fuse is lit by the *Freya* affair, and the time is running out."

"Then why cannot Chancellor Busch be told of Rudin's ultimatum?" asked Munro. "He'd realize that the Treaty of Dublin, which affects his country traumatically, is more important than the *Freya*."

"Because," cut in Sir Nigel, "even the news that Rudin has made the ultimatum is secret. If even that got out, the world would realize the affair must concern more than just a dead airline captain."

"Well, gentlemen, this is all very interesting," said Mrs. Carpenter. "Indeed, fascinating. But it does not help solve the problem. President Matthews faces two alternatives: permit Chancellor Busch to release Mishkin and Lazareff, and lose the treaty. Require these two men to remain in jail, and lose the *Freya* while gaining the loathing of nearly a dozen European governments and the condemnation of the world.

"So far, he has tried a third alternative, that of asking Prime Minister Golen to return the two men to jail in Germany after the release of the *Freya*. The idea was to seek to satisfy Maxim Rudin. It might have; it might not. In fact, Benyamin Golen refused. So that was that.

"Then *we* proposed a third alternative, that of storming the *Freya* and liberating her. Now that has become impossible. I fear there are no more alternatives, short of doing what we suspect the Americans have in mind."

"And what is that?" asked Munro.

"Blowing her apart by shellfire," said Sir Nigel Irvine. "We have no proof of it, but the guns of the *Moran* are trained right on the *Freya*."

"Actually, there *is* a third alternative. It might satisfy Maxim Rudin, and it should work," suggested Munro.

"Then please explain it," commanded the Prime Minister.

Munro did so. It took barely five minutes. There was silence.

"I find it utterly repulsive," said Mrs. Carpenter at last.

"Ma'am, with all respect, so did I when I was forced to expose my agent to the KGB," Munro replied stonily. Ferndale shot him a warning look.

"Do we have such devilish equipment available?" Mrs. Carpenter asked Sir Nigel.

He studied his fingertips.

"I believe the specialist department may be able to lay its hands on that sort of thing," he said quietly.

Joan Carpenter inhaled deeply.

"It is not, thank God, a decision I would need to make. It is a decision for President Matthews. I suppose it has to be put to him. But it should be explained person-to-person. Tell me, Mr. Munro, would you be prepared to carry out this plan?"

Munro thought of Valentina walking out into the street, to the waiting men in gray trench coats.

"Yes," he said, "without a qualm."

"Time is short," she said briskly, "if you are to reach Washington tonight. Sir Nigel, have you any ideas?"

"There is the five o'clock Concorde, the new service to Boston," he said. "It could be diverted to Washington if the President wanted it."

Mrs. Carpenter glanced at her watch. It read four P.M.

"On your way, Mr. Munro," she said. "I will inform President Matthews of the news you have brought from Moscow, and ask him to receive you. You may explain to him personally your somewhat . . . macabre proposal. If he will see you at such short notice."

Lisa Larsen was still holding her husband five minutes after he entered the cabin. He asked her about home and the children. She had spoken to them two hours earlier; there was no school on Saturday, so they were staying with the Dahl family. They were fine, she said. They had just come back from feeding the rabbits at Bogneset. The small talk died away.

"Thor, what is going to happen?"

"I don't know. I don't understand why the Germans will not release those two men. I don't understand why the Americans will not allow it. I sit with prime ministers and ambassadors, and they can't tell me, either."

"If they don't release the men, will that terrorist . . . do it?" she asked.

"He may," said Larsen thoughtfully. "I believe he will try. And if he does, I shall try to stop him. I have to."

"Those fine captains out there, why won't they help you?"

"They can't, snow mouse. No one can help me. I have to do it myself, or no one else will."

"I don't trust that American captain," she whispered. "I saw him when I came on board with Mr. Grayling. He would not look me in the face."

"No, he cannot. Nor me. You see, he has orders to blow the *Freya* out of the water."

She pulled away from him and looked up, eyes wide.

"He couldn't," she said. "No man would do that to other men."

"He will if he has to. I don't know for certain, but I suspect so. The guns of his ship are obviously trained on us. If the Americans thought they had to do it, they would do it. Burning up the cargo would lessen the ecological damage, destroy the blackmail weapon."

She shivered and clung to him. She began to cry.

"I hate him," she said.

Thor Larsen stroked her hair, his great hand almost covering her small head.

"Don't hate him," he rumbled. "He has his orders. They all have their orders. They will all do what the men far away in the chancelleries of Europe and America tell them to do."

"I don't care. I hate them all."

He laughed as he stroked her, gently reassuring.

"Do something for me, snow mouse."

"Anything."

"Go back home. Go back to Ålesund. Get out of this place. Look after Kurt and Kristina. Keep the house ready for me. When this is over, I am going to come home. You can believe that."

"Come back with me. Now."

"You know I have to go. The time is up."

"Don't go back to the ship," she begged him. "They'll kill you there."

She was sniffing furiously, trying not to cry, trying not to hurt him.

"It's my ship," he said gently. "It's my crew. You know I have to go."

He left her in Captain Preston's armchair.

As he did so, the car bearing Adam Munro swung out of Downing Street, past the crowd of sightseers who hoped to catch a glimpse of the high and the mighty at this moment of crisis, and turned through Parliament Square for the Cromwell Road and the highway to Heathrow.

Five minutes later Thor Larsen was buckled by two Royal Navy seamen, their hair awash from the rotors of the Wessex above them, into the harness.

Captain Preston, with six of his officers and the four NATO captains, stood in a line a few yards away. The Wessex began to lift.

"Gentlemen," said Captain Preston. Five hands rose to five braided caps in simultaneous salute.

Mike Manning watched the bearded sailor in the harness being borne away from him. From a hundred feet up, the Norwegian seemed to be looking down, straight at him.

He knows, thought Manning with horror. Oh, Jesus and Mary, he knows.

Thor Larsen walked into the day cabin of his own suite on the *Freya* with a submachine carbine at his back. The man he knew as Svoboda was in his usual chair. Larsen was directed into the one at the far end of the table.

"Did they believe you?" asked the Ukrainian.

"Yes," said Larsen. "They believed me. And you were right. They were preparing an attack by frogmen after dark. It's been called off."

Drake snorted.

"Just as well," he said. "If they had tried it, I'd have pressed this button without hesitation, suicide or no suicide. They'd have left me no alternative."

At ten minutes before noon, President William Matthews laid down the telephone that had joined him for fifteen minutes to the British Premier in London, and looked at his three advisers. They had each heard the conversation on the Ampli-Vox.

"So that's it," he said. "The British are not going ahead with their night attack. Another of our options gone. That just about leaves us with the alternative of blowing the *Freya* to pieces ourselves. Is the warship on station?"

"In position, gun laid and loaded," confirmed Stanislaw Poklewski.

"Unless this man Munro has some idea that would work," suggested Robert Benson. "Will you agree to see him, Mr. President?"

"Bob, I'll see the devil himself if he can propose some way of getting me off this hook," said Matthews.

"One thing at least we may now be certain of," said David Lawrence. "Maxim Rudin was not overreacting. He could do nothing other than what he has done, after all. In his fight with Yefrem Vishnayev, he, too, has no aces left. How the hell did those two in Moabit Prison ever get to shoot Yuri Ivanenko?"

"We have to assume the one who leads that group on the *Freya* helped them," said Benson. "I'd dearly love to get my hands on that Svoboda."

"No doubt you'd kill him," said Lawrence with distaste.

"Wrong," said Benson. "I'd enlist him. He's tough, ingenious, and ruthless. He's taken ten European governments and made them dance like puppets."

It was noon in Washington, five P.M. in London, as the late-afternoon Concorde hoisted its stiltlike legs over the concrete of Heathrow, lifted its drooping spear of a nose toward the western sky, and climbed through the sound barrier toward the sunset.

The normal rules about not creating the sonic boom until well out over the sea had been overruled by orders from Downing Street. The pencil-slim dart pushed its four screaming Olympus engines to full power just after takeoff, and a hundred fifty thousand pounds of thrust flung the airliner toward the stratosphere.

The captain had estimated three hours to Washinton, two hours ahead of the sun. Halfway across the Atlantic he told his Boston-bound passengers with deep regret that the Concorde would make a stopover of a few moments at Dulles International Airport, Washington, before heading back to Boston, for "operational reasons."

It was seven P.M. in Western Europe but nine in Moscow when Yefrem Vishnayev finally got the personal and highly unusual Saturday evening meeting with Maxim Rudin for which he had been clamoring all day.

The old director of Soviet Russia agreed to meet his Party

theoretician in the Politburo meeting room on the third floor of the Arsenal building.

When he arrived, Vishnayev was backed by Marshal Nikolai Kerensky, but he found Rudin supported by his allies, Dmitri Rykov and Vassili Petrov.

"I note that few appear to be enjoying this brilliant spring weekend in the countryside," he said acidly.

Rudin shrugged. "I was in the midst of enjoying a private dinner with two friends," he said. "What brings you, Comrades Vishnayev and Kerensky, to the Kremlin at this hour?"

The room was bare of secretaries and guards; it contained just the five power bosses of the Soviet Union in angry confrontation beneath the globe lights in the high ceiling.

"Treason," snapped Vishnayev. "Treason, Comrade Secretary-General."

The silence was ominous, menacing.

"Whose treason?" asked Rudin.

Vishnayev leaned across the table and spoke two feet from Rudin's face.

"The treason of two filthy Jews from Lvov," he hissed. "The treason of two men now in jail in Berlin. Two men whose freedom is being sought by a gang of murderers on a tanker in the North Sea. The treason of Mishkin and Lazareff."

"It is true," said Rudin carefully, "that the murder last December by these two of Captain Rudenko of Aeroflot constitutes—"

"Is it not also true," asked Vishnayev menacingly, "that these two murderers also killed Yuri Ivanenko?"

Maxim Rudin would dearly have liked to shoot a sideways glance at Vassili Petrov by his side. Something had gone wrong. There had been a leak.

Petrov's lips set in a hard, straight line. He, too, now controlling the KGB through General Abrassov, knew that the circle of men aware of the real truth was small, very small. The man who had spoken, he was sure, was Colonel Kukushkin, who had first failed to protest his master, and then failed to liquidate his master's killers. He was trying to buy his career, perhaps even his life, by changing camps and confiding to Vishnayev.

"It is certainly suspected," said Rudin carefully. "Not a proven fact."

"I understand it *is* a proven fact," snapped Vishnayev.

"These two men have been positively identified as the killers of our dear comrade, Yuri Ivanenko."

Rudin reflected on how intensely Vishnayev had loathed Ivanenko and wished him dead and gone.

"The point is academic," said Rudin. "Even for the killing of Captain Rudenko, the two murderers are destined to be liquidated inside their Berlin jail."

"Perhaps not," said Vishnayev with well-simulated outrage. "It appears they may be released by West Germany and sent to Israel. The West is weak; it cannot hold out for long against the terrorists on the *Freya*. If those two reach Israel alive, they will talk. I think, my friends—oh, yes, I truly think we all know what they will say."

"What are you asking for?" said Rudin.

Vishnayev rose. Taking his example, Kerensky rose, too.

"I am *demanding*," said Vishnayev, "an extraordinary plenary meeting of the full Politburo here in this room tomorrow night at this hour, nine o'clock. On a matter of exceptional national urgency. That is my right, Comrade Secretary-General?"

Rudin nodded slowly. He looked up at Vishnayev from under his eyebrows.

"Yes," he growled, "that is your right."

"Then until this hour tomorrow," snapped the Party theoretician, and stalked from the chamber.

Rudin turned to Petrov.

"Colonel Kukushkin?" he asked.

"It looks like it. Either way, Vishnayev knows."

"Any possibility of eliminating Mishkin and Lazareff inside Moabit?"

Petrov shook his head.

"Not by tomorrow. No chance of mounting a fresh operation under a new man in that time. Is there any way of pressuring the West not to release them at all?"

"No," said Rudin shortly. "I have brought every pressure on Matthews that I know how. There is nothing more I can bring to bear on him. It is up to him now, him and that damned German Chancellor in Bonn."

"Tomorrow," said Rykov soberly, "Vishnayev and his people will produce Kukushkin and demand that we hear him out. And if by then Mishkin and Lazareff are in Israel . . ."

At eight P.M. European time, Andrew Drake, speaking

through Captain Thor Larsen from the *Freya*, issued his final ultimatum.

At nine A.M. the following morning, in thirteen hours, the *Freya* would vent one hundred thousand tons of crude oil into the North Sea unless Mishkin and Lazareff were airborne and on their way to Tel Aviv. At eight P.M., unless they were in Israel and identified as genuine, the *Freya* would blow herself apart.

"That's positively the last straw!" shouted Dietrich Busch when he heard the ultimatum ten minutes after it was broadcast from the *Freya*. "Who does William Matthews think he is? No one—absolutely no one—is going to force the Chancellor of the Federal Republic of Germany to carry on with this charade. It is over!"

At twenty past eight, the West German government announced that it was unilaterally releasing Mishkin and Lazareff the following morning at eight A.M.

At eight-thirty, a personal coded message arrived on the U.S.S. *Moran* for Captain Mike Manning. When decoded, it read simply: "Prepare for fire order seven A.M. tomorrow."

He screwed it into a ball in his fist and looked out through the porthole toward the *Freya*. She was lit like a Christmas tree, flood and arc lights bathing her towering superstructure in a glare of white light. She sat on the ocean five miles away, doomed, helpless; waiting for one of her two executioners to finish her off.

While Thor Larsen was speaking on the *Freya*'s radiotelephone to Maas Control, the Concorde bearing Adam Munro swept over the perimeter fence at Dulles International Airport, flaps and undercarriage hanging, nose high, a delta-shaped bird of prey seeking to grip the runway.

The bewildered passengers, like goldfish peering through the tiny windows, noted only that she did not taxi toward the terminal building, but simply hove to, engines running, in a parking bay beside the taxi track. A gangway was waiting, along with a black limousine.

A single passenger, carrying no mackintosh and no hand luggage, rose from near the front, stepped out of the open door, and ran down the steps. Seconds later the gangway was withdrawn, the door closed, and the apologetic captain announced that they would take off at once for Boston.

Adam Munro stepped into the limousine beside the two

burly escorts and was immediately relieved of his passport. The two Secret Service agents studied it intently as the car swept across the expanse of tarmac to where a small helicopter stood in the lee of a hangar, rotors whirling.

The agents were formal, polite. They had their orders. Before he boarded the helicopter, Munro was exhaustively frisked for hidden weapons. When they were satisfied, they escorted him aboard and the whirlybird lifted off, heading across the Potomac for Washington and the spreading lawns of the White House. It was half an hour after touchdown at Dulles, three-thirty on a warm Washington spring afternoon, when they landed, barely a hundred yards from the Oval Office windows.

The two agents escorted Munro across the lawns to where a narrow street ran between the big gray Executive Office Building, a Victorian monstrosity of porticos and columns intersected by a bewildering variety of different types of window, and the much smaller, white West Wing, a squat box partly sunken below ground level.

It was to a small door at the basement level that the two agents led Munro. Inside, they identified themselves and their visitor to a uniformed policeman sitting at a tiny desk. Munro was surprised; this was all a far cry from the sweeping facade of the front entrance to the residence on Pennsylvania Avenue, so well-known to tourists and beloved of Americans.

The policeman checked with someone by house phone, and a woman secretary came out of an elevator several minutes later. She led the three past the policeman and down a corridor, at the end of which they mounted a narrow staircase. One floor up, they were at ground level, stepping through a door into a thickly carpeted hallway, where a male aide in a charcoal-gray suit glanced with raised eyebrows at the unshaven, disheveled Englishman.

"You're to come straight through, Mr. Munro," he said, and led the way. The two Secret Service agents stayed with the woman.

Munro was led down the corridor, past a small bust of Abraham Lincoln. Two staffers coming the other way passed in silence. The man leading him veered to the left and confronted another uniformed policeman sitting at a desk outside a white, paneled door, set flush with the wall. The policeman examined Munro's passport again, looked at his appearance with evident disapproval, reached under his desk and pressed a button. A buzzer sounded, and the aide pushed at the door. When it opened, he stepped back and ushered Munro past him. Munro took two paces forward and found himself in the Oval Office. The door clicked shut behind him.

The four men in the room were evidently waiting for him, all four staring toward the curved door now set back in the wall where he stood. He recognized President William Matthews, but this was a President as no voter had ever seen him: tired, haggard, ten years older than the smiling, confident, mature but energetic image on the posters.

Robert Benson rose and approached him.

"I'm Bob Benson," he said. He drew Munro toward the desk. William Matthews leaned across and shook hands. Munro was introduced to David Lawrence and Stanislaw Poklewski, both of whom he recognized from their newspaper pictures.

"So," said President Matthews, looking with curiosity at the English agent across his desk, "you're the man who runs the Nightingale."

"*Ran* the Nightingale, Mr. President," said Munro. "As of twelve hours ago, I believe that asset has been blown to the KGB."

"I'm sorry," said Matthews. "You know what a hell of an ultimatum Maxim Rudin put to me over this tanker affair. I had to know why he was doing it."

"Now we know," said Poklewski, "but it doesn't seem to change much, except to prove that Rudin is backed right into a corner, as we are here. The explanation is fantastic: the murder of Yuri Ivanenko by two amateur assassins in a street in Kiev. But we are still on that hook. . . ."

"We don't have to explain to Mr. Munro the importance of the Treaty of Dublin, or the likelihood of war if Yefrem Vishnayev comes to power," said David Lawrence. "You've read all those reports of the Politburo discussions that the Nightingale delivered to you, Mr. Munro?"

"Yes, Mr. Secretary," said Munro. "I read them in the original Russian just after they were handed over. I know what is at stake on both sides."

"Then how the hell do we get out of it?" asked President Matthews. "Your Prime Minister asked me to receive you because you had some proposal she was not prepared to discuss over the telephone. That's why you're here, right?"

"Yes, Mr. President."

At that point, the phone rang. Benson listened for several seconds, then put it down.

"We're moving toward the crunch," he said. "That man Svoboda on the *Freya* has just announced he is venting one hundred thousand tons of oil tomorrow morning at nine European time—that's four A.M. our time. Just over twelve hours from now."

"So what's your suggestion, Mr. Munro?" asked President Matthews.

"Mr. President, there are two basic choices here. Either Mishkin and Lazareff are released to fly to Israel, in which case they talk when they arrive there and destroy Maxim Rudin and the Treaty of Dublin; or they stay where they are, in which case the *Freya* will either destroy herself or will have to be destroyed with all her crew on board her."

He did not mention the British suspicion concerning the real role of the *Moran*, but Poklewski shot the impassive Benson a sharp glance.

"We know that, Mr. Munro," said the President.

"But the real fear of Maxim Rudin does not concern the geographical location of Mishkin and Lazareff. His real concern is whether they have the opportunity to address the world on what they did in that street in Kiev five months go."

William Matthews sighed.

"We thought of that," he said. "We have asked Prime Minister Golen to accept Mishkin and Lazareff, hold them incommunicado until the *Freya* is released, then return them to Moabit Prison, even hold them out of sight and sound inside an Israeli jail for another ten years. He refused. He said if he made the public pledge the terrorists demanded, he would not go back on it. And he won't. Sorry, it's been a wasted journey, Mr. Munro."

"That was not what I had in mind," said Munro. "During the flight, I wrote the suggestion in memorandum form on airline notepaper."

He withdrew a sheaf of papers from his inner pocket and laid them on the President's desk.

President Matthews read the memorandum with an expression of increasing horror.

"This is appalling," he said when he had finished. "I have no choice here. Or rather, whichever option I choose, men are going to die."

Adam Munro looked across at him with no sympathy. In

his time he had learned that, in principle, politicians have little enough objection to loss of life, provided that they personally cannot be seen publicly to have had anything to do with it.

"It has happened before, Mr. President," he said firmly, "and no doubt it will happen again. In the Firm we call it 'the Devil's Alternative.' "

Wordlessly, President Matthews passed the memorandum to Robert Benson, who read it quickly.

"Ingenious," he said. "It might work. Can it be done in time?"

"We have the equipment," said Munro. "The time is short, but not too short. I would have to be back in Berlin by seven A.M. Berlin time, ten hours from now."

"But even if we agree, will Maxim Rudin go along with it?" asked the President. "Without his concurrence the Treaty of Dublin would be forfeit."

"The only way is to ask him," said Poklewski, who had finished the memorandum and passed it to David Lawrence. The Boston-born Secretary of State put the papers down as if they would soil his fingers.

"I find the idea cold-blooded and repulsive," Lawrence said. "No United States government could put its imprimatur to such a scheme."

"Is it worse than sitting back as twenty-nine innocent seamen in the *Freya* are burned alive?" asked Munro.

The phone rang again. When Benson replaced it he turned to the President.

"I feel we may have no alternative but to seek Maxim Rudin's agreement," he said. "Chancellor Busch has just announced Mishkin and Lazareff are being freed at oh-eight-hundred hours, European time. And this time he will not back down."

"Then we have to try it," said Matthews. "But I am not taking sole responsibility. Maxim Rudin must agree to permit the plan to go ahead. He must be forewarned. I shall call him personally."

"Mr. President," said Munro. "Maxim Rudin did not use the hot line to deliver his ultimatum to you. He is not sure of the loyalties of some of his inner staff inside the Kremlin. In these faction fights, even some of the small fry change sides and support the opposition with classified information. I believe this proposal should be for his ears alone or he will feel bound to refuse it."

"Surely there is not the time for you to fly to Moscow through the night and be back in Berlin by dawn?" objected Poklewski.

"There is one way," said Benson. "There is a Blackbird based at Andrews that would cover the distance in the time."

President Matthews made up his mind.

"Bob, escort Mr. Munro to Andrews Air Force Base. Alert the crew of the Blackbird there to prepare for takeoff in one hour. I will personally call Maxim Rudin and ask him to permit the airplane to enter Soviet airspace, and to receive Adam Munro as my personal envoy. Anything else, Mr. Munro?"

Munro took a single sheet from his pocket.

"I would like the Company to get this message urgently to Sir Nigel Irvine so that he can take care of the London and Berlin ends," he said.

"It will be done," said the President. "Be on your way, Mr. Munro. And good luck to you."

CHAPTER EIGHTEEN

2100 to 0600

WHEN THE HELICOPTER rose from the White House lawn, the Secret Service agents were left behind. An amazed pilot found himself bearing the mysterious Englishman in the rumpled clothes, and the Director of the CIA. To their right, as they rose above Washington, the Potomac River glittered in the late-afternoon sun. The pilot headed due southeast for Andrews Air Force Base.

Inside the Oval Office, Stanislaw Poklewski, invoking the personal authority of President Matthews in every sentence, was speaking to the base commander there. That officer's protestations died slowly away. Finally, the national security adviser handed the phone to William Matthews.

"Yes, General, this is William Matthews and those are my orders. You will inform Colonel O'Sullivan that he is to prepare a flight plan immediately for a polar route direct from Washington to Moscow. Clearance to enter Soviet airspace unharmed will be radioed to him before he quits Greenland."

The President went back to his other telephone, the red machine on which he was trying to speak directly to Maxim Rudin in Moscow.

At Andrews, the commander himself met the helicopter as it touched down. Without the presence of Robert Benson, whom the Air Force general knew by sight, it was unlikely he would have accepted the unknown Englishman as a passenger on the world's fastest reconnaissance jet, let alone his orders to allow that jet to take off for Moscow. Ten years after it entered service, it was still on the secret list, so sophisticated were its components and systems.

"Very well, Mr. Director," he said finally, "but I have to tell you that in Colonel O'Sullivan we have one very angry Arizonan."

He was right. While Adam Munro was taken to the pilot clothing store to be issued with a *g*-suit, boots, and goldfish-bowl oxygen helmet, Robert Benson found Colonel George T. O'Sullivan in the navigation room, cigar clamped in his teeth, poring over maps of the Arctic and eastern Baltic. The Director of Central Intelligence might outrank him, but he was in no mood to be polite.

"Are you seriously ordering me to fly this bird clean across Greenland and Scandinavia, and into the heart of Rooshia?" he demanded truculently.

"No, Colonel," said Benson reasonably. "The President of the United States is ordering you to do it."

"Without my navigator–systems operator? With some goddam Limey sitting in his seat?"

"The 'goddam Limey' happens to bear a personal message from President Matthews to President Rudin of the USSR which has to reach him tonight and cannot be discussed in any other way," said Benson.

The Air Force colonel stared at him for a moment.

"Well," he conceded, "it better be goddam important."

At twenty minutes before six, Adam Munro was led into the hangar where the aircraft stood, swarming with ground technicians preparing her to fly.

He had heard of the Lockheed SR-71, nicknamed the Blackbird due to its color; he had seen pictures of it, but never the real thing. It was certainly impressive. On a single, thin nosewheel assembly, the bulletlike nose cone thrust upward at a shallow angle. Far down the fuselage, wafer-thin wings sprouted, delta-shaped, being both wings and tail controls all in one.

Almost at each wing tip, the engines were situated, sleek pods housing the Pratt & Whitney JT-11-D turbofans, each capable with afterburner of throwing out thirty-two thousand pounds of thrust. Two knifelike rudders rose, one from atop each engine, to give directional control. Body and engines resembled three hypodermic syringes, linked only by the wing.

Small white U.S. stars in their white circles indicated its nationality; otherwise the SR-71 was black from nose to tail.

Ground assistants helped him into the narrow confines of the rear seat; he found himself sinking lower and lower until the side walls of the cockpit rose above his ears. When the canopy came down, it would be almost flush with the fuselage to cut down drag effect. Looking out, he would see only directly upward to the stars.

The man who should have occupied that seat would have understood the bewildering array of radar screens, electronic countermeasure systems, and camera controls, for the SR-71 was essentially a spy plane, designed and equipped to cruise at altitudes far beyond the reach of most interceptor fighters and rockets, photographing what it saw below.

Helpful hands linked the tubes sprouting from his suit to the aircraft's systems: radio, oxygen, anti-*g*-force. He watched Colonel O'Sullivan lower himself into the seat in front of him and begin attaching his own life-support systems with accustomed ease. When the radio was connected, the Arizonan's voice boomed in his ears.

"You Scotch, Mr. Munro?"

"Scottish, yes," said Munro into his helmet.

"I'm Irish," said the voice in his ears. "You a Catholic?"

"A what?"

"A Catholic, for chrissake."

Munro thought for a moment. He was not really religious at all.

"No," he said, "Church of Scotland."

There was evident disgust up front.

"Jesus, twenty years in the United States Air Force and I get to chauffeur a Scotch Protestant."

The triple-perspex canopy capable of withstanding the tremendous air-pressure differences of ultra-high-altitude flight was closed upon them. A hiss indicated the cabin was now fully pressurized. Drawn by a tractor somewhere ahead of the nosewheel, the SR-71 emerged from the hangar into the evening light.

Heard from inside the aircraft, the engines, once started, seemed to make only a low, whistling sound. Outside, the ground crew shuddered even in their earmuffs as the boom echoed through the hangars.

Colonel O'Sullivan secured immediate clearance for takeoff even while he was running through his seemingly innumerable pre-takeoff checks. At the start of the main runway, the Blackbird paused, rocked on its wheels as the colonel lined her up; then Munro heard his voice:

"Whatever God you pray to, start now, and hold tight."

Something like a runaway train hit Munro squarely across the broad of the back; it was the molded seat in which he was strapped. He could see no buildings to judge his speed, just the pale blue sky above. When the jet reached 150 knots, the nose left the tarmac; half a second later the main wheels parted company, and O'Sullivan lifted the undercarriage into its bay.

Clean of encumbrances, the SR-71 tilted back until its jet efflux pipes were pointing directly down at Maryland, and it climbed. It climbed almost vertically, powering its way to the sky like a rocket, which was almost what it was. Munro was on his back, feet toward the sky, conscious only of the steady pressure of the seat on his spine as the Blackbird streaked toward a sky that was soon turning to dark blue, to violet, and finally to black.

In the front seat, Colonel O'Sullivan was navigating, which is to say, following the instructions flashed before him in digital display by the aircraft's on-board computer. It was feeding him altitude, speed, rate of climb, course and heading, external and internal temperatures, engine and jet-pipe temperatures, oxygen flow rates, and approach to the speed of sound.

Somewhere below them, Philadelphia and New York went by like toy towns; over northern New York State they went through the sound barrier, still climbing and still accelerating. At eighty thousand feet, five miles higher than the Concorde flew, Colonel O'Sullivan cut out the afterburners and leveled his flight attitude.

Though it was still not quite sundown, the sky was a deep black, for at these altitudes there are so few air molecules from which the sun's rays can reflect that there is no light. But there are still enough such molecules to cause skin friction on a plane like the Blackbird. Before the state of Maine and the Canadian frontier had passed beneath them, they had adopted a fast-cruise speed of almost three times the speed of sound. Before Munro's amazed eyes, the black skin of the SR-71, made of pure titanium, began to glow cherry-red in the heat.

Within the cockpit, the aircraft's own refrigeration system kept its occupants comfortably cool in their *g*-suits.

"Can I talk?" asked Munro.

"Sure," said the pilot laconically.

"Where are we now?"

"Over the Gulf of St. Lawrence," said O'Sullivan, "heading for Newfoundland."

"How many miles to Moscow?"

"From Andrews, four thousand eight hundred fifty-six miles."

"How long for the flight?"

"Three hours and fifty minutes."

Munro calculated. They had taken off at six P.M. Washington time, eleven P.M. European time. That would be one A.M. in Moscow on Sunday, April 3. They would touch down at around five A.M. Moscow time. If Rudin agreed to his plan, and the Blackbird could bring him back to Berlin, they would gain two hours by flying the other way. There was just time to make Berlin by dawn.

They had been flying for just under one hour when Canada's last landfall at Cape Harrison drifted far beneath them and they were over the cruel North Atlantic, bound for the southern tip of Greenland, Cape Farewell.

"Mr. President Rudin, please hear me out," said William Matthews. He was speaking earnestly into a small microphone on his desk, the so-called hot line, which in fact is not a telephone at all. From an amplifier to one side of the microphone, the listeners in the Oval Office could hear the mutter of the simultaneous translator speaking in Russian into Rudin's ear in Moscow.

"Maxim Andreevich, I believe we are both too old in this business, that we have worked too hard and too long to secure peace for our peoples, to be frustrated and cheated at this late stage by a gang of murderers on a tanker in the North Sea."

There was silence for a few seconds; then the gruff voice

of Rudin came on the line, speaking in Russian. By the President's side a young aide from the State Department rattled off the translation in a low voice.

"Then, William, my friend, you must destroy the tanker, take away the weapon of blackmail, for I can do no other than I have done."

Bob Benson shot the President a warning look. There was no need to tell Rudin the West already knew the real truth about Ivanenko.

"I know this," said Matthews into the mike. "But I cannot destroy the tanker, either. To do so would destroy me. There may be another way. I ask you with all my heart to receive this man who is even now airborne from here and heading for Moscow. He has a proposal that may be the way out for us both."

"Who is this American?" asked Rudin.

"He is not American, he is British," said President Matthews. "His name is Adam Munro."

There was silence for several moments. Finally the voice from Russia came back grudgingly.

"Give my staff the details of his flight plan—height, speed, course. I will order that his airplane be allowed through, and will receive him personally when he arrives. *Spakoinyo notch*, William."

"He wishes you a peaceful night, Mr. President," said the translator.

"He must be joking," said William Matthews. "Give his people the Blackbird's flight path, and tell Blackbird to proceed on course."

On board the *Freya*, it struck midnight. Captives and captors entered their third and last day. Before another midnight struck, Mishkin and Lazareff would be in Israel, or the *Freya* and all aboard her would be dead.

Despite his threat to choose a different cabin, Drake was confident there would be no night attack from the Marines, and elected to stay where he was.

Thor Larsen faced him grimly across the table in the day cabin. For both men the exhaustion was almost total. Larsen, fighting back the waves of weariness that tried to force him to place his head in his arms and go to sleep, continued his solo game of seeking to keep Svoboda awake, too, pinpricking the Ukrainian to make him reply.

The surest way of provoking Svoboda, he had discovered, the surest way of making him use up his last remaining reserve of nervous energy, was to draw the conversation to the question of Russians.

"I don't believe in your popular uprising, Mr. Svoboda," he said. "I don't believe the Russians will ever rise against their masters in the Kremlin. Bad, inefficient, brutal they may be; but they have only to raise the specter of the foreigner, and they can rely on that limitless Russian patriotism."

For a moment it seemed the Norwegian might have gone too far. Svoboda's hand closed over the butt of his gun; his face went white with rage.

"Damn and blast their patriotism!" he shouted, rising to his feet. "I am sick and tired of hearing Western writers and liberals go on and on about this so-called marvelous Russian patriotism.

"What kind of patriotism is it that can feed only on the destruction of other people's love of homeland? What about *my* patriotism, Larsen? What about the Ukrainians' love for their enslaved homeland? What about Georgians, Armenians, Lithuanians, Estonians, Latvians? Are they not allowed any patriotism? Must it all be sublimated to this endless and sickening love of Russia?

"I hate their bloody patriotism. It is mere chauvinism, and always has been, since Peter and Ivan. It can exist only through the conquest and slavery of other, surrounding nations."

He was standing over Larsen, halfway around the table, waving his gun, panting from the exertion of shouting. He took a grip on himself and returned to his seat. Pointing the gun barrel at Thor Larsen like a forefinger, he told him:

"One day, maybe not too long from now, the Russian empire will begin to crack. One day soon, the Rumanians will exercise *their* patriotism, and the Poles and Czechs. Followed by the East Germans and Hungarians. And the Balts and Ukrainians, the Georgians and Armenians. The Russian empire will crack and crumble, the way the Roman and British empires cracked, because at last the arrogance of their mandarins became insufferable.

"Within twenty-four hours I am personally going to put the cold chisel into the mortar and swing one gigantic hammer onto it. And if you or anyone else gets in my way, you'll die. And you had better believe it."

He put the gun down and spoke more softly.

"In any case, Busch has acceded to my demands, and this time he will not go back on his promise. This time, Mishkin and Lazareff *will* reach Israel."

Thor Larsen observed the younger man clincially. It had been risky; he had nearly used his gun. But he had also nearly lost his concentration; he had nearly come within range. One more time, one single further attempt, in the sad hour just before dawn . . .

Coded and urgent messages had passed all night between Washington and Omaha, and from there to the many radar stations that make up the eyes and ears of the Western alliance in an electronic ring around the Soviet Union. Distant eyes had seen the shooting star of the blip from the Blackbird moving east of Iceland toward Scandinavia on its route to Moscow. Forewarned, the watchers raised no alarm.

On the other side of the Iron Curtain, messages out of Moscow alerted the Soviet watchers to the presence of the incoming plane. Forewarned, no fighters scrambled to intercept it. An air highway was cleared from the Gulf of Bothnia to Moscow, and the Blackbird stuck to its route.

But one fighter base had apparently not heard the warning; or hearing it, had not heeded it; or had been given a secret command from somewhere deep inside the Defense Ministry, countermanding the Kremlin's orders.

High in the Arctic, east of Kirkenes, two Mig-25s clawed their way from the snow toward the stratosphere on an interception course. These were the 25-E versions, ultramodern, better powered and armed than the older version of the seventies and the 25-A.

They were capable of 2.8 times the speed of sound, and of a maximum altitude of eighty thousand feet. But the six Acrid air-to-air missiles that each had slung beneath its wings would roar on, another twenty thousand feet above that. They were climbing on full power with afterburner, leaping upward at over ten thousand feet per minute.

The Blackbird was over Finland, heading for Lake Ladoga and Leningrad, when Colonel O'Sullivan grunted into the microphone.

"We have company."

Munro came out of his reverie. Though he understood

little of the technology of the SR-71, the small radar screen in front of him told its own story. There were two small blips on it, approaching fast.

"Who are they?" he asked, and for a moment a twinge of fear moved in the pit of his stomach. Maxim Rudin had given his personal clearance. He wouldn't revoke it, surely. But would someone else?

Up front, Colonel O'Sullivan had his own duplicate radar scanner. He watched the speed of approach for several seconds.

"Mig-twenty-fives," he said. "At sixty thousand feet and climbing fast. Those goddam Rooshians. Knew we should never have trusted them."

"You turning back to Sweden?" asked Munro.

"Nope," said the colonel. "President of the U.S. of A. said to git you to Moscow, Limey, and you are going to Moscow."

Colonel O'Sullivan threw his two afterburners into the game; Munro felt a kick as from a mule in the base of the spine as the power increased. The Mach counter began to move upward, toward and finally through the mark representing three times the speed of sound. On the radar screen the approach of the blips slowed and halted.

The nose of the Blackbird rose slightly; in the rarefied atmosphere, seeking a tenuous lift from the weak air around her, the aircraft slid through the eighty-thousand-foot mark and kept climbing.

Below them, Major Pyotr Kuznetsov, leading the two-plane detail, pushed his two Tumansky single-shaft jet engines to the limit of performance. His Soviet technology was good, the best available, but he was producing five thousand fewer pounds of thrust with his two engines than the twin American jets above him. Moreover, he was carrying external weaponry, whose drag was acting as a brake on his speed.

Nevertheless, the two Migs swept through seventy thousand feet and approached rocket range. Major Kuznetsov armed his six missiles and snapped an order to his wingman to follow suit.

The Blackbird was nudging ninety thousand feet, and Colonel O'Sullivan's radar told him his pursuers were over seventy-five thousand feet and nearly within rocket range. In straight pursuit they could not hold him on speed and altitude, but they were on an intercept course, cutting the corner from their flight path to his.

"If I thought they were escorts," he said to Munro, "I'd let the bastards come close. But I just never did trust Rooshians."

Munro was sticky with sweat beneath his thermal clothing. He had read the Nightingale file; the colonel had not.

"They're not escorts," he said. "They have orders to see me dead."

"You don't say," came the drawl in his ear. "Goddam conspiring bastards. President of the U.S. of A. wants you alive, Limey. In Moscow."

The Blackbird pilot threw on the whole battery of his electronic countermeasures. Rings of invisible jamming waves radiated out from the speeding black jet, filling the atmosphere for miles around with the radar equivalent of a bucket of sand in the eyes.

The small screen in front of Major Kuznetsov became a seething snowfield, like a television set when the main tube blows out. The digital display showing him he was closing with his victim and when to fire his rockets was still fifteen seconds short of firing time. Slowly it began to unwind, telling him he had lost his target somewhere up there in the freezing stratosphere.

Thirty seconds later the two hunters keeled onto their wing tips and dropped away down the sky to their Arctic base.

Of the five airports that surround Moscow, one of them, Vnukovo II, is never seen by foreigners. It is reserved for the Party elite and their fleet of jets maintained at peak readiness by the Air Force. It was here, at five A.M. local time, that Colonel O'Sullivan put the Blackbird onto Russian soil.

When the cooling jet reached the parking bay, it was surrounded by a group of officers wrapped in thick coats and fur hats, for early April is still bitter in Moscow before dawn. The Arizonan lifted the cockpit canopy on its hydraulic struts and gazed at the surrounding crowd with horror.

"Rooshians," he breathed. "Messing all over my bird." He unbuckled and stood up. "Hey, get your mother-loving hands off this machine, ya hear?"

Adam Munro left the desolate colonel trying to prevent the Russian Air Force from finding the flush caps leading to the refueling valves, and was whisked away in a black limousine, accompanied by two bodyguards from the Kremlin staff. In the car he was allowed to peel off his *g*-suit and dress again in his trousers and jacket, both of which had spent the journey rolled up between his knees and looked as if they had just been machine-washed.

Forty-five minutes later the Zil, preceded by the two motorcycle outriders who had cleared the roads into Moscow, shot through the Borovitsky Gate into the Kremlin, skirted the Great Palace, and headed for the side door to the Arsenal Building. At two minutes to six, Adam Munro was shown into the private apartment of the leader of the USSR, to find an old man in a dressing gown, nursing a cup of warm milk. He was waved to an upright chair. The door closed behind him.

"So you are Adam Munro," said Maxim Rudin. "Now, what is this proposal from President Matthews?"

Munro sat in the straight-backed chair and looked across the desk at Maxim Rudin. He had seen him several times at state functions, but never this close. The old man looked weary and strained.

There was no interpreter present. Rudin spoke no English. In the hours while he had been in the air, Munro realized, Rudin had checked his name and knew perfectly well he was a diplomat from the British Embassy who spoke Russian.

"The proposal, Mr. Secretary-General," Munro began in fluent Russian, "is a possible way whereby the terrorists on the supertanker *Freya* can be persuaded to leave that ship without having secured what they came for."

"Let me make one thing clear, Mr. Munro. There is to be no more talk of the liberation of Mishkin and Lazareff."

"Indeed not, sir. In fact, I had hoped we might talk of Yuri Ivanenko."

Rudin stared back at him, face impassive. Slowly he lifted his glass of milk and took a sip.

"You see, sir, one of those two *has* let something slip already," said Munro. He was forced, to strengthen his argument, to let Rudin know that he, too, was aware of what had happened to Ivanenko. But he could not indicate he had learned it from someone inside the Kremlin hierarchy, just in case Valentina was still free.

"Fortunately," he went on, "it was to one of our people, and the matter has been taken care of."

"Your people?" mused Rudin. "Ah, yes, I think I know who your people are. How many others know?"

"The Director General of my organization, the British Prime Minister, President Matthews, and three of his senior advisers. No one who knows has the slightest intention of revealing this for public consumption. Not the slightest."

Rudin seemed to ruminate for a while.

"Can the same be said for Mishkin and Lazareff?" he asked.

"That is the problem," said Munro. "That has always been the problem since the terrorists—who are Ukrainian émigrés, by the way—stepped onto the *Freya*."

"I told William Matthews, the only way out of this is to destroy the *Freya*. It would cost a handful of lives, but save a lot of trouble."

"It would have saved a lot of trouble if the airliner in which those two young killers escaped had been shot down," rejoined Munro.

Rudin looked at him keenly from under beetle eyebrows.

"That was a mistake," he said flatly.

"Like the mistake tonight in which two MIG-twenty-fives almost shot down the plane in which I was flying?"

The old Russian's head jerked up.

"I did not know," he said. For the first time, Munro believed him.

"I put it to you, sir, that destroying the *Freya* would not work. That is, it would not solve the problem. Three days ago Mishkin and Lazareff were two insignificant escapees and hijackers, serving fifteen years in jail. Now they are already celebrities. But it is assumed their freedom is being sought for its own sake. We know different.

"If the *Freya* were destroyed," Munro went on, "the entire world would wonder why it had been so vital to keep them in jail. So far, no one realizes that it is not their imprisonment that is vital, it is their silence. With the *Freya*, her cargo, and her crew destroyed in order to keep them in jail, they would have no further reason to stay silent. And because of the *Freya*, the world would believe them when they spoke about what they had done. So simply keeping them in jail is no use anymore."

Rudin nodded slowly.

"You are right, young man," he said. "The West Germans would give them their audience; they would have their press conference."

"Precisely," said Munro. "This, then, is my suggestion."

He outlined the same train of events that he had described to Mrs. Carpenter and President Matthews over the previous twelve hours. The Russian showed neither surprise nor horror, just interest.

"Would it work?" he asked at last.

"It has to work," said Munro. "It is the last alternative. They have to be allowed to go to Israel."

Rudin looked at the clock on the wall. It was past six-forty-five A.M. Moscow time. In fourteen hours he would have to face Vishnayev and the rest of the Politburo. This time there would be no oblique approach; this time the Party theoretician would put down a formal motion of no confidence. His grizzled head nodded.

"Do it, Mr. Munro," he said. "Do it and make it work. For if it doesn't, there will be no more Treaty of Dublin, and no more *Freya*, either."

He pressed the bell push, and the door opened immediately. An immaculate major of the Kremlin praetorian guard stood there.

"I shall need to deliver two signals: one to the Americans, one to my own people," said Munro. "A representative of each embassy is waiting outside the Kremlin walls."

Rudin issued his orders to the guard major, who nodded and escorted Munro out. As they were passing through the doorway, Maxim Rudin called:

"Mr. Munro."

Munro turned. The old man was as he had found him, hands cupped around his glass of milk.

"Should you ever need another job, Mr. Munro," he said grimly, "come and see me. There is always a place here for men of talent."

As the Zil limousine left the Kremlin by the Borovitsky Gate at seven A.M., the morning sun was just tipping the spire of St. Basil's Cathedral. Two long black cars waited by the curb. Munro descended from the Zil and approached each in turn. He passed one message to the American diplomat and one to the British. Before he was airborne for Berlin, the instructions would be in London and Washington.

On the dot of eight o'clock the bullet nose of the SR-71 lifted from the tarmac of Vnukovo II Airport and turned due west for Berlin, a thousand miles away. It was flown by a thoroughly disgusted Colonel O'Sullivan, who had spent three hours watching his precious bird being refueled by a team of Soviet Air Force mechanics.

"Where do you want to go now?" he called through the intercom. "I can't bring this into Tempelhof, ya know. Not enough room."

"Make a landing at the British base at Gatow," said Munro.

"First Rooshians, now Limeys," grumbled the Arizonan. "Dunno why we don't put this bird on public display. Seems everyone is entitled to have a good look at her today."

"If this mission is successful," said Munro, "the world may not need the Blackbird anymore."

Colonel O'Sullivan, far from being pleased, regarded the suggestion as a disaster.

"Know what I'm going to do if that happens?" he called. "I'm going to become a goddam cabdriver. I'm sure getting enough practice."

Far below, the city of Vilnius in Lithuania went by. Flying at twice the speed of the rising sun, they would be in Berlin at seven A.M. local time.

It was half past five on the *Freya*, while Adam Munro was in a car between the Kremlin and the airport, that the intercom from the bridge rang in the day cabin.

Drake answered it, listened for a while, and replied in Ukrainian. From across the table Thor Larsen watched him through half-closed eyes.

Whatever the call was, it perplexed the terrorist leader, who sat with a frown, staring at the table, until one of his men came to relieve him in the guarding of the Norwegian skipper.

Drake left the captain under the barrel of the submachine gun in the hands of his masked subordinate and went up to the bridge. When he returned ten minutes later, he seemed angry.

"What's the matter?" asked Larsen. "Something gone wrong again?"

"The West German Ambassador on the line from The Hague," said Drake. "It seems the Russians have refused to allow any West German jet, official or private, to use the air corridors out of West Berlin."

"That's logical," said Larsen. "They're hardly likely to assist in the escape of the two men who murdered their airline captain."

Drake dismissed his colleague, who closed the door behind

him and returned to the bridge. The Ukrainian resumed his seat.

"The British have offered to assist Chancellor Busch by putting a communications jet from the Royal Air Force at their disposal to fly Mishkin and Lazareff from Berlin to Tel Aviv."

"I'd accept," said Larsen. "After all, the Russians aren't above diverting a German jet, even shooting it down and claiming an accident. They'd never dare fire on an RAF military jet in one of the air corridors. You're on the threshold of victory; don't throw it away for a technicality. Accept the offer."

Bleary-eyed from weariness, slow from lack of sleep, Drake regarded the Norwegian.

"You're right," he conceded. "They might shoot down a German plane. In fact, I have accepted."

"Then it's all over but the shouting," said Larsen, forcing a smile. "Let's celebrate."

He had two cups of coffee in front of him, poured while he was waiting for Drake to return. He pushed one halfway down the long table; the Ukrainian reached for it. In a well-planned operation it was the first mistake he had made. . . .

Thor Larsen came at him down the length of the table with all the pent-up rage of the past fifty hours unleashed in the violence of a maddened bear.

The partisan recoiled, reached for his gun, had it in his hand and was about to fire. A fist like a log of cut spruce caught him on the left temple, flung him out of his chair and backward across the cabin floor.

Had he been less fit, he would have been out cold. He was very fit, and younger than the seaman. As he fell, the gun slipped from his hand and skittered across the floor. He came up empty-handed, fighting, to meet the charge of the Norwegian, and the pair of them went down again in a tangle of arms and legs, fragments of a shattered chair, and two broken coffee cups.

Larsen was trying to use his weight and strength, the Ukrainian his youth and speed. The latter won. Evading the grip of the big man's hands, Drake wriggled free and went for the door. He almost made it; his hand was reaching for the knob when Larsen launched himself across the carpet and brought both his ankles out from under him.

The two men came up again together, a yard apart, the Norwegian between Drake and the door. The Ukrainian lunged with a foot, caught the bigger man in the groin with a kick that doubled him over. Larsen recovered, rose again, and threw himself at the man who had threatened to destroy his ship.

Drake must have recalled that the cabin was virtually soundproof. He fought in silence, wrestling, biting, gouging, kicking, and the pair rolled over the carpet amid the broken furniture and crockery. Somewhere beneath them was the gun that could have ended it all; in Drake's belt was the oscillator, which, if the red button on it was pressed, would certainly end it all.

In fact it ended after two minutes; Thor Larsen pulled one hand free, grasped the head of the struggling Ukrainian, and slammed it into the leg of the table. Drake went rigid for half a second, then slumped limply. From just below his hairline a thin trickle of blood seeped down his forehead.

Panting with weariness, Thor Larsen raised himself from the floor and looked at the unconscious man. Carefully he eased the oscillator from the Ukrainian's belt, held it in his left hand, and crossed to the one window in the starboard side of his cabin that was secured closed with butterfly-headed bolts. One-handed, he began to unwind them. The first one flicked open; he started on the second. A few more seconds, a single long throw, and the oscillator would sail out of the porthole, across the intervening ten feet of steel deck, and into the North Sea.

On the floor behind him, the young terrorist's hand inched over the carpet to where his discarded gun lay. Larsen had the second bolt undone and was swinging the brass-framed window inward when Drake lifted himself painfully onto one shoulder, reached around the table, and fired.

The crash of the gun in the enclosed cabin was earsplitting. Thor Larsen reeled back against the wall by the open window and looked first at his left hand, then at Drake. From the floor the Ukrainian stared back in disbelief.

The single shot had hit the Norwegian captain in the palm of his left hand—the hand that held the oscillator—driving shards of plastic and glass into the flesh. For ten seconds both men stared at each other, waiting for the series of rumbling explosions that would mark the end of the *Freya*.

They never came. The soft-nosed slug had fragmented the detonator device into small pieces, and, in shattering, it had not had time to reach the tonal pitch needed to trigger the detonators in the bombs below decks.

Slowly the Ukrainian climbed to his feet, holding onto the table for support. Thor Larsen looked at the steady stream of blood running from his broken hand down to the carpet. Then he looked across at the panting terrorist.

"I have won, Mr. Svoboda. I have won. You cannot destroy my ship and my crew."

"You may know that, Captain Larsen," said the man with the gun, "and I may know that. But they"—he gestured to the open porthole and the lights of the NATO warships in the predawn gloom across the water—"thev don't know that. The game goes on. Mishkin and Lazareff *will* reach Israel."

CHAPTER NINETEEN

0600 to 1600

MOABIT PRISON in West Berlin comprises two sections. The older part predates the Second World War. But during the sixties and early seventies, when the Baader-Meinhof gang spread a wave of terror over Germany, a new section was added. Into it were built ultramodern security systems, the toughest steel and concrete, television scanners, electronically controlled doors and grilles.

On the upper floor, David Lazareff and Lev Mishkin were awakened in their separate cells by the governor of Moabit at six A.M. on the morning of Sunday, April 3, 1983.

"You are being released," he told them brusquely. "You are being flown to Israel this morning. Takeoff is scheduled for eight o'clock. Get ready to depart; we leave for the airfield at seven-thirty."

Ten minutes later the military commandant of the British Sector was on the telephone to the Governing Mayor of West Berlin.

"I'm terribly sorry, Herr Burgomeister," he told the Berliner, "but a takeoff from the civil airport at Tegel is out of the question. For one thing, the aircraft, by agreement between our governments, will be a Royal Air Force jet, and the refueling and maintenance facilities for our aircraft are far better at our own airfield at Gatow. For a second reason, we are trying to avoid the chaos of an invasion by the press, which we can easily prevent at Gatow. It would be hard for you to do this at Tegel Airport."

Privately, the Governing Mayor was somewhat relieved. If the British took over the whole operation, any possible disasters would be their responsibility.

"So what do you want us to do, General?" he asked.

"London has asked me to suggest to you that these blighters be put in a closed and armored van inside Moabit, and be driven straight into Gatow. Your chaps can hand them over to us in privacy inside the wire, and of course we'll sign for them."

The press was less than happy. Over four hundred reporters and cameramen had camped outside Moabit Prison since the announcement from Bonn the previous evening that their release would take place at eight. They desperately wanted pictures of the pair leaving for the airport. Other teams of newsmen were staking out the civil airport at Tegel, seeking vantage points for their telephoto lenses high on the observation terraces of the terminal building. They were all destined to be frustrated.

The advantage of the British base at Gatow is that it occupies one of the most outlying and isolated sites inside the fenced perimeter of West Berlin, situated on the western side of the broad Havel River, close up against the border with Communist East Germany, which surrounds the beleaguered city on all sides.

Inside the base there had been controlled activity for hours before dawn. Between three and four o'clock an RAF version of the HS-125 executive jet, known as the Dominie, had flown in from Britain. It was fitted with long-range fuel tanks that would extend its range to give it ample reserves to fly from Berlin to Tel Aviv over Munich, Venice, and Athens without ever entering Communist airspace. Its 500-mile-per-hour cruising speed would enable the Dominie to complete the 2,200-mile journey in just over four hours.

Since landing, the Dominie had been towed to a quiet hangar, where it had been serviced and refueled.

So keen were the press on watching Moabit and the airport at Tegel that no one noticed a sleek black SR-71 sweep over the East Germany–West Berlin border in the extreme corner of the city and drop onto the main runway at Gatow at just three minutes after seven o'clock. This aircraft, too, was quickly towed to an empty hangar, where a team of mechanics from the U.S. Air Force at Tempelhof hurriedly closed the doors against prying eyes and began to work on it. The SR-71 had done its job. A relieved Colonel O'Sullivan found himself at last surrounded by his fellow countrymen; next destination: his beloved U.S. of A.

His passenger left the hangar and was greeted by a youthful RAF squadron leader waiting with a Land Rover.

"Mr. Munro?"

"Yes." Munro produced his identification, which the Air Force officer scanned closely.

"There are two gentlemen waiting to see you in the mess, sir."

The two gentlemen could, if challenged, have proved that they were low-grade civil servants attached to the Ministry of Defense. What neither would have cared to concede was that they were concerned with experimental work in a very secluded laboratory, whose findings, when such were made, went immediately into a top-secret classification.

Both men were neatly dressed and carried attaché cases. One wore rimless glasses and had medical qualifications, or had had until he and the profession of Hippocrates had parted company. The other was his subordinate, a former male nurse.

"You have the equipment I asked for?" asked Munro without preamble.

For an answer, the senior man opened his attaché case and extracted a flat box no larger than a cigar case. He opened it and showed Munro what nestled on a bed of cotton inside.

"Ten hours," he said. "No more."

"That's tight," said Munro. "Very tight."

It was seven-thirty on a bright, sunny morning.

The Nimrod from Coastal Command still turned and turned fifteen thousand feet above the *Freya.* Apart from observing the tanker, its duties also included that of watching the oil slick of the previous noon. The gigantic stain was still moving sluggishly on the face of the water, still out of range of the emulsifier-spraying tugs, which were not allowed to enter the area immediately around the *Freya* herself.

After spillage the slick had drifted gently northeast of the tanker on the one-knot tide toward the northern coast of Holland. But during the night it had halted, the tide had moved to the ebb, and the light breeze had shifted several points. Before dawn the slick had come back, until it had passed the *Freya* and lay just south of her, two miles away from her side in the direction of Holland and Belgium.

On the tugs and firefighting ships, each loaded with its maximum capacity of emulsifier concentrate, the scientists from Warren Springs prayed the sea would stay calm and the wind light until they could move into operation. A sudden change in wind, a deterioration in the weather, and the giant slick could break up, driven before the storm toward the beaches either of Europe or of Britain.

Meteorologists in Britain and Europe watched with apprehension the approach of a cold front coming down from the Denmark Strait, bringing cold air to dispel the unseasonable heat wave, and possibly wind and rain. Twenty-four hours of squalls would shatter the calm sea and make the slick uncontrollable. The ecologists prayed the descending cold snap would bring no more than a sea fog.

On the *Freya,* as the minutes to eight o'clock ticked away, nerves became even more strained and taut. Andrew Drake, supported by two men with submachine guns to prevent another attack from the Norwegian skipper, had allowed Captain Larsen to use his own first-aid box on his hand. Gray-faced with pain, the captain had plucked from the pulped meat of his palm such pieces of glass and plastic as he could, then bandaged the hand and placed it in a rough sling around his neck. Drake watched him from across the cabin, a small adhesive plaster covering the cut on his forehead.

"You're a brave man, Thor Larsen, I'll say that for you," he said. "But nothing has changed. I can still vent every ton of oil on this ship with her own pumps, and before I'm halfway through, the Navy out there will open fire on her and complete the job. If the Germans renege again on their promise, that's just what I'll do at nine."

At precisely seven-thirty the journalists outside Moabit Prison were rewarded for their vigil. The double gates on Klein Moabit Strasse opened for the first time, and the nose of a blank-sided armored van appeared. From apartment windows across the road, the photographers got what pictures they could, which were not very many, and the stream of press cars started up, to follow the van wherever it would go.

Simultaneously, television remote-broadcast units rolled their cameras, and radio reporters chattered excitedly into their microphones. Even as they spoke, their words went straight to the various capital cities from which they hailed, including that of the BBC man. His voice echoed into the day cabin of the *Freya,* where Andrew Drake, who had started it all, sat listening to his radio.

"They're on their way," he said with satisfaction. "Not long to wait now. Time to tell them the final details of their reception in Tel Aviv."

He left for the bridge; two men remained to cover the *Freya*'s captain, slumped in his chair at the table, struggling with an exhausted brain against the waves of pain from his bleeding and broken hand.

The armored van, preceded by motorcycle outriders with howling sirens, swept through the twelve-foot-high steel-mesh gates of the British base at Gatow, and the pole barrier descended fast as the first car bulging with newsmen tried to follow it through. The car stopped with a squeal of tires. The double gates swung to. Within minutes a crowd of protesting reporters and photographers were at the wire clamoring for admittance.

Gatow contains not only an air base; it has an Army unit as well, and the commandant was an Army brigadier. The men on the gate were from the Military Police, four giants with red-topped caps, peaked down to the bridge of the nose, immovable and immune.

"You cannot do this," yelled an outraged photographer from *Der Spiegel.* "We demand to see the prisoners take off."

"That's all right, Fritz," said Staff Sergeant Brian Farrow comfortably. "I've got my orders."

Reporters rushed to public telephones to complain to their editors. They complained to the Governing Mayor, who sympathized earnestly and promised to contact the base commander at Gatow immediately. When the phone was quiet, he leaned back and lit a cigar.

Inside the base, Adam Munro, accompanied by the wing commander in charge of aircraft maintenance, walked into the hangar where the Dominie stood.

"How is she?" Munro asked of the warrant officer (technical) in charge of the fitters and riggers.

"Hundred percent, sir," said the veteran mechanic.

"No, she's not," said Munro. "I think if you look under one of the engine cowlings, you'll find an electrical malfunction that needs quite a bit of attention."

The warrant officer looked at the stranger in amazement, then across to his superior officer.

"Do as he says, Mr. Barker," said the wing commander. "There has to be a technical delay. The Dominie must not be ready for takeoff for a while. But the German authorities must believe the malfunction is genuine. Open her up and get to work."

Warrant Officer James Barker had spent thirty years maintaining aircraft for the Royal Air Force. Wing commanders' orders were not to be disobeyed, even if they did originate with a scruffy civilian who ought to be ashamed of the way he was dressed, not to mention that he badly needed a shave.

The prison governor, Alois Bruckner, had arrived in his own car to witness the handover of his prisoners to the British, and their takeoff for Israel. When he heard the aircraft was not yet ready, he was incensed and demanded to see it for himself.

He arrived in the hangar, escorted by the RAF base commander, to find Warrant Officer Barker head and shoulders into the starboard engine of the Dominie.

"What is the matter?" he asked in exasperation.

Warrant Officer Barker pulled his head out.

"Electrical short circuit, sir," he told the official. "Spotted it during a test run of the engines just now. Shouldn't be too long."

"These men must take off at eight o'clock, in ten minutes' time," said the German. "At nine o'clock the terrorists on the *Freya* are going to vent a hundred thousand tons of oil."

"Doing my best, sir. Now, if I could just get on with my job?" said the warrant officer.

The base commander steered Herr Bruckner out of the hangar. He had no idea what the orders from London meant, either, but orders they were, and he intended to obey them.

"Why don't we step across to the officers' mess for a nice cup of tea?" he suggested.

"I don't want a nice cup of tea," said the frustrated Herr Bruckner. "I want a nice takeoff for Tel Aviv. But first I must telephone the Governing Mayor."

"Then the officers' mess is just the place," said the wing commander. "By the way, since the prisoners can't really remain in that van much longer, I've ordered them to the Military Police station cells in Alexander Barracks. They'll be nice and comfortable there."

It was five to eight when the BBC radio correspondent was given a personal briefing by the RAF base commander about the technical malfunction in the Dominie, and his report cut clean into the eight A.M. news as a special flash seven minutes later. It was heard on the *Freya*.

"They'd better hurry up," said Drake.

Adam Munro and the two civilians entered the Military Police cells just after eight o'clock. It was a small unit, used only for the occasional Army prisoner, and there were four cells in a row. Mishkin was in the first, Lazareff in the fourth. The junior civilian let Munro and his colleague enter the corridor leading to the cells, then closed the corridor door and stood with his back to it.

"Last-minute interrogation," he told the outraged MP sergeant in charge. "Intelligence people." He tapped the side of his nose. The MP sergeant shrugged and went back to the orderly room.

Munro entered the first cell. Lev Mishkin, in civilian clothes, was sitting on the edge of the bunk bed, smoking a cigarette. He had been told he was going to Israel at last, but he was still nervous and uninformed about most of what had been going on these past three days.

Munro stared at him. He had almost dreaded meeting him. But for this man and his crazy schemes to assassinate Yuri Ivanenko in pursuit of some far-off dream, his beloved Valentina would even now be packing her bags, preparing to leave for Rumania, the Party conference, the holiday at Mamaia Beach, and the boat that would take her to freedom. He saw again the back of the woman he loved going through the plate-glass doors to the Moscow street, the man in the trench coat straightening up and beginning to follow her.

"I am a doctor," he said in Russian. "Your friends, the Ukrainians who have demanded your release, have also insisted you be medically fit to travel."

Mishkin stood up and shrugged. He was unprepared for the four rigid fingertips that jabbed him in the solar plexus, did not expect the small canister held under his nose as he gasped for air, and was unable to prevent himself from inhaling the aerosol vapor that sprayed from the nozzle of the can as he inhaled. When the knockout gas hit the lungs, his legs buckled without a sound, and Munro caught him beneath the armpits before he reached the floor. Carefully he was laid on the bed.

"It'll act for five minutes, no more," said the civilian from the Defense Ministry. "Then he'll wake with a fuzzy head but no ill effects. You'd better move fast."

Munro opened the attaché case and took out the box containing the hypodermic syringe, the cotton, and a small bottle of alcohol. Soaking the cotton in the alcohol, he swabbed a portion of the prisoner's right forearm to sterilize the skin, held the syringe to the light and squeezed until a fine jet of liquid rose into the air, expelling the last bubble.

The injection took less than three seconds, and ensured that Lev Mishkin would remain under its effects for almost two hours, longer than necessary but a period that could not be reduced.

The two men closed the cell door behind them and went down to where David Lazareff, who had heard nothing, was pacing up and down, full of nervous energy. The aerosol spray worked with the same instantaneous effect. Two minutes later he had also had his injection.

The civilian accompanying Munro reached into his breast pocket and took out a flat tin box. He held it out.

"I leave you now," he said coldly. "This isn't what I am paid for."

Neither hijacker knew, nor would ever know, what had been injected into them. In fact it was a mixture of two narcotics called pethidine and hyoscine by the British, and meperidine and scopolamine by the Americans. In combination they have remarkable effects.

They cause the patient to remain awake, albeit slightly sleepy, willing and able to be obedient to instructions. They also have the effect of telescoping time, so that coming out from their effects after almost two hours, the patient has the impression of having suffered a dizzy spell for several seconds. Finally, they cause complete amnesia, so that when the effects wear off, the patient has not the slightest recall of anything that happened during the intervening period. Only a reference to a clock will reveal that time has passed at all.

Munro reentered Mishkin's cell. He helped the young man into a sitting position on his bed, back to the wall.

"Hello," he said.

"Hello," said Mishkin, and smiled. They were speaking in Russian, but Mishkin would never remember it.

Munro opened his flat tin box, extracted two halves of a long, torpedo-shaped capsule called a spansule, such as is often used as a cold remedy, and screwed the two ends together.

"I want you to take this pill," he said, and held it out with a glass of water.

"Sure," said Mishkin, and swallowed it without demur.

From his attaché case Munro took a battery-operated wall clock and adjusted a timer at the back. Then he hung it on the wall. The hands read eight o'clock but were not in motion. He left Mishkin sitting on his bed, and returned to the cell of the other man. Five minutes later the job was finished. He repacked his bag and left the cell corridor.

"They're to remain in isolation until the aircraft is ready for them," he told the MP sergeant at the orderly room desk as he passed through. "No one to see them at all. Base commander's orders."

For the first time Andrew Drake was speaking in his own voice to the Dutch Premier, Jan Grayling. Later, English linguistics experts, analyzing the tape recording made of the conversation, would place the accent as having originated within a twenty-mile radius of the city of Bradford, England, but by then it would be too late.

"These are the terms for the arrival of Mishkin and Lazareff in Israel," said Drake. "I shall expect no later than one hour after the takeoff from Berlin an assurance from Premier Golen that they will be fulfilled. If they are not, I shall regard the agreement as null and void.

"One: the two are to be led from the aircraft on foot and at a slow pace past the observation terrace on top of the main terminal building at Ben-Gurion Airport.

"Two: access to that terrace is to be open to the public. No controls of identity or screening of the public is to take place by the Israeli security force.

"Three: if there has been any switch of the prisoners, if any look-alike actors are playing their part, I shall know within hours.

"Four: three hours before the airplane lands at Ben-Gurion, the Israeli radio is to publish the time of its arrival and inform everyone that any person who wishes to come and witness their arrival is welcome to do so. The broadcast is to be in Hebrew and English, French and German. That is all."

"Mr. Svoboda," Jan Grayling cut in urgently, "all these demands have been noted and will be passed immediately to the Israeli government. I am sure they will agree. Please do not cut contact. I have urgent information from the British in West Berlin."

"Go ahead," said Drake curtly.

"The RAF technicians working on the executive jet in the hangar at Gatow airfield have reported a serious electrical fault developed this morning in one of the engines during testing. I implore you to believe this is no trick. They are working frantically to put the fault right. But there will be a delay of an hour or two."

"If this is a trick, it's going to cost your beaches a deposit of one hundred thousand tons of crude oil," snapped Drake.

"It is not a trick," said Grayling urgently. "All aircraft occasionally suffer a technical fault. It is disastrous that this should happen to the RAF plane right now. But it has, and it will be mended—is being mended, even as we speak."

There was silence for a while as Drake thought.

"I want takeoff witnessed by four different national radio reporters, each in live contact with his head office. I want live reports by each of that takeoff. They must be from the Voice of America, Deutsche Welle, the BBC, and France's ORTF. All in English and all within five minutes of takeoff."

Jan Grayling sounded relieved.

"I will ensure the RAF personnel at Gatow permit these four reporters to witness the takeoff," he said.

"They had better," said Drake. "I am extending the venting of the oil by three hours. At noon we start pumping one hundred thousand tons into the sea."

There was a click as the line went dead.

Premier Benyamin Golen was at his desk in his office in Jerusalem that Sunday morning. The Sabbath was over, and it was a normal working day; it was also past ten o'clock, two hours later than in Western Europe.

The Dutch Prime Minister was barely off the telephone before the small unit of Mossad agents who had established themselves in an apartment in Rotterdam were relaying the message from the *Freya* back to Israel. They beat the diplomatic channels by more than an hour.

It was the Premier's personal adviser on security matters who brought him the transcript of the *Freya* broadcast and laid it silently on his desk. Golen read it quickly.

"What are they after?" he inquired.

"They are taking precautions against a switch of the prisoners," said the adviser. "It would have been an obvious ploy—to make up two young men to pass for Mishkin and Lazareff at first glance, and effect a substitution."

"Then who is going to recognize the real Mishkin and Lazareff here in Israel?"

The security adviser shrugged.

"Someone on that observation terrace," he said. "They have to have a colleague here in Israel who can recognize the men on sight—more probably someone whom Mishkin and Lazareff themselves can recognize."

"And after recognition?"

"Some message or signal will presumably have to be passed to the media for broadcasting, to confirm to the men on the *Freya* that their friends have reached Israel safely. Without that message, they will think they have been tricked and go ahead with their deed."

"Another of them? Here in Israel? I'm not having that," said Benyamin Golen. "We may have to play host to Mishkin and Lazareff, but not to any more. I want that observation terrace put under clandestine scrutiny. If any watcher on that terrace receives a signal from these two when they arrive, I want him followed. He must be allowed to pass his message, then arrest him."

On the *Freya* the morning ticked by with agonizing slowness. Every fifteen minutes Andrew Drake, scanning the wave bands of his portable radio, picked up English-language news broadcasts from the Voice of America or the BBC World Service. Each bore the same message: there had been no takeoff. The mechanics were still working on the faulty engine of the Dominie.

Shortly after nine o'clock the four radio reporters designated as the witnesses to the takeoff were admitted to the Gatow Air Base and escorted by Military Police to the officers' mess, where they were offered coffee and biscuits. Direct telephone facilities were established to their Berlin offices, whence radio circuits were held open to their native countries. None of them met Adam Munro, who had borrowed the base commander's private office and was speaking to London.

In the lee of the cruiser *Argyll* the three fast patrol boats *Cutlass, Sabre,* and *Scimitar* waited at their moorings. On the *Cutlass* Major Fallon had assembled his group of twelve Special Boat Service commandos.

"We have to assume the powers-that-be are going to let the bastards go," he told them. "Sometime in the next couple of hours they'll take off from West Berlin for Israel. They should arrive about four and a half hours later. So, during this evening or tonight, if they keep their word, those terrorists are going to quit the *Freya.*

"Which way they'll head, we don't know yet, but probably toward Holland. The sea is empty of ships on that side. When they are three miles from the *Freya,* and out of possible range for a small, low-power transmitter-detonator to operate the explosives, Royal Navy experts are going to board the *Freya* and dismantle the charges. But that's not our job.

"We're going to take those bastards, and I want that man Svoboda. He's mine, got it?"

There was a series of nods, and several grins. Action was what they had been trained for, and they had been cheated of it. The hunting instinct was high.

"The launch they've got is much slower than ours," Fallon resumed. "They'll have an eight-mile start, but I reckon we can take them three to four miles before they reach the coast. We have the Nimrod overhead, patched in to the *Argyll.* The *Argyll* will give us the directions we need. When we get close to them, we'll have our searchlights. When we spot them, we take them out. London says no one is interested in prisoners. Don't ask me why; maybe they want them silenced for reasons we know nothing about. They've given us the job, and we're going to do it."

A few miles away, Captain Mike Manning was also watching the minutes tick away. He, too, waited on news from Berlin that the mechanics had finished their work on the engine of the Dominie. The news in the small hours of the morning, while he sat sleepless in his cabin awaiting the dreaded order to fire his shells and destroy the *Freya* and her crew, had surprised him. Out of the blue, the United States government had reversed its attitude of the previous sundown; far from objecting to the release of the men from Moabit, far from being prepared to wipe out the *Freya* to prevent that release, Washington now had no objection. But his main emotion was relief, waves of pure relief that his murderous orders had been rescinded, unless. . . . Unless something could still go wrong. Not until the two Ukrainian Jews had touched down at Ben-Gurion Airport would he be completely satisfied that his orders to shell the *Freya* to a funeral pyre had become part of history.

At a quarter to ten, in the cells below Alexander Barracks at Gatow airfield, Mishkin and Lazareff came out from the effects of the narcotic they had ingested at eight o'clock. Almost simultaneously the clocks Adam Munro had hung on the wall of each cell came to life. The sweep hands began to move around the dials.

Mishkin shook his head and rubbed his eyes. He felt sleepy, slightly muzzy in the head. He put it down to the broken night, the sleepless hours, the excitement. He glanced at the clock on the wall; it read two minutes past eight. He knew that when he and David Lazareff had been led through the orderly room toward the cells, the clock there had said eight exactly. He stretched, swung himself off the bunk, and began to pace the cell. Five minutes later, at the other end of the corridor, Lazareff did much the same.

Adam Munro strolled into the hangar where Warrant Officer Barker was still fiddling with the starboard engine of the Dominie.

"How is it going, Mr. Barker?" asked Munro.

The long-service technician withdrew himself from the guts of the engine and looked down at the civilian with exasperation.

"May I ask, sir, how long I am supposed to keep up this playacting? The engine's perfect."

Munro glanced at his watch.

"Ten-thirty," he said. "In one hour exactly, I'd like you to telephone the aircrew room and the officers' mess and report that she's fit and ready to fly."

"Eleven-thirty it is, sir," said Warrant Officer Barker.

In the cells, David Lazareff glanced again at the wall clock. He thought he had been pacing for thirty minutes, but the clock said nine. An hour had gone by, but it had seemed a very short one. Still, in isolation in a cell, time plays strange tricks on the senses. Clocks, after all, are accurate. It never occurred to him or Mishkin that their clocks were moving at double speed to catch up on the missing hundred minutes in their lives, or that they were destined to synchronize with the clocks outside the cells at eleven-thirty precisely.

At eleven, Premier Jan Grayling in The Hague was on the telephone to the Governing Mayor of West Berlin.

"What the devil is going on, Herr Burgomeister?"

"I don't know," shouted the exasperated Berlin official. "The British say they are nearly finished with their damn engine. Why the hell they can't use a British Airways airliner from the civil airport I don't understand. We would pay for the extra cost of taking one out of service to fly to Israel with two passengers only."

"Well, I'm telling you that in one hour those madmen on the *Freya* are going to vent a hundred thousand tons of oil," said Jan Grayling, "and my government will hold the British responsible."

"I entirely agree with you," said the voice from Berlin. "The whole affair is madness."

At eleven-thirty Warrant Officer Barker closed the cowling of the engine and climbed down. He went to a wall phone and called the officers' mess. The base commander came on the line.

"She's ready, sir," said the technician.

The RAF officer turned to the men grouped around him, including the governor of Moabit Prison and four radio reporters holding telephones linked to their offices.

"The fault has been put right," he said. "She'll be taking off in fifteen minutes."

From the windows of the mess they watched the sleek little executive jet being towed out into the sunshine. The pilot and copilot climbed aboard and started both engines.

The prison governor entered the cells of the prisoners and informed them they were about to take off. His watch said eleven-thirty-five. So did the wall clocks.

Still in silence, the two prisoners were marched to the MP Land Rover and driven with the German prison official across the tarmac to the waiting jet. Followed by the air quartermaster sergeant who would be the only other occupant of the Dominie on its flight to Ben-Gurion, they went up the steps without a backward glance and settled into their seats.

At eleven-forty-five, Wing Commander Peter Jarvis opened both the throttles and the Dominie climbed away from the runway of Gatow airfield. On instructions from the air-traffic controller, it swung cleanly into the southbound air corridor from West Berlin to Munich and disappeared into the blue sky.

Within two minutes, all four radio reporters were speaking to their audiences live from the officers' mess at Gatow. Their voices went out across the world to inform their listeners that forty-eight hours after the demands were originally made from the *Freya*, Mishkin and Lazareff were airborne and on their way to Israel and freedom.

In the homes of thirty officers and seamen from the *Freya* the broadcasts were heard; in thirty houses across Scandinavia, mothers and wives broke down and children asked why Mummy was crying.

In the small armada of tugs and emulsifier-spraying vessels lying in a screen west of the *Argyll* the news came through, and there were sighs of relief. Neither the scientists nor the seamen had ever believed they could cope with a hundred thousand tons of crude oil spilling into the sea.

In Texas, oil tycoon Clint Blake caught the news from NBC over his Sunday morning breakfast in the sun and shouted "About goddam time, too!"

Harry Wennerstrom heard the BBC broadcast in his penthouse suite high over Rotterdam and grinned with satisfaction.

In every newspaper office from Ireland to the Iron Curtain the Monday morning editions of the dailies were in preparation. Teams of writers were putting together the whole story from the first invasion of the *Freya* in the small hours of Friday until the present moment. Space was left for the arrival of Mishkin and Lazareff in Israel, and the freeing of the *Freya* herself. There would be time before the first editions went to press at ten P.M. to include most of the end of the story.

At twenty minutes past twelve, European time, the State of Israel agreed to abide by the demands made from the *Freya* for the public reception and identification of Mishkin and Lazareff at Ben-Gurion Airport in four hours' time.

In his sixth-floor room at the Avia Hotel, three miles from Ben-Gurion Airport, Miroslav Kaminsky heard the news on the piped-in radio. He leaned back with a sigh of relief. Having arrived in Israel late Friday afternoon, he had expected to see his fellow partisans arrive on Saturday. Instead, he had listened by radio to the change of heart by the German government in the small hours, the delay through the morning, and the venting of the oil at noon. He had bitten his fingernails down, helpless to assist, unable to rest, until the final decision to release them after all. Now for him, too, the hours were ticking away until touchdown of the Dominie at four-fifteen European time, six-fifteen in Tel Aviv.

On the *Freya,* Andrew Drake heard the news of the takeoff with a satisfaction that cut through his weariness. The agreement of the State of Israel to his demands thirty-five minutes later was by way of a formality.

"They're on their way," he told Larsen. "Four hours to Tel Aviv and safety. Another four hours after that—even less if the fog closes down—and we'll be gone. The Navy will come on board and release you. You'll have proper medical help for that hand, and you'll have your crew and your ship back. . . . You should be happy."

The Norwegian skipper was leaning back in his chair, deep black smudges under his eyes, refusing to give the younger man the satisfaction of seeing him fall asleep. For him it was still not over—not until the poisonous explosive charges had been removed from his holds, not until the last terrorist had left his ship. He knew he was close to collapse. The searing pain from his hand had settled down to a dull, booming throb that thumped up the arm to the shoulder, and the waves of exhaustion swept over him until he was dizzy. But still he would not close his eyes.

He raised his eyes to the Ukrainian with contempt.

"And Tom Keller?" he asked.

"Who?"

"My third officer, the man you shot out on the deck on Friday morning."

Drake laughed.

"Tom Keller is down below with the others," he said. "The shooting was a charade. One of my own men in Keller's clothes. The bullets were blanks."

The Norwegian grunted. Drake looked across at him with interest.

"I can afford to be generous," he said, "because I have

won. I brought against the whole of Western Europe a threat they could not face, and an exchange they could not wriggle out of. In short, I left them no alternative. But you nearly beat me; you came within an inch of it.

"From six o'clock this morning when you destroyed the detonator, those commandos could have stormed this ship any time they pleased. Fortunately, they don't know that. But they might have done if you'd signaled to them. You're a brave man, Thor Larsen. Is there anything you want?"

"Just get off my ship," said Larsen.

"Soon now, very soon, Captain."

High over Venice, Wing Commander Jarvis moved the controls slightly and the speeding silver dart turned a few points east of south for the long run down the Adriatic.

"How are the clients?" he asked the quartermaster sergeant.

"Sitting quietly, watching the scenery," said the QMS over his shoulder.

"Keep 'em like that," said the pilot. "The last time they took a plane trip, they ended up shooting the captain."

The QMS laughed.

"I'll watch 'em," he promised.

The copilot tapped the flight plan on his knee.

"Three hours to touchdown," he said.

The broadcasts from Gatow had also been heard elsewhere in the world. In Moscow the news was translated into Russian and brought to a table in a private apartment at the privileged end of Kutuzovsky Prospekt where two men sat at lunch shortly after two P.M. local time.

Marshal Nikolai Kerensky read the typed message and slammed a meaty fist onto the table.

"They've let them go!" he shouted. "They've given in. The Germans and the British have caved in. The two Jews are on their way to Tel Aviv."

Silently, Yefrem Vishnayev took the message from his companion's hand and read it. He permitted himself a wintry smile.

"Then tonight, when we produce Colonel Kukushkin and his evidence before the Politburo, Maxim Rudin will be finished," he said. "The censure motion will pass; there is no doubt of it. By midnight, Nikolai, the Soviet Union will be ours. And in a year, all Europe."

The marshal of the Red Army poured two generous slugs of Stolichnaya vodka. Pushing one toward the Party theoretician, he raised his own.

"To the triumph of the Red Army!"

Vishnayev raised his vodka, a spirit he seldom touched. But there were exceptions.

"To a truly Communist world!"

CHAPTER TWENTY

1600 to 2000

OFF THE COAST south of Haifa, the little Dominie turned its nose for the last time and began dropping on a straight-in course for the main runway at Ben-Gurion Airport, inland from Tel Aviv.

It touched down after exactly four hours and thirty minutes of flight, at four-fifteen European time. It was six-fifteen in Israel.

At Ben-Gurion the upper terrace of the passenger building was crowded with curious sightseers, surprised in a security-obsessed country to be allowed free access to such a spectacle.

Despite the earlier demands of the terrorists on the *Freya* that there be no police presence, officers of the Israeli Special Branch were there. Some were in the uniform of El Al staff, others selling soft drinks, or sweeping the forecourt, or at the wheels of taxis. Detective Inspector Avram Hirsch was in a newspaper delivery van, doing nothing in particular with bundles of evening papers that might or might not be destined for the kiosk in the main concourse.

After touchdown, the Royal Air Force plane was led by a ground-control jeep to the apron of tarmac in front of the passenger terminal. Here a small knot of officials waited to take charge of the two passengers from Berlin.

Not far away an El Al jet was also parked, and from its curtained portholes two men with binoculars peered through the cracks in the fabric at the row of faces atop the passenger building. Each had a walkie-talkie set to hand.

Somewhere in the crowd of several hundred on the observation terrace Miroslav Kaminsky stood, indistinguishable from the innocent sightseers.

One of the Israeli officials mounted the few steps to the Dominie and went inside. After two minutes he emerged, followed by David Lazareff and Lev Mishkin. Two young hotheads from the Jewish Defense League on the terrace unfurled a placard they had secreted in their coats and held it up. It read simply WELCOME and was written in Hebrew. They also began to clap, until several of their neighbors told them to shut up.

Mishkin and Lazareff looked up at the crowd on the terrace above them as they were led along the front of the terminal building, preceded by a knot of officials and with two uniformed policemen behind them. Several of the sightseers waved; most watched in silence.

From inside the parked airliner the Special Branch men peered out, straining to catch any sign of recognition from the refugees toward one of those at the railing.

Lev Mishkin saw Kaminsky first and muttered something quickly in Ukrainian out of the side of his mouth. It was picked up at once by a directional microphone aimed at the pair of them from a catering van a hundred yards away. The man squinting at the riflelike microphone did not hear the phrase; the man next to him in the cramped van, with the earphones over his head, did. He had been picked for his knowledge of Ukrainian. He muttered into a walkie-talkie, "Mishkin just made a remark to Lazareff. He said, quote, 'There he is, near the end, wearing the blue tie,' unquote."

Inside the parked airliner the two watchers swung their binoculars toward the end of the terrace. Between them and the terminal building the knot of officials continued their solemn parade past the sightseers.

Mishkin, having spotted his fellow Ukrainian, looked away. Lazareff ran his eyes along the line of faces above him, spotted Miroslav Kaminsky, and winked. That was all Kaminsky needed; there had been no switch of prisoners.

One of the men behind the curtains in the airliner said, "Got him," and began to speak into his walkie-talkie.

"Medium height, early thirties, brown hair, brown eyes,

dressed in gray trousers, tweed sports jacket, and blue tie. Standing seven or eight feet from the far end of the observation terrace, toward the control tower."

Mishkin and Lazareff disappeared into the building. The crowd on the roof, the spectacle over, began to disperse. They poured down the stairwell to the interior of the main concourse. At the bottom of the stairs a gray-haired man was sweeping cigarette butts into a trash can. As the column swept past him, he spotted a man in a tweed jacket and blue tie. He was still sweeping as the man strode across the concourse floor.

The sweeper reached into his trash cart, took out a small black box, and muttered, "Suspect moving on foot toward exit gate five."

Outside the building Avram Hirsch hefted a bundle of evening newspapers from the back of the van and swung them onto a dolly held by one of his colleagues. The man in the blue tie walked within a few feet of him, looking neither to right nor left, made for a parked rented car, and climbed in.

Detective Inspector Hirsch slammed the rear doors of his van, walked to the passenger door, and swung himself into the seat.

"The Volkswagen Golf over there in the car park," he said to the van driver, Detective Constable Moishe Bentsur. When the rented car left the parking area en route for the main exit from the airport complex, the newspaper van was two hundred yards behind it.

Ten minutes later Avram Hirsch alerted the other police cars coming up behind him. "Suspect entering Avia Hotel car park."

Miroslav Kaminsky had his room key in his pocket. He passed quickly through the foyer and took the elevator to his sixth-floor room. Sitting on the edge of the bed, he lifted the telephone and asked for an outside line. When he got it, he began to dial.

"He's just asked for an outside line," the switchboard operator told Inspector Hirsch, who was by her side.

"Can you trace the number he's dialing?"

"No, it's automatic for local calls."

"Blast!" said Hirsch. "Come on." He and Bentsur ran for the elevator.

The telephone in the Jerusalem office of the BBC was answered at the third ring.

"Do you speak English?" asked Kaminsky.

"Yes, of course," said the Israeli secretary at the other end.

"Then listen," said Kaminsky, "I will say this only once. If the supertanker *Freya* is to be released unharmed, the first item in the six o'clock news on the BBC World Service, European time, must include the phrase 'no alternative.' If that phrase is not included in the first news item of the broadcast, the ship will be destroyed. Have you got that?"

There were several seconds of silence as the young secretary to the Jerusalem correspondent scribbled rapidly on a pad.

"Yes, I think so. Who is this?" she asked.

Outside the bedroom door in the Avia, Avram Hirsch was joined by two other men. One had a short-barreled shotgun. Both were dressed in airport staff uniform. Hirsch was still in the uniform of the newspaper delivery company: green trousers, green blouse, and green peaked cap. He listened at the door until he heard the tinkle of the telephone being replaced. Then he stood back, drew his service revolver, and nodded to the man with the shotgun.

The gunner aimed once, carefully, at the door lock and blew the whole assembly out of the woodwork. Avram Hirsch went past him at a run, moved three paces into the room, dropped to a crouch, gun held forward in both hands, pointed straight at the target, and called on the room's occupant to freeze.

Hirsch was a Sabra, born in Israel thirty-four years earlier, the son of two immigrants who had survived the death camps of the Third Reich. Around the house in his childhood the language spoken was always Yiddish or Russian, for both his parents were Russian Jews.

He supposed the man in front of him was Russian; he had no reason to think otherwise. So he called to him in Russian. "*Stoi. . . .*" His voice echoed through the small bedroom.

Miroslav Kaminsky was standing by the bed, the telephone directory in his hand. When the door crashed open, he dropped the book, which closed, preventing any searcher from seeing which page it had been open at, or what number he might have called.

When the cry came, he did not see a hotel bedroom outside Tel Aviv; he saw a small farmhouse in the foothills of the Carpathians, heard again the shouts of the men with the green insignia closing in on the hideaway of his group. He looked at Avram Hirsch, took in the flash of green from his peaked cap and uniform, and began to move toward the open window.

He could hear them again, coming at him through the bushes shouting their endless cry: "*Stoi. . . . Stoi. . . . Stoi. . . .*" There was nothing to do but run, run like a fox with the hounds behind him, out through the back door of the farmhouse and into the undergrowth.

He was running backward, through the open glass door to the tiny balcony, when the balcony rail caught him in the small of the back and flipped him over. When he hit the parking lot fifty feet below, his back, pelvis, and skull were shattered. From over the balcony rail, Avram Hirsch looked down at the broken body and muttered to Detective Constable Bentsur:

"What the hell did he do that for?"

The service aircraft that had brought the two specialists to Gatow from Britain the previous evening returned westward soon after the takeoff of the Dominie from Berlin for Tel Aviv. Adam Munro hitched a lift on it, but used his clearance from the Cabinet Office to require that it drop him off at Amsterdam before going on to England.

He had also ensured that the Wessex helicopter from the *Argyll* would be at Schiphol to meet him. It was half past four when the Wessex settled back onto the afterdeck of the missile cruiser. The officer who welcomed him aboard glanced with evident disapproval at his appearance, but took him to meet Captain Preston.

All the Navy officer knew was that his visitor was from the Foreign Office and had been in Berlin supervising the departure of the hijackers to Israel.

"Care for a wash and brush-up?" he asked.

"Love one," said Munro. "Any news of the Dominie?"

"Landed fifteen minutes ago at Ben-Gurion," said Captain Preston. "I could have my steward press your suit, and I'm sure we could find you a shirt that fits."

"I'd prefer a nice thick sweater," said Munro. "It's turned damn cold out there."

"Yes, that may prove a bit of a problem," said Captain Preston. "There's a belt of cold air moving down from Norway. We could get a spot of sea mist this evening."

The sea mist, when it descended just after five o'clock, was a rolling bank of fog that drifted out of the north as the cold air followed the heat wave and came in contact with the warm land and sea.

When Adam Munro, washed, shaved, and dressed in borrowed thick white Navy sweater and black serge trousers, joined Captain Preston on the bridge just after five, the fog was thickening.

"Damn and blast!" said Preston. "These terrorists seem to be having everything their own way."

By half past five the fog had blotted out the *Freya* from vision, and swirled around the stationary warships, none of which could see each other except on radar. The circling Nimrod above could see them all, and the *Freya*, on its radar, and was still flying in clear air at fifteen thousand feet. But the sea itself had vanished in a blanket of gray cotton. Just after five the tide turned again and began to move back to the northeast, bearing the drifting oil slick with it, somewhere between the *Freya* and the Dutch shore.

The BBC correspondent in Jerusalem was a staffer of long experience in the Israeli capital and had many and good contacts. As soon as he learned of the telephone call his secretary had taken, he called a friend in one of the security services.

"That's the message," he said, "and I'm going to send it to London right now. But I haven't a clue who telephoned it."

There was a grunt at the other end.

"Send the message," said the security man. "As to the man on the telephone, we know. And thanks."

It was just after four-thirty when the news flash was broadcast on the *Freya* that Mishkin and Lazareff had landed at Ben-Gurion.

Andrew Drake threw himself back in his chair with a shout.

"We've done it!" he yelled at Thor Larsen. "They're in Israel!"

Larsen nodded slowly. He was trying to close his mind to the steady agony from his wounded hand.

"Congratulations," he said sardonically. "Now perhaps you can leave my ship and go to hell."

The telephone from the bridge rang. There was a rapid exchange in Ukrainian, and Larsen heard a whoop of joy from the other end.

"Sooner than you think," said Drake. "The lookout on the funnel reports a thick bank of fog moving toward the whole area from the north. With luck we won't even have to wait until dark. The fog will be even better for our purpose. But when we do leave, I'm afraid I'll have to handcuff you to the table leg. The Navy will rescue you in a couple of hours."

At five o'clock the main newscast brought a dispatch from Tel Aviv to the effect that the demands of the hijackers of the *Freya* in the matter of the reception at Ben-Gurion Airport of Mishkin and Lazareff had been abided by. Meanwhile, the Israeli government would keep the two from Berlin in custody until the *Freya* was released, safe and unharmed. In the event that she was not, the Israeli government would regard its pledges to the terrorists as null and void, and return Mishkin and Lazareff to jail.

In the day cabin on the *Freya*, Drake laughed.

"They won't need to," he told Larsen. "I don't care what happens to me now. In twenty-four hours those two men are going to hold an international press conference. And when they do, Captain Larsen, when they do, they are going to blow the biggest hole ever made in the walls of the Kremlin."

Larsen looked out of the windows at the thickening mist.

"The commandos might use this fog to storm the *Freya*," he said. "Your lights would be of no use. In a few minutes you won't be able to see any bubbles from frogmen underwater."

"It doesn't matter anymore," said Drake. "Nothing matters anymore. Only that Mishkin and Lazareff get their chance to speak. That was what it was all about. That is what makes it all worthwhile."

The two Jewish-Ukrainians had been taken from Ben-Gurion Airport in a police van to the central police station in Tel Aviv and locked in separate cells. Prime Minister Golen was prepared to abide by his part of the bargain—the exchange of the two men for the safety of the *Freya*, her crew, and her cargo. But he was not prepared to have Svoboda trick him.

For Mishkin and Lazareff it was the third cell in a day, but both knew it would be the last. As they parted in the corridor, Mishkin winked at his friend and called in Ukrainian, "Not next year in Jerusalem—but tomorrow."

From an office upstairs, the chief superintendent in charge of the station made a routine call to the police doctor to give the pair a medical examination, and the doctor promised to come at once. It was half past seven Tel Aviv time.

The last thirty minutes before six o'clock dragged by like years on the *Freya*. In the day cabin, Drake had tuned his radio to the BBC World Service and listened impatiently for the six o'clock newscast.

Azamat Krim, assisted by three of his colleagues, shinnied down a rope from the taffrail of the tanker to the sturdy fishing launch that had bobbed beside the hull for the past two and half days. When the four of them were standing in the launch's open waist, they began preparations for the departure of the group from the *Freya*.

At six o'clock the chimes of Big Ben rang out from London, and the evening news broadcast began.

"This is the BBC World Service. The time is six o'clock in London, and here is the news, read to you by Peter Chalmers."

A new voice came on. It was heard in the wardroom of the *Argyll*, where Captain Preston and most of his officers were grouped around the set. Captain Mike Manning tuned in on the *Moran;* the same newscast was heard at 10 Downing Street, in The Hague, Washington, Paris, Brussels, Bonn, and Jerusalem. On the *Freya*, Andrew Drake sat motionless, watching the radio unblinkingly.

"In Jerusalem today, Prime Minister Benyamin Golen said that following the arrival earlier from West Berlin of the two prisoners David Lazareff and Lev Mishkin, he would have no alternative but to abide by his pledge to free the two men, provided the supertanker *Freya* was freed with her crew unharmed. . . ."

"No alternative!" shouted Drake. "That's the phrase! Miroslav has done it!"

"Done what?" asked Larsen.

"Recognized them. It's them, all right. No switching has taken place."

He slumped back in his chair and exhaled a deep sigh.

"It's over, Captain Larsen. We're leaving, you'll be glad to hear."

The captain's personal locker contained one set of handcuffs, with keys, in case of the necessity physically to restrain someone on board. Cases of madness have been known on ships. Drake slipped one of the cuffs around Larsen's right wrist and snapped it shut. The other went around the table leg. The table was bolted to the floor. Drake paused in the doorway and laid the keys to the handcuffs on top of a shelf.

"Good-bye, Captain Larsen. You may not believe this, but I'm sorry about the oil slick. It would never have happened if the fools out there had not tried to trick me. I'm sorry about your hand, but that, too, need not have happened. We'll not see each other again, so good-bye."

He closed and locked the cabin door behind him and ran down the three flights of stairs to A deck and outside to where his men were grouped on the afterdeck. He took his transistor radio with him.

"All ready?" he asked Azamat Krim.

"As ready as we'll ever be," said the Crimean Tatar.

"Everything okay?" he asked the Ukrainian-American who was an expert on small boats.

The man nodded.

"All systems go," he replied.

Drake looked at his watch. It was twenty past six.

"Right. Six-forty-five, Azamat hits the ship's siren, and the launch and the first group leave simultaneously. Azamat and I leave ten minutes later. You've all got papers and clothes. After you hit the Dutch coast, everyone scatters. It's every man for himself."

He looked over the side. By the fishing launch, two inflatable Zodiac speedboats bobbed in the fog-shrouded water. Each had been dragged out from the fishing launch and inflated in the previous hour. One was the fourteen-foot model, big enough for five men. The smaller, ten-foot model would take two comfortably. With the forty-horsepower outboards behind them, they would make thirty knots over a calm sea.

"They won't be long now," said Major Simon Fallon, standing at the forward rail of the *Cutlass*.

The three fast patrol boats, long since invisible from the *Freya,* had been pulled clear of the western side of the *Argyll* and now lay tethered beneath her stern, noses pointed to where the *Freya* lay, five miles away through the fog.

The Marines of the SBS were scattered, four to each boat, all armed with submachine carbines, grenades, and knives.

One boat, the *Sabre,* also carried on board four Royal Navy explosives experts, and this boat would make straight for the *Freya* to board and liberate her as soon as the circling Nimrod had spotted the terrorist launch leaving the side of the supertanker and achieving a distance of three miles from her. The *Cutlass* and *Scimitar* would pursue the terrorists and hunt them down before they could lose themselves in the maze of creeks and islands that make up the Dutch coast south of the Maas.

Major Fallon would head the pursuit group in the *Cutlass.* Standing beside him, to his considerable disgust, was the man from the Foreign Office, Mr. Munro.

"Just stay well out of the way when we close with them," Fallon said. "We know they have submachine carbines and handguns, maybe more. Personally, I don't see why you insist on coming at all."

"Let's just say I have a personal interest in these bastards," said Munro, "especially Mr. Svoboda."

"So have I," growled Fallon. "And Svoboda's mine."

Aboard the *Moran,* Mike Manning had heard the news of the safe arrival of Mishkin and Lazareff in Israel with as much relief as Drake on the *Freya.* For him, as for Thor Larsen, it was the end of a nightmare. There would be no shelling of the *Freya* now. His only regret was that the fast patrol boats of the Royal Navy would have the pleasure of hunting down the terrorists when they made their break. For Manning the agony he had been through for a day and a half parlayed itself into anger.

"If I could get my hands on Svoboda," he told his gunnery officer, Lieutenant Commander Olsen, "I'd happily wring the bastard's neck."

As on the *Argyll,* the *Brunner,* the *Breda,* and the *Montcalm,* the *Moran*'s radar scanners swept the ocean for signs of the launch moving away from the *Freya*'s side. Six-fifteen came and went, and there was no sign.

In its turret the forward gun of the *Moran,* still loaded, moved away from the *Freya* and pointed at the empty sea three miles to the northeast.

At ten past eight Tel Aviv time, Lev Mishkin was standing in his cell beneath the streets of Tel Aviv, when he felt a pain in his chest. Something like a rock seemed to be growing fast inside him. He opened his mouth to scream, but the air was cut off. He pitched forward, face down, and died on the floor of the cell.

There was an Israeli policeman on permanent guard outside the door of the cell, and he had orders to peer inside at least every two or three minutes. Less than sixty seconds after Mishkin died, his eye was pressed to the judas hole. What he saw caused him to let out a yell of alarm, and he frantically rattled the key in the lock to open the door. Farther up the corridor, a colleague in front of Lazareff's door heard the yell and ran to his assistance. Together they burst into Mishkin's cell and bent over the prostrate figure.

"He's dead," breathed one of the men. The other rushed into the corridor and hit the alarm button. Then they ran to Lazareff's cell and hurried inside.

The second prisoner was doubled up on the bed, arms wrapped around himself as the paroxysms struck him.

"What's the matter?" shouted one of the guards, but he spoke in Hebrew, which Lazareff did not understand. The dying man forced out four words in Russian. Both guards heard him clearly and later repeated the phrase to senior officers, who were able to translate it.

"Head . . . of . . . KGB . . . dead."

That was all he said. His mouth stopped moving; he lay on his side on the cot, sightless eyes staring at the blue uniforms in front of him.

The ringing bell brought the chief superintendent, a dozen other officers of the station staff, and the doctor, who had been drinking coffee in the police chief's office.

The doctor examined each rapidly, searching mouths, throats, and eyes, feeling pulses and listening to chests. When he had done, he stalked from the second cell. The superintendent followed him into the corridor; he was a badly worried man.

"What the hell's happened?" he asked the doctor.

"I can do a full autopsy later," said the doctor, "or maybe it will be taken out of my hands. But as to what has happened, they've been poisoned, that's what happened."

"But they haven't eaten anything," protested the policeman. "They haven't drunk anything. They were just going to have supper. Perhaps at the airport . . . or on the plane . . . ?"

"No," said the doctor, "a slow-acting poison would not work with such speed, and simultaneously. Body systems vary too much. Each either administered to himself, or was administered, a massive dose of instantaneously fatal poison, which I suspect to be potassium cynanide, within the five to ten seconds before they died."

"That's not possible," shouted the police chief. "My men were outside the cells all the time. Both prisoners were thoroughly examined before they entered the cells. Mouths, anuses—the lot. There were no hidden poison capsules. Besides, why would they commit suicide? They'd soon have had their freedom."

"I don't know," said the doctor, "but they both died within seconds of that poison's hitting them."

"I'm phoning the Prime Minister's office at once," said the chief superintendent grimly, and strode off to his office.

The Prime Minister's personal security adviser, like almost everyone else in Israel, was an ex-soldier. But the man whom those within a five-mile radius of the Knesset called simply "Barak" had never been an ordinary soldier. He had started as a paratrooper under the paracommander Rafael Eytan, the legendary Raful. Later he had transferred, to serve as a major in General Arik Sharon's elite 101 Unit until he stopped a bullet in the kneecap during a dawn raid on a Palestinian apartment block in Beirut.

Since then he had specialized in the more technical side of security operations, using his knowledge of what he would have done to kill the Israeli Premier, and then reversing it to protect his master. It was he who took the call from Tel Aviv and entered the office where Benyamin Golen was working late, to break the news to him.

"Inside the cell itself?" echoed the stunned Premier. "Then they must have taken the poison themselves."

"I don't think so," said Barak. "They had every reason to want to live."

"Then they were killed by others?"

"It looks like it, Prime Minister."

"But who would want them dead?"

"The KGB, of course. One of them muttered something about the KGB, in Russian. It seems he was saying the head of the KGB wanted them dead."

"But they haven't been in the hands of the KGB. Twelve hours ago they were in Moabit Prison. Then for eight hours in the hands of the British. Then two hours with us. In our hands they ingested nothing—no food, no drink, nothing. So how did they take in an instant-acting poison?"

Barak scratched his chin, a dawning gleam in his eye.

"There is a way, Prime Minister. A delayed-action capsule."

He took a sheet of paper and drew a diagram.

"It is possible to design and make a capsule like this. It has two halves; one is threaded so that it screws into the other half just before it is swallowed."

The Prime Minister looked at the diagram with growing anger.

"Go on," he commanded.

"One half of the capsule is of a ceramic substance, immune both to the acidic effects of the gastric juices of the human stomach and to the effects of the much stronger acid inside it. And strong enough not to be broken by the muscles of the throat when it is swallowed.

"The other half is of a plastic compound, tough enough to withstand the digestive juices, but not enough to resist the acid. In the second portion lies the cyanide. Between the two is a copper membrane. The two halves are screwed together; the acid begins to burn away at the copper wafer. The capsule is swallowed. Several hours later, depending on the thickness of the copper, the acid burns through. It is the same principle as certain types of acid-operated detonators.

"When the acid penetrates the copper membrane, it quickly cuts through the plastic of the second chamber, and the cyanide floods out into the body system. I believe it can be extended up to ten hours, by which time the indigestible capsule has reached the lower bowel. Once the poison is out, the blood absorbs it quickly and carries it to the heart."

Barak had seen his Premier annoyed before, even angry. But he had never seen him white and trembling with rage.

"They send me two men with poison pellets deep inside them," he whispered, "two walking time bombs, triggered to die when they are in our hands? Israel will not be blamed for this outrage. Publish the news of the deaths immediately. Do you understand? At once. And say a pathology examination is under way at this very moment. That is an order."

"If the terrorists have not yet left the *Freya,*" suggested Barak, "that news could reverse their plans to leave."

"The men responsible for poisoning Mishkin and Lazareff should have thought of that," snapped Premier Golen. "But any delay in the announcement and Israel will be blamed for murdering them. And that I will not tolerate."

The fog rolled on. It thickened; it deepened. It covered the sea from the coast of East Anglia across to Walcheren. It embalmed the flotilla of tugs bearing the emulsifier that were sheltering west of the warships, and the Navy vessels themselves. It whirled around the *Cutlass, Sabre,* and *Scimitar* as they lay under the stern of the *Argyll,* engines throbbing softly, straining to be up and away to track down their prey. It shrouded the biggest tanker in the world at her mooring between the warships and the Dutch shore.

At six-forty-five all the terrorists but two climbed down into the larger of the inflatable speedboats. One of them, the Ukrainian-American, jumped into the old fishing launch that had brought them to the middle of the North Sea, and glanced upward.

From the rail above him, Andrew Drake nodded. The man pushed the starter button, and the sturdy engine coughed into life. The prow of the launch was pointed due west, her wheel lashed with cord to hold her steady on course. The terrorist gradually increased the power of the engine, holding her in neutral gear.

Across the water, keen ears, human and electronic, had caught the sound of the motor; urgent commands and questions flashed among the warships, and from the *Argyll* to the circling Nimrod overhead. The spotter plane looked to its radar but detected no movement on the sea below.

Drake spoke quickly into his walkie-talkie, and far up on the bridge, Azamat Krim hit the *Freya*'s siren button.

The air filled with a booming roar of sound as the siren blew away the silence of the surrounding fog and the lapping water.

On his bridge on the *Argyll,* Captain Preston snorted with impatience.

"They're trying to drown the sound of the launch engine," he observed. "No matter; we'll have it on radar as soon as it leaves the *Freya*'s side."

Seconds later the terrorist in the launch slammed the gear into forward, and the fishing boat, its engine revving high, pulled violently away from the *Freya*'s stern. The terrorist leaped for the swinging rope above him, lifted his feet, and let the empty boat churn out from under him. In two seconds it was lost in the fog, plowing its way strongly toward the warships to the west.

The terrorist swung on the end of his rope, then lowered himself into the speedboat where his four companions waited. One of them jerked at the engine's lanvard: the outboard coughed and roared. The five men in it gripped the hand-holds, and the helmsman pushed on the power. The inflatable dug its motor into the water, cleared the stern of the *Freya,* lifted its blunt nose high, and tore away across the calm water toward Holland.

The radar operator in the Nimrod high above spotted the steel hull of the fishing launch instantly; the rubber-compound speedboat gave no reflector signal.

"The launch is moving," he told the *Argyll* below him. "Hell, they're coming straight at you."

Captain Preston glanced at the radar display on his own bridge.

"Got 'em," he said, and watched the blip separating itself from the great white blob that represented the *Freya* herself.

"He's right, she's boring straight at us. What the hell are they trying to do?"

On full power and empty, the fishing launch was making fifteen knots. In twenty minutes it would be among the Navy ships, then through them and into the flotilla of tugs behind them.

"They must think they can get through the screen of warships unharmed, and then lose themselves among the tugs in the fog," suggested the first officer, beside Captain Preston. "Shall we send the *Cutlass* to intercept?"

"I'm not risking good men, however much Major Fallon may want his personal fight," said Preston. "Those bastards have already shot one seaman on the *Freya,* and orders from the Admiralty are quite specific. Use the guns."

The procedure that was put into effect on the *Argyll* was smooth and practiced. The four other NATO warships were politely asked not to open fire, but to leave the job to the *Argyll.* Her fore and aft five-inch guns swung smoothly onto target and opened fire.

Even at two miles, the target was small. Somehow it survived the first salvo, though the sea around it erupted in spouts of rising water when the shells dropped. There was no spectacle for the watchers on the *Argyll,* nor for those crouched on the three patrol boats beside her. Whatever was happening out there in the fog was invisible; only the radar could see every drop of every shell, and the target boat rearing and plunging in the maddened water. But the radar could not tell its masters that no figure stood at the helm, no men crouched terrified in her stern.

Andrew Drake and Azamat Krim sat quietly in their two-man speedboat close by the *Freya* and waited. Drake held onto the rope that hung from her rail high above. Through the fog they both heard the first muffled boom of the *Argyll*'s guns. Drake nodded at Krim, who started the outboard engine. Drake released the rope, and the inflatable sped away, light as a feather, skimming the sea as the speed built up, its engine noise drowned by the roar of the *Freya*'s siren.

Krim looked at his left wrist, where a waterproof compass was strapped, and altered course a few points to south. He had calculated forty-five minutes at top speed from the *Freya* to the maze of islands that make up North and South Beveland.

At five minutes to seven, the fishing launch stopped the *Argyll*'s sixth shell, a direct hit. The explosive tore the launch apart, lifting it half out of the water and rolling both stern and aft sections over. The fuel tank blew up, and the steel-hulled boat sank like a stone.

"Direct hit," reported the gunnery officer from deep inside the *Argyll* where he and his gunners had watched the uneven duel on radar. "She's gone."

The blip faded from the screen; the illuminated sweep arm went around and around but showed only the *Freya* at five miles. On the bridge, four officers watched the same display, and there were a few moments of silence. It was the first time for any of them that their ship had actually killed anybody.

"Let the *Sabre* go," said Captain Preston quietly. "They can board and liberate the *Freya* now."

The radar operator in the darkened hull of the Nimrod peered closely at his screen. He could see all the warships, all the tugs, and the *Freya* to the east of them. But somewhere beyond the *Freya*, shielded by the tanker's bulk from the Navy vessels, a tiny speck seemed to be moving away to the southeast; it was so small it could almost have been missed; it was no bigger than the blip that would have been made by a medium-size tin can; in fact it was the metallic cover to the outboard engine of a speeding inflatable. Tin cans do not move across the face of the ocean at thirty knots.

"Nimrod to *Argyll*, Nimrod to *Argyll* . . ."

The officers on the bridge of the guided-missile cruiser listened to the news from the circling aircraft with shock. One of them ran to the wing of the bridge and shouted the information down to the sailors from Portland who waited on their patrol launches.

Two seconds later the *Cutlass* and *Scimitar* were away, the booming roar of their twin diesel marine engines filling the fog around them. Long white plumes of spray rose from their bows; the noses rose higher and higher, the sterns deeper in the wake, as the bronze screws whipped through the foaming water.

"Damn and blast them," shouted Major Fallon to the Navy commander who stood with him in the tiny wheelhouse of the *Cutlass*, "how fast can we go?"

"On water like this, over forty knots," the commander shouted back.

Not enough, thought Adam Munro, both hands locked to a stanchion as the vessel shuddered and bucked like a runaway horse through the fog. The *Freya* was still five miles away, the terrorists' speedboat another five beyond that. Even if they overhauled at ten knots, it would take an hour to come level with the inflatable carrying Svoboda to safety in the creeks of Holland, where he could lose himself. But he would be there in forty minutes, maybe less.

Cutlass and *Scimitar* were driving blind, tearing the fog to shreds, only to watch it form behind them. In any crowded sea, it would be lunacy to use such speed in conditions of zero visibility. But the sea was empty. In the wheelhouse of each launch, the commander listened to a constant stream of information from the Nimrod via the *Argyll:* his own position and that of the other fast patrol launch; the position in the fog ahead of them of the *Freya* herself; the position of the *Sabre*, well away to their left, heading toward the *Freya* at a slower speed; and the course and speed of the moving dot that represented Svoboda's escape.

Well east of the *Freya*, the inflatable in which Andrew Drake and Azamat Krim were making for safety seemed to be in luck. Beneath the fog the sea had become even calmer, and the sheetlike water enabled them to increase speed even more. Most of their craft was out of the water, only the shaft of the howling engine being deep beneath the surface. A few feet away in the fog, passing by in a blur, Drake saw the last remaining traces of the wake made by their companions ten minutes ahead of them. It was odd, he thought, for the traces to remain on the sea's surface for so long.

On the bridge of the *Moran,* which was lying south of the *Freya,* Captain Mike Manning also studied his radar scanner. He could see the *Argyll* away to the northwest of him, and the *Freya* a mite east of north.

Between them, the *Cutlass* and the *Scimitar* were visible, closing the gap fast. Away to the east he could spot the tiny blip of the racing speedboat, so small it was almost lost in the milky complexion of the screen. But it was there. Manning looked at the gap between the refugee and the hunters charging after it.

"They'll never make it," he said, and gave an order to his executive officer. The five-inch forward gun of the *Moran* began to traverse slowly to the right, seeking a target somewhere through the fog.

A seaman appeared at the elbow of Captain Preston, still absorbed in the pursuit through the fog as shown by his own scanner. His guns, he knew, were useless; the *Freya* lay almost between him and the target, so any shooting would be too risky. Besides, the bulk of the *Freya* masked the target from his own radar scanner, which could not, therefore, pass the correct aiming information to the guns.

"Excuse me, sir," said the seaman.

"What is it?"

"Just come over the news, sir. Those two men who were flown to Israel today, sir. They're dead. Died in their cells."

"Dead?" queried Captain Preston incredulously. "Then the whole bloody thing was for nothing. Wonder who the hell could have done that. Better tell that Foreign Office chappie when he gets back. He'll be interested."

The sea was still flat calm for Andrew Drake. There was a slick, oily flatness to it that was unnatural in the North Sea. He and Krim were almost halfway to the Dutch coast when their engine coughed for the first time. It coughed again several seconds later, then repeatedly. The speed slowed, the power reduced.

Azamat Krim gunned the engine urgently. It fired, coughed again, and resumed running, but with a throaty sound.

"It's overheating," he shouted to Drake.

"It can't be," yelled Drake. "It should run at full power for at least an hour."

Krim leaned out of the speedboat and dipped his hand in the water. He examined the palm and showed it to Drake. Streaks of sticky brown crude oil ran down to his wrist.

"It's blocking the cooling ducts," said Krim.

"They seem to be slowing down," the operator in the Nimrod informed the *Argyll*, which passed the information to the *Cutlass*.

"Come on," shouted Major Fallon, "we can still get the bastards!"

The distance began to close rapidly. The inflatable was down to ten knots. What Fallon did not know, nor the young commander who stood at the wheel of the racing *Cutlass*, was that they were speeding toward the edge of a great lake of oil lying on the surface of the ocean. Or that their prey was chugging right through the center of it.

Ten seconds later Azamat Krim's engine cut out. The silence was eerie. Far away they could hear the boom of the engines of *Cutlass* and *Scimitar* coming toward them through the fog.

Krim scooped a double handful from the surface of the sea and held it out to Drake.

"It's our oil, Andriy. It's the oil we vented. We're right in the middle of it."

"They've stopped," said the commander on the *Cutlass* to Fallon beside him. "The *Argyll* says they've stopped. God knows why."

"We'll get 'em!" shouted Fallon gleefully, and unslung his Ingram submachine gun.

On the *Moran*, gunnery officer Chuck Olsen reported to Manning, "We have range and direction."

"Open fire," said Manning calmly.

Seven miles to the south of the *Cutlass*, the forward gun of the *Moran* began to crash out its shells in steady, rhythmic sequence. The commander of the *Cutlass* could not hear the shells, but the *Argyll* could, and told him to slow down. He was heading straight into the area where the tiny speck on the radar screens had come to rest, and the *Moran* had opened fire on the same area. The commander eased back on his twin throttles; the bucking launch slowed, then settled, chugging gently forward.

"What the hell are you doing?" shouted Major Fallon. "They can't be more than a mile or so ahead."

The answer came from the sky. Somewhere above them, a mile forward from the bow, there was a sound like a rushing train as the first shells from the *Moran* homed in on their target.

The three semi-armor-piercing shells went straight into the

water, raising spouts of foam but missing the bobbing inflatable by a hundred yards.

The starshells had proximity fuzes. They exploded in blinding sheets of white light a few feet above the ocean surface, showering gentle, soft gobbets of burning magnesium over a wide area.

The men on the *Cutlass* were silent, seeing the fog ahead of them illuminated. Four cables to starboard, the *Scimitar* was also hove to, on the very edge of the oil slick.

The magnesium dropped onto the crude oil, raising its temperature to and beyond its flashpoint. The light fragments of blazing metal, not heavy enough to penetrate the scum, sat and burned in the oil.

Before the eyes of the watching sailors and Marines the sea caught fire; a gigantic plain, miles long and miles wide, began to glow, a ruddy red at first, then brighter and hotter.

It lasted for no more than fifteen seconds. In that time the sea blazed. Over half of a spillage of twenty thousand tons of oil caught fire and burned. For several seconds it reached five thousand degrees centigrade. The sheer heat of it burned off the fog for miles around in a tenth of a minute, the white flames reaching four to five feet high off the surface of the water.

In utter silence the sailors and Marines gazed at the blistering inferno starting only a hundred yards ahead of them; some had to shield their faces or be scorched by the heat.

From the midst of the fire a single candle spurted, as if a petrol tank had exploded. The burning oil made no sound as it shimmered and glowed for its brief life.

From the heart of the flames, carrying across the water, a single human scream reached the ears of the sailors:

"Shche ne vmerla Ukraina. . . ."

Then it was gone. The flames died down, fluttered, and waned. The fog closed in.

"What the hell did that mean?" whispered the commander of the *Cutlass*. Major Fallon shrugged.

"Don't ask me. Some foreign lingo."

From beside them, Adam Munro gazed at the last flickering glow of the dying flames.

"Roughly translated," he said, "it means 'The Ukraine will live again.' "

EPILOGUE

IT WAS eight P.M. in Western Europe but ten in Moscow, and the Politburo meeting had been in session for an hour.

Yefrem Vishnayev and his supporters were becoming impatient. The Party theoretician knew he was strong enough; there was no point in further delay. He rose portentously to his feet.

"Comrades, general discussion is all very well, but it brings us nowhere. I have asked for this special meeting of the Presidium of the Supreme Soviet for a purpose, and that is to see whether the Presidium continues to have confidence in the leadership of our esteemed Secretary-General, Comrade Maxim Rudin.

"We have all heard the arguments for and against the so-called Treaty of Dublin, concerning the grain shipments the United States had promised to make to us, and the price—in my view, the inordinately high price—we have been required to pay for them.

"And finally we have heard of the escape to Israel of the murderers Mishkin and Lazareff, men who it has been proved to you beyond a doubt were responsible for assassinating our dear comrade, Yuri Ivanenko. My motion is as follows: that the Presidium of the Supreme Soviet can no longer have confidence in the continued direction of the affairs of our great nation by Comrade Rudin. Comrade Secretary-General, I demand a vote on the motion."

He sat down. There was silence. Even for those participating, far more for the smaller fry present, the fall of a giant from Kremlin power is a terrifying moment.

"Those in favor of the motion?" asked Maxim Rudin.

Yefrem Vishnayev raised his hand. Marshal Nikolai Kerensky followed suit. Vitautas the Lithuanian did likewise. There was a pause of several seconds. Mukhamed the Tajik raised his hand. The telephone rang. Rudin answered it, listened, and replaced the receiver.

"I should not, of course," he said impassively, "interrupt a vote, but the news just received is of some passing interest.

"Two hours ago Mishkin and Lazareff both died, instantaneously, in cells beneath the central police station of Tel Aviv. A colleague fell to his death from a hotel balcony window outside that city. One hour ago the terrorists who had hijacked the *Freya* in the North Sea—to liberate these men—died in a sea of blazing petrol. None of them ever opened their mouths. And now none of them ever will.

"We were, I believe, in the midst of voting on Comrade Vishnayev's resolution. . . ."

Eyes were studiously averted; gazes were upon the table.

"Those against the motion?" murmured Rudin.

Vassili Petrov and Dmitri Rykov raised their hands. They were followed by Chavadze the Georgian, Shushkin, and Stepanov.

Petryanov, who had once voted for the Vishnayev faction, glanced at the raised hands, caught the drift of the wind, and raised his own.

"May I," said Komarov of Agriculture, "express my personal pleasure at being able to vote with the most complete confidence in favor of our Secretary-General."

He raised his hand. Rudin smiled at him.

Slug, thought Rudin. I am personally going to stamp you into the garden path.

"Then with my own vote the issue is denied by eight votes to four," said Rudin. "I don't think there is any other business?"

There was none.

Twelve hours later, Captain Thor Larsen stood once again on the bridge of the *Freya* and scanned the sea around him.

It had been an eventful night. The British Marines had found and freed him twelve hours before, on the verge of collapse. Royal Navy demolitions experts had carefully lowered themselves into the holds of the supertanker and plucked the detonators from the dynamite, bringing the charges gently up from the bowels of the ship to the deck, whence they were removed.

Strong hands had turned the steel cleats to the door behind which his crew had been imprisoned for sixty-four hours, and the liberated seamen had whooped and danced for joy. All night they had been putting through personal calls to their parents and wives.

The gentle hands of a Royal Navy doctor had laid Thor Larsen on his own bunk and tended the wounds as well as conditions would allow.

"You'll need surgery, of course," the doctor told the Norwegian. "And it'll be set up for the moment you arrive by helicopter in Rotterdam."

"Wrong," said Larsen on the brink of unconsciousness. "I will go to Rotterdam, but I will go on the *Freya*."

The doctor had cleaned and swabbed the broken hand, sterilizing against infection and injecting morphine to dull the pain. Before he was finished, Thor Larsen slept.

Skilled hands had piloted the stream of helicopters that landed on the *Freya*'s helipad amidships through the night, bringing Harry Wennerstrom to inspect his ship, and the berthing crew to help her dock. The pumpman had found his spare fuses and repaired his cargo-control pumps. Crude oil had been pumped from one of the full holds to the vented one to restore the balance; the valves had all been closed.

While the captain slept, the first and second officers had examined every inch of the *Freya* from stem to stern. The chief engineer had gone over his beloved engines foot by foot, testing every system to make sure nothing had been damaged.

During the dark hours, the tugs and firefighting ships had started to spray their emulsifier concentrate onto the area of sea where the scum of the vented oil still clung to the water. Most had burned off in the single brief holocaust caused by the magnesium shells of Captain Manning.

Just before dawn, Thor Larsen had awakened. The chief steward had helped him gently into his clothes, the full uniform of a senior captain of the Nordia Line that he insisted on wearing. He had slipped his bandaged hand carefully down the sleeve with the four gold rings, then hung the hand back in the sling around his neck.

At eight A.M. he stood beside his first and second officers on the bridge. The two pilots from Maas Control were also there, the senior pilot with his independent "brown box" navigational aid system.

To Thor Larsen's surprise, the sea to the north, south, and west of him was crowded. There were trawlers from the Humber and the Schelde, fishermen up from Lorient and Saint-Malo, Ostende and the coast of Kent. Merchant vessels flying a dozen flags mingled with the warships of five NATO navies, all of them hove to within a radius of three miles and outward from that.

At two minutes past eight, the gigantic propellers of the *Freya* began to turn, the massive anchor cable rumbled up from the ocean floor. From beneath her stern a maelstrom of white water appeared.

In the sky above, four aircraft circled, bearing television cameras that showed a watching world the sea goddess coming under way.

As the wake broadened behind her, and the Viking helmet emblem of her company fluttered out from her yardarm, the North Sea exploded in a burst of sound.

Little sirens like tin whistles, booming roars and shrill whoops echoed across the water as over a hundred sea captains commanding vessels from the tiny to the grand, from the harmless to the deadly, gave the *Freya* the traditional sailor's greeting.

Thor Larsen looked at the crowded sea about him and the empty lane leading to Euro Buoy 1. He turned to the waiting Dutch pilot.

"Mr. Pilot, pray set course for Rotterdam."

On Sunday, April 10, 1983, in St. Patrick's Hall, Dublin Castle, two men approached the great oak refectory table that had been brought in for the purpose, and took their seats.

In the Minstrel Gallery the television cameras peered through the arcs of white light that bathed the table and beamed their images across the world.

Dmitri Rykov painstakingly scrawled his name for the Soviet Union on both copies of the Treaty of Dublin and passed the copies, bound in red Morocco leather, to David Lawrence, who signed for the United States.

Within hours the first grain ships, waiting off Murmansk and Leningrad, Sebastopol and Odessa, moved forward to their berths.

A week later the first Warsaw Pact units along the Iron Curtain began to load their gear to pull back east from the barbed-wire line.

On Thursday the fourteenth, the routine meeting of the Politburo in the Arsenal Building of the Kremlin was far from routine.

The last man to enter the room, having been delayed outside by a major of the Kremlin guard, was Yefrem Vishnayev.

When he came through the doorway, he observed that the faces of the other eleven members were all turned toward him. Maxim Rudin brooded at the center place at the top of the T-shaped table. Down each side of the stem were five chairs, and each was occupied. There was only one chair left vacant. It was the one at the far end of the stem of the table, facing up the length of it.

Impassively, Yefrem Vishnayev walked slowly forward to take that seat, known simply as the Penal Chair. It was to be his last Politburo meeting.

On April 18 a small freighter was rolling in the Black Sea swell, ten miles off the shore of Rumania. Just before two A.M. a fast speedboat left the freighter and raced toward the shore. At three miles it halted, and a Marine on board took a powerful flashlight, pointed it toward the invisible sands, and blinked a signal: three long dashes and three short ones. There was no answering light from the beach. The man repeated his signal four times. Still there was no answer.

The speedboat turned back and returned to the freighter. An hour later it was stowed below decks and a message was transmitted to London.

From London another message went in code to the British Embassy in Moscow: "Regret Nightingale has not made the rendezvous. Suggest you return to London."

On April 25 there was a plenary meeting of the full Central Committee of the Communist Party of the Soviet Union in the Palace of Congresses inside the Kremlin. The delegates had come from all over the Soviet Union, some of them many thousands of miles.

Standing on the podium beneath the outsized head of Lenin, Maxim Rudin made them his farewell speech.

He began by outlining to them the crisis that had faced their country twelve months earlier; he painted a picture of famine and hunger to make their hair stand on end. He went on to describe the brilliant feat of diplomacy by which the Politburo had instructed Dmitri Rykov to meet the Americans in Dublin and gain from them grain shipments of unprecedented size, along with imports of technology and computers, all at minimal cost. No mention was made of concessions on arms levels. He received a standing ovation for ten minutes.

Turning his attention to the matter of world peace, he reminded one and all of the constant danger to peace that was posed by the territorial and imperialistic ambitions of the capitalist West, occasionally aided by enemies of peace right there within the Soviet Union.

This was too much; consternation was unconfined. But, he went on with an admonishing finger, the secret conspirators with the imperialists had been uncovered and rooted out, thanks to the eternal vigilance of the tireless Yuri Ivanenko, who had died a week earlier in a sanatorium after a long and gallant struggle against a serious heart ailment.

When the news of his death broke, there were cries of horror and compassion for the departed comrade who had saved them all. Rudin raised a regretful hand for silence.

But, he told them, Ivanenko had been ably assisted before his heart attack the previous October, and replaced since his infirmity began, by his ever loyal comrade-in-arms Vassili Petrov, who had completed the task of safeguarding the Soviet Union as the world's first champion of peace.

There was an ovation for Vassili Petrov.

Because the conspiracies of the antipeace faction, both inside and outside the Soviet Union, had been exposed and destroyed, Rudin went on, it had been possible for the USSR, in its unending search for détente and peace, to curb its arms-building programs for the first time in years. More of the national effort could thenceforward be directed toward the production of consumer goods and social improvement, thanks solely to the vigilance of the Politburo in spotting the antipeace faction for what they were.

This time the applause extended for another ten minutes.

Maxim Rudin waited until the clapping was almost over before he raised his hands; then he dropped his speaking tone.

As for himself, Rudin said, he had done what he could, but the time had come for him to depart.

The stunned silence was tangible.

He had toiled long—too long, perhaps—bearing on his

shoulders the most onerous burdens, which had sapped his strength and his health.

On the podium, his shoulders slumped with the weariness of it all. There were cries of "No! No!"

He was an old man, Rudin said. What did he want? Nothing more than any other old man wanted. To sit by the fire on a winter's night and play with his grandchildren. . . .

In the diplomatic gallery the British head of Chancery whispered to the Ambassador:

"I say, that's going a bit strong. He's had more people shot than I've had hot dinners."

The Ambassador raised a single eyebrow and muttered back:

"Think yourself lucky. If this were America, he'd produce his bloody grandchildren on the stage."

And so, concluded Rudin, the time had come for him to admit openly to his friends and comrades that the doctors had informed him he had only a few more months to live. With his audience's permission he would lay down the burden of office and spend what little time remained to him in the countryside he loved so much, with the family who were the sun and the moon to him.

Several of the women delegates were crying openly by now.

One last question remained, said Rudin. He wished to retire in five days, on the last day of the month. The following morning was May Day, and a new man would stand atop Lenin's Mausoleum to take the salute of the great parade. Who would that man be?

It should be a man of youth and vigor, of wisdom and unbounded patriotism; a man who had proved himself in the highest councils of the land but was not yet bowed with age. Such a man, Rudin proclaimed, the peoples of the fifteen Soviet Socialist Republics were lucky to have, in the person of Vassili Petrov. . . .

The election of Petrov to succeed Rudin was carried by acclamation. Supporters of alternative candidates would have been shouted down had they tried to speak. They did not even bother.

Following the climax of the hijacking in the North Sea, Sir Nigel Irvine had wished Adam Munro to remain in London, or at least not to return to Moscow. Munro had appealed personally to the Prime Minister to be allowed one last chance to ascertain whether his agent, the Nightingale, was safe. In view of his role in ending the crisis, his wish had been granted.

Since his meeting in the small hours of April 3 with Maxim Rudin, it was evident that his cover was completely blown and that he could not function as an agent in Moscow.

The Ambassador and the head of Chancery regarded his return with considerable misgivings, and it was no surprise when his name was carefully excluded from any diplomatic invitations, or that he could not be received by any representative of the Soviet Ministry of Foreign Trade. He hung about like a forlorn and unwanted party guest, hoping against hope that Valentina would contact him to indicate she was safe.

Once he tried her private telephone number. There was no answer. She could have been out, but he dared not risk it again. Following the fall of the Vishnayev faction, he was told he had until the end of the month. Then he would be recalled to London, and his resignation from the Firm would be gratefully accepted.

Maxim Rudin's farewell speech caused a furor in the diplomatic missions, as each informed its home government of the news of Rudin's departure and prepared position papers on his successor, Vassili Petrov. Munro was excluded from this whirl of activity.

It was therefore all the more surprising when, following the announcement of a reception in St. George's Hall in the Great Kremlin Palace on the evening of April 30, invitations arrived at the British Embassy for the Ambassador, the head of Chancery, and Adam Munro. It was even hinted during a phone call from the Soviet Foreign Ministry to the embassy that Munro was confidently expected to attend.

The state reception to bid farewell to Maxim Rudin was a glittering affair. Over a hundred of the elite of the Soviet Union mingled with four times that number of foreign diplomats from the Socialist world, the West, and the Third World. Fraternal delegations from Communist parties outside the Soviet bloc were also there, ill at ease amid the full evening dress, military uniforms, stars, orders, and medals. It could have been a tsar who was abdicating, rather than the leader of a classless workers' paradise.

The foreigners mingled with their Russian hosts beneath the three thousand lights of the six spreading chandeliers, exchanging gossip and congratulations in the niches where the great tsarist war heroes were commemorated with the other Knights of St. George. Maxim Rudin moved among them like an old lion, accepting the plaudits of well-wishers from one hundred fifty countries as no more than his due.

Munro spotted him from afar, but he was not included in the list of those presented personally, nor was it wise for him to approach the outgoing Secretary-General. Before midnight, pleading a natural tiredness, Rudin excused himself and left the guests to the care of Petrov and the others from the Politburo.

Twenty minutes later Adam Munro felt a touch at his arm. Standing behind him was an immaculate major in the uniform of the Kremlin's own praetorian guard. Impassive as ever, the major spoke to him in Russian.

"Mr. Munro, please come with me."

His tone permitted of no expostulation. Munro was not surprised. Evidently, his inclusion in the guest list had been a mistake; it had been spotted, and he was being asked to leave.

But the major headed away from the main doors, passed through into the high, octagonal Hall of St. Vladimir, up a wooden staircase guarded by a bronze grille, and out into the warm starlight of Upper Savior Square.

The man walked with completely confident tread, at ease among passages and doorways well known to him, although unseen by most.

Still following, Munro went across the square and into the Terem Palace. Silent guards were at every door; each opened as the major approached, and closed as they passed through. They walked straight across the Front Hall Chamber and to the end of the Cross Chamber. Here, at a door at the far end, the major paused and knocked. There was a gruff command from inside. The major opened the door, stood aside, and indicated that Munro should enter.

The third chamber in the Terem Palace, the so-called Palace of Chambers, is the Throne Room, the holy of holies of the old tsars, the most inaccessible of all the rooms. In red, gilt, and mosaic tiles, with parquet floor and deep burgundy carpet, it is lush but smaller and warmer than most of the other rooms. It was the place where the tsars worked or received emissaries in complete privacy. Standing staring out through the Petition Window was Maxim Rudin. He turned as Munro entered.

"So, Mr. Munro, you will be leaving us, I hear."

It had been twenty-seven days since Munro had seen him before, in dressing gown, nursing a glass of milk, in his personal apartments in the Arsenal. Now he was in a beautifully cut charcoal-gray suit, almost certainly from Savile Row, London, bearing the two orders of Lenin and Hero of the Soviet Union on the left lapel. The Throne Room suited him better this way.

"Yes, Mr. President," said Munro.

Maxim Rudin glanced at his watch.

"In ten minutes, Mr. ex-President," he remarked. "Midnight, I officially retire. You also, I presume, will be retiring?"

The old fox knows perfectly well that my cover was blown the night I met him, thought Munro, and that I also have to retire.

"Yes, Mr. President. I shall be returning to London tomorrow, to retire."

Rudin did not approach him or hold out his hand. He stood across the room, just where the tsars had once stood, in the room representing the pinnacle of the Russian Empire, and nodded.

"Then I shall wish you farewell, Mr. Munro."

He pressed a small onyx bell on a table, and behind Munro the door opened.

"Good-bye, sir," said Munro. He had half turned to go, when Rudin spoke again.

"Tell me, Mr. Munro, what do you think of our Red Square?"

Munro stopped, puzzled. It was a strange question for a man saying farewell. Munro thought, and answered carefully.

"It is very impressive."

"Impressive, yes," said Rudin, as if weighing the word. "Not, perhaps, so elegant as your Berkeley Square, but sometimes, even here, you can hear a Nightingale sing."

Munro stood motionless as the painted saints on the ceiling above him. His stomach turned over in a wave of nausea. They had got her, and, unable to resist, she had told them all, even the code name and the reference to the old song about the Nightingale in Berkeley Square.

"Will you shoot her?" he asked dully.

Rudin seemed genuinely surprised.

"Shoot her? Why should we shoot her?"

So it would be the labor camps, the living death, for the

woman he loved and had been so near to marrying in his native Scotland.

"Then what will you do to her?"

The old Russian raised his eyebrows in mock surprise.

"Do? Nothing. She is a loyal woman, a patriot. She is also very fond of you, young man. Not in love, you understand, but genuinely fond—"

"I don't understand," said Munro. "How do you know?"

"She asked me to tell you," said Rudin. "She will not be a housewife in Edinburgh. She will not be Mrs. Munro. She cannot see you again—ever. But she does not want you to worry for her, to fear for her. She is well, privileged, honored, among her own people. She asked me to tell you not to worry."

The dawning comprehension was almost as dizzying as the fear. Munro stared at Rudin as the disbelief receded.

"She was yours," he said quietly. "She was yours all along. From the first contact in the woods, just after Vishnayev made his bid for war in Europe. She was working for you. . . ."

The grizzled old Kremlin fox shrugged.

"Mr. Munro," growled the old Russian, "how else could I get my messages to President Matthews with the absolute certainty that they would be believed?"

The impassive major with the cold eyes drew at his elbow; he was outside the Throne Room, and the door closed behind him. Five minutes later he was shown out, on foot, through a small door in the Savior Gate onto Red Square. The parade marshals were rehearsing their roles for May Day. The clock above his head struck midnight.

He turned left toward the National Hotel to find a taxi. A hundred yards later, as he passed Lenin's Mausoleum, to the surprise and outrage of a militiaman, he began to laugh.

ABOUT THE AUTHOR

Frederick Forsyth lives in London with his wife and two sons. He is the author of *The Biafra Story, The Day of the Jackal, The Odessa File, The Dogs of War, The Shepherd, The Devil's Alternative,* and the short story collection *No Comebacks.* His most recent novel is *The Fourth Protocol.*